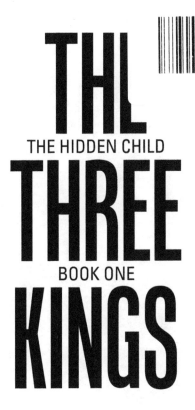

THE
THE HIDDEN CHILD
THREE
BOOK ONE
KINGS

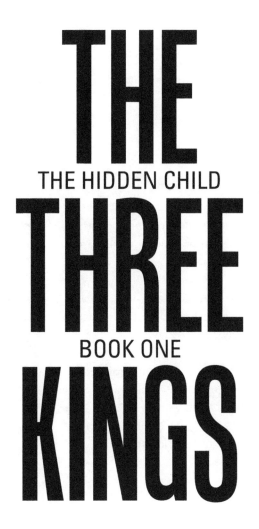

THE THREE KINGS

THE HIDDEN CHILD

BOOK ONE

FRANCISCO BURBANO

Library of Congress Control Number: 2019919502
ISBN: Hardcover   978-1-7960-7307-2
                   Softcover   978-1-7960-7308-9
                   eBook   978-1-7960-7306-5

Rev. date: 01/24/2020

To order additional copies of this book, contact:
Xlibris
1-888-795-4274
www.Xlibris.com
Orders@Xlibris.com
620011

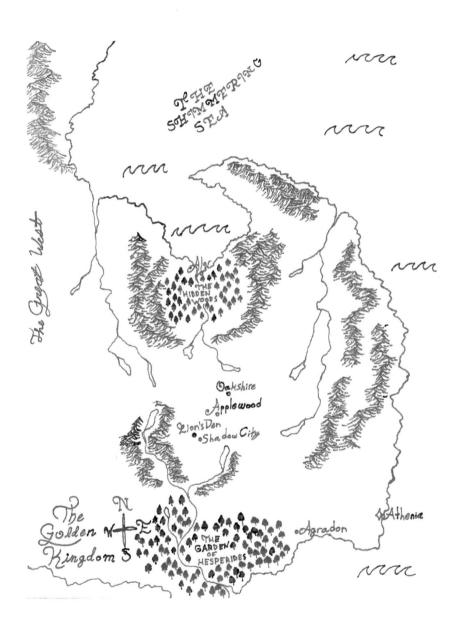

THE SHIMMERING SEA

The Great West

Aloc
THE HIDDEN WOODS

Oakshire
Applewood
Lion's Den
Shadow City

The Golden Kingdom

N
W E
S

THE GARDEN OF HESPERIDES

Agradon

Athenia

ADAM GROANED AS morning sunshine washed his room. He caught himself sweating and breathing heavily as he shot up, thirsty and tired. The dreams. Those damn dreams. They were destroying him. He couldn't get rid of them. Nothing would help. He reached around hysterically until he found the cup of water, he had not finished the previous night.

He drank immediately then took a deep breath. After a few moments, Adam slowly sat on his bed, with his elbows resting on his knees, silently thinking about his dream. His curse. That's what he called it. That's what his mother called it.

He laid on his bed in a stone room that wasn't very large. Only large enough for a few people. On the bed next to his, Adam's mother lay asleep. He rubbed his eyes and groaned quietly, trying not to wake her.

The bodies, the mountain and the fire. The light in his hand. What did it all mean? He had no idea, but he figured there was a meaning behind it. He always wanted to find answers to it. He had dreaded going to sleep each night in fear that they would return. As he feared, they always did.

He stood up and the floor creaked. His mother shifted under her sheets at the sound of the creaking wood. She was a light sleeper and Adam was worried what his mother would do if she woke up. Once, she was so angry that she beat Adam with a wooden board until it broke over his back. Luckily, he survived, but he never forgave his abusive mother, nor can he forget the terrible things that she did to him.

She would constantly beat him and laugh at him. He hated her, just as much as she hated him. Unfortunately, telling her that wouldn't have made her care. She was a rude and disgusting woman. She ruled over her household with an iron fist. It was strange how she never looked like the type of horrible person she was. She had curly black hair that she would often leave resting over her shoulders. Her green eyes would show anyone that she was a kind and loving person. Her attitude outside of the house was different as well. If someone were to approach her on the street, she would greet them kindly, and treat them with respect. That was a lie of course. All a ploy to get more clients.

Adam's mother worked at a brothel in the city. She was a prostitute. She was obviously different at home. A tyrannical, hate filled woman. It was worse since Adam lived only with her and no one else. He never knew his father; he was told he died when Adam was still a baby. Adam hated his home, which is why he rarely spent time there. He slept in his own house some of the time, but he would sneak out early in the morning or late at night to be with his friends or anywhere else besides his home: a home that did not feel like a home should.

He didn't want to face his mother, or any of her clients who didn't treat him any differently. His mother was often mad about it, other times she didn't care, but when Adam came back to his house, she was either absent, or asleep, which would allow Adam to get away with his unauthorized trips without repercussions.

He'd much rather explore the city than to stay in his own house. It wasn't much better though. His city was difficult to live in.

It was difficult time to be alive. Alor was an overpopulated city with too many mouths and scarcely enough to go around. It was last city in the world. All the other ones were destroyed over one hundred centuries ago.

Some people said it was because of a war between the gods of Olympus and the Titans that had ruined the world. Each punch that one would throw would cause massive waves to fly over cities. Each step they took would cause earthquakes around the earth, but Adam never believed it. He knew the real cause for all the destruction in the world was due to natural disasters. Ones that were not caused by celestial beings fighting amongst themselves. Gods were all fake in his eyes, simply stories told by humanity to give itself a purpose on this world.

The skies were always grey, there was rarely any sunshine. Rain was a regular thing and diseases were common. Adam would often hear old, crazy hermits shouting on the streets that it was the end of time, that the world would soon collapse, and considering Adam had never known anything else apart from this sad, destroyed city, he often believed them, to his dread.

He stepped out of his house and into the city. He wore a brown wool tunic, woolen breeches and leather sandals. He immediately began to make his way to the grove where his friends always were. They seemed to be the only thing he really appreciated about his life. The world was dying, and he knew it. Most people did. Unlike anyone else however, he welcomed it. He wanted this pathetic wasteland he and thousands of others called home to fall. That way there could be a possibility for a better one. At least that is what he hoped.

He constantly wished for a better life for him and his friends. He wanted to live outside the city walls. Perhaps all the monsters and diseases that had been rumored about had subsided during the past century. He hoped maybe his last moments of life won't be locked away in this shit pile of a city. He never liked his home. The people were rude, the life expectancy was short, and several other things piled on to his hatred for this wretched town. He wasn't angry at it. He was sad that he never got to experience anything else. Abuse and misery. That was all he knew.

He was going to find Chase and Kathrine. He had to tell them about the dream. It was unlike any other. It was vivid. Clear as clean water and meaning to tell something.

He walked through the busy streets, still sweating and slightly disoriented from the dream, or rather nightmare. These dreams were always haunting him, keeping him hostage overnight. No matter what he tried, he couldn't get rid of them.

Why me? He asked himself. What did he do to deserve these horrid visions? Chase and Kathrine had to know about it. Chase and Kathrine were his closest friends. They also lived similar lives as Adam. Living only behind the city walls all their lives and never knowing anything else. They, however, were not as upset about it all the time. If they were, they were doing a damn good job at hiding it. They were always happy. Adam tried to match their attitude as much he could when he was with them. He didn't want them to match his depression. He had a sad life, but he was always grateful for his friends. They kept his spirits as high as they could be.

He walked through the busy streets of the city as buzzing crowds of people surrounded him. He passed beggars in the street, their arms extended to receive coin or food. He passed a leper weeping below the shadow of a balcony, his brown skin riddled with boils. Cobblestone buildings lined the streets. Small stone houses were built close together as merchants in reed huts tried what they could to sell things like food, clothes and old jewelry to people. It seemed to Adam as if every bloody piece of silver that the merchants could get their hands on was "the best in all the land". Hand maidens or servants patted old, dirty rags from the windows above to clean them. Old men and women sat on chairs on the sidewalks and smoked their pipes, and carriage drivers directed their horses to the stables.

It is late then, Adam concluded, horses and carriages were not allowed in the streets until after midday. Adam was surprised he had slept almost all day. On the east end of the small city, the docks were filled with fishermen and sailors. Adam couldn't see it that well through the heads of all the people, but he was familiar enough with the city to imagine it. The sky was a calm, light grey, as usual and the winds were faintly blowing gravel from the roads into Adam's sandals. On the north side of the city, behind Adam, a massive one-hundred-foot-tall marble and quarts castle stood.

The Citadel was where lord Adameious lived. He was lazy man who cared for only himself. He never helped with the problems of the lower class, he just sat on his throne eating away his days and worries. At least, that's what Adam imagined he did. He rarely ever appeared outside his castle. None of the common folk were allowed in there either. It seemed as if the Citadel was there for show and no other reason.

Surrounding the whole city, a huge stone wall blocked off all access to the outside world. It stood seven hundred feet tall, so the commoners said. Its tips touched the clouds and green vines snaked down its bricks.

Oh, what Adam would give to be on the other side of that wall. He did not know for certain what was on the other side, but if it were better than this city and its residents, he would be happy. He continued his path as people were all talking, kids were playing and of course, the very few satyrs that were around, were being yelled at or disrespected by the people.

They were sweet creatures, with hearts of gold and souls filled with kindness. Of course, nobody payed them much attention to find it out.

Adam was friends with many of them. He didn't listen to what other people said about them of course. No one else really cared for the nature spirits. To them, satyrs are just hairy, homeless animals. That of course led to more violence and division in an already violent and divided city.

They were peaceful beings. Adam had seen humans steal more.

Chase was one of these satyrs. He was a kind soul that always put others before himself. In Alor, that was dangerous, but he did not care. Near the southern end of the city, and off to the east near the docks, a massive forest of trees with dark, leaves covered the area. No stone buildings were built there, only wooden huts. All the cities' satyrs and nymphs lived here. The humans who were found with them were banished there as "punishment". So, the satyrs and nymphs had to cross to the part of the city where they were unwanted and treated harshly, in order to get necessities like water and food. They had no wells of clean water, and they ate no meat, as was expected of creatures who were spiritually connected to the forest and all its inhabitants.

Chase did not exactly help to calm the conflict. He was always angering someone, but he was skilled in always managing to get away safely. He and Adam had met a few years past. When Adam was seven, he was walking these streets with his mother and he got lost in a crowd. Panicking and breaking into tears, he was eventually helped by the young satyr. He helped him to his mother and even got him a bit of food to eat. When Adams mother had found out he was with a satyr, she beat him and then locked him in the basement for three days without food or water.

She deemed it fit as punishment for being with a satyr. She constantly told Adam how terrible they were. It wasn't fair, Adam hated how she talked about them. They didn't deserve it at all. But what could they do to stop it?

Adam stayed friends with Chase but never let his mother know.

Kathrine was a different story. Kathrine was the second half of the duo that made up Adam's pair of friends. She was kind and caring, but she was wild and unpredictable. She stole often and didn't hesitate to have a drinking contest against any man ignorant enough to insult her. She was no lady. She knew how to take care of herself. She was scrappy. She never really fit in with any of the girls so she tried to make friends with the boys. They rejected her because of her gender, so she decided to make friends with satyrs and nymphs. They didn't care that she was different. That's why Adam preferred them over humans. He still had the occasional human friend that also accepted the satyrs and nymphs as friends, but not many. He remembered Bird, the boy with the hooked nose he was friends with, who was always happy when he was around the peaceful satyrs, but he died last winter to a fever.

Adam's mother loved Kathrine, even more than she loved Adam. Kathrine had lost her parents at a very young age. Orphaned and homeless, his mother took her in one day and she grew up living with Adam. Adam's mother had wanted a daughter, and seeing a young girl with no parents to care for her, she saw a golden opportunity. That was something Adam envied, being an orphan. He considered it would be much better than living with no father and an abusive mother that hated him. His mother had told him that Adam's father had been killed in a fishing accident before Adam could walk. She talked about him very rarely and when she did, she spoke in a tone that implied that she hated him. She was glad he was gone. Adam wondered how so much hatred could fit in a single woman.

Kathrine eventually left and Adam's mother was devastated. As a result, she took her anger out on Adam, again, beating him and even cutting his face with a piece of broken glass. He still had the scar underneath his left eye. He never got mad at his friends for what happened to him because of them. He was mad at his mother for doing those things. He brushed off the thought and continued through the city.

Turning a corner and entering an alleyway, Adam already heard laughter and music from the other side of the alley. When it opened, a huge courtyard filled with satyrs and nymphs greeted him. Tall trees surrounded the courtyard, looming over the dancing satyrs with a canopy of dark reddish colors crawling over the green leaves. Built on the thick branches were wooden shacks. Adam noticed some familiar faces in the crowd.

Clio and Philocrates danced in the courtyard. Julius was another satyr friend of Adam's who was dancing with his friend Eavy in the middle of the courtyard and an old satyr named Diocles sat having a conversation with two nymphs and another satyr.

"Adam, my boy!" Diocles noticed him.

He spoke with glee as he smiled with bright, white teeth. He had a brown beard with black dreadlocks and umber skin. On top of his head, two curled horns sprouted from his scalp. He had brown furry goat legs that ended in cloven hooves. Adam had a special place for Diocles in his heart. Growing up without a father was difficult, but Diocles had filled that void. It was Diocles who taught Adam what he knew about the world. Diocles taught him and Chase how to read. Kathrine had never shown interest in reading. That, coupled with the

fact that Adam's mother would never let her out of the house to spend
times with satyrs and nymphs, ultimately left her unable to read. She
was never jealous of Adam's skills. She never cared much for books.
Adam loved reading. He did not own any books, but Diocles always
had some. How he managed to get them, Adam never knew, but
Diocles always had them. They told tales of oceans and valleys and
monsters from past ages that were slain by famous heroes. They had
maps of the world, calling it Alanos, and the continents and countries
and cities and thousands of different cultures and languages that
decorated them all.

Adam wanted to see them, but he knew he couldn't. With nothing
more than a few pieces of paper stuck between two leather sheets,
Adam was mesmerized by a world he could never see.

"What can I do for ya?" He asked, Adam hugged him.

"Can you tell me where Chase is?"

Without hesitation Diocles immediately answered. "In the bar, he's
been in there for a while."

Adam turned around to where Diocles pointed to, across the
sand courtyard stood a small building made from reed, wood and
hardened mud.

Even from the outside Adam could smell the terrible odors wafting
from the bar.

In one corner of the building, a group of drunken satyrs and even
some men were dancing around like merry fools, shouting or laughing
hysterically at a stupid joke one of them said. Not all people thought
of the satyrs as filth. One of the men was even unconscious, his head
drooping over his shoulders as his friends danced around him singing
songs in Senewan, the tongue of the satyrs. They screamed and cursed
in a wasted trance. Adam chuckled. "*Oyon von thooroo, aye! Oyon von
thoorah, aye!*" They sang; *a drink for the gentlemen, a drink for the ladies!*

In the middle was a small serving table with two people sitting on
the chairs in front of it. An old satyr and Chase. Behind the counter,
a young nymph was cleaning mugs with a soggy cloth.

Adam ignored the howling hooligans that were the drunken morons in the back as he sat next to Chase. He pulled up a chair next to his friend and ordered a cup of beer. The alcohol would help with the pain his nightmare had left him with.

Adam and Chase exchanged greetings as Adam took a seat.

Chase looked at him while sipping on a second cup.

"I uh.... I was looking for you." Adam hesitated.

"Hm. For what?"

Adam crossed his arms with the glass sitting in front of him.

"I had another nightmare last night," he said, gloomily.

"Oh.... I ... I thought they were done."

"They were never done. They come back every night, again and again. It seemed familiar, like it was connected to another one."

Chase sighed, "Adam, I think maybe we should seek out the priestess, again. Maybe she can help."

"No. We already tried that. I'm not spending any more coin on useless information."

"It's not useless, besides, maybe it'll work this time. You even told me they seemed like something more... mystical." Chase said, but Adam still didn't believe the priestess would help.

Last time they went to the priestess, she told him to contact his "dream giver". How the hell was he supposed to do that? He didn't even know if there was even something giving him his dreams, let alone how to find them. She wouldn't tell him anymore information.

"I don't think so. She'll tell me the same thing. I promise you." Adam told Chase.

"Come on give it one shot. I'll pay. We can't have these cursed things coming back. They hurt you, like a poison that courses through your veins before you wake. Who knows what would happen if they got worse?"

What happened that morning, when he was hyperventilating, was only a small, but bitter taste of what could truly happen. He was reluctant but he saw the outcome. At best he lives the rest of his life with these terrible nightmares, forever dreading the time he was to sleep. At worst his breath would stop, and he would die from fear or shock, and that could be any day. Adam had a feeling it was going to happen sooner rather than later. Neither outcome was something that Adam enjoyed.

As if almost reading his thoughts, Chase raised his eyebrows. "So," he said while shaking his glass, "hat do you mean it seemed connected? What happened in this one?"

He explained the dream from last night to Chase, and the more he spoke the more fluently he remembered it.

Adam talked about it with such vividness and clarity that the images returned to his head as if he were seeing it for the first time. He looked up at Chase, but only saw the landscape that had been in his dream.

It started in a field. A large field covered in tall, dead grass. It spread for miles in every direction, and no matter where Adam looked, he only saw more grass. Fire was covering a lot of it. Burning patches of grass washed the dark landscape in light. Dead bodies covered it as well. Adam was horrified. He collapsed onto his knees as he saw the wounds the bodies had. Severe burns, sword gashes, arrow holes, and giant bite marks across some of their bodies. He couldn't focus on what made them, or if it was coming for him, he simply focused on the hot tears that rolled down his face, and in his eyes that heavily blurred out the image. In front of him was a mountain so large, that it's top blended in with the clouds, and from its base, a building made of quarts and marble exploded with screams of what sounded like hundreds of men crying for.... battle?

He understood it; he was in the middle of a war. But which one? And who were they fighting? He hadn't heard or read of any of any battle in front of a mountain. He saw nothing living around him. He only heard the noises. He noticed a lot of the bodies around him were black as coal and boney, as if starved, almost... skeletal. They weren't human.

Then, the mountain burst into flames with the power of an active volcano and the sound of a thousand thunderclaps. The earth rumbled and the shockwave sent Adam hurdling backwards several hundred yards. The clouds became pitch black as blue lightning flashed in the inky sky.

Lava, fire, rocks, smoke, dust and ash rained down from the obliterated mountain. The smoldering dust at the summit was now visible and from it, a massive roar came. It shook the ground and curdled Adam's blood.

Then... he woke up. Strange, but the one he had had before was even stranger. Usually the dreams are simple. He sees the mountain and hears the roars and the dragons attack him, but these were the only two where more had happened.

That one had started on the top of a mountain instead of the bottom. It wasn't on fire, so Adam figured it was different, or at least hoped it wasn't going to explode with him on it. The war zone was behind him, he could hear it over his shoulders, but could not see the bottom. In front of him stood a large man. He was massive, almost thirty feet tall, Adam estimated. He was dressed in bright golden armor and his face was covered by a golden helmet. The only features visible were two blue eyes that crackled with electricity. In one hand he held a shield that was broken is two. The other half lay smoking on the ground. In the other hand he held a large club. The end was as big as a carriage, and the shield was the size of two. He threw the rest of the destroyed shield onto the ground as he raised his club over his head and swung it towards Adam. Suddenly, a bright light took everything away. It was all white. Then Adam woke up.

Chases words snapped him back to reality: "wow" he said, astonished. His eyes were wide open, but his eyebrows were low, almost like he was imagining the dream himself. "That's... terrifying." Chase attempted to sound sympathetic, but Adam knew it would not sound terrifying to someone who had never seen it themselves.

"What if the priestess tells us the same thing, she did last time, Chase?"

"We will make them tell us more. I promise, I just don't want you to end up damaged by something you may see in those things. Or worse...."

Adam was still reluctant, but he finally agreed. "Very well, we will go to the priestess. But I don't have coin..."

"Were you not listening? I will pay. Don't worry," Chase said while finishing his glass with a smile, "Now let's go find Kathrine."

After finishing their glasses and leaving the bar, Adam thought about his trip to the priestess.

He didn't like the odds of him coming out without the slightest idea of how to get rid of these nightmares, but it was the only option he had.

They walked out of the satyr-and-nymph filled plaza back onto the busy streets of Alor. Carriages strolled by as men and women walked and talked on the streets. The busy market was still buzzing with people as Chase and Adam travelled to Katherine's house.

She was most likely there, but she was unpredictable. She was used to the streets, she was born on them and raised by them. When Adam and his mother took her in, they fed her, gave her bed and even new clothes. Adam's mother re sewed his clothing to be fit for a girl. He was left with little to wear afterwards. He was never mad at Kathrine though.

She eventually went back to living on the streets, however she never said why. She simply stopped living at Adam's house and took over an abandoned one at the outskirts of the city. Neither Adam nor his mother were pleased with the decision. To Adam's mother, she had been a daughter, but to Adam, she was nothing like a sister. They shared a bond, a strong one. The thought of her face made his heart dance, and the sound of her voice was music, and when she spoke his name, it was his favorite song of all. He did not want to believe in love, not in a city like this. Love meant the bearing of children, and he did not want to show this city to an innocent child.

They walked past the courtyard, eventually returning to the streets. As Chase walked along side Adam, his fur swayed in the wind. Chase was taller than Adam, maybe about three inches. He had somewhat beefy arms and a broad chest. He wore brown, wool tunic and nothing covering his goatish back legs. He had pointed ears and small round ended horns that grew from his small afro. He told Adam about a girl he had met with, a kind nymph named Naomi. He spoke highly of her and was telling his story as they walked through the streets. She was kind, and beautiful and funny, but she was evidently not very bright, laughing at all the things that Chase said, even if they were not jokes.

They passed by a group of bearded men all drinking and smoking pipes. They looked at Chase annoyed and disgusted. They spat and cursed. One of them called to Adam, "Hey, boy!" He said. "What the hell do you think you are doing with that thing?" He laughed, then had another drink.

Adam turned to him, "He has done nothing to harm you, you fool!" People like this always made Adam angry. They were so arrogant and ignorant. His words burst from his mouth like flames. Chase put a hand on his shoulder, trying to call him away from the drunkards.

The man's smile melted into an angry glare. "What did you just call me?" He grunted as he pushed against his chair to stand up. "You should know better than to call a man that, and hang around the likes of this animal." He gestured to Chase as if he were filth.

He walked toward the pair.

Chase chuckled, unamused, and he stepped "What did you say?"

The man opened his mouth to speak, but the only sound he made was a grunt as Chase's fist flew into his nose. "You should know better than to call me an animal, you filth!" said Adam, intimidatingly.

The man's colleagues on the porch sat on their chairs shocked and without words. The rude man's black mustache and beard were now covered in blood from his nose and lip. He spat at the feet of the boys and proceeded back to his porch. Not turning around, the man began to say, "you know you are an animal, nothing but game from the forest. An ugly drunken beast!" The ugly drunken beast of a man said.

Adam could see the sad acceptance in Chases eyes as the angry man spoke every word.

The man simply continued, "you come anywhere near here again I'll kill ya! You dirty goat! You hear me? I'll kill ya!" His voice, fortunately, was eventually blocked out by the sound of passing by people and carriages.

Adam tapped Chase on the shoulder, "Are you alright?"

He cursed in Senewa and took a deep, shaky breath. "Yes… I'm fine. It's not the first time this has happened." It was sad, but true. Many people in Alor hated satyrs and nymphs because of their differences. Many people made little to no effort in hiding their bigoted ways. Many times, throwing stones and hateful comments a plenty to either. Not all residents of the city were like this, but the people who were did not hold back when it came to hurting members of either race. Verbally or physically. Chase had grown up around it. He didn't look like it, but he was several decades older than Adam. He looked to be the same age as Adam, but satyrs matured much quicker than humans. He was maybe thirty or forty in his own years, and over the years that Chase had lived in Alor, he had developed a sense of dignity and searched for nothing except respect from people. Still, when he was faced with the hateful ways of the bigoted many, he did nothing but walk away. What more was he to do? If he reacted with violence, he would only be proving the point that the bigots were trying to make. He left the problems be, but Adam knew they affected him.

That was not to say he was incapable of doing anything. He was tough and he knew how to fight. It was often that Chase would find himself in the middle of a quarrel with a couple of delinquents from around the city. He never started fights, but he knew how to end them.

"Don't worry about them." Adam said, "One day they'll have what they deserve."

"I suppose, but what of it. What happened has happened. Let's just focus on finding Kathrine." Chase said. Adam didn't like him changing the subject. He wanted to talk to Chase about the troubles that came with being different in a world that feared "different". He wondered where all that anger went. Whether it had left, or whether it was covered by a sheet of positivity until Chase found something to take it out on. Adam knew it was a serious matter, but he also knew that no one would help them. Satyrs were very disliked in the city. Parents even told their children to stay away from them, so growing up, and being best friends with one, Adam had little other friends aside from Chase and Kathrine. Being close with a member of a minority times like these did not help with his popularity, but he didn't care. Chase was funny, loyal and kind. He was a great friend, so, Adam was proud to call him one.

They continued walking and were about to turn a corner onto a road when suddenly a girl came running around the side of the building next to them and slammed straight into Adam. Knocking both Adam and Chase to the ground with a loud grunt, Adam noticed it was Kathrine. She shot up so quick that Adam could barely distinguish her face. Her voice was recognizable though. She looked down at him then helped them up with a hurry. His back was now facing the alley Kathrine had come out of.

"Come on let's go!" She cried, now facing Adam with his back to the road. "What? Where are we going?" Adam asked, concerned.

"Don't ask questions, I'll tell you when we get there. In the meantime," her eyes flew wide open as she saw something behind Adam.

"Run!"

Katherine nearly got run over by a carriage but somehow slid underneath it's wagon and continued sprinting down the path across the road. Adam and Chase had to wait until the carriage past to be able to cross.

It is then when Adam heard "get back here, you little brats!" He turned around as best he could while still running and noticed a man chasing them down the block. He picked up his pace until he was caught up with Kathrine. They had to run through crowds of people and merchant huts.

Turning another corner into a dead-end alley was when they stopped. They looked down, on the bottom corner was a hole large enough for a person to crawl through.

"Where are we going?" Adam asked.

"Shut up. He'll hear us." She whispered. "Follow me." She got on all fours and began to crawl into the small tunnel. Then, from inside, her voice echoed out.

"Come on you idiots!" she said. Chase made a face that said he obviously meant he didn't want to follow her. "You are insane," he said," you better not expect me to get in there." He turned around and began to walk out of the alley.

"Meet me at your house later when you 're done screwing around—" his face lit up. And then the man came running around the corner cursing and a club in his hand. Running back to Adam, Chase shouted at him to get in the tunnel.

"Get in! Get in!" He cried. Following his orders, Adam got on all fours and crawled as fast as he could through the tight tunnel. Chase quickly followed. And the sound of the man's voice on the other side eventually died out. After crawling for a few feet through the tight, dark tunnel, Adam made it to the other side only to notice Katherine walking calmly to a small building surrounded by a circular patch of grass. It was her house. This must have been a shortcut.

Adam followed her.

Katherine's house was at the end of the city, as far away as responsibility and society as possible, which wasn't far. It was a stone building with holes as windows and a wooden door. The flat roof was only 7 feet above the ground. Kathrine seemed to like it and so did Adam. It was small and warm. Besides, it had a bed and a fireplace, so it wasn't too bad. They walked in and got comfortable. Chase immediately looking for anything containing water, he was completely out of breath and holding his chest.

"The well is in the field." Kathrine said, obviously noticing his dehydration.

Chase cut to the exit and ran to the field behind the house. Adam and Kathrine stayed alone in the house. The inside was small. Just a few seats around the place and a metal pot suspended over a fireplace by sticks in the middle. In the corner furthest from the door sat a bed, next to it was a desk drawer made of rotting wood.

Adam looked at Kathrine. Her hazel hair was braided and sat over her shoulder. She had bright green eyes and wore a regular brown tunic. A piece of clothing made for boys. The girls her age and women usually wore long white gowns or longer tunics that had a subtle purple color. She didn't care. She wore whatever she wanted. Besides, as she was always on the run from merchants and other people, running in a tunic would be much easier than running than anything else.

"So, care to explain why we were running from that man?" He asked while panting.

She didn't say anything and instead only took a bag of food and fruit from behind her back with a smirk. Adam's eyes widened. "Oh," he said. She opened it and tossed an apple to Adam. He caught it and took a wet chomp. Kathrine then reached into the bag and took out a small doughball. Her favorite. She munched on multiple of those while Chase drowned himself in drinking water in the backyard. She pulled a second bag and shook it. Metal coins jingled inside.

Adam looked at her, "These were his?"

Kathrine nodded, "He's a merchant. I saw him selling these and I decided to maybe borrow some. Anyways," she said while taking a bite out of another doughball.

"Why were you and Chase on the streets?"

Adam continued eating his apple. "We were looking for you," he said to her, "Chase and I were going to go find the priestess again. I was wondering if you wanted to come?"

Kathrine's eyes widened, "You had another one? What happened? Are you okay?"

He didn't want to worry her, he didn't like it when she was worried, and she didn't either.

"I'm fine, don't worry; but I just don't want it to happen again. It worries me every time I have one. It of makes me feel like something is going to happen. I know it sounds foolish, but Chase said he'll pay, and that he'll make them say more if they just screw us off."

"Is that what you want to do?" Kathrine asked him.

"I don't think I have any other choice."

"That's not true."

"Then name another option."

Kathrine hesitated. Adam looked at her, disappointed. He knew she was just trying to make him feel better, but he did know she was lying. He had no other choice.

Chase opened the door and sat on the seat next to Adam's.

"Hey when did you two get food?" He asked.

Kathrine then tossed him a pear and another doughball. He immediately began to eat. Chase looked at Adam with a full mouth. "Did you tell her?"

"Yes." He answered.

"Good," he wiped his pear juice covered hands on his tunic, "let's go."

"Let's think about this," Kathrine interrupted. "Is this even going to work?"

Adam shrugged, "It has to." Chase agreed.

"And if it doesn't?" She said, "the dreams will keep coming and you would have just lost money for nothing. It doesn't make sense to do something that we've already tried. We could go to the priests in the citadel. They might help."

Chase waved his hand, "the Citadel never allows townsfolk to enter. And all those priests are all false and a bunch of cheats anyways. I've never seen one leave the castle, and what the hell would they do anyways? The priestess has actual abilities. We know this, we've seen her use them."

It was true, magic was no stranger to the residents of the city. None of the townsfolk knew how to use it but the priestess, because she was the only one who had it.

"We also know that she gave us useless information last time. Why would this time be any different?" Said Kathrine.

"We'll pay more." Chase said.

"That won't matter. She'll take your money and leave you with the same cryptic horseshit. It's a cheat." She looked at Adam. "Do you remember what she told you last time?"

"Yes, but how is that going to help?" Adam asked.

"Well, have you ever stopped to do what she told you to?"

"She told me to find the "dream giver" or something. It won't help." Kathrine rolled her eyes.

"We're out of options. Priestess it is!" Chase said. Adam agreed.

Kathrine, while reluctant, eventually gave in, and together they left the house, still on the lookout for the man with the club.

They returned to the courtyard where Adam followed Chase down a path leading a small reed hut. Opening the wooden door Chase entered and quickly grabbed a small brown sack. It made a jingling noise when he lifted it and Adam figured it was Chase's money, made from working for the non-bigoted merchants and stealing from the bigoted ones. Making their way to the center of the city, they passed people and there wasn't any sign of the club wielding man in the area.

The city of Alor was a large city located in the southern part of the continent of Vulna, Old maps Adam had seen in the old libraries gave him a lot of information, but all of it was false. Due to circumstances on the outside world, it was isolated after an old king demanded walls be put up to protect the residents of the cities from the elements of the outside world, thousands of years before Adam was born. Monsters, bandits, incoming armies (if any left) making their way to war or anything else that surrounded the area was locked out to prevent any death. The city was basically built inside a seven hundred-foot-tall solid stone fence. To the western side of the city, the castle stood nearly one hundred feet tall and was entirely made of quartz and marble. But where they were meant to keep intruders out, they were also made to keep residents inside.

Fields of flowers and tall grass dotted the landscape adding an element of beauty to the boring city. To the eastern side, near the docks, a massive cliff nearly jutted straight down on a steep slope. The houses and temples and stores and other buildings were built to near edge of the cliff, called Elder's Ridge. The cliff rounded out on the sides making the slopes on either side of the cliff much easier to descend. Mountains so tall that the summit was covered in clouds stood behind these slopes and they acted as the rest of the barrier surrounding the cliff. On the bottom of the crater, a huge lagoon sat peacefully as small fishing boats, fishermen and others gathered fresh drinking water and fish to eat.

The city was as beautiful as it could possibly be, which unfortunately was not much; However, living one's entire life inside one designated area without ever leaving or knowing what lies beyond can make one thirst for more. Adam wanted to leave it behind. Even is the rest of the world had ended.

When they found the building where the priestess worked, Chase handed Adam the pouch.

"Good luck." He said.

Kathrine patted his back and agreed with Chase. Adam took a deep breath and entered. They could not come with him. They would simply be kicked out as the magic being done was for Adam's sake.

From the outside, it still looked as ominous as Adam remembered. The walls and entrance were covered in purple and teal silk cloths, the inside wasn't much different. The walls and ceilings were all covered in purple cloths. There was no source of light apart from eight lit candles that sat in the middle of the room, which was dangerous, with all the cloth around, but he figured magic might be playing a role in controlling the fire... The floor was quarts and behind closed curtains lay the rest of the building: unknown to his eyes.

He stepped forward cautiously and asked is anyone was there. No response.

He asked again. More silence. Then a voice spoke.

"Hello," it said. The voice was raspy and almost echoing. As if it were coming out of the walls. Then an elderly lady wearing a purple and red cloak and hood, came out from behind the curtains. She looked up to show a wrinkled, hideous face. When she spoke, only three yellow teeth were visible, and her fingers were long, skinny and ended with long, grotesque fingernails. When she spoke again, her voice echoed.

"What may I do for you child?"

He hesitated, "I... I want you to cure me from my dreams."

The lady paused. "You again? I thought I already told you how to rid yourself of these nightmares."

"You didn't tell me anything. Only to "seek out my dream giver" or something. I don't know what that means. I want more information!"

She smiled, "That was perfectly good information dear. He is waiting for you, I saw it. However, if you insist on additional information: more information requires more payment, darling." She assured him.

Adam reached in his pocket and took out the brown sack. He threw in down in the middle of the ring of candles and the lady laughed.

"There you go," he said, "now talk."

The lady, with a snap of her disgusting fingers, made the sack vanish and then reappear in her hands.

"I hope you realize, boy, that you shall not receive anything from anyone asking like that." She said. Walking back into the other room.

Adam's eyes widened. "Hey wait!" He yelled. "I paid, give me my information."

He heard rummaging and the shifting of objects from behind the curtain.

"Quit your yammering boy!" Said the lady," I've only gone to retrieve the items to help your problem."

She placed a stone bowl into the middle of the ring and then placed a poppy, a glass bottle of water, and a small cup of white dust. She looked at Adam with a careless smile.

"The poppy is the flower of the god of dreams, Morpheus. Did you know that?" She said while grinding the ingredients together in the bowl. She sat down and encouraged Adam to do the same. Both on either side of the ring of candles.

Adam paused, "You... you still believe in the gods?".

She nodded, "Of course I do, if they were all dead, our existence as we know it would be destroyed. We live in a difficult world, but life has never been easy. We are always counting our mistakes, but we never count our blessings. We are alive, and we have each other. Look at the children in the fields of this city. They roam carelessly, playing with whomever, they wish. For this we have the gods to thank."

Adam sat speechless. He never considered what the lady was saying. He never really believed in the gods. And if he did, he couldn't thank them for a thing. His life was miserable, and he blamed the gods. The beliefs of their existence were beginning to diminish around the time he was born. By now, they were almost completely gone. She told him the people had each other, but that didn't count for shit in here.

"Here you go." The ladies ominous voice snapped him back to the present moment. She handed him the cloudy red solution.

Adam looked at the bowl. "Last time I was here you never made me drink anything."

"It is not for drinking boy," she said, "You came to me because you did not know how to contact, he who gives you your dreams. This," She signaled to the bowl, "should help you find him."

"What does it do?" Adam asked.

She said nothing and simply reached behind her, with another toothless cackle.

A ceramic jar appeared out of thin air with a puff of purple smoke. She reached her claw like fingers into it, and pulled out a black powder, it was shining and had bright little shining grains in it. It was spark powder, he realized.

The priestess scooped one half with one hand and poured the second half onto her second hand, then she tossed both into the stone bowl. Then she took a candle and simply pulled out fire. Adam thought he was hallucinating, but he rubbed his eyes and it was still happening, she curved her fingers and took a piece of the flame in her hands, without burning herself. Then, as she spoke and incantation in and some ancient language that Adam did not understand, she tossed it into the bowl.

Sparks flew, light flashed, and Adam nearly fell back. It was like a firework went off inside the tent.

"Hmm," said the lady. "Now, take my hand." Adam stared at the smoking bowl and placed the back of his hand on the palm of the lady, reluctantly. She whispered something in the ancient language while rocking back and forth with closed eyes. She continued and then opened her eyes to Adam's bewilderment. Her entire eyes began to glow. Adam's body felt lighter. He felt like he was drifting in a never-ending abyss.

He was without words; every time he opened his mouth his voice would not come out. The lady's voice was still going chanting something in the other language. She kept getting louder and louder and finally Adam thought he had rid himself from these horrible nightmares. Finally, no more staying up at night trying to make sense of it all. No more terrible thoughts. He was free. Then the room faded into dark.

When light returned to the tent, it was from the smoke of the bowl. It glowed a light pinkish color. The lady sat across Adam with her legs crossed and her eyes closed, then she opened them and began waving her arms around the smoke.

Adam's eyes widened as the pink clouds began to shift. They formed to create the face of a man. They turned and twisted around in the middle of the tent until Adam could distinguish the blurry face of a bearded man.

"He is a powerful man, the man you wish to meet. A man you have wished to meet for quite some time."

The clouds shifted again until they formed a mountain figure. On top of the mountain were twelve beams of white light,

"He will be past the golden apples. Beyond the greatest festivities and past the golden protector. Behind a fine feast. Beyond the city from which you came, beyond the walls that forbid exit." Then, the smoke faded, and they were back in the dark. The candles caught fire again and light returned.

"What the hell? You couldn't do this last time?" Adam squealed.

"You didn't pay for it." Said the priestess with a laugh.

Her smile faded when the clouds returned from the bowl. They floated to the top of the tent and despite the priestess trying to swat them out of existence, they would not dissipate. Adam was worried, and scared.

It shifted around until the face in the smoke was nothing more than a group of shapeless clouds.

Adam pursed his lips, "what the hell?"

He turned to the woman, who had a hand worryingly over her mouth.

A flash of light burst from the smoke, sending everything and everyone flying back several feet.

Adam collapsed to the floor and looked at the priestess. She was breathing heavily but otherwise she seemed fine. "Hm," she said.

Adam's eyes widened, "what did you do?"

The lady scratched her chin. "Something is coming. I see them. They are on their way her. They travel fast, and we summoned them."

Adam paused, "wait what? That doesn't make any sense. How did we? What exactly is coming? Wait what about my dreams? Are they done? Did you cure me?"

"I apologize but it seems to be the opposite, we have made them worse."

He raised his eyebrows. "What? But you saw him. You can tell me how to find him!" He argued. "Isn't he going to make them go away?"

She looked around, with a puff of purple smoke, a feather and paper appeared in front of her. She began to write, "take this boy. It will help you!" She handed Adam the paper, "Now go! Warn the others. They are coming! They will destroy Alor. Run! Now!"

Then suddenly a gust of wind and a flash of light washed over Adam's face. He was blinded for a quick second then realized some smoke in the air. Not much, only enough to come from a.... candle.

They were put out by the curtains for doors. Adam turned around. He hesitated. Chase and Katherine's voices were now approaching him. He felt dizzy and then they woke him up.

He sat up so quickly he gave himself a sharp neck pain. The lady was rubbing her eyes in the corner, and on his way to the tent was the man with the club, and he looked furious. Adam tucked the paper in his pant pockets. Chase and Kathrine lifted him up and they all began to run.

Sprinting as fast they could to avoid the man, who Adam finally got a good look at. He had a scruffy beard and mustache and brown, fair hair. He was tall and a bit pudgy. Like a large child. His arms were long and bulky, and he was dressed in an apron from the baking store he had come from. The apron sat over his brown wool tunic and sandals. He yelled at the three before picking up speed and catching up to them.

They ran through more crowded streets, cutting multiple corners to throw him off, but to no success. So much was happening, and he still didn't have an answer. Worst of all, he still had the dreams. According to the priestess.

"Ah hell, this again?" Chase said annoyed.

"Shit!" Adam screamed. "I thought we lost him!"

"Well he found us again!"

They turned another corner and then entered a large marble courtyard as they noticed people following them. The crowd began to get tighter, harder to move through. Then they made it to the end. It ended on the edge of the cliff with columns on either side. The railing was covered with people looking onto the horizon. They curved through people and the crowds they made, and they finally lost the man.

However, they realized their problems might had gotten greater. The crowds of people seemingly got larger with every passing second, their voices could be heard asking strange questions.

"What are those?" One lady said.

"Demons!" Screamed another.

Adam noticed that closing in on either side of the courtyard, through the corridors that lead to the marketplace, armored guards immediately called for the people's cooperation in evacuating the building. He was caught off when suddenly a green cloud flew up behind him and he fell over the railing. More likely, he was thrown. By the cloud? Adam had no time to think. The fading screaming of the guard and then the thump of him making impact with the ground at the bottom of the cliff caused an immediate stampede. The priestess was right about something coming.

People went sprinting, grabbing their children or completely abandoning the whole group. They were screaming and they split up the three. Adam went to follow the crowd when a sharp pain split. He turned around and continued running, leaving Adam on the ground. Chase was on the other side of the platform, pushing and shoving his way and trying to reach Kathrine who had already left with most of the screaming crowd. Adam curled up into a ball with his head in between his knees and his hands over his head. He breathed heavily as groups of people still tried to run past, over, or on top of him.

The large green cloud flew above the open canyon and then somehow engaged a fight with the armed guards.

The guards were all wearing matching uniforms with silver chain mail armor with solid breastplates and chain mail pants over red fabric ones. They had sheathed swords strapped to their belts and spears with red tunics underneath the armor. With an order from the first guard, the rest engaged, throwing their spears at the clouds. The weapons flew and travelled through the clouds, which were about up to Adam's waist in height and had a disgusting, poison green color, but the spears did not come out the other side. They simply vanished into thin air once they hit the clouds. Then, with a gust of wind, the spears went flying in the opposite direction directly to the guards, impaling them straight through the torso. Adam was horrified and he felt like throwing up. At this point, the entire platform had been evacuated. Except for the guards he was the only one there. So, he decided to pick himself up, hold back his vomit and get the hell out of there.

A larger group of guards, about thirty to forty, scrambled into the entrance of the building and began fighting the clouds. One of them noticed Adam trying to leave and went to aid him with the help of two other guards for protection. The panicked screams of residents were noticeable even through the thick marble walls of the building. They ran to him as he got up on all fours. The loud "thunks" of the spears and other weapons piercing the armors of the guards made Adam paranoid.

They got to the exit and left the building as fast as they could when a group of more guards came bounding into the building with a massive crossbow being pulled by horses. They loaded the bolt in a haste.

There were only two guards helping Adam now, the third one being lost in the heat of the fight. They had shields and swords over Adam, protecting him and as soon as they got far enough, they stopped.

One of the guards looked at Adam with his hand on the boy's shoulder, "Are you hurt?" He asked.

Adam looked up, shocked and terrified but unhurt. He wanted to find his friends, he wanted to know if they were ok. The soldiers turned around and began to run to the building when one of them stopped in his tracks. He asked his colleague, "Do you hear that?" They paused for a sound.

"No." The second guard replied.

"Exactly," Said the first. Adam stood in the middle of the sidewalk completely stunned. He couldn't move. Those things, whatever they were, were the things that the priestess had warned about. He wondered if that vision had anything to do with it.

He tried to move his feet, but they were seemingly glued to the ground. Men and women stood looking at the building waiting for something to happen. No screams or sounds of combat were audible. Adam took a small step backwards.

The two guards in front of Adam rushed to the aid of their friends but as soon as they took one step forward a large boom shook the ground.

"The crossbow," Adam whispered to himself.

Another loud boom, then a third. The people around him began shaking and making nervous sounds.

Then the building exploded, and Adam flew backwards.

With an immense eruption of steel and rock, the wall of the building blew into pieces. The crossbow was seen through the large whole in the wall, smoking and facing them. He wiped the dust from his face and coughed. He looked through the whole in the wall and gasped. The bodies of the dead soldiers were littered around the entire platform.

For a moment the only sounds heard were the concerned noises of the citizens and the faint curse from a man or woman.

Then the streets burst into a massive storm of screams, and shouts, as the two green clouds flew through the whole and immediately killed the two guards that helped Adam by throwing a spear and a sword at each of them. The clouds flew higher as Adam got to his feet. He couldn't take his eyes off of what was happening. Once they reached a point, they believed was high enough, around twenty or thirty feet off the ground, the clouds unfurled and shifted to reveal their true forms. They were the most grotesquely disgusting creatures Adam had ever seen.

They were both about Adam's height, with a thin bony build. Their skin was rough and had a deep green color to it. Their bony hands ended with long, nimble, skeletal fingers tipped with long, sharp claws. Their eyes glowed red and their mouths were filled with razor sharp teeth. Swaying behind them was a long scary tail and they had sharp talons that looked... metallic.

Even the bat wings that sprouted from their shoulder blades was not the strangest thing they had. That title went to their heads. The backs of their necks and a crest in it that stretched to the top of their head like a cobra's crown. In between their neck and their crest, a nest of living serpents seemed to be connected to them by the tail. Green venomous vipers.

When they spoke, their long, slit tongue hung from their slimy mouths, "Where is it Stheno?" One asked its companion. The second monster looked at the first, "it will not simply show itself to us," Said the first monster. "We must find it. Smell it's blood."

The crowds of people continued running past Adam. Adam, he simply stood there, not knowing what to do. He was frozen. He knew that if he stood there he would die, but his feet just didn't move.

The second monster, who was called Stheno sniffed the air, seemingly unfazed by the cowering people.

"Euryale," It said to the first, "It is close." Adam realized that they had come here to hunt him. He was they're prey. He summoned them therefore he would be they're primary target. But what about the priestess? She helped as well.

He still could not move but then someone from behind him startled him. It was Kathrine and she was out of breath.

"We need to leave now! What the hell are those?" She cried while looking at the horrid creatures.

"Let's go now!" Chase was following Kathrine and was also exhausted. Following the direction of the crowd, the three sprinted away from the monsters as they began to glide above of the crowd. They're large scaly bat wings ripped through the air like blades and they held their hands out in front of them.

Adam recognized them. He had heard stories long ago. They were gorgons, monstrous creatures that terrorized the land with their exceptional killing ability and venomous breath. They were more horrendous in person then they were depicted in stories.

They made their way to Katherine's house, still following the direction of the remainders of the cowering crowd. The beasts were still flying above them.

"What the hell was that? What on earth were those things?" She said.

"Gorgons," Chase said. "Poisonous monsters."

"Oh shit..." said Adam, still trying to catch his breath.

"Are they coming for us?"

"Hell, if I know!" Snapped Kathrine.

"Hey, calm down. This never would have happened if you—*"

Kathrine interrupted him, "No! This never would have happened if you didn't want to go get information you already knew!"

"But I didn't —*."

"I don't care." She snapped. "We were out, so they attacked us."

"Fine, be like this, but right now we need to worry about those things in the city. The priestess said something about calling them here, I just don't know how, or why. But maybe this can help." He pulled out the crumpled piece of paper the priestess wrote on. He folded it open and stared at her writing.

Past the golden apples.
Past the festivities.
Past the impenetrable defender.
Past a fine feast.
Past the city from which you came.
Past the walls that forbid exit.

Kathrine took out of Adam's hands, "What is this?"

Adam scratched his head, "I had a vision. It was a mountain in clouds of smoke. If we follow it, she said it could lead us to the dream giver."

Kathrine squinted at the paper with frustration, "past a fine feast? City from which you came? Walls? Exit?" She mumbled faintly, "That means Alor! You expect to leave?"

"Yes! It's a chance, and it's something we've always wanted!"

Kathrine scowled, "You wanted!" She corrected.

Chase stepped forward, "That's enough!" He snapped. "We can't focus on that right now. Those things are outside and they're wrecking the city. Adam, tell us what happened in the tent. You said this was the priestesses work, and that you had a vision? How?"

Adam began to pace. "I don't know entirely how. She started doing this weird ritual. She hadn't done it last time, so I thought it would work."

He explained what happened in his vision. "It was her magic, so I thought nothing of it. But then she said something about summoning them. Next thing I know I'm running into the city from killer bat women."

Chase held his hair with stress. "Shit, oh shit. Okay so we know the ritual summoned them. But how the hell do we, I don't know, unsummon them?"

"The priestess most likely knows." Kathrine said. "But we don't know where she is."

Chase's eyes opened and he jolted up and towards the door.

"Where the hell do you think you are going?" Asked Adam.

"The satyrs and nymphs on the other side. I need to see if they're ok. They're my family." He said worryingly.

Adam raised his eyebrows. "No, you can't do that. You'll die."

"I'll be quick. I promise." He said as he shoved objects away from the entrance of the house.

For a moment, when he opened it, the screams of faraway citizens could be heard. It felt like catastrophe.

Adam and Kathrine stood there, waiting for their friend to come back from near certain death, in the middle of the House.

Adam turned to her. "Look I'm so tired of this. You're always stealing. When are you going to realize that there's a better way to live?"

"When you show me. You know damn well that's not true so shut up!" She snapped. "Besides, where is this coming from?"

Adam put the piece of paper in his pocket again, "If you hadn't stolen from that man, we wouldn't have ended up away from the priestess's tent, and maybe we could have found a way to solve this problem." Kathrine scowled at him and stood up, "When are you going to realize that I steal for us. I steal so that we can eat. What do you do?! All you do is mope about and cry about your stupid dreams. They aren't going away! Accept it. Argh! Sometimes you just make me want to punch you in the face."

"Kathrine, it doesn't matter what I do."

"Yes, it does! I do the wrong things for the right reasons. Can't you see that? You don't do anything!"

Adam looked at the ground, and said nothing. He always fought with Kathrine. She was hardheaded and stubborn. But she was still close with Adam. Despite being his opposite, Adam never really connected with anyone else the same way he did with Kathrine. Adam couldn't fight the way she was. He was more of an outsider. He loved reading. Kathrine did not even know how to read. And maybe deep down, he knew that she was right.

He read them all the time. His favorites were the stories he'd heard about the creatures in the outside world, and how the earth looked thousands of years ago. Long before the creation of humanity, it was green and full of life.

That was not the case nowadays. He wanted to say something to her, but when she was angry, he knew it was best for him to leave her alone.

Several minutes had passed since Chase had first left. But suddenly, with a loud thud, Chase made it into the room, sweating and breathing heavily. "What happened??" Adam asked. Him and Kathrine walked over to him.

"They're destroying everything. They flew over the citadel and wrecked the walls. They threw guards everywhere and the marketplace is in ruins. We need to stay silent. I know they're close. I can smell them."

Kathrine opened her mouth to speak but Chase covered her mouth.

"Shh. They're here..." he pointed to the ceiling with his free hand and Kathrine removed the first. The three listened closely as a series of clicks could be heard on the roof. As if a bird was poking at it with its beak, trying to find sticks for its nest. The silence was unbearable. They crouched down next to the furniture trying not to make a sound. Then, three loud clicks could be heard, each one louder than the last.

The ceiling collapsed as one of the monsters from outside could be seen diving into the building.

Her claws pierced into Adam's clothes and Kathrine screamed for it to let him go. The monster, the second gorgon: Stheno, lifted Adam above the ground and began to take him away. She was fast.

He was lifted through the destroyed roof, but he stopped the kidnapping by hanging on to the side of the hole left in the stone ceiling. Chase and Kathrine stood on the inside, pulling him and not letting go by any means. Adam screamed with pain and the gorgon and his friends fought for who was going to win him. His torso was filled with pain. His sweat trickled down his arms and through the cracks in his fingers. He began to slip as Chase and Kathrine still held onto his clothes. But they were beginning to lose their grip as well. He could feel his sweat mix with his blood as the jagged hole cut up his palms. Adam's grasp on the ceiling was lost eventually and he saw the horrified look of Chase and Kathrine's face become smaller and smaller as he flew further away from them.

Within a matter of seconds, he was already on the other side of the city: near the canyon. Where the gorgons first attacked.

His mind was racing. If she dropped him, he would surely die, if she didn't, she would take him back to wherever she came from and simply delay the inevitable. A projectile went flying past his face and Adam realized it was an arrow. He looked behind him to notice the guards and soldiers of the city firing arrows through bows and crossbows. With every one that pierced the skin of her wings, Stheno began to lower, to the point where Adam would not die if the dropped him. She managed to dodge many of the incoming arrows. That still didn't make his predicament much better. The arrows flew close to him and nearly struck him in his torso, if it wasn't for a quick maneuver to dodge the arrow by the gorgon Adam would have been hit.

Another flying arrow pierced the leathery skin between the bones of the gorgon's wings, causing her to plummet to the ground, dropping Adam in the process. It fell into the middle of the streets while Adam fell onto a merchant's hut and crushed it, rolling over it and eventually ending up on the dusty ground. Adam heard a loud crunch in his ear but felt no pain. He got up and continued running, now with both monsters behind him. The second one appearing from behind another merchant's hut, bursting through it and throwing food and wood everywhere. Adam ran to the end the of the city to the hills that lead to the bottom of the canyon. Stheno followed by foot because of her damaged wing and Euryale flying above.

She zoomed towards him with blazing speed, however a quick dodge on Adam's hand cause her to land face first in the ground and go tumbling down the slope to the water below. Stheno may have had an eagle's talons for feet, but she was nowhere near slow. She caught up with him quickly and nearly caught him, he managed to get to the bottom before she grabbed him.

"I'll rip you to shreds!" She shrieked...

He dashed to the boats and could see more guards coming around the opposite slope. He sprinted towards and they all took aim with spears, bows, and cannons, but not only to the monster, they aimed at him as well.

Before Adam could process everything, a scream could be heard behind him and emerging from the water was Euryale. She shrieked and blazed towards Adam. She was about three inches away from him when the guards opened fire.

The explosion the cannon had made launched him and both gorgons in different directions. He went left, towards the cliff wall, and the gorgons landed in the water. The guards quickly subdued Euryale, quickly slitting her throat with a blade from one of the guard's belts, killing her. Her companion however, she was already getting up from out of the water. Her appearance was even more disgusting from before because the explosion caused her right arm and half her face to melt off, along with multiple snakes, which left nothing but bloody tentacle like appendages sticking out from beneath her crest. She lunged at Adam and he dodged by rolling away from her pounce. Her metal claws managed to grab his foot, they dug into his skin, he bled out as she still waited to take his life.

He closed his eyes and accepted his fate when suddenly, a guard came to his aid. He stabbed his spear through what remained of the monster's face. It let out a loud shriek with the weapon in her face, then fell to the ground, dead.

Adam breathed heavily as all the effects of the battle hit him at once, his shoulder erupted with pain, his foot felt like it was burning and bruised.

He then let out a loud scream and closed his tired eyes as the guards lifted him up. Then, the world faded to black.

2

HE WOKE UP in a field, wind lightly blowing through his hair. It was cold. He was dressed normally but his wounds were all gone. He lay there, confused. Adam got up. He looked around but for miles he could only see the same thing. More grass. It covered hills and groves. Mountains loomed over the valley.

He looked over the mountains. The sky was a deep purple color with blue lights and white stars sparkling in the darkness. The seemed as if it were lower, closer to the earth than usual. It beautifully shined over the night and gave the landscape a sense of magic. Adam thought to himself: "is this the afterlife."

Had he died? In the attack on the city, did the gorgons kill him? He thought about what this could mean. He left that boring life, but he had also left everything good about that life: Kathrine, Chase, his other friends. He never got to see what was on the other side of that wall. It didn't matter anymore. It was all probably the exact way the elders described it, dangerous, disgusting, foul.

He didn't believe this was the end, however. He was alone. If this was the afterlife, why was he alone? No person was visible for miles.

He stepped forward, towards the mountains. The ground shifted and the landscape moved as he walked. The ground moved towards him, but he didn't even flinch. He looked down and noticed he was standing in a new spot than originally. He took one step forward, but moved over half a quarter of a mile. He took another step and the ground blurred with speed once again and Adam found himself closer to the mountains. He began to sprint and within a matter of minutes he was at the base of the mountain. Adam looked at the mountain and wondered if it was the one in his old dreams.

His dreams. He thought about it. This could be just another dream. Either that, or Adam really was dead... he pushed the thought aside. He was hesitant to believe it, there were no horrifying sights, despite the fact that the priestess said they were going to get worse. It was peaceful. He liked it. It still felt like a dream. Because it had sights and aspects that were never seen in real life. However, he felt everything around him. His dreams were always so profoundly realistic. He could feel the cold grass rubbing against his feet. The wind blew gentle breezes through this short hair. He felt his face take the breath of the wind, it refreshed him.

He began to climb the mountain and suddenly the shifting of reality stopped. He moved normally, slowly placing one foot behind another as he continued his ascent. The rocks were slippery, as if a recent rainfall had showered them, adding a sheet of water that made them impossible to climb.

He stared at the summit. Then ascended.

Along the way, Adam thought about what he might see at the summit. Was this the mountain in his dreams? It was probable. However, it had no dead bodies. Nor fire, nor lakes of blood covering the land. Regardless it did seem familiar. He had seen it before. Perhaps in another dream. But he couldn't think of it. Most of them, except for some, were almost completely forgotten about. Others had become nothing more than bits and pieces of a forgotten nightmare that once kept Adam hostage during the night. It felt like a few minutes had passed since he first woke up in this strange place. He knew that, it was more like a few hours. He looked up at what remained of the mountain, what was yet to be climbed. Not much. He was almost at the top. Under normal circumstances his hands would have begun to bleed, or he would slip on the wet rocks and fall from a height that would kill him. He was now at a point taller than any building in Alor, yet, the sight of any living creatures was never there. He couldn't see any birds, animals, people. It was a ghost land. He felt like the last man on earth.

Within around fifteen more minutes of climbing the wet mountain he reached the summit. The view at the summit was beautiful on one side, it was empty of life, but it had a beautiful charm to it. The way that the purple sky lit up the miles and miles of grass as it ever so satisfyingly swayed in the wind was mesmerizing. But when Adam turned, he wished that he had stayed at the foot of the mountain.

He now knew that this was a nightmare. He hoped for it. On the other side of the mountain was a city. Destroyed and in ruins. Stone columns stood at varying feet before eventually ending in a crushed, destroyed top with the rest of the fallen buildings scattered throughout. It seemed as if this city was hit by multiple earthquakes or crushed by something huge. The essence of death and destruction could be felt in the mere presence of the city. He looked around him. That's all he could see. The valley was almost completely dark except for the many red puddles of sparking flames that dotted the entire valley. Around the fire, scorched, black skeletons were burning and melting. It was almost completely silent except for the faint crackling of the far away flames. This was the horrific sight he was expecting, but prayed that it never came. When he descended it became worse?

Still on top of the mountain, Adam took a single step forward, however, like how he approached the mountain before, the ground shifted, his ears were flooded with the noise of the ground he was standing on shifting. In front of him, dust and rocks shifted out of the way like water. Eventually, they had formed a smooth path suitable for walking on. He took another step forward when the ground shifted again.

Rocks underneath him began moving forward. They lifted him slightly however he never lost balance. Almost floating on a cloud of rocks, he descended the mountain to a small courtyard nearer to the center of the city. He passed small fires and more destroyed buildings. He looked at the bodies, some were large: meaning adults. But when

Adam noticed some of the other skeletons he fell to his knees and began to cry.

He sat there horrified as smaller skeletons surrounded him. Children, infants. This was a massacre. This city was attacked by an army. It was evident by the number of bodies that the army that attacked had taken no prisoners. Neither had they lost any of their own men. None of the bodies were wearing battle armor. All were wearing togas and casual clothes stained with blood and peppered with holes. Who would do this? Much of the damage could not have been done by humans alone. They had something on their side. Something dangerous. He noticed how the buildings looked. Architecture he had seen before. Then he saw one more body. The skeleton was charred and covered in dust. But on the top of its skull, were a pair of horns. Adam gasped as a tear ran down his cheek.

This was Alor. That skeleton was a satyr.

He sat there, slowly making a puddle of his tears bigger and bigger.

"They are not all here. Some of them escaped." Said a voice. "They will all go to the golden city."

Adam looked up to see a man. A tall man, he had a long white beard with long white hair and blue eyes. He wore a long red cloak that seemed old and dirty. Underneath, a regular tunic. "Many of them got lucky." He reassured.

Adam looked at the horrific sight.

"How is this lucky? They were tortured and killed. This is terrible"

"It could have been worse. Much, much worse."

Adam considered the things he was saying. Then realized he might have had a point. This was not the place in his other dreams.

"Those bodies deserved what they received however." Said the man. Adam looked at him.

"How could you say that? These were children, kids. Innocent men and women. They did not even have a way to defend themselves."

"I was talking about the bodies in your other dream. The one you were just thinking of."

Adam paused. "How...how did you know that? Who are you?"

"I am no one. I have many names but none of them are important. I'm sorry to talk to you like this. It is the best I could reach. Please forgive me."

Adam stood confused then remembered what the priestess said to him.

"You were the man she was talking about; you are the person who gives me my dreams." He said.

The man nodded. "You are a smart boy. I see that the priestesses magic had worked, as I hoped it would." Adam paused. A sudden group of emotions assaulted him at once. Anger and sadness made him want to hurt the man for all the pain and suffering he had caused him. However, now that he knew who was giving him these nightmares, he could finally stop them. Instead he simply let one word come out of his mouth.

"Why?"

"He fears you. You are the only one who can stop him. I would tell you more if I could, but I cannot, not right now. Believe that. But believe me also when I say, that, Adam, you are part of a world much larger than your own. You just don't understand it yet."

Adam processed what he was saying. He stood there not knowing what to do or what to say. This was only a dream, how could he tell that every word that was coming out of this man's mouth wasn't a lie followed by a second that simply wanted him to believe it so he could wake up and return to that horrid reality for the rest of his life and wonder where it all went?

There was another thing, how did he know he wasn't dead? Those monsters had wounded him terribly, they could have killed him. Maybe they did. He knew now that it was the magic that summoned them, but why didn't they kill immediately. He knew they could have easily.

However, they tried to fly off with him instead. They didn't want him dead. He wondered why...

"He wanted you."

"Who did?"

"The one who corrupts your dreams. All the things you see in your dreams. The horrific sights. It's all because of him, and I am near powerless to stop it. He sent the gorgons after you, that is why they didn't kill you. He wanted you." He said, looking towards the ground with a frown.

This man could hear Adam's thoughts, he was cautious of anything he thought about going forward.

"What is his name?"

The man paused, he stared at his sandals as if contemplating to tell Adam or not. It wasn't his fault. This "thing", this person that the man had mentioned had somehow infiltrated his mind. This thing was in his head.

"I cannot tell you. He will kill both of us. He will win." Said the man.

Adam waited for the man to something else. Anything else, but instead the sky dematerialized. As if it were made of paper, the entire sky folded up and crumbled in seconds before returning back its normal state. Adam looked at the man, hoping for an explanation. Instead, the ground began to rumble. What was left of the ruined buildings suddenly melted into dunes of sand. The skeletons began turning into ashes as the wind blew more and more away. The black ashes began to glow as if being lit by a fire. They formed together to make a massive cloud of fiery black dust. Thousands of particles swirling into one solid being. In the center, two groups of ashes suddenly completely burst into flames forming red eyes. The front elongated making a snout and in a matter of seconds what seemed like a black, molten dragon was standing in front of Adam and the man. It was several feet long and almost 20 feet tall, it was covered in flames and looked at Adam with an open mouth. It's teeth we're made of the metal of the weapons what been used to kill the citizens.

"Adam...." said the man.

Adam turned to him.

"Run."

With that order the two began to sprint in the opposite direction as the dragon. Adam could feel the heat singe the hair on the back of his neck as the dragon blasted the courtyard in flames. It sounded more like a destructive hiss than an explosion.

Out of the destroyed remains of the building came out the dragon, now with multiple heads courtesy of the dust from the buildings it had just destroyed. The flames on its body turned blue as it charged up another blast. Adam turned a corner to avoid being consumed by the fire and thankfully, the dragon missed. The man now came running towards Adam with a large silver sword made of shining steel. He jumped in front of the dragon and stabbed the creature in between the eyes. Instead of a wound, in the place where the blade had hit, the dragon's ashes began to glow white and eventually burn out.

"Go Adam!" Yelled the man.

"You need to wake up! Adam wake up!"

Adam stood shocked as the man swung at the beast with the shining blade, creating more and more of the glowing wounds. He focused on what was happening and wanted to wake up. He was caught in a problem. While still hiding behind a wall facing opposite the dragon he thought. Could he die here? If he woke up, he knew almost for certain that he would die. The gorgons had given him multiple stab wounds in his leg and had also broken his arm. They had thrown him from several stories, and he landed on buildings. The alternative was not much desired, if he stayed in this vision, and the dragon got to him, it would do much worse than break bones and cut his feet. It would burn him to death. If it desires not to eat it. However, a thought popped in his mind. Usually in his dreams, in the moment when he is about to be killed by anything, he wakes up. He concluded that attempting to stay alive in this dream world.

As he thought, the loud explosions of the dragon blasting flame at the bearded man shook the ground and the howling pain from the stabs the man gave him curdled Adam's blood. Adam also thought about another possibility, how did he know this man wasn't trying to kill him? Stopping the dragon only to do it himself. He didn't know who the man was, but he could tell he was powerful. That he had been in battle. Maybe he was a warrior, or a soldier. Adam saw a warrior when he looked at him. A strong, dangerous man. But also a kind and caring one. A man who would release hell upon those who wrong him. Adam did nothing to upset him, so maybe he wasn't trying to kill him. Adam didn't want to find out.

A loud explosion rocked Adam's ears as the man flew back into the wall in front of Adam, chipping off the corner and landing in the dusty remains next to it. He got back up almost immediately and was about to charge at the monster again when he noticed Adam.

What a pathetic sight he must have been, he thought to himself, a teenage boy crying and cowering like an infant who was just yelled at. He was covered in dust and ashes. Warm tears rolled down his face as he held his hands over his head, protecting himself from falling rocks.

The warrior's eyes widened, and he was about to speak when the creature howled. A boom and crunch sound erupted from it and then suddenly a large chunk of rocky debris was flung at the man as if it were a small stone. It destroyed the building behind the man as he quickly grabbed Adam in his arms and ran, still holding Adam. He ran with great speed and remained in the air for seconds at a time, as if he was hopping. However, he was hoping for a longer period than any regular human. He was almost floating. The man dropped Adam when they were far enough away from the beast.

"What on earth are you still doing here?" He cried. "I told you to wake up!" Adam never took that as an order, simply as a statement. Maybe a metaphor for something, he realized now that wasn't the case.

"Can you not wake up?" He asked, crouching behind an old waterless fountain.

"I don't.... know. I don't know how. "Adam said. Crouching behind him.

Following them into the courtyard of the fountain the dragon burst through a pair of walls that were smaller than itself, causing rocks and debris to fly in all directions.

Then to Adam's surprise. It spoke.

"Child..." It said.

Adam preferred a mouth that spewed flames than one that had a voice like that. When it spoke, what seemed like a million sinister voices spoke simultaneously causing every bone in Adam's body to shake.

"I find it amusing how you do not know so many things. Has the king of fools forgotten an explanation?" It snarled.

The man next to Adam clenched his fist. Adam was still covering his head, and the man gestured for him to remain silent, so Adam guessed the monster hadn't found them yet. In front of Adam, more destroyed bricks and wrecked buildings converted to dust and hundreds of swirls of sand and dust flew over his head and he guessed that they added to the creature's body. Adam could hear the collection of materials sticking to his body, and each other, creating things he did not want to imagine. The sound of the monster's metal claws hitting the hard ground repeated in Adam's ears. The dragon spoke again.

"Tell me boy, do you know what this is? Any of this? This man, myself, the very ground you walk on... what is it?"

Adam looked at the man. Who seemed as if he had done something wrong? He looked at the ground and tightened his fist. His sword was held in his other hand and he turned to Adam.

"Take this," he handed the boy his blade. "When you are ready, use it." He held Adam's right hand as Adam received the blade with his left. He took it by the hilt and tightened his grip on it. As the skin of the tips of his fingers tightened around the hilt, Adam felt a surge of power shoot through his spine. The sword was perfect. The blade was perfectly designed for slashing and slicing. Adam noticed the whole thing was made of iron; most swords he saw had leather hilts. But not this one, in had a hilt made of a silver metal that seemed incredibly light. Adam waved the blade around, and it felt as if the weapon had become a feather. Nothing more than an extension of his body. Something that he could move with nothing more than a reflex. He knew the sword was made for him.

"Look at me." Said the man. Adam focused on him. He noticed things he never did before, the center of the man's eyes were a pure, colorless white rather than black. His irises were the lightest color of blue Adam had ever seen. A calm sky colors. No sky he had ever seen, but looking into the man's eyes, he felt as if he now knew what he was missing. The man's breath smelled of fresh air.

"Listen to me very carefully. When you wake, follow the boy and the man. Whatever you do, trust in him. Trust in me. Please Adam, promise me that."

Adam didn't know this man, yet, as he sat there in front of him, he felt as if this man was someone he could trust. He felt as if denying would bring him possibly even more suffering. This was the man who had given him his dreams. They were never pleasant, but maybe he could do something with that information. He could, maybe one day he could rid that monster from everything and finally take control of his nightmares, leaking them into whatever he wanted. Every word that came out the man's mouth was a riddle, one which seemed to have no answer; however, he looked the man in his eyes and complied.

"I promise." He said, firmly.

"Good," Said the man. "Now, raise your weapon and step forward.

Immediately, everything Adam had thought before went up in flames. This man was trying to kill him.

"No, I am not." Said the man, Adam forgot he could read his thoughts.

"I don't know about this. Maybe you could—*" Adam was cut off by an explosion that sent them both flying. When the dust settled and Adam opened his eyes, the creature stood above the man's unconscious body. His center head had a mouth that was flaming. His appearance had changed. He now had three heads also made of dust and ashes, and a broken line pattern covered his body and it showed fire and heat on the other side, giving the monsters body a molten lava kind of look.

"This is sad," It said, still in the same sinister voice. "It brings tears to my eyes, how you both believe in pathetic stories." He turned to Adam and Adam scoured the area for the weapon. In the corner of his eye he noticed a bright light and slowly signaled to it for the man to realize. It was a sword. The creature stood in between of them and looked at Adam.

Slowly, three long black tendrils shot out of his body, and after becoming somewhat used to their new form, the ashes shot at Adam with blinding speed. He dodged and ran for the blade. One of the tendrils swung at his feet and he fell as the dragon's mouth began to smoke and fire up. He reached for the sword, which was stuck in the ground, and he took it by the hilt. He turned to the monster. The creature simply smiled and continued to smoke. Adam could faintly hear the man scream, as the fire from the mouth of the dragon surrounded him. It blinded him and he lifted the weapon for protection. Instead the light erupted into an even brighter one once they hit. The man's scream faded away as the rumbling in Adam's ears blasted louder and louder. Then suddenly everything stopped, and the world turned black.

Adam opened his eyes and his surroundings appeared as a blurry fuzz. Pain suddenly filled his body and his senses rushed back to functioning normally. He screamed for minutes and rolled in pain before he even realized where he was. He lay there slowly noticing more and more about his surroundings. How the walls had cracks scattered around in random spots. The room was dry, like it hasn't seen water in decades. Adam was thirsty. His mouth begged for water but when he attempted to say something no sounds came out. His damaged body made him realize that he wasn't in a dream anymore, this was reality.

He tried his best to not look around or move to drastically. Whenever he turned his neck, he could feel and hear the severed halves of his collar bone graze against each other. He screamed in agony.

A voice came from nearby and it said

"Shut up. I'm trying to sleep. Be in pain quieter."

Adam was breathing heavily and heard it. His pupils quickly darted from one corner of his eye to another.

"Where am I?" He asked faintly.

He doubted the voice was going to hear him. He spoke so quietly, nearly whispering. He wasn't even sure he heard a voice to begin with, maybe he was just hallucinating.

There was a pause of silence. For a moment or two, the owner of the voice began to shuffle things around. Moving slowly as if he was getting up from his sleep in the morning.

"The citadel prisons." It replied. "They brought you in yesterday morning. You've been quiet for quite a while." The voice was smooth. It didn't seem like the person speaking was old or grizzled. So if Adam guessed, he'd say the owner was somewhere near his age. His first thought was Mason, his childhood bully. He always got into trouble, but there was a fat chance of that, Mason never got caught. Then he remembered what the man in his dream had said, the *boy and the man*.

"Do you even know what you're in here for?" The voice asked. "I stole some stuff so they through me in here. I had to though. My friends and I needed to eat." He giggled; Adam was sure now that it was only a kid.

He remembered the incident with the baker.

He moved up towards the wall in order to comfort himself, and he noticed that his arm was wrapped in gauze and had a sling. His ankle was also covered in gauze, but it had bloody stains bleeding through the white bandages. He began to breath heavily, but calmed down and managed to answer the voices message.

"I... I stole as well." Adam answered.

"Oh, okay. What's your name?"

"Adam."

"Nice to meet you, I'm Hexus."

Adam slowly moved his head from looking to one side to looking towards the other. He lay on a large stone rectangle in the corner of a stone room. The bottom edges and corners had plants and small leaves sprouting from the cracks. Odd, since Adam couldn't find water anywhere. About seven feet away from Adam, steel bars blocked anyway he could get out.

"I need, help. I broke something."

"I know. The way you screamed said so. I broke my arm once. It hurt, a lot. But back then I had my friends to help me.

"In here, you're not going to get anything but a beating if you keep screaming." Hexus continued, "I saw them bring you in, you were covered in bandages. You got patched up maybe yesterday morning. What the hell happened to you anyways?"

He paused, "I... I can barely remember. I think I got attacked."

"Weird how they would lock you up if you were the one who got attacked. This city is corrupt. Your king kinda sucks. But I've seen worse cities." Said Hexus.

The boy was right about Adam getting locked up, and about his city, but it took Adam a minute to process what he said, "You... you've been to other cities? There are other cities?"

"Of course, there are! Thousands, and I've been all over."

Adam's brain exploded with knowledge. And questions.

"What are they like? Do they have better cities than this? How far away is the nearest? Can you get me out of here?" He remembered the priestess's paper, which was no longer in his pocket. He couldn't find the sword that the man had given him either, thought that one was probably elsewhere.

"Slow down, slow down! One at a time." Adam agreed and began the questions.

"How long have you been in here?" He asked Hexus.

"About two days. I stole something remember, I didn't murder anyone or anything like that. So, I doubt I'll be in here long. My friend should be here any minute to break me out. Oh... I wasn't supposed to say that." Adam heard a slap, he figured Hexus put his hands over his mouth. This kid was bringing up more questions than answers.

"You are going to be broken out?"

"No."

"But you just said..."

"I didn't say anything."

It took Adam a second for him to realize that the boy was trying to cover up his mistake.

"Okay, Fine."

"Hm."

There was a pause before Adam spoke again.

"What's his name?" Adam asked Hexus.

"Who?"

"Your friend."

Hexus paused. "Norris." Looks like he gave up trying to keep a secret.

"He better hurry up."

There was a second pause. Then Hexus said "I hope he does." The boy was waiting for a man. *A good sign* thought Adam.

"So, what are these other cities like?" Adam asked, still with the question lingering in his mind.

"They're lovely! Full of people, but they all know that the other cities exist. Why are you lot different?"

"I don't know, I was raised with the assumption that this is the last city. Nobody has ever been outside the walls. We all thought it was a wasteland."

Hexus laughed. "Wasteland? It's beautiful! Well some parts. I have been to some wastelands. They aren't exactly the best, but the parts that aren't wastelands are quite nice. There are mountains, forests, lakes, valleys. It's amazing! I'm sorry you've never seen it, you should though."

"It's fine. Hearing about it is nice enough. Wait you said you've been to wastelands. Are you... and explorer?" He hoped the words that exited the boys mouth next were a "yes I am" rather than, "no, child, I'm simply mad."

"That's a word for it. I travel from place to place." He answered instead.

"Do you have a destination?"

"Yes, but I can't tell you."

"Why not?"

"My friend told me I can't tell anyone because we don't want other people there."

"Oh." Adam said gloomily, "Must be a pretty cool place if you don't want anyone there."

"I guess, I'm sorry I can't tell you."

Adam was a little upset over the fact, but he could respect it.

"It's ok. So... how did you and your friend get in?"

"The city?"

"Yeah."

"Well there was a rock formation on the other side. We just climbed that. We needed food, so we came here." It was the nearest city.

"Nearest to what?"

"My friends set up camp nearby."

"Nearby?"

"Never mind. Let's change the subject. So, who exactly attacked you?"

"Gorgons."

A third pause lasted longer than any other before it, "what did you say?"

"Gorgons. I know, it's queer and I'm lucky to be alive."

"Shit!"

"What?"

"How are you still alive?! Gorgon poison kills its victims in under twenty-four hours!"

"I don't know... they didn't seem to want to kill me, they kept saying something about, needing "it" alive. Maybe they mistaken me for someone else. Or maybe they wanted to kill me but never got the chance."

Adam knew that wasn't the case, but he was reluctant to tell this stranger about his dream.

"Why would they want to kill you?"

"Because I summoned them. Through some magic."

"You have magic?" The boy said excitedly.

"No, it was a priestess. I was trying to get rid of something."

"Dreams?"

Adam froze. He had never told Hexus that he had dreams. He had no idea what to say.

"Yes, actually. How did you know?"

Hexus paused. "I um... I have them, too. Priestesses don't really work, I've tried. Nothing really does." He said with a chuckle.

Adam widened his eyes. He knew Hexus wasn't a crazy person now. He knew that these were the two that the man in the dream spoke of. Everything he had previously thought he knew was being warped into new information by this new boy that he just met. Hexus took his lessons of his memories and twisted them to create the truth that Adam had wanted for long: the dreams do mean something. He figured they had to. Exactly what, was still unknown but Adam was going to find it out. Hexus maybe had different dreams. But the fact that he knew right away what Adam was talking about meant that he had experience with them. He knew something that Adam didn't, but that he intended on finding out. He thought about what answers this might give him. Everything was flooding his mind. He lay on his makeshift bed silently, breathing heavily. Hexus was also silent, most likely waiting for Adam to break the silence.

He did, knowing that the things that he was going to ask might scare him.

"What are they about?"

"They're different from time to time." Hexus said, nervously. "Sometimes I see other people, sometimes I see monsters. But I do remember this one time. It was a mountain, and an explosion. It was crazy."

Adam gasped. "What else did you see?"

"I once saw a war. It was huge. I was fighting in it. My friends were there, and a couple of other people I had never seen before.I could see the battlefield. It was covered in bodies, and fire. It was scary."

"Yeah, it is." Adam said.

"What do you see?"

"Almost the same things you do. I was on that mountain."

"This is great. Norris would love to hear about this."

"What?"

"Alright, here's my plan." Hexus said, making Adam pay close attention.

"Tomorrow morning, we are going to be checked in since we are part of the new group of inmates. The guards are going to give us a tour and other things along those lines. After that, go to the main courtyard. We need to talk. This is so exiting! I'm going to tell you everything. Then, when Norris comes. I promise you I'm going to get you out of here. But for now, get some sleep. Goodnight, and try not to scream that much."

Adam lay still. In shock, but also happy. All these answers, finally. Maybe those Gorgons were a blessing in disguise. He rested well knowing that he would be filled in on everything he missed about these dreams. And how he would maybe be able to see the outside world for the first time in his life.

Adam wondered where his friends were. Worrying about him surely. But he didn't think they were going to make an effort to break him out. Especially since Kathrine was still most likely mad at him. She thought he brought this on the city. Did he though? Was it really his fault? He figured the king must have thought the same thing. They wouldn't have put him in here for nothing.

Adam had a headache; it was already nighttime. And reaching to if not totally.

Adam had been unconscious for almost two days. But he didn't remember doing anything after the gorgon attack or before the dream. It all seemed to happen almost within the same hour. Thoughts raced through his head. How to escape, what to do after he does. Hexus said he would see the world, but Adam was reluctant to do so without his friends. Kathrine had even said that it was something *he* had always wanted; he was left confused. They have always had the same dream he had, at least that's what he thought.

Predictably, he didn't sleep. He feared falling asleep. More dreams. He processed what that man had said in his dream. He thought about the creature that had somehow "infiltrated" his dream, entered his mind.

Everything bad about these dreams, everything that had made them nightmares, were because of that massive pile of living ashes. What did it want with him? So many things had been going wrong since the attack. Even before that. The lady told him to "seek out his dream giver" and now that he kind of knew who it was, and how to find him, he still had questions. He was no closer to finding out how to do anything to stop the nightmares. He needed to get to that man again if he even had a chance of changing anything. Maybe Hexus could help. He had them too, maybe he saw this one. He wondered if the place that Hexus said he was heading too, was the same place that Adam would find his dream giver. He had no idea, but he figured he wouldn't get anything done sitting in this cell.

Earlier than he believed, morning rolled around. The sound of metal clanging together filled his ears while an old, demanding voice ordered him to wake up.

"Off your ass! Now!" Said the guard.

Adam turned to face him. He couldn't see anything beyond the bars covering his escape last night because there was no light. Now he saw much more. Beyond his cell, an open, indoor, courtyard sat in the middle of four walls of three floors of cells. Prisoners were walking inside and talking amongst themselves. The walls were all a dirty and unwashed rock that had been covered in red stains over time. He felt sick to his stomach just thinking about where they came from.

The guard in front of Adam's cell screamed the same thing into Hexus's cell. All the cell doors were opened with the sound of jangling keys. Adam heard faint footsteps and a click, then out of the cell next to Adam's a young boy walked out. He was Adam's age. Maybe younger. He had short, dark, coarse hair and dark skin. His eyes were a fiery red and he smiled at Adam like an innocent child. He was dressed in a brown tunic and sandals with a brown wool pair of pants. He awkwardly waved best he could while in handcuffs. The guard pushed him out of the way, walked into Adam's cell and forcibly sat him up. Adam begged him to stop before he hurt Adam, but when the guard moved, he felt no pain. He was about to think about that but then the guard slapped a pair of thick, metal cuffs on his wrists. The guard pushed him out and he began walking next to Hexus.

"Hey, how's your arm?"

"Fine. Still hurts, but it's better than it was yesterday."

"That's good."

"It is."

He wanted to ask Hexus to tell him about the dreams and everything that he knew about them, but he didn't want to rush him. Hexus also said the poison of the gorgons would have killed him in under twenty-four hours. But he was still alive. And he didn't feel like there was a deadly toxin flowing through his bloodstream. His collar bone had seemed to heal in less than three days. But how? What saved him? As usual, he didn't know. But he intended on finding out.

Hexus and Adam continued down an elevated hallway that was visible from the courtyard. At the end there was a staircase that led to the center. Adam looked up to see rectangular rings of cells. Maybe two or three more rings above where he was. He couldn't count how many exactly because of his angle. Many inmates were escorted from their cells and forced to walk down into the space center of the rectangle. It was filled with inmates that were talking amongst themselves or working out by lifting hundreds of pounds worth of metal rings on the end of a long shaft that they pushed and pulled towards and away from their chest. They made it to the bottom of the stairs and turned to enter the courtyard. It was filled with men that looked like they had been through war. Most of them were almost double Adam's age, size and weight. They could easily kill him if they felt like it.

"Look." Hexus said.

Hexus pointed to a man talking with a guard in front of Adam's cell.

The man's hair was short and fair, he was fat and short. Behind him two guards stood ready for orders. The guard that was speaking to the man pointed into the courtyard and Adam's heart began to beat louder and harder. The fat man examined Adam and raised his eyebrows.

The guard behind Adam poked him with an elbow.

"Alright, girls!" He shouted. "Get in line!"

The men in the courtyard all obeyed and stood angrily in a single file line. The fat man looked down at them all from his position on the elevated walkway.

"Welcome, newcomers." He spoke with a high pitched, weasel like voice. "Welcome to the brig. I have things to do so I'll make this quick. My name is Rufus, and I am the warden here. This is not a prison, simply a holding area. In the sense that, it is holding you criminals before you get sent to city hall for judgment. Shall you be deemed allowed to; you will return to the city after completing a short sentence here. If not, you will be sent to the city prison. It is located at the base of the mountains that lay on the other side of the lagoon. However, let me say this. This is not a real prison, but it will act like one, and you all will be treated as real inmates. Step out of line, or disobey any of the guards or myself, and there will be dire consequences. Am I understood?"

A moment of silence passed over the group before the warden repeated.

"Am I understood?" He shouted.

"Yes sir." Said the men. Adam was the only one who remained silent, which cause the warden to stare at him with annoyance.

Adam took a deep breath. "Yes sir." He muttered.

The warden smirked. "Good, now, follow Sir Deon as he takes you to the initiation room."

The men turned and began to follow the guard in front. They were taken to the showers, where they were washed and given new clothes. After that, they walked into a bigger room, with multiple inmates staring at them with anticipation to kill them probably. They all looked like the men in Adam's group, big, mean, and dangerous. Adam kept walking at Hexus's side with his new uniform. Black togas were all they were as they entered the new room which looked like a dining area. Along the end of the room, a table sat with two men on the other side serving disgusting wads of brownish mush to hungry inmates. They sat down at tables and nearly inhaled the food.

They were let go in the middle of the room, with the guard telling them to enjoy sarcastically. Then he walked off with a stupid smile on his face.

Hexus got up and wiped his lip with the back of his hand.

"Come with me, we need to talk." He said as he walked towards an empty table.

The room looked like a bigger version of his cell. The cobblestone walls and floor were riddled with cracks that allowed flora to grow from the soil beneath and push out to reveal green leaves. Adam looked up to see columns upon columns of abandoned cells and figured that this must have been the main room of the prison at one point. The inmates continued to do what they were doing before Adam and his group walked in. They smoked pipes, talked or arm wrestled. For something that was only a "holding area" it sure had a lot of inmates.

Hexus's eyes glittered, as he looked at Adam's arm. "So, it's gone? The pain in your arm."

"Yeah, kind of. But that's not what I want to talk about. You know something," Adam hesitated. "You ask me all these things, but I feel like you already have an answer."

"So...?"

"So, do you?"

"Well the thing is, I think that I have them, but I cannot simply *give* them, not in front of everything. No one can know about us. It's strange, I know your one of us, but making sure is even

"Us?" Adam asked. "Who exactly is "Us"?" Adam asked him.

Hexus looked around to see if anyone heard him.

"We don't exactly know what we are, but not far from here, my friends and I have set up camp. And if I'm thinking right, then Adam, you belong to something bigger than this!" His eyes lit up with curiosity. Adam paused; those were the same words that the man in his dream had said.

"Who's we? And why can nobody know about you."

"My friends and I are different. We've seen things, we can do things that other people can't. If I'm right, and you are the person who I think you are, we need to leave now. Follow me."

Hexus and Adam cut through the groups of inmates and entered a small area underneath a platform that held up cells. They cut a corner and the further they walked, the darker the area got. Eventually, their surroundings were completely dark.

Then, from in front of Hexus, a source of light sparked into sight. It lit up most of the room and Adam could see that he was in an old cell, one that quite evidently hadn't been used in years. The walls were stone and there were no bars at the entrance, more grass and other forms of plants managed to sprout through small cracks in the floor. Small patches of moss dotted the walls, and rats and bugs crawled around the place. Adam felt like throwing up.

Hexus turned around. Adam jumped back. His eyes widened, and his knees buckled. From the palm of Hexus's hand, a bright red flame was crackling. Adam grabbed whatever he could reach and swung it at Hexus. A stick flew across the air and Hexus simply dodged it.

"Hey wait, calm down!"

Adam stuttered; he was lost for words.

"You, you're..."

"Yeah I know. Adam don't panic,"

"Guards!" Adam began to run towards the exit before Hexus threw the ball of fire in front of him, cutting off his path and throwing him back. A large wall of fire was left. Hexus tackled Adam and wrestled him onto the ground. Hexus had been in fights before, Adam was older than he, but Hexus held him down with ease. The light from the fire illuminated his face. He was sweating, and Adam could see in Hexus's eyes that he wasn't happy doing this. He grabbed Adam by the collar, slammed him onto the wall and covered his mouth with a hand.

"Shut up! If they find out what I can do, they'll kill me."

Adam struggled to get free but Hexus placed a leg over his so he couldn't move, with one hand he covered Adam's mouth and with the other, he kept the flame lit.

Adam breathed heavily, "Listen, I don't want to hurt you. So, stay quiet and stay calm. I know this is scary, but you need to listen to me. Do you understand?"

Adam nodded with a muffled "Yes".

Hexus slowly moved away and Adam didn't move. Adam was shocked, Hexus was cautious, slowly backing away from Adam. Adam didn't know what to do. He just stared at Hexus in shock. He was terrified. Something he had gotten used to over the past few days. His life had become stranger than any story he had ever heard in his life.

"Are you...? A demon? What.... What are you?" Adam trembled and stuttered.

"I told you, I don't know. But I need to get us both out of here." He took a step closer and Adam tried his best with his back against the wall to crawl away from Hexus.

"It's alright." He held a handout.

Adam reluctantly took it, it was warm, but miraculously it wasn't burnt.

"What's going on."

"Listen to me Adam, what I'm about to tell you, it might scare you, so brace yourself." Hexus raises his eyebrows.

"Yeah ok." Adams was still shaking with adrenaline, but he was slowly calming down.

"I'm not the only one who can do this. I told you already, my friends are different. We can each do something different."

"You... you don't know what you are?"

"No, but we do know some things. All of us, we were once children like you. We lived normal lives and thought we were nothing special. I used to be a farmer, my mother owned a farm, and made my brother and I work there a lot. I had to leave them after my city was attacked by gorgons."

"Gorgons?"

"Yeah. The ones that attacked you, they attacked me, they attacked a lot of us, and they were all found by Eric."

"Eric? Who's Eric?"

"Eric's the one who found us all. We don't know much about him, but we know that he wants to help us. Him and Norris."

"Wait, you guys are a group of people who were all attacked by gorgons? So, what, they like to attack people, it's just a coincidence."

"Well some of us were attacked by the gorgons, others were attacked by other things, but that's the thing, we were all attacked! After that, a series of events led us to where we are today. In that group under the control of Eric. It's connected, all of it, can't you see? It must be the same for you!"

"What? No. It's not connected, how could it be, it's all just a coincidence."

"Look at the fire I have in my hand, you still think that this doesn't mean anything? I learned to do this after I was attacked.

Adam observed it, he was skeptical and obviously frightened. He doubted his own statement but maybe it was because he wanted to. He just wanted to get rid of his dreams. That's not what he wanted to do, or be. He wasn't exactly fine with living in this city, not always. He wanted to see the world and travel to different places, but Alor was peaceful, and it was his home. He couldn't just leave it over an assumption. If he was going to leave, he wanted to see the places that the world had to offer. Not travel the land with a group of strangers. He was torn apart by the decision.

Adam didn't know if he was what Hexus was talking about, Hexus didn't even know for sure. There would be things that he wouldn't miss, like his mother's constant abuse or the rude people. But what about his friends, and all the times they hung out together, that wouldn't work anymore. Unless they went with him, he doubted that thought.

"You're not convinced?" Hexus read Adam's face. "I am not lying to you, I promise."

"A promise isn't going to prove anything."

"What about the dreams?"

"What about them?"

"You said you had them."

"You do to..." Adam was weary about where Hexus was going with that.

"So, does everyone else. They see the same things you do. It starts off fine. Everything is green and beautiful, next it's dark and covered in dark things, and death and things. And a big creature with blood red eyes. Have you ever seen that?"

Adam stood still. He was lost for words.

More people had these dreams, then he was going to get an answer. He couldn't pass on that opportunity. The answers weren't with Hexus, maybe they were with this mysterious person Eric. Maybe Eric was the person the man in Adam's dream was talking about. But he still worried about other aspects of the dream, like the skeletons and the dragon. He was also too familiar with the red eyed creature. It had been in several of his dreams.

"Say I decide to go with you, how are we supposed to get out of this prison?"

"That's what I'm worried about. I have no idea, escaping never really been my area of expertise. We could wait for Norris, but I have no idea how long that could take. He doesn't know that I got arrested and I'm not able to tell him."

"What if—" Adam was cut off by an abrupt gasp. He turned around to see an old man peeking past a corner. He stared at the flame in Hexus's hand and his eyes widened. He turned around screaming for the guards. He was fast for an old man. Hexus raced towards him, jumping at his legs before he was completely out of Adam's sight. Hexus held onto one of his feet but the old man slipped out, still screaming uncontrollably, Hexus pulled him towards himself, and Adam ran towards him. He reached over to help Hexus when the man kicked him in the face, Adam fell back and Hexus chased him. The old man made it to the center of the courtyard, limping all the way there. The rest of the inmates looked at Hexus and the old man suspiciously as guards stood ready on the ledges. The man waved his arms around the air.

"He held a flame! I saw, with my own two eyes! He held a flame! He's a demon! A beast from Erebor!"

With every word he screamed, the inmates gathered around, each one more interested in Hexus then the last.

The man continued screaming about Hexus while pointing at him as Adam stayed at his side. The inmates walked towards them with a look that told Adam he was in danger.

"Is he lying?" One inmate asked him.

Hexus stuttered, "Yes he is, I don't know what he's talking about."

"He's stuttering." The inmates friend pointed out as he nodded his head. They were tall and angry, most likely scared. They closed in on the boys and began chanting for Hexus to show them.

"Do it!"

"Show us!"

"Make one right now!"

Some inmates began pumping their fists as others backed away.

"I don't know what you're talking about. I can't do any of that."

The first inmate walked closer to them with a stern face. He looked down at Hexus and Adam.

"Do it now."

"I... I can't."

Suddenly, the man grabbed Hexus by the collar and raised him above the ground. Reacting quickly, Hexus raised his hand and brought it down on the man's wrist, making a small stream of smoke drift up from Hexus's fist. He hid it behind his back, and looked at the man, who was rubbing his sore wrist.

"Got a little fight in you?" He gazed up and noticed the cloud of smoke that was wafting from behind Hexus's back.

"Get his hands." He ordered. Multiple inmates closed in on them and two of them grabbed Hexus's hands on either side. He struggled to get free. Adam tried to pull him free, but the bigger men just pushed him aside with ease.

The guards looked down at the calamity and moved towards the crowd.

Hexus was shouting and squirming, the man that Hexus hit punched him in the stomach and Hexus reeled.

The guards quickly cane separating the crowd. Those who resisted were forcefully taught otherwise with quick jabs to the forehead or arms. The guards finally got to Hexus and removed all three men restraining Hexus from the boy. The men fought back best they could with yells and curses, but the guards knew better than to engage someone in combat over a petty insult. A guard looked down at the winded body of Hexus and ordered him to look up. Hexus raised his head to face the man and immediately rolled back. The guard stepped forward with his hand on his sword hilt. Adam stared in confusion as Hexus rolled away from the man. He sat on the floor pushing himself away from the guard with his palms and his heels. The guard readied a sword.

Hexus grabbed a nearby rock and chucked it at the guard. The guard swerved out of the way and marched towards Hexus. Adam tried to hold him back, holding onto his arms and tugging at his cloths. The guard's strength eventually overtook him, and he was pushed aside. His sword flashed. His colleagues rushed to his side, and even inmates closed in on Hexus.

Suddenly, a wall of flames blocked their path. The crowd exploded into a collective gasp and backed up immediately and Adam widened his eyes. Multiple people shouted and gasped at the flash fire and covered their eyes and on the other side of the wall was Hexus, holding a ball of fire in his hand.

3

GUARDS ON THE railings rushed forward and launched arrows from bows and crossbows. Hexus dodged and destroyed them in midair with flames. He did not attack the inmates who hurled insults at him, though he wanted to. He would kill them, and when Norris arrived, he would kill Hexus. He tried to ignore the insults.

They threw rocks and food at Hexus. He dodged as much as he could, but a stone struck him in the head. He flinched, and flames from his hand jumped up and towards the crowd. They all jumped as Hexus bled from his forehead.

Adam ducked to avoid the flames. He threw himself to the ground.

"Hexus," Adam yelled, "what are you doing!"

"Tell them to stop!" Blood trickled from the cut on his head. Not much, but enough to be noticeable.

The warden came barreling from the top balcony and stared daggers at the scene below. He cursed and ordered the guards to continue firing.

Adam called to him, "Stop this!"

The hysteria was far too loud for the warden to hear Adam. More guards poured in from all sides. Adam tried to stop as many as he could. He would push things in their way to make them trip, and even tackled one himself.

He tugged on the soldier's uniform, trying to prevent him from getting to Hexus. The guard turned and slammed an elbow into

Adam's nose. Adam let go and the guard sprinted forward towards Hexus. He felt dizzy, his nose suddenly cold. He took his hand away and saw red dripping from his fingers. He wiped the blood of his lips and rushed upwards to help Hexus. His head was spinning, and he felt his body tumble forward.

"Let... him... go..." he tried to say. The words were jumbled and mixed.

His vision doubled and he stood by and watched as the guards carried Hexus away. The warden screamed orders at them, words that sounded faraway and echoey to Adam.

4

KATHRINE WAS SURPRISED at how little Chase could sit still. She stared at him and trying not to laugh, as he always flinched whenever the nymphs placed bandages on his cuts. He made strange and loud noises and Kathrine nearly burst out laughing. She contained herself though.

The two of them were at the gardens of the nymphs. It was a small garden in the middle of the woods that belonged to the nature spirits that lived in the city. Chase had grown up here and his surroundings gave him nostalgia. Kathrine liked coming here often as well. It was a nice and peaceful escape from the people in the city. They sat inside a large tent that held many satyrs, nymphs and other creatures. The walls were nothing more than a white curtain keeping out the leaves and plants that would scud across the forest floor with the wind. Tables holding medical supplies were scattered all around the tent. The Dryads, forest nymphs, were helping all the wounded with the cuts and wounds they acquired from the gorgon attack. Around them, many satyrs lay injured from the calamity. Humans were also helping, men and women who weren't as thick headed as the others to realize that satyrs and nymphs weren't anything to be feared or disrespected. Diocles had helped many injured, by leading them here and healing them himself, but the humans offered nothing. Kathrine was disappointed, but not surprised. The humans seldom cared for the nymphs and satyrs. They would leave them to care for themselves.

The sight made Kathrine want to cry. She held back tears looking at the injured. The bloody bandages that were tied around her arm were irritating and a Dryad named Ophelia was stitching up a gash on her leg with a threading needle. The potion she had drank made her legs numb.

Chase lay on the bed next to her. He had several cuts on his arms and chest and a swollen eye. He winced with pain as the nymphs rubbed remedies on his body. There was not enough of the potion for all. The nymph helping him laughed as she spread a clear, glowing thick liquid across the injuries. They gave him a bag full of the material to put over his black eye.

"When did you get these?" Asked Ophelia.

"Those monsters burst through my roof. The rocks fell, and we got cut."

"And hit in the face with those rocks." Chase said, wincing as his nurse lightly pressed his black eye.

Ophelia giggled. "He can't handle a thing, can he?"

Kathrine laughed. "No, he can't. He's a child."

"Shut up!" Chase snapped, breathing heavily. Kathrine and Ophelia just laughed.

"So," The nymph helping Chase began, "that attack was terrifying. It's terrible that they went for that boy."

"Neveah!" Ophelia cried, "don't talk about that in front of them, they knew him." She tried her best to silence were words so that only her sister could hear.

Neveah gasped, "I am so, so-"

"It's fine..." Kathrine said, trying to make Neveah feel better. "It's ok, we're fine. Really..."

"I'm so sorry." Said Neveah.

Kathrine said nothing more. She lowered her head silently. The last thing she did thing she did with Adam was fight. She didn't know what to think. She had cried all night because she thought about where Adam was. She knew he was still alive, but she was told he was being moved to the prison. The guards told her that he had out the lives of the innocent in jeopardy because he summoned the gorgons. Not to mention that the baker probably ratted on him as well. She tried explaining but they just brushed her off. Chase refused to eat, or sleep or do anything. He blamed himself for what happened to his friend. Kathrine knew it wasn't his fault, Kathrine knew it wasn't anyone's fault. But that didn't stop her from feeling guilty. She couldn't have done anything about him going to the priestess, but now she now realized how much she regretted spending her last moments with Adam as an argument. She pulled out the piece of paper that fell out of Adam's pocket when he was dragged out of the house.

She stared down at her bleeding bandages. They didn't hurt anymore, but she still wanted to replace the bandages. She felt the skin and soft touch of Ophelia, which snapped her back to what was going on.

"Why don't we change the subject?" She asked, with a compassionate smile. Nymphs were beautiful creatures. Ophelia and Neveah were sisters and they looked nearly identical. The only difference was they're eye color. Ophelia had bright, ocean blue eyes that reminded Kathrine and Chase of the sky. Of course, it would remind them of the ocean, except they had never seen the ocean, only stories. Neveah's eyes were a golden color that glimmered when she looked towards a light. Other than that, they looked the same. Both had long, flowing hazel colored hair, with tan, almost bronze colored skin and beautiful faces. They wore flowing silk dresses and had a crown of roses, lotuses, dahlias and other flowers perched on the top of their head.

"Yes, of course." Kathrine replied. She continued to talk with the nymphs about other things, while Chase stared into space.

He remained silent, only making sounds of pain when his injuries hurt to much.

Neveah apologized. "What are you thinking about?" She noticed Chase drifting off into space.

"I don't know..." he replied. Still staring into space. Neveah's eyes gleamed with curiosity.

"Nothing...Everything." He said. He was usually a relaxed person, rarely worried about things. Not really the type to be worried by anything. But this circumstance angered and annoyed him. One thousand thoughts passed his mind. All of them about Kathrine and Adam. He was always around. They were his closest friends. He would give his life for theirs, and although they didn't say it, he knew that Kathrine and Adam would do the same. They were more than friends really. They were family. They were all there for each other when no one else was.

"Your friend?" Neveah asked.

Chase chuckled, "uhh, yes. I... was just remembering things."

"Old memories. Your best ones with him?"

"Both of them." He nodded towards Kathrine, who was talking with Ophelia.

"You love them."

"Of course, I do."

She giggled, "Of course you do. I figured, since your souls are intertwined."

"What." Chase stopped.

"Yeah, I can see it, I've been practicing. It's an old type of Woodmagic, my grandmother teaches me."

Chase stuttered, "that's a myth. It's not real."

"On the contrary. It's very real. I learn it all the time. It happens when two or more people are close. They respect and care for each other. I can see now that you and your friends are very close. Loyal to one another, and strong together."

"I don't know—*"

His thoughts were cut off by the sound of Kathrine's voice.

"Right, Chase?" She asked.

Chase tried to focus on what she had been saying.

"Hmm?" He asked.

"I asked how long we've been friends, I said around eight years, right?"

"I...think so." He said unsure.

His thoughts drifted towards the new subject. But he still tried his best to focus on Adam. He had cried for hours last night, so had Kathrine. His eyes were red and puffy by the morning. But now, he didn't feel sad, he felt more... empty, and angry. Very angry. Like he had lost a part of himself. He knew it wasn't like himself to not speak, he was always upbeat and clever with jokes. He always made Kathrine and Adam laugh. But he didn't feel like speaking.

So instead he sat quietly.

Chase considered what Neveah had said. He never did anything to believe that he and Adam were intertwined. The way that Neveah had worded it made him think of a bunch of people sitting around during a ritual to intertwine their souls, but maybe it was just a connection thing. He had heard stories about souls intertwining. The old satyrs would tell the younger ones about two mythical heroes, who defeated an evil king. Their souls were intertwined and that helped them communicate and stuff. It was hearing the other persons voice in your head. He always loved that story, but he never believed that it happened. It was just a story. And he treated it as such.

Regardless, he was skeptical. The heroes were close, he and Adam were as well, but he couldn't connect the dots between a fictional story and real life, and assume that he had shared, special abilities with Adam just because he had a hunch that Neveah was right. It was ludicrous. But he tried it anyways.

He felt his fur softly shift with the wind.

Communication? He closed his eyes and tried to picture it. He tried to imagine Adam, wherever he was. Or maybe, a black space, an empty void. With just Adam inside. Nothing. His mind and vision were both blank. He couldn't picture anything. Kathrine's voice snapped him back to reality.

"Are you alright?" She asked. He opened his eyes, to see her looking at him confused. Neveah and Ophelia had left and were washing the blood out of the rags they used to aid the two.

"Yes," Chase answered, "why wouldn't I be?"

"Don't lie to me Chase." She lowered her eyebrows.

"I... I'm not, lying." he lied.

Kathrine reached out to wipe a tear from Chases face. He raised his eyebrows, he hadn't even noticed it sitting there, yet there it was, resting on his cheek, only to be removed by Kathrine's finger. Chase guessed his thoughts about Adam had made his eyes water. She put a hand on his shoulder, then pulled him in for a hug.

"I miss him too." She said.

"I know." Chase noticed the next tear, and the next one falling down his face. But he never bothered to wipe them away, he just let them flow, and fall to the ground.

Kathrine pushed away. She took a deep breath.

She had bruises all over her body from last night. When she saw Adam's unconscious body being carried away, she got angry and attacked the guards. She furiously kicked, punched and hit the guards, who were unbothered by her actions. She was eventually taken off the guards and hit with multiple batons as they left for the citadel with Adam's body and the dead bodies of the gorgons following them in a wagon. She was left hurt, and angry.

She was scared for Adam, but she was also mad at him. He had been so stupid and decided to do the same thing he had done many times before. She tried to warn him. But no matter how much she thought about what went on, she was mad at herself for starting that fight with Adam. Now he was left nearly dead and in prison for trying to rid himself of terrible nightmares.

She clenched her fists at the thought. He would have told her to leave the guards alone. Adam hated seeing people hurt. That's why he never fought anyone. Not that he could fight people. Adam was a fit kid, but he wasn't very good at hitting. Chase and Kathrine were fine with roughing someone up if they deserved it. Kathrine remembered the time she and Chase had fought some kids that had beat up Adam. She remembered the time clearly.

The three boys had kicked and punched Adam until he was bleeding and winded on the ground. He had been beat for no less than a few minutes but nothing too terrible. Regardless, he fought back. He threw punch after punch, not even injuring his attackers, who were nearly three years his senior. Adam was nothing if not brave, or stupid. Kathrine and Chase eventually arrived at the scene and Chase smiled at the boys.

"You want some?" The first boy asked. His name was Mason, a boy who had picked on Adam before. He was accompanied by his two friends, Skunk and Atreus. The second boy was named skunk because he often smelled foul, which was common for kids who grew up without the constant nagging of parents. His white hair added to the nickname. Mason stepped forward. He wore a dirty brown tunic and sandals. Skunk wore the same thing, but in an all-black color. Atreus stood behind mason wearing a brown shirt and grey pants.

"What are you looking at, goat?" Mason snapped at Chase. Chase smiled and stepped forward.

"I see three idiots beating on another who does not even fight back." He chuckled. His laughter was cut off by Mason's fist hitting his nose. Chase backed up, dazed. He quickly regained his balance and looked at mason with a bloody nose. Behind the three boys, Adam laughed.

"You've done it now." He said.

Chase launched himself at Mason and quickly began dealing with all three boys at the same time. Kathrine joined in at one point, tripping Skunk, making him fall onto Atreus and punching Mason right in the jaw. There was a cracking noise and the three boys lay dazed and embarrassed in the middle of the alley where they had beat up Adam.

Adam had to be taken care of by the nymphs after that. He had a black eye, and bruises all over his legs and arms. He thanked his friends.

"Why didn't you tell us about Mason." Kathrine asked.

"Because I don't need your help." He said through a bloody lip.

"Because you can't fight? Brother, I can barely fight." Chase said, while gnawing on a blade of grass.

"What are you talking about? You fed them your knuckles!" Adam said with enthusiasm. Chase chuckled.

"Chase is just stupid. He throws himself into fights and just swings his arms around until he hits something." That last part was true, Chase was careless but brave. He was willing to do the dumbest things for his friends. But the first was a bit of a lie. Chase didn't go around looking for fights, but he did occasionally brawl with whoever decided to put themselves in harm's way and threaten Chase's friends. He barely fought people who bothered him.

"Whatever you do, I wish I could do it." Adam began, "I can't fight, I'm a coward." He said. Kathrine held his cheek.

"Don't say that. We know you aren't." She said. "Your brave for taking all three." Adam smiled. Kathrine heart melted whenever she saw him smile. She never showed it, but she cared a lot for Adam. He was her first love when they were younger, but he had never known. Of course, she never told him, but eventually she grew out of her feelings for him. At least, that's what she told herself. She loved the way he laughed, the way he looked at her, she loved the way he loved people. He didn't want anyone to go through pain. He was kind, sweet, and adorable. She did wonder if he thought the same way about her, but most of time she ignored the thought.

She remembered kissing Adam on the cheek soon after seeing him smile that day.

Chase woke her up.

"Yeah, I miss him too." He said, "This place is corrupt, they arrested him for nothing. He didn't do anything wrong. If anything, he's the victim. I say we walk in there and demand that they free him." He cried. Neveah and Ophelia laughed.

Chase was a lovable fool most of the time. The kind of person you'd love to have a drink with. He was quick with jokes and a damn loyal friend. But he wasn't so bright. He wasn't stupid, despite what Kathrine may joke about. He just didn't think things all the way through before he spoke. Most of the time it was hilarious, but other times, it was just plain ridiculous. This was one of those times.

Kathrine slapped her forehead.

"Chase," She said, "they'll kill us. We can't walk in there and do anything. The king would call it trespassing and immediately order out execution."

Under his breath chase cursed. "Sons of bitches." Kathrine agreed. King Adameious was a coward and a careless person. He only cared about himself and would do nothing to fix the poverty and lack of food and that plagued Alor. He focused more on his shiny jewelry and eating boatloads of delicious meals knowing damn well that all that was being sold in the market was old fruit and bread.

Neveah twisted a lock of her hair with her fingers, "it's getting late. Maybe you two should rest. You'll need it. In the morning, we'll have breakfast ready for you."

Chase's mouth watered; he hadn't noticed how hungry he was until Neveah brought up food.

"She's right. I'm tired and hungry." He stretched his arms and yawned, as if to demonstrate his fatigue. "See you tomorrow." He said with a smile as he waved at Kathrine and pulled his blanket over his head.

Neveah sat at the foot of Kathrine's bed.

"I know how angry you must be at that king. I am too, but there's nothing that we can do. Get some sleep, it will get your mind off it."

Kathrine nodded and said goodbye and thanks to the sisters as they walked away. She leaned back and stared at the stars in the night sky. It had become nigh time quickly. Maybe she just thought so because she had spent her whole day in the nymph's nursery. Despite all the thoughts going through her head, she shut her eyes, and gave in to the soothing feeling of slumber.

5

NORRIS WALKED CALMLY by the side of the wall. He knew that was the quickest way into the prison, thanks to his time interrogating the guards he had kidnapped. It was the middle of the night. Crickets were chirping in the distance, their songs like lullabies to him. He took another swig of wine. Blackale, one of his favorites. Most of the city was asleep, they all set up torches outside their houses to illuminate the path walk that led to the castle for anyone that was walking on the streets at night. Watch towers stood over the sides of the castle, inside, two or three torches through light from the small opening at the top of them, built for shooting at incoming invaders with bows and crossbows.

He stood in a blind spot, underneath the ledge that was on the top of the watch tower. He ran left, towards a wall that led to the entrance. He took the grapple line from the side of his belt and swung it around until it was moving at a fast-enough speed for him to throw it and grapple onto the edge of the wall.

The wall was a crosswalk from the side of the castle to one of the watch towers. The citadel was truly a spectacular sight.

In front of the main entrance, a quartz and limestone fountain sat in the middle of a huge courtyard. The entire building was at least 100 feet tall with a domed roof on the main middle building and four watch towers closest to the main structure. Two on either sides and another two on the other side of a tall wall that was connected to the large barrier that encased the city. He remembered how difficult it was for him and Hexus to climb over the wall. It was nearly two hundred feet, little did the residents know that on the other side, hills of rock and grass had formed. Which was strange, the other cities he had were never as isolated as this one.

He had been sent to Alor to gather food for the others, but then Hexus had to get himself in trouble and locked in the basement of the citadel. Now he had to break the idiot out of prison. Maybe he would meet that important person that Eric told him about the night before.

The middle building of the citadel had maybe six or seven balconies and a terrace on the bottom of the domed roof. Behind it, a large building maybe 70 or 80 feet tall stood. It was connected to the main building but was different in shape. Parts of the towers that poked above it, the man could see over the wall. The entire citadel was made of quartz, marble, limestone, polished granite and some stone bricks. Some of the citadel balconies had shimmering gemstones shining on the edges, adding a tough of luxury to the creation. He finally got the rope with the three-sided hook on the end to hook onto the edge of the wall after multiple seconds of swinging it around.

After pulling twice to see if it was stable and safe to climb, he placed his feet on the side and began to pull himself up. Once he made it to the top, six guards greeted him with unsheathed swords and spears. One even had a crossbow. They were dressed the same way the guards at the entrance of the citadel were, with red uniforms and silver and black armor. The chest plates had a black rim with a silver interior and the same went for the arm and leg pads. Their helmets had three ridges on top of their heads, but the leader had red metal horns on each side and a white visor connected to the top of his helmet by a purple stripe.

"Who are you? What are you doing on the wall?" Asked the first guards.

He starred over the balconies and noticed the unconscious bodies of his colleagues at the entrance. The ones that were left there by the man. The guards then lifted their spears and swords at the man's chest.

He raised his hands in surrender. "You might want to..." he paused, lifted his face mask to his nose and brought out the grenade with his other hand, he carefully uncapped it and threw it towards the guards. "Duck!" He shielded his face as a bright light engulfed the walkway. He shut his eyes. When he opened them again, he could see smoke billowing all over the place. He looked up, the guards were all stunned and coughing because of the flash stinker. Not the best name, but Hexus, who designed the grenade, was only 13. He was brilliant with tools, but he wasn't very mature.

The soldiers quickly regained their senses. Norris stayed quiet until he could sneak past them, he didn't want to leave any more evidence for him being here. He made it halfway before the first guard yelled "Where are you?" The guard picked up his spear. Feeling around with its butt until he could finally open his eyes. He saw the man, named Norris move the slightest and so he charged him, his spear ready. Norris rolled over the spear tip, his back moving against the staff. He unsheathed his sword halfway and slammed it into the back of the guard's head, knocking him unconscious. He fell to the ground and the rest of his colleagues came charging. Norris dodged the first one by ducking as his sword swung at Norris's face. The second attack was more difficult to dodge, the leader came at him with his spear facing directly to Norris's stomach. Norris knocked his spear to the ground with the blade of his sword. Then picked it back up by rolling it onto his toe as and throwing his leg up so that the momentum would launch the spear upwards. He caught it in midair and swung the butt to the third oncoming guard.

"You try to sneak in once and end up doing this nonsense." He whispered to himself.

The third one fell over and didn't move. Norris then heard a quick whistle and threw himself to the ground. He heard a *thunk*. When he looked up, an arrow was lodged inside the leader guard behind him. He jumped up and he ran to the guard with the crossbow. Norris tossed the spear to him but didn't throw it. He wasn't trying to kill anyone. The guard behind him was fortunately simply incapacitated, the arrow having been stuck in his leg.

The guard with the cross bow dropped his weapon to catch the incoming spear. Using the opportunity, he gave himself, Norris flung himself at the man with his knee stuck out. He threw the guard to the ground, and punched him once more in the face. The two last remaining guards ran to the side of the closest watch tower to warn other soldiers. Norris couldn't let that happen, so he picked up the crossbow and quickly shot them both in the leg. Then he got up, dusted himself off and continued his way to free his friend inside the castle.

Adam woke up in cell. He didn't know what time it was but judging by the crickets that he heard and the minimal light coming into his view, he believed it to be the middle of the night. He couldn't sleep. Not because of his dreams. He didn't have one.

Lucky me, he thought to himself. A rare occurrence, but a welcome one.

He couldn't sleep because of the constant dread and worry of what they might be doing to Hexus. Torture to make him talk about what he was. What he did. How he did it. Adam didn't want to think of it. But the question did linger in the back of his head. What was Hexus? Could he be a god? Adam heard stories of the gods being able to have powers like that. Hexus summoned flames, Adam thought of Hephaestus: the god of fire. Maybe Hexus was Hephaestus in disguise. It would be unusual but not unheard of. Gods usually take human form to find love. But for one to take the form of a person at Hexus's age? Unlikely. But not impossible. But if he was a god... he wouldn't had let himself be arrested. He would smite those who dared to accuse him of anything. Also, he didn't believe that a god would have been scared when facing a king. The only thing greater than a king was a god. Adam remembered something that the man in his dream and Hexus had both said, "You are part of a bigger world." Or something along those lines. Adam was something as well? He wasn't a god, he knew that, but he knew he was different. The injuries he healed from were too great. He wasn't at all what he thought he was. He always noticed that he was a quick healer. He thought about the time that Kathrine and chase had saved him from mason and his goons. He had healed from his wounds within almost an hour of getting them. He never thought much of it, he was a fast healer. But he had also never realized how much he had survived. The time his mother beat him with the wooden stick and broke his back, he healed from that in less than three days. The more he thought about it, the more he realized how hard it was to permanently hurt him.

He wondered, "maybe that's my gift." Hexus had said that the kids he knew had special abilities, the way that he could control flames. Maybe Adam's was healing quickly. After all, his nose was no longer bleeding.

He tried to go back to sleep but the thoughts kept coming. Hexus said something about his friend coming to get him. Granted, he denied saying anything, but Adam knew better. Hexus was going to be broken out, but when? And by who? He figured his friend, was this new man different as well? Would Adam be able to leave with Hexus. Would Hexus even be able to leave? Who knew what they were doing to him? Wherever he was. They could have him in maximum security. That could jeopardize everything. Adam wanted to leave, but not without Hexus. He only met him two days ago, but he knew that he could trust him.

Norris raced through the hundreds of corridors, taking out as many guards as he could. He didn't have time to think of what was going to happen once he found Hexus and got out. Those guards would be back up by then. He was going to sneak in and sneak back out, but he had already made an impact and there was no going back. He paused every so often to take another drink of the Blackale.

He tried to incapacitate the guards for as long as possible: tying them together, knocking them out or injuring their legs, so that they couldn't run. But he couldn't do all of them. He left a few because he knew that now that he was inside the castle, he only had a few minutes to find Hexus and get the hell out of there, before he was overpowered.

Most of the halls were several feet tall but only a few feet wide, although they varied in size, and every second that Norris was running through them, he felt as if he was heading deeper and deeper into a changing labyrinth. He had circled back to places he had already been to multiple times. A prison would not be over the ground, and that was the only place to look. An idea came to Norris's head.

He circled back to a previous room, which wasn't hard. They were everywhere. It felt like he wasn't going anywhere. He dressed himself in the uniform of one of the guards he took out and put his old clothes in his satchel which he threw out the window onto the bridged he has crossed before. It was hard to fit his brown tunic and blue cape into the bag with the black breeches, but he managed. His Sabre was still sheathed and strapped to his side. He exited the room and looked for the nearest guard.

He walked around the castle for around half an hour until he finally found a legion of soldiers. They were dressed the same as him, so he blended in well. They were jogging in formation in the direction of the bridge where Norris had entered. If they found the bag, it would be taken away. That was the least of his worries. He ran to the group. Pulling aside one of the guards, he asked where the prison was.

"Why?"

"I um.. I'm from the east wing, I have orders straight from the warden to watch over the inmates."

"Wouldn't you know where the prison is then? If you're from the east wing?"

"I uh... um..." Norris began to stutter. The torches that lit up the corridors gleamed in his eyes. Sweat trickled down his forehead. He couldn't knock the guard out; the others were within earshot. He stayed as calm as possible and tried to come up with an idea, even so, he gripped the hilt of his Sabre slightly.

"I'm new." He said, immediately he regretted saying that as it was the dumbest thing he could have said.

The guard raised his eyebrow.

"Alright," he said. "Go to the very bottom of the eastern tower than it should be at the bottom of a stairwell." Norris softened his grip on the sword.

"My thanks."

"Of course." Said the guard, with sarcasm.

Norris turned to leave when another guard came dashing around the corner towards them. He was younger than Norris, maybe fresh out of his teens. He walked towards the other guards panting hard.

"Rondus!" He yelled, "There... there were six men outside... all unconcious. And I found this." He held up Norris's bag. Norris paused. The guard took the bag and examined it. He looked at the boy.

"Where was this?"

"The bridge, on the western wing." He answered. There was a rope too. It was a grapple, it hung on the side. Someone got into the castle."

Norris's heart was pounding. If he kept walking maybe they wouldn't bother him. He looked more and more suspicious the more and more he walked, however.

"Who are you?" Asked the guard. Immediately, Norris knew he was talking to him. He didn't say a word, and simply began to sprint. His loud footsteps echoed all throughout the prison. They had caught him. His time was running out.

Hexus looked around. There was no way Norris was going to be able to get him out. The walls that surrounded him were pure iron. Hexus figured it was a maximum-security cell. His hands were extremely uncomfortable as they were bonded with metal cuffs that covered his fingers. He felt cold, which was odd, but he figured that that was their plan. He couldn't summon any flames here. He had accidentally done so to protect Adam. Hexus knew what he was, but Adam didn't. Hexus was only trying to protect him. He wondered if Norris had left without him. It had been three days. He was still in this prison. The shackles encase his wrist, he couldn't reach the, with his palms to melt them and he couldn't move his hands because to their grip.

He stood exhausted in the middle of the room with the shackles having chains that kept him from moving. His feet were bonded at the ankle with shackles. He stood in a starfish position and looked down, sadly. He admitted the fact that Norris was never going to come. He might as well accept the fact that he'll rot in his cell with all the rest of the inmates. He shivered. There was no point in coming up with an escape plan. He was trapped and the prison was probably riddled with guards. Hexus heard a loud creaking noise behind him. That was the door.

"Who is it?" He asked.

The warden stepped in front of him.

"Hello." He said. "I see you are aware of our new maximum-security area. Do you like it?"

"Where's Adam?" He cried.

"Hm, he's fine. He's in his cell, along with the rest of the inmates. The ones you didn't burn at least."

"Let me go or else!" Hexus said, trying to ignore the fact that the warden had just old him that he had just killed countless men.

"Threatening me won't work child. You cannot leave those bonds on your own. You nearly killed yourself in that little stunt, I doubt you have enough strength to break through these. It's made for the most dangerous of prisoners. You just so happen to be one of them. For starters, you can do things. Abnormal things. So, this is what is going to happen, you are going to tell me what you are, and what Adam is, because he survived something that should have killed him immediately, or at least in a matter of days. So, tell me or else there will be dire consequences. I'll ask this once. What exactly are you?"

"I am not afraid of you."

The warden nodded to someone behind Hexus. With a pound crank, the shackles around Hexus began to rotate. Now his knuckles were facing downward. Cold overwhelmed Hexus' body as he gasped for air when one of the warden's men had thrown a bucket of water at him.

"I would hate to ask again. What... are... you?"

"I... am—*" he strained.

Hexus was interrupted by a guard running into the room. He was panting.

"What is the meaning of this?" The warden asked the guard.

"There is an intruder. He already took out a third of the eastern guards and a fifth of the western guards."

He looked up and took a breath.

"I will be back child." He warned Hexus. "Lock down the perimeter, I want all soldiers looking for the intruder, sound the alarm!" At that moment, that sound of a gong being struck echoed through the halls of the prison.

They slammed the door behind Hexus and all he was thinking of was a single name.

Adam was startled by loud banging noises. He looked around but was greeted with the darkness that still lay over the prison. Suddenly a loud thud that came from Adam's left side made him fall to the ground. The lights to the prison were all lit one by one by incoming guards. He sat confused as the siren noise filled his ears. He covered his ears, but it was no use. The sound of footsteps could be heard despite the siren. He heard men, and guards screaming about someone that had entered the prison and attacked them. Adam made it to the bars of his cell as more and more guards noticed something that was out of Adam's sight. The prisoners cheered as faint thumps were heard. From Adam's angle of sight, a guard went flying into the bars of one of the cells and passed out. He was then pulled through the bars by the arms of inmates as several more thuds could be heard in unison with screams. More thumps were heard, and the inmates cheered louder. The thumps went silent, then another guard flew into the bars of Adam's cell on the second level. He flew over the railing and hit the bars with a loud bang. Adam jumped back and the cheers from the spectating prisoners grew louder. A man jumped up onto the railing with relative ease. Fingers were seen underneath the elevated railing followed by arms that pulled up a man. He was dark, with a round head of coarse hair. Much older than Adam, maybe in his late 20s.

He wore a prison guard outfit but fought against the guards. "He's infiltrating the prison!" Adam thought

"He's Hexus's escape plan," he figured. The man grabbed the guard by the collar and lifted him up over the railing. Then put his arm on the guard's waist and flipped him over so that he was upside down.

"Where is my friend?"

"I don't know! Please don't let me go!" The guard pleaded with tears running down his face.

Adam raised his eyebrows.

"Wait," he said.

The man turned around to show his face properly, he had dark eyes with black facial hair.

Adam contemplated moving forward as the man had a very intimidating look in his eyes. He had been through combat, that much was clear with a glance. Adam stood up and looked at the man with determination.

"What?" He growled. The shouts from the crowd turned from a loud mess of cheering and whistling to a simultaneous chant for the man to drop the guard.

"I...I can help you find your friend." Adam told him.

"What? Who are you?"

"I know Hexus."

"I don't know who you are, who are you?" He repeated.

"My name is Adam, I can help you, but you have to let me out of here."

The man, without hesitation, dropped the guard. His scream was abruptly stopped by the cement at the bottom breaking his fall, along with many of his bones. Then he wailed, which thankfully meant that he wasn't dead. The inmates howled with approval.

"No. I don't know you, nice try."

"I can help you find him. You're Norris, right? He mentioned you. The guards are going to be here any minute. We need to go. Please, I can help you."

The man hesitated but he stopped and reached for his sword.

Faint words were heard as Norris spoke under his breath, "dammit Hexus!" He said.

Adam backed away as the Norris unsheathed his blade and swung, Adam covered his face but felt nothing hit him. Instead he heard two loud shrieks followed by a loud clang. Adam looked up to realize Norris had cut through the bars. He stood on the other side of the whole clenching his sword.

"Rest assured, if you play me, I'll leave you here. Let's go."

Adam nodded and ran off with the man. They descended the stairs as Norris picked up a crossbow and fired it at incoming prison guards. He knocked another arrow as more men came racing up the stairs along with the warden. Once he saw Adam he stood silently.

"Wait," He said. "I—*" his words were ended abruptly by a punch to the face courtesy of Adam's fist. Adam leaned back, observing his now sore knuckles. The warden's fat body leaned backwards and lost balance. He fell down the stairs taking three guards with him. Norris jumped in and knocked out the two remaining guards.

They continued down the stairs and thought a series of hallways. Each one leading to a dead end. Adam was confused, they had taken Adam in this direction. This place was a maze. Norris turned to him with angry eyes.

"I thought you said you could help me!" Shouted Norris.

"I...I can. They brought him down here, I saw them."

More guards raced in their direction and Norris took them all down with ease. He unsheathed a dagger from his belt and firmly walked towards Adam, obviously with negative intentions. He grunted and took Adam by the collar. Norris threw him across the hallway. Adam skidded across the floor and waited for his vision to become clear again. Adam ran but Norris was quickly in pursuit. The man took him by the neck and all Adam could see was the tip of a knife headed towards his face. He closed his eyes and suddenly, a loud thump filled his ears. He felt Norris's cold hand leave his back but felt something pulling on his clothes. He opened his eyes to see Norris's blade pierce a hole in Adam's clothes, pinning him to the wall behind him. He was unharmed.

Norris was breathing heavily.

"I knew it. Stay out of my way." He warned.

"No...no wait I can help you!"

"Shut up!"

Norris sprinted away to other corridors to find his friend, while Adam stood there. He attempted to move the dagger that pinned him. But no matter how much he hit it, or took it by the hilt to move it, it didn't shift. More guards came rushing into the hallway and noticed Adam. They pulled the sword out from the wall, releasing Adam, but immediately bonded him with handcuffs and walked off with him.

Norris was going to kill Hexus.

Norris and Eric specifically told him to stay hidden and out of trouble. But not only did the idiot have to get himself arrested, all for a damn fruit, but he also managed to spill the fact that Norris was rescuing him from this prison to a random kid. Norris clenched his fists. Hexus had better have a good excuse. He eventually found his way to a dark hallway leading down another level surrounded by guards. He easily incapacitated most of them until he descended the stairs. Greeting him at the base of the staircase was five guards all holding crossbows directly pointing at Norris's chest. They stood in front of a large metal door that was obviously housing something important or dangerous on the other side, otherwise they wouldn't be defending it.

He found Hexus. Norris rolled his eyes. The room he was in was small, and didn't have anything he could hide behind.

"Stop at once!" The first guard ordered.

Norris placed his arms above his head and got on his knees. He waited for the guards to come over to his side and try to place handcuffs on his wrists, and as soon as the first one managed to get to his side he swept his leg and the guard fell over. Norris quickly grabbed his crossbow and fired it at the second guard. The arrow stuck into his leg and he fell to the ground, screaming in pain. The third attempted to come up behind him and knock him out with the butt of his crossbow, but Norris blocked it with his weapon and punched the guard in the face. The last two remaining guards took a step forward before Norris held up the first unconscious guard, and pointed the crossbow to his ear.

"Stop!" He shouted. "Take one more step, and I'll fire." The two men halted.

"Open the door, or else." He nudged the tip of the crossbow into the man's skin, softly. He didn't want to kill anyone while he was in the city. They had just come here for food, and supplies. They were all waiting on the other side of the wall with Pormant.

The two guards in front of Norris reluctantly opened the door. Norris was correct in his assumption. On the other side of the door, was Hexus, being suspended by metal chains in a starfish position.

Norris held up the crossbow up to the two guards. "Okay, now free him. He placed his finger on the trigger and realized how stern his face was. He was just angry that Hexus got him into this whole ordeal, but he knew what the guards were thinking: We should stay on his good side. Intimidation: the best way to deliver orders.

He was beginning to get really annoyed. The guards got Hexus down from his chains and pushed him over to Norris. Hexus smiled, but his face of amusement was immediately drowned in a look of embarrassment as he stared at Norris annoyed complexion.

"You will regret this." The hostage said.

"I know. I already do." Norris said, while staring very sternly at Hexus. The boy chuckled as Norris threw his hostage to the ground and ran up the stairs. They didn't talk to each other until they turned a corner and noticed Adam being taken away by a pair of guards. They all immediately attacked the two as soon as they saw them. Hexus dodged all the stabs and slashes that were aimed at him and launched two punches at the guard holding Adam.

Adam ducked as the guard went flying into the hallway behind him. Norris made quick work of the remaining guards as Hexus got Adam's handcuffs off by melting the center. Adam just snapped the rest of it off his wrist.

"What are you doing?" Norris shouted at Hexus, as he picked up his blade and sheathed it at his side. "We need to leave him in his cell!"

"I'm freeing him. Obviously."

Norris scoffed. "Why?"

"Because he's one of us!" Hexus said with a smile. Norris remained quiet and raised his eyebrows. His eyes were wide open: the special person Eric told him about.

Adam felt like he should have said something but instead he remained silent.

Norris stood still and quiet for another moment before snapping out of his thoughts and dashing for the storage building. They ran to a door at they're left side and stepped into a room that held several hundred wooden boxes with things like clothes and personal belongings that were owned by the inmates, on several shelves. Adam didn't do with anything on him, exempt the paper the priestess wrote. But he didn't have time to look for a single sheet of paper in all this mess. Hexus rummaged through several the boxes, throwing rags of clothes and objects to the ground. He then found a box that held his belongings and immediately ordered for Norris and Hexus to run to the nearest exit. They dashed past groups of guards that had been looking for them and made it to a doorway that led to the bridge in between the main building and a watchtower that Norris had first arrived at. Hexus was still carrying his box. An entire legion of heavily armed guards came racing down the stairs of the main building, so they had to think fast.

"There!" Adam shouted, pointing to the forest, which lay a couple hundred feet from their current position.

"Jump now!" Hexus shouted as he noticed more and more guards exiting the building.

"Where the hell do these guys keep coming from?" Adam said, annoyed.

"I don't want to find out!" Norris shouted, throwing himself from the ledge of the bridge and landing on the ground with a quiet thump. Hexus dropped his box to the ground, then followed and landed in a somersault. Adam began with a running start, which was hardly necessary, and launched himself from the edge. He immediately regretted his running start. His head made a steep dip and as he tried to move, a pain filled his spine. He looked up then realized he was on the ground. Not a very graceful landing.

They dashed down the city and through corners and alleys. A couple minutes before making it to the forest, they lost of the guards that were pursuing them.

"We lost them. We need to go now!" Hexus said, as they walked into the woods.

Norris pinned him to the wall angrily, Adam lunged at him but before he could do anything, Norris had placed his blade under Adam's chin in the blink of an eye. "What the hell do you think you're doing?" He asked. "Telling a random kid about us! Are you out of your mind? We can't just take him with us. What makes you think he's one of us."

Through muffled words, Hexus spoke, "He survived the gorgons, they attacked him and he survived. He healed from a broken bone in two days, Norris! He's one of us. I know it!"

"You decided to put our entire plan in jeopardy over an idea? You truly are a great fool, that much I know." He let go of Hexus, and lowered his weapon.

"It's not just an idea. He has the dreams too!" Hexus said.

Norris froze. He said nothing for exactly five minutes. They sat in silence in the middle on the woods, under a pine tree. After a while Norris stood up and began furiously punching the very pine tree they were hiding behind. The bark of the tree began flying off with every strike. Norris took a wineskin from his satchel and breathed heavily.

Adam waited for Norris to swiftly kill him, as a single drop of nervous sweat trickled down his neck. Instead, Norris said nothing and looked at Adam. He observed him with curiosity and concern. It made Adam feel uncomfortable.

He sighed.

"Okay," he said. "Let's go."

6

THE LAST PLACE Adam wanted to go was his own house. But he knew that if he was to go anywhere with these two, he would need to get a few things. The three of them jogged down the city streets, cautious of citizens or soldiers. A knot formed in Adam's throat as he observed the ruined buildings that riddled the city. The people in his city were quite divided. There wasn't much of a social difference, as most people that didn't live in the citadel were poor, but many people simply never talked to others. So, Adam was glad to see people helping the wounded. He realized how close they become when worst comes to pass.

They dashed past destroyed houses, restaurants and other buildings until they made it to the stone building Adam reluctantly called home. It was strange how out of hundreds of buildings in the city, his house was of the few that remained untouched.

He turned to Hexus and Norris, "I have to go in alone. If something happens, I'll run out."

"No," Norris said, "If something happens, we need to end it then and there. Hexus, go with him. I'll stay out here and keep watch for guards.

"Fine," Adam agreed.

He slowly and carefully opened the door with a loud creek and winced at the noise. The inside was completely quiet and dark. Then, a dim orange light swept across the house. Adam looked back to Hexus, who held up a flame on his index finger as if his hand was a candle and his fingernail the wick.

"Still kind of odd to me how you can do that." Adam said with a quiet laugh.

Hexus smiled, "you'll get used to it." He said.

They crept inside, careful to not make any noise. After a couple steps in, the turned a corner into the bedroom. Next of Adam's perfectly made bed, his mother lay asleep in hers. He looked around the room. The chest in the corner was his goal. Inside were clothes, a satchel, a canteen and a cloak.

"You stay here," he whispered Hexus, "I'll get the stuff and we can go."

Hexus nodded silently. Adam entered the pitch-black room.

He made his way to the wooden chest with cautiousness and tried to open it, but there was a problem. It was locked, and his mother had the key.

Norris stood outside the door of Adam's house with one hand on his Sabre and the other ready to unplug his canteen. He hadn't used his ability in front of Adam yet, because he didn't want to trust a stranger with the knowledge of his powers. Even though Hexus seemed to do so quickly. He was annoyed at how easily Hexus was to dupe. The more he stayed in this city, the more he wondered how on earth this random kid could be the important to them. He felt rustling under his shirt. Out of his collar popped a golden-brown weasel with black eyes and a pink nose and a white underbelly. His Vàninëll, animal protector.

"Hey Bugbush," he said to his weasel. "Sorry I'm taking so long, I got sidetracked."

The weasel chirped.

Norris returned to observing his surroundings. The weasel was a friend Norris made when he and Eric were young. After the day where Norris's loved ones were slaughtered, him and Eric went on the run and Norris found a mother rodent caring for her children in the middle of the snow. After he took care of them, they were able to leave, but Bugbush never did. He stayed with Norris, and Norris never complained. He was a useful and loyal little creature. Norris truly loved him.

He looked up when he heard rustling in the trees in front of him. He felt a breeze flow through his hair.

"Get back in." He ordered Bugbush.

He replied with a squeak then buried himself in Norris's shirt.

Norris got onto his knees and lifted his face mask. He was still in the prison guard uniform, but he kept the face mask to hide his visage, and of course for little more than dramatic effect, after all, the guards already knew what he looked like. He kept his hand on his Sabre.

"Hurry up," he whispered.

Adam reached his hand out towards his mother's nightstand, where the key to the chest lay. She snored into her pillow on her bed and for the first time ever, she seemed, at peace. Her black wavy hair was a mess around her head, and her pale white skin almost glowed.

Adam stared at her. He knew that she wasn't always the way she is. After Adam's father left them, she descended into a pool of hatred and anger. Adam had never met his father and he wasn't even sure if he left, or if he died. But all he knew, is that if we were alive, Adam would give him a piece of his mind.

He grabbed the key and turned to the chest. Adam stopped abruptly when he noticed the light. Through the cracks in the lid of the chest, a bright, white light shined from within. He breathed heavily. Adam slowly approached the wooden container and placed the key in the lock. He moved it around until he could hear the click and then he threw open the lid. Inside, Adam found the source of the light. A silver rod lay on top all of his clothes. The same rod he saw in his dream. The one the king had, with all the ancient designs on it, except, he saw no blade. Just a six-inch silver rod.

"Let's go!" Hexus said.

Adam remembered why he was here in the first place.

He reached under the clothes until he found a satchel and a backpack. He put the wineskin and rod in the satchel and the clothes in the backpack quickly. The last object left in the chest was a flute that

Chase had made for him when they were little. Adam never learned how to play but he knew Chase would like it. He took it, stuffed in the satchel along with the canteen and rod and stuffed the clothes in the backpack. Then he stood up, and an unwelcome voice was heard. "Adam? The hell are you doing? It's the middle of the night! I thought they took you." She said. Why was acting so concerned? She didn't care.

"Where are you going?" She asked. Adam didn't want to answer. He was afraid of the consequences. He heard her bedsheets ruffling behind him. He didn't dare look back.

"WHERE ARE YOU GOING?" His mother shouted. He flinched and so did Hexus.

"What was that?" She stepped towards Adam. "Look at me when I'm talking to you, you're a miserable little rat."

He reluctantly turned around. Adam looked up at his mother. She was taller than he was but only by a short bit. Her hair was messy, and she smelled of smoke and dirt, but Adam was not going to say anything.

A sharp, hot pain erupted from his right cheek. He fell to the ground after his mother slapped him.

"If you don't put those things back in the chest this instant, I swear by my own mother I will give you more than a slap." She said.

Adam felt a hot tear run down his cheek. His mother simply scoffed.

"Crying? Really? You are weaker than I deemed you to be, then." She chuckled. Her eyes widened when she saw his clothes. The black tunic and pants. "Those are the prison's clothes. But if you are here...?" She connected the invisible dots and had an evil gleam in her eyes.

She began towards the door and completely ignored Hexus.

She opened the door and did the unexpected. "GUARDS!" She yelled, "GUARDS THERE ARE DELINQUENTS IN MY HOME! PLEASE, HELP M—!" Her sentence was cut off by Hexus placing a hand over her mouth and tossing her inside. He slammed the door shut and yelled for Adam "We need to go!" He yelled. His hands blazed to life. "Stay down!" He told Adam's mother, who was already getting up. She used the kitchen counter to help herself up.

"You have a reward I assume? I want it." She snorted.

"Are you not concerned for you own son? He was nearly killed by monsters only DAYS ago?!" Hexus asked her, his hands still flaming. He illuminated nearly the whole room with his flames.

"Good riddance to him." She said, panting. "He has been nothing but a burden to me. I deserve better. His father was a coward and an idiot for leaving his disgusting hide with me!" She growled.

Adam balled his fists; he wiped the tear from his face.

"You don't deserve to call yourself a mother. You not a mother." He told her, standing next to Hexus. "You are a pathetic, sad, horrible woman. A terrible person. I would rather die than stay with you!" He said.

With those words, he made a cut. A deep, painful cut in his mother's soul that would not ever heal. He meant every word he had said. She didn't have the right to bring up Adam's father. She was most likely the thing that drove him away.

Adam stood tall and proud and exclaimed his actions.

"I'm leaving Alor with Hexus, and my friends. And I am grateful that I won't need to ever see your miserable face ever again."

His mother stood feet away from him, with an expression growing more horrified and disrespected with each passing syllable that came from her own son.

She bared her teeth, "how dare you insult me..."

Hexus noticed her hand moving unnaturally, as if she was reaching for something behind her.

"You are but a child. And clearly that slap wasn't harsh enough a punishment for your actions." She seemed to observe the scar on Adam's face. "That scar," she smiled sinisterly "I remember that scar. That was indeed a good punishment. And believe me when I say that your actions today... have called for another one!" A clanging noise was heard when she moved.

She lunged at the boys holding a kitchen knife in the air. Adam froze, petrified with fear. Hexus stepped in.

He had fought a lot of things: Cyclopes, gorgons, even other human soldiers. But a mortal older woman, never. He anticipated what she fought like, however. She was slow, sloppy and not very coordinated. She wildly swung the knife hoping to cut into something. Hexus found it pretty easy to dodge her attacks. He stepped back as she stepped forward, and had one only been staring at their feet, it would appear as though they were dancing. He eventually felt a counter behind him. He looked back to see a pan and other dirty dishes. Which immediately gave him an idea.

"You won't take my son! He must be punished!" She yelled. One obvious thing about combat: you should never make it clear when you will attack your opponent. He ducked as she stabbed at his previous position. Knocking the pan over with his feet, he tossed it to Adam, who took it and threw a long, hard swing.

With a loud clang, Adam's mother fell to the ground, unconscious. He stared at the kitchen appliance he had just used to hit his mother. He could not express what he felt in that instance. Happiness, anger, distress, horror, and sick were all pretty good attempts. But there was something more. A burning feeling deep within Adam's soul that had not seen the light of day in years: pride.

His thoughts were cut off by Hexus, "Adam.... Adam we have to go!" He said.

Adam caught himself staring at his unconscious abuser. He noticed several things in that moment. He focused on Hexus's words echoing in his brain, he focused on the head of sweat that slowly made its way down his neck and he focused on how the hand holding the frying pan went from quivering to still.

He took one final deep breath, "okay..." he said, "let's go".

Hexus carefully opened the front door and peered outside for a slight second, then signaled for Adam to follow him.

Adam gulped and stared at the boy in the doorway. He lifted his leg and took a step away from his home, with no intentions of ever going back.

7

CHASE SLEPT DECENTLY well until he was awaken in the middle of the night by a little child with red eyes.

He lay still in his bed next to Kathrine's. He wondered a lot about Adam's dreams when he was asleep. He knew Kathrine was never really bothered by them, unless they were bothering Adam. But Chase, he was more curious than anything. Adam explained all his dreams to him, but Chase always felt like he never imagined them correctly. He got the basic idea often.

They are all terrible visions that encouraged Adam to remain awake for days at a time. But that didn't stop Chase from wondering what it would be like to have them. He knew it made him sound like a terrible person, because of the strain it has on Adam's body and mind. But he still wondered it.

Most of his dreams were the normal, meaningless nonsense that everyone else's dreams were. Just regular boring visions about the satyr living a normal day in Alor before a group of thugs attack a random merchant shop and it's up to Chase to track them down and stop them. Then the towns people would worship him and accept him as a resident of the city. That's how he realized that they were dreams, when the people accepted him for who he was and not what they saw. He had never been respected by anyone besides others in the satyr community. Kathrine and Adam were exceptions.

Inside the community he was well respected, he was brave and kind. And he always managed to put a smile on everyone's faces with a joke or two. He put other people in front of him when it came to things like eating or drinking in times of great need, which, in Alor, were common.

The elderly nymphs called him "Pan's heir", which basically meant he was a kind satyr. Pan was the god of the wild and master of satyrs. The elderly and the nature spirits still believed in the gods of course, but most of the humans did not. With the condition that everyone was in, it was difficult to believe that an all loving higher power was controlling everything else and making everything the way it was. If the gods did exist, Chase figured they would at least try to help. After all, all living things are a result of the gods' work. But alas, poor harvests meant Demeter, the goddess of the grain, was absent and no catches after days of hunting in the great woods meant Artemis the goddess of the hunt was gone as well. If they were gone, why would the others be real? If Chase was a god, he would make sure that bellies were full, and the skies were blue. The equality that satyrs desperately deserve would be a priority as well of course.

Chase found it weird how even in times of great struggle, people were still willing to segregate every living thing in different groups that basically explained your importance in society. The thought of how people could hate someone so much and so hard, who had done nothing to anger them in the first place was beyond Chase.

There was a slight breeze outside that cooled Chase's wounds, making his fur shuffle with the direction of the wind. It was cold. And dark. But Chase liked it, it felt peaceful. At least it did. Until Chase felt two hands press against his arms and shake him vigorously.

He opened his eyes and noticed a pairs of big brown eyes staring back at him. He nearly fell off the bed with surprise. He shouted which consequently woke up Kathrine. She shot up with a jolt and noticed the same thing Chase did. She was then tackled by a hug from Adam. She swiftly punched him in the stomach, quickly sending him flinching backwards. But once she saw his face, she held him closer with a harder hug.

"Adam!" A wave of happiness washed over Chase.

"Hi." The boy at the foot of Chase's bed waved and gave an ear to ear grin with bright white teeth. He stood next to a tall dark man with a stern face. As if the two strangers weren't a concern for either Chase or Kathrine, Adam began to say, "I'm glad to see you," he said, still hugging Kathrine.

He pulled away and walked to Chase's bed. They hugged each other before Adam finally addressed the elephant in the room. He pointed to the two strangers.

"This is Hexus," he said. The boy raised his hand and happily repeated, "hi!" several times. "And this is Norris." He signaled towards the tall man, who stayed silent and raised a finger from his crossed arms without lifting his hand, in salutaion. "They helped me out of jail." Adam said that as if it were a regular thing to say.

Chase and Kathrine flinched. "They what?" They both said simultaneously.

"I don't have a lot of time. None of us do. We need to go now."

"What," Kathrine said. "Wait hold on. You get arrested for two days, meet a strange pair in prison and then break out of said prison!" She cried. Chase was worried she might wake up some of the other wounded, who were sleeping in the area. "What the hell is going on?" She asked.

Adam pinched the bridge of his nose and sighed. The tall man, Norris, was peering around windows and corners, he paced back and forth as if he was looking for something, it made Chase uncomfortable.

"I'll explain later, but we need to get out of the city."

Chase looked at him with surprise. He wasn't sure if he heard him correctly. His brain nearly exploded. "Get out of what?" He cried, "What the hell are you talking about?" He demanded to know.

Adam looked at Hexus, who was staring into space with his mouth wide open and thinking about something else. What it might be?

Chase had no clue, but he wasn't interested anyways. Adam sighed and turned to them, "Can you two walk?" He asked.

They looked at each other, "Chase might need some aid, but I can walk just fine." Kathrine said. She was right, without the help of a crutch, pain rushed up his leg and he could barely walk. Adam rushed over to an unoccupied bed nearby and took a single crutch from on top of it. He handed it to Chase, and with help from Adam, he was able to at least limp.

They exited the tent and headed towards a tall building that was built into the side of a tree. The tree was a forty foot tall oak with long branches that ended in groups of green leaves. It was down the sidewalk from the medical tent. A couple yards, it wasn't a long walk, but it was a strange one. Norris and Hexus guided the way, and Adam, Chase and Kathrine followed them. All of them except for Chase and Kathrine were looking around for something that seemed to worry them. Again, Chase felt on edge, especially with the way both Norris and Hexus kept their hands on their blades. As if they were ready to draw them if the situation called for it. They made it to the base of the tree. It had birch wood planks that were stuck on one side of the tree, sailing up around the trunk, making a staircase. At the top, amongst many, waving hands of leaves, a wooden shack rested of the thick oak branches. The windows were nothing but holes in the small, square building. Chase remembered this place well. He and his friends had built it.

They ascended the spiral of wooden planks, which led to a small trapdoor on the bottom of the shack, of course Chase needed help. When Norris pushed it open, cobwebs stretched from the floor of the shack to the edge of the trapdoor. They all entered one by one. When Chase entered, a wave of nostalgia washed over him. The walls, ceiling and roof were all made of oak planks that were held together by iron nails. Chase looked around. The room they were in was small. A rectangle with a single bed in the corner that was far too small for anyone of his age to sleep in. The four windows were simply holes that were built into the walls, and next to them, a door. It wasn't much of a door, just another hole that was about the height of a human being. No handle or anything. On the other side of the door was a small balcony. It had a wooden fence on the perimeter but was empty. Adam looked back to Norris and Hexus.

"Can you give us a minute?" He asked "I have to talk to them."

Norris scowled, "Adam we don't have time. We have to—*" Hexus held him back. Norris and he shared a silent conversation.

"Five minutes. You have five minutes, then we leave, with or without you." Norris said.

Adam nodded. Norris and Hexus walked off the balconies and into the room.

Adam looked at his friends, and was immediately tackled by a hug from Kathrine.

"You gave me a heart attack, I'm glad you're ok." He held his arms around her for a silent moment and then pulled away.

"You two must listen to me."

Chase and Kathrine looked at him with concern.

"We can get out of this place. We can leave Alor." He said with an exited smile.

Chase and Kathrine paused. Chase wondered if he had heard him right.

"Hold on," he said. "Start from the beginning."

Adam told them about how he met a man in one of his dreams. The man had told him that he will have to trust a man that will show him a world that he has never known. A world much bigger than any of them could understand. He told them about his broken arm, and how he healed from it in two days. How Hexus could control flames, and that somewhere out those walls, there is a camp of people that all have the same dreams as Adam.

Every word that came out of Adam's mouth took another breath from Chase's lungs. He felt dizzy, and held on to his crutches a bit tighter.

"Don't you guys understand? These people can help, we can leave this place. Is that not what you have always wanted?"

Chase had always wanted to see the world, but now that the opportunity was staring him in the face, he didn't know whether to charge at it, or run away. He could live without Alor, all the people in it, the racism, the difficulty that came with living there. But at the same time, this was his home. He thought about the decision, but there wasn't much of a contest. He looked at Adam in the eye and told him, "I'm coming with you." They both shared a smile and hugged each other. The two then stared at Kathrine, who was staring at the night sky.

"How do we know we can trust them?" She asked.

"We don't. But don't you think an opportunity like this is too big to give up?"

Chase didn't like how Adam admitted that he barely trusted these people, but he remained with his decision. There was a whole world out there, and he was going to be able to see it. His wildest dreams were going to come true. He walked into the room behind them, inside, Hexus sat on the bed, playing with a small mechanism he had pulled out of his backpack, while Norris leaned against the wall with his eyes closed.

"You," he pointed to Hexus. The boy looked up with confusion. "Come out here." Chase said. The boy tucked the devise he was fidgeting with into his backpack and walked out onto the balcony.

"What's up? Can we go now?" He asked.

"Everything that Adam is saying, about the dreams, the cities, and the fire, is it true?"

The boy stayed silent for a moment, then he looked up.

"Yes." He said. "A couple hours south from here, my friends set up camp and sent me and Norris to get supplies and food, but we got sidetracked, and I ended up in jail. Anyways, my friends are like Adam. The dreams, the ability to heal from wounds super quickly, it's all true."

"We weren't supposed to tell anyone about this," Said a voice from behind Hexus. Chase turned to see Norris in the doorway. "Our leader, Eric, he tells us that we can't tell anyone because his dreams say so. Something about, mass panic or something. But Adam, he's different, he's one of us. And he won't leave without you two. We need him, and that means we need you. Trust me, I'm not happy about this, but he needs to come with us."

Chase looked at Kathrine, who was still staring at the sky.

"I've decided," he said. "I'm going to go pack my things."

Hexus smiled crazily. Norris nodded at Kathrine, "what about the girl?"

Chase could feel Kathrine's scowl without even looking at her. "'The girl' has a name!" She growled. "And I haven't decided yet."

"Well you might want to hurry that up." Hexus said quietly, "you see, the guards obviously aren't so happy that we broke out of their prison." He pulled out the object from before and began to fidget with it again, as if it calmed his nerves.

Chase looked at Adam, "we'll be back, you two stay here." He said. Adam nodded.

Chase, Norris and Hexus left the building as Adam and Kathrine stayed on the balcony. Deciding whether, they were going to leave Alor forever.

8

KATHRINE STOOD ON her tiptoes, trying to look beyond the walls on the horizon, but no matter how much she wanted to, she couldn't see.

Adam placed his hand on her shoulder. They were alone in their old treehouse, the one they had built many years ago. Kathrine wondered why Adam decided to bring them up here, but she never complained. She forgot how much she liked it up there. She liked the breeze flowing through her hair.

They stayed silent for a couple minutes. Kathrine didn't know what to say, and Adam was waiting for an answer. Her neutrons were firing faster than her brain could handle. Her head brought up a thousand things at once.

She was scared to speak, then she felt Adam's hand touch hers, and her heart raced. She was genuinely happy to have him back. She was worried sick, and she felt bad about the fight that they had had. She was being rational, they had already tried that, and they were low on money, but Chase had managed to make a few silver pieces by working for Diocles. She didn't want to think about it. But she thought about her situation, on one hand, she would be able to leave this place and leave all her problems along with it. But she did not trust neither Hexus nor Norris, not yet. They could do something to her friends, and if she wouldn't be able to stop them, she didn't want to think about it. But the thought lingered in her mind no matter what. She felt the slight breeze flow through her hazel hair which was now resting over her shoulders. She looked down at the city beneath them. The area that belonged to the satyrs and nymphs was a huge valley about a third the size of the whole city. All around the valley, forests lakes and hills covered the land in a sheet of dark green. It would have been a beautiful sight if most of the trees had green leaves instead of brown, crinkly leaves. Some of the, were completely green, and it made Kathrine smile. A couple miles in front of her, a thin, blue river separated the human city from the woodland valley. It twisted through the valley and ended in a blue pool of water in the West. She studied Adam's hands. They were had small cuts in some places and were bruised in others. She looked at his face. He pretended not to notice her looking at him, but Kathrine could read him like a book. The way he slowly tapped his foot up and down, the way he bit his lip. He wanted to leave as soon as possible, he wanted to leave now, and he was hoping that Kathrine would come with him.

"You really want to go, don't you?" She asked Adam. He stopped the tapping and quit chewing on his lip.

"I do. But... I won't go without you." He held her hand. And her heart was beating a million miles a minute. She was shocked. Adam would leave all of his wildest dreams for her. He would leave everything in a heartbeat, all she had to do was say the word.

But she didn't want that. She didn't want to get in the way of Adam and his freedom. She stayed silent and stared up at the sky. Her cheeks felt warm as she heard the faint chirping of a cricket.

She wondered what it would be like to be a star. All people wanted of you was that you stayed in the sky and stayed lit. To not have a care in the world, just stand around and not have to worry about anything or anyone. You already knew everything you were going to know because you could see the whole world. Now she could be that star, but her mind was still declining the offer. She didn't want to know what she would do if something happened to Adam. She should be there to help him. Her soul was ripped in two. The decision was excruciating.

Almost half an hour had past and neither of them had said a word. She had already made up here mind, but she didn't want to say it. She wanted to stay in this moment forever, staring at the night sky with Adam. But she couldn't, so she turned to him.

"I'm sorry. About before. I was being...difficult."

"No, it's ok. It was all my fault." Adam said.

"But I shouldn't have said that. You know I would want to go with you, but what if something happens. This is the biggest decision of our entire lives. None of our people have seen the outside world for over a century."

He remained silent for a moment, then turned to her, "then we run."

"What?"

"We run. If something goes wrong, we will run. See the world together, by ourselves."

The thought made Kathrine's heart nearly stop beating all together. She looked up at her star once more, "I assume the guards are looking for you and the others, right?" She asked.

He nodded, "We caused them a bit of trouble, couple hours ago we lost a group of about maybe twenty men. They don't like us very much."

"The way you talk about these two, you trust them, don't you?"

"Hexus and Norris? A little, at least I trust that their telling the truth. But we won't know for sure unless we go." He had an empathetic look in his blue eyes. Kathrine stared at them with butterflies in her stomach. Sure, Adam wasn't a strong kid. He barely knew how to fight; he had always relied on her and Chase to help in a random fights that he got into. The guys always underestimated Kathrine because she was a girl. She usually just shrugged it off because by the end of the fight, they were on the ground with Kathrine standing proudly over them. But regardless, Adam tried. And what he lacked in fighting ability, he more than made up for in bravery. He always said something when it came to insensitivity about satyrs, or if some thugs were roughhousing a shop or something. And he never threw the first punch. He never managed to hurt anyone with the punches he did throw, but Kathrine always wondered if he did it because he felt like he needed to prove his worth. Which wasn't necessary, she and Chase both cared deeply for him, whether they had to save his ass every once and a while.

"Isn't this what you wanted?" He asked her, his voice had an ounce of annoyance in it. "Didn't you want to leave?"

Kathrine knew that she wanted to go, but deep down, she wanted to stay. She wished she was as easy to convince as Chase, who had gone off with Norris and Hexus nearly an hour ago. Wait... "oh gods!" She thought to herself. "It's been nearly an hour". She wondered if Chase was okay with the two. She wasn't really concerned about the boy, he seemed harmless and kind of a sweetheart maybe. But Kathrine kept that comment that Adam had made about the boy being to control flames very close to her. It was more Norris that put her off, he was tall, kind of lean and muscular and he didn't really enjoy the thought of taking three strangers to wherever they're destination was.

Kathrine continued to stare at the night sky and say nothing. They probably would have stayed longer if chase and the others hadn't burst onto the balcony.

They turned around to see Hexus and Chase panting in the doorways. They were both sweating and Chase was wearing a backpack. Behind his head, three brown wool sleeping bags were strapped to the backpack via rope and to his side was a satchel containing who knows what.

"They... they found us." Hexus said in between deep breathes. "We have.... To go."

"Where's Norris?" Adam asked.

"He's holding them off," Chase replied. "But I don't know how long we might have."

Adam stared at Kathrine with worried eyes.

Her heart raced. Her hands were shaking. She couldn't speak.

Suddenly her train of thought was cut off by the door on the inside of the treehouse floor swung open. A city guard wearing a red uniform and holding a sword propped his head up from underneath. Immediately, before the guard could say anything, Hexus ran into the room and kicked him in the nose, sending the guard tumbling down the stairs and onto the ground below. He looked back at them with desperate eyes.

"We have to go now!" He shouted. All three stared at Kathrine and the gaze from the three sets of eyes made her nervous. She had to think quickly, they could all die in a matter of minutes if they didn't leave now. Kathrine saw no other way.

"Ok." She said quietly. "I'll go."

A look of joy washed over Adam's face. He threw his arms over Kathrine and hugged her. Then they both exited the treehouse in search of Norris.

They descended the ladder and immediately saw dozens of city officers scrambling from one corner of Kathrine's eyes to another. They pushed satyrs and nymphs out of their ways as they shouted for where the kids were.

A knot formed in her stomach as she saw the officers mistreating the innocent people. It infuriated her.

"Where is Norris?" Adam asked.

"We lost him ... there!" Hexus pointed to a man that was single handedly holding off maybe two dozen guards. He moved with speed and skill, slicing, punching and grabbing anything around him that could be used to his advantage. It made Kathrine wonder even more about who these people might be. Norris jumped from the roof of a stone building on to a barrage of soldiers. Before the men attempted to attack, Norris took them out in seconds. Tripping some with his sword, punching others, jumping out of the way of more and making them jump onto their comrades. Kathrine watched in awe. She knew a little bit how to fight, but not in any way like that.

Hexus jumped in and launched a glowing object from his hand (that had seemingly come out of nowhere) and to a second group of incoming guards. It took a moment for Kathrine to realize that what he had thrown at them was a ball of flames. He shouted in a barbaric manner as he threw more balls of fire at the guards. Some exploded in front of the groups, sending dozens of heavily armored troops flying into the sky. Others simply hit the soldiers poking blank and knocked them back several yards.

Kathrine, Chase and Adam simply stared at the two strangers fend off an entire army.

Kathrine noticed a guard regaining consciousness behind Norris and Hexus. Not knowing what she was doing, she began to spring at the guard as he began to lift his weapon. She jumped and as her feet left the ground, she cursed herself and asked what she was doing. With a thud from the sound of Kathrine's elevated knee crashing into the side of the guard's helmet, the man crumpled.

Hexus turned around. "Thanks." He said with a smile.

Kathrine smiled back, but it faded as soon as she saw another group of soldiers closing in on them with speed. Norris stepped in front of them and stood in front of them with his arms out at both sides. He clenched his fists and suddenly a ball of water formed in front of him as he moved his arms. He controlled the liquid with authority. He waved his arms back and forth in swaying motions, then he jumped at the guards, taking them all out with a single swipe of his hand, that sent the ball of water flying into them. Suddenly, a small sphere of water had turned into a wave big enough to send them all flying. They were all taken away with the current and Norris set his hands down with a deep breath. Everyone stared at him in awe, except Hexus, who probably already knew he could do that.

"Why didn't you do that earlier?" Chase asked.

Norris ignored him, "Follow me." He ordered.

They ran past groups of angry guards, confused citizens and several buildings until they were on the complete opposite side of the city.

Kathrine noticed her house becoming smaller and smaller as they ran.

"Wait!" She said. "I have to get something!"

"I already took everything for all of us!" Chase cried while signaling to his large backpack. Then he pointed to the group of guards chasing them. "We need to leave! NOW!"

Kathrine winced; she knew what she needed to get.

"No, you didn't." She told him. Chase screamed with annoyance as Kathrine ran directly in the direction of the guards towards her house.

She threw open what was left of the door. After the gorgon attack, it had been reduced to a half destroyed wooden plank on weak hinges. She rummaged through a cabinet that was still intact before finding what she was looking for. Under a pile of neatly folded clothes for boys, was a golden bracelet. In had designs all over it, and inscriptions swirling around the large ring. It was the last thing that Kathrine had from her mother.

She slipped it on her wrist, and she figured while she was there, she might as well get more things. She grabbed a nearby leather satchel and threw in random pieces of clothing, as well as her bag of food that she had stolen on the day of the gorgon attack. Her mind was racing, she paused in the middle of her room and thought if she was missing anything. But before she could leave, a voice snapped her back to the moment.

"There's one! She with them!" One guard shouted to another as they ran for Kathrine's doorway. One of them was swept away in a wave of fire while the other was thrown to the ground by Chase, who threw his body against the guard. He picked up the two swords that the men were holding and handed one to Kathrine. She caught it and grunted.

"You're crazy! Let's go!" He said.

Kathrine grinned and ran after him. Chase, Hexus and Kathrine caught up with Adam and Norris at the base of the wall. A solid barrier of solid stone that was one hundred feet tall. Its shadow caused a feeling of dread to wash over the group.

Norris turned to Hexus, "do you have the blackpowder?" He asked.

The boy rummaged through a satchel that was at his side.

"Yes, yes, quit your yapping! Give me a moment?" He said calmly.

Norris turned to Kathrine and Adam, who was now holding the second blade that Chase had picked up.

"You two, come with me." He ran towards the crowd of incoming guards while Hexus attached two small iron spheres to the stone wall with the help of a chisel he had pulled from his bag. Kathrine raced next to Norris who raised his blade to attack the guards. She did the same and immediately cut the shaft of the spear of one guard. She kicked him in the stomach, which sent him tumbling back into more guards. She felt the adrenaline rush through her body as her limbs controlled themselves. She, slashed, punched, kicked and hit as many guards as she could. She had no idea what she was doing but she liked it. The rush all of this made her feel invincible. She came face to face with another guard, who was holding his spear with anger. Then, she noticed his face turn to horror as a loud boom came from behind Kathrine. She felt the ground tremble beneath her feet. She turned to see Chase and Hexus standing in front of a massive, smoking whole right where Hexus had placed the iron spheres. They were both plugging their ears with their fingers and screamed at the others to follow. Kathrine looked down and noticed that the man in front of her was still conscious, and charging. Then, Norris came in between the two and slammed the hilt of his sword towards the guard's helmet. He fell to the ground.

She looked behind her and noticed a bow and quiver filled with arrows lying next to the unconscious body of a guard. Intrigue fell over her as she took both objects and slipped them to her back. She picked up what remained of the arrows in the dirt and dashed towards the rest of the group. She made it to the edge of the wall and froze.

She... She could see the other side! Her heart raced. Suddenly none of the guards behind them mattered. The world froze, and Kathrine could only hear the faint beating of her heart and the light crackling of some of the fire that the explosion had created. Her eyes glossed over and she held back tears. She didn't know why she was crying, maybe it was from sadness that she was leaving the only home she knew. But she ended up on the conclusion that it was in awe. Through the whole in the solid stone one-hundred-foot wall she saw the outside world. It was nothing like people described it. Green hills washed the valley in a beautiful carpet of grass. Though it was late at night, Kathrine could still see the forests of trees that dotted the landscape. The stars and the moon gave the beautiful sight a wonderful silvery glow.

"Kathrine!" yelled a voice. She stirred. She suddenly remembered where she was and what she was doing.

"Kathrine!" Adam cried again.

She looked at him, they were already on the other side of the crater. Adam ran back and grabbed her wrist. He pulled her and she followed his lead until they made it several yards from the hole in the wall. Kathrine's awe was almost doubled from the new views.

To the north, several mountains were visible on the horizon, their massive size made Kathrine wonder how she never saw them before. To the east, a massive sea stretched as far as the eye could see. The shine from the moon made gave it a silvery shine. It led streams of water that created rivers and lakes in varying locations. Kathrine realized the lagoon at the base of Alor, was from the ocean: a lagoon from a river leading away from the sea. She wondered if that sea had a name. Even the air felt different. It carried a faint humidity, probably from the proximity to the water.

Her eyes couldn't believe what they were seeing, and the air had seemed to have disappeared from her lungs.

They were still running, and Kathrine wondered if Chase and Adam felt the same way that she did. Everything was so... beautiful.

They dashed down a hill and made it to the shore of a small river, one that was a long stretch of water from the ocean hundreds of miles to the east.

Norris looked back. The guards were still pursuing them. Behind them, hundreds of confused and shocked citizens slowly began to exit the wall one by one. Kathrine kept her gaze fixed on the group of guards. To her left and right, the river seemed to stretch for miles. The only way to the other side, was to swim through it.

"Where's Pormant?" Hexus asked.

Norris yelled. "I left him next to the wall. Aw hell! Okay, Hexus get these two across the lake." He gestured to Kathrine and Adam. "You!" He pointed to Chase, "come with me!"

The two groups separated. Chase ran off with Norris to get this Pormant fellow as Kathrine, Adam and Hexus crossed the stream. The water was cold, and a bit deep. It touched up to their chins, and it was several meters across.

They swam as best they could, keeping everything with them. Once they made to the other side, at the bottom of a small hill, was the entrance to a forest. Two large oak trees were bent in shape directions so that they crossed each other forming a large X out of bark. They raced to the bottom and waited and stopped for breath behind the giant X.

"They'll be here soon; we need to wait."

Hexus walked back up the hill to see what was happening, several emotions, crossed his face. First it was confusion, then worry, then fright. A whistling sound grew closer as suddenly and arrow flew above their heads and became stuck in the bark of an oak tree with a *thunk*.

Kathrine was breathing heavily. Adam rested his hands on his knees and was slumped over. Then his back began to twitch. Kathrine wondered what was wrong. Then he looked up, revealing a bright smile. It took a moment for Kathrine to realize that he was laughing.

He stared at her with glee then tackled her with a hug.

"We made it. We did this. We're free."

Those words echoed in her head as she wrapped her arms around Adam and hugged him back.

Kathrine felt a drop of water fall over her. She looked up to see if it was going to rain, but the canopy of the trees above blocked out the sky. She felt a second drop. Then a third. Suddenly she and the two boys were underneath a hail of water droplets, as if it were raining solely on them. They ran up the hill to see if Norris and Chase were anywhere near, only to see the two riding... a donkey? The drops of water had come from the thirty-foot-tall tidal wave that Norris had created. Everyone stared in awe as Norris thrust his hands forward and launched the wave into the group of guards, sending them tumbling back several yards in an explosion of water.

Norris stood on the other side of the river, where the guards were. He moved his hands back and forth and called a small wave that carried him and Chase and their newfound friend, which Kathrine guessed was Pormant across the other side of the river.

They made it to the other side, and Norris looked at them.

"They're in the forest, we need to go."

Kathrine looked behind her. The guards were already recovering, and the citizens were flooding out from the whole in the Great Wall. Then, she ran into the forest, and turned her back on the city of Alor.

9

ADAM'S BRAIN HURT.

So many things had happened at once. He wasn't sure if he had processed everything that had happened back at the prison. What scared him most is Hexus's loss of control. He had nearly killed dozens of guards. He scared Adam. He wondered if it was too late to return. He figured as much because of what they did to the guards. Adam had been thrown in prison for putting the people in danger. He figured that this was worse, and returning was suicide.

No turning back now.

He felt multiple emotions, happiness, worry, fear, relief. All of them had piled up on the last over the past hour or so. His mind immediately returned to his dream. He remembered the man, standing in front of the ruins of Alor. What had happened to it? He didn't want to think about. He remembered what the man had said, about Adam coming to a decision soon. And having to follow a man. He figured Norris was that man. He had single handedly taken out nearly a hundred guards over the course of that past few hours. Adam wondered if he was going to one day be able to fight like that. He felt useless during the fight with the guards. He, Kathrine and Norris had held back a group of soldiers while Chase and Hexus tended to a case of blackpowder. The priestess was right about the dreams not leaving, and maybe they were going to get worse, the dead bodies from his most recent dreams seemed to prove that, but he wondered what part of the ritual had summoned the gorgons. A lot of it made no sense to him.

Now, the fact that he was on his way to meet a group of people that could help him, and the fact that there were people outside the walls gave him a splitting headache.

He tried to think straight. So, Norris had the ability to control water, and Hexus, fire. And possibly more, that Adam had no idea of. Maybe these people had similar abilities, maybe one could control the air, and another, the earth. He wondered how many there were, and what exactly he would do after he got rid of his dreams. He wondered if he could even get rid of them. Was it even possible?

They walked through the forest for the most part in silence, before they were stopped by Norris.

"Wait," he put his hand up. "Do you hear that?"

Adam tried to focus; he couldn't hear anything.

"No."

"There's a lake about a mile from here. If we keep walking north, maybe we could reach it before nightfall, and make it to the others around the same time."

Adam's heart raced. They were close.

They kept walking through the thick forest. It probably wasn't anything new for Hexus and Norris, but Adam and his friends were in awe. About thirty feet above them, the shade from hundreds of oak branches prevented most of the new rainfall to get to them, with the exception of a few occasional droplets. The sticks and twigs cracked underneath Adam's feet and most of Adam's vision was dark apart from the torch that Norris held at the front of the group and the flame that Hexus kept lit in the palm of his hand. The red flame rested on his hand without trouble, Adam wondered, "is he fireproof"?

Adam decided to talk to him. Maybe he could help him with most of his confusion.

"Hey," he murmured to Hexus.

Hexus faced him. "Concerned about something?"

"So, about these people, who are they exactly?" With that question, a wave of intrigue washed over Adam's friends. They walked closer to Hexus.

"I told you, I don't know. None of us do."

Kathrine knit her eyebrow. "You don't know who you are?"

"We don't know what we are." He corrected, "We're different." He held up his fire higher, as an example. As if they need it.

"Where are you guys from?" Chase asked.

"We're from all over, I'm from a farming family in the north, Norris is from a clan of—*" Norris turned to him with a warning look, that put Adam on edge. Hexus refrained from finishing his sentence.

"We're from all over." He repeated, ignoring his previous statement.

Norris stared at his shoes, he held Pormant by a lead connected to the donkey's collar.

Hexus sighed, "Adam," he said, his voice was quiet, "what do you see?"

Adam paused, "I'm not following."

Norris stared at him like he had just said a terrible joke. "In your dreams. What do you see in your dreams?"

Adam felt a jolt go up his spine, Kathrine placed her hand on his shoulder. Chase and Hexus stayed silent.

"I... uh," he didn't know what to say. At least he didn't know what to say first. There were so many things he saw.

"I see...bad things." He managed. Norris looked up.

"Hm." He said, "what kind of bad things?"

"D...death. And monsters. And, this, m...mountain." He tried to control his sudden stutter. He was worried he had said something when Norris winced at the word, "mountain".

"Ok." He said, as if nothing had happened.

Adam looked at Kathrine, she seemed to be holding something back. Adam could see it in her eyes.

"What do you see?" She asked. "Hexus said you guys have dreams too. Do you?"

Adam felt like one of Hexus's bombs had gone off in his stomach.

Norris looked at her, "We do. And we see the same things. Sometimes they're different. But most of the time," he looked at Adam, "it's the mountain." He turned back and continued walking. Adam now knew why Hexus had stopped speaking about Norris's past. He didn't trust Adam, nor his friends, not until he knew if he truly saw the same things they did.

"What does it mean?" Adam asked. "Any of it?"

"We don't know," Hexus said. "We can't control them, we don't know where they come from, but we do know something." He said, with a twinkle in his eye. He opened his mouth and bared his bright white teeth in a wide smile.

"Which is...?" Kathrine asked, annoyed.

"They're leading us somewhere." Norris answered.

"It's like a map, but in your brain." Hexus said, pointing to his head.

"Where is this somewhere?" Chase asked. Norris turned back to him now with annoyance in his eyes. He swallowed more of his wine, he seemed to do that a lot.

"Why do you two ask so many questions? You two don't have the dreams, don't you? Why do you care so much? The only reason I won't leave you behind is because this kid doesn't want you two to go." He jabbed a thumb at Adam. "And he's the only person we need." He turned back a round and continued into the forest.

Kathrine had a sudden flame in her eye. Anything she was holding back, was about to come out.

"If he goes with you, were coming too. And you can't change that!" She shouted.

"Besides, what the hell do you need him for?" Chase asked.

Norris rolled his eyes, "Not me you idiot goat. Us. We need him. The group. We need one more, but I never thought it would be a kid like this. But since he has the same dreams, I guess I have no choice but to bring him. Because once we get all the people we need, we might actually learn where these dreams are taking us."

"Whoever gives us the dreams, once talked with Norris and Eric." Hexus said.

"They said that they need to gather a group of eleven *special people.* We already had eight, plus Eric and Norris, that was ten. And now you! That makes eleven," he paused and stared at his fingers. "I think."

"You talked with the dream giver?" Adam asked with awe.

"They're not called that, but yes."

"What did they look like? Was he a king?"

"Yes. You saw him?"

"Yes. In a dream I had in the prison. He told I would have to follow you. He called you the *Dragonarcher.*"

Norris seemed to question that statement. But he sighed and looked at Adam, "The *Dragonarcher* is Eric. He told you to find Eric. I will take you to him, because now you are a part of our group. Whether you like it or not. I don't think I can say the same about the girl and the goat." He nodded behind him.

"What does *that* mean?!" Kathrine asked, angrily.

Norris stepped over a bush, into an opening in the woods. They followed him into a small area the size of Kathrine's house. Or... her old house, Adam figured.

A ring of rocks and dirt circled a small lake that was maybe a couple feet deep. The surrounding trees had blocked it out before, but now Adam could see the rising sun. On the opposite side of them, across the lake, was a group of tall rocks. The rainfall splashed in the lake in rings of tiny waves. Chase unslung his pack and took out a small object. His backpack really was huge. It held several things that they would all need. Food, water, clothes, sleeping bags, a tent and a couple of Chase's personal belongings. He had always liked to make music, so he brought his flute, pipes and a small wooden bowl with a piece of animal skin stretched over the top: a drum.

The small object that he had taken out was a waterskin. A circular bottle with a small mouth hole at the top. He dipped it in the lake and immediately the water began to flow into the canteen with a barrage of bubbles.

"I mean that since you two don't have dreams," Norris's voice snapped Adam back to their previous conversation, "you're technically not a part of our group. Or at least, not going to be excepted. I'm just being honest."

Adam shuffled toward Hexus, "is Norris always this much of an asshole?" Pormant brayed at that.

He raised his eyebrows as if he was tired of answering that question. "No, not really. He's always like that at first. But once you get to know him, he's a really funny dude."

"So what if we don't have dreams!" Kathrine snapped at Norris. He remained calm and filled his own bottle with the lake water, despite Kathrine's rising tone.

"We can still help." She assured him.

He smirked. "Help with what, you're friend over there doesn't even know that this water is dirty," Norris swayed his arm over the water and a stream of clear, blue liquid emerged from the musky lake. Chase paused and immediately emptied his water bottle and spat out what was in his mouth.

Norris laughed. Adam wondered if he would one day get cool powers like Hexus and Norris. Maybe it was healing, he remembered how quickly he had recovered from his broken shoulder in the prison. He liked the idea of him having powers.

"Well Chase is an idiot!" Kathrine immediately looked at him and regretted her words. He shouted back at her "HEY!"

She winced and turned her attention back towards Norris, who was now helping Chase with his water. Maybe he was a kind person, but he had a funny way of showing it. He made a blob of clean water float up and out of the lake and into the mouth of the donkey. Pormant, was a brown and grey donkey that had several pounds of equipment on his back. Packs and pouches as well as things that looked like satchels designed for donkeys. Adam felt bad for it, but the animal showed no signs of a struggle.

Kathrine grunted and turned into the woods.

"Where are you going?" Adam asked.

"I'm going to go find firewood. Because I'm useful." She pointed proudly at her chest.

Norris laughed, Adam got the feeling that he just enjoyed annoying Kathrine. They all knew she was useful, Adam especially. She was smart, resourceful and always knew what to do. But sometimes her mind was clouded by her emotions. Adam never saw it as a weakness, more of a flaw. He knew there wasn't much better, but the word "weakness" always sounded insulting while a "flaw" was something you could better. Although there were few things that were a flaw about Kathrine. In Adam's book, she was nearly perfect. He never said that out loud, but he knew better than to tease her.

"First of all," Norris began. "It has not yet even stopped raining, so the fire would go out. That is, if you manage to find pieces of wood dry enough to burn in the wet forest. Besides," he stood up and wiped the mud off his shins, "the group is near. They'll have anything we need. So we should get moving." He grabbed the reins on Pormant and lightly tugged at them. Kathrine grunted, annoyed.

Hexus followed he washed his face in the water. He dried himself off with his shirt, revealing a large tattoo on his left arm. A circle with several swirls above it that resembled a flame. This boy really liked fire.

"Whoa," Adam said. He'd never seen a person so young with a tattoo.

Hexus looked at him. Then he smiled. "You like it? It's a fireball, I thought it would be cool since, y'know, the whole fire thing I got going on. Eleon gave it to me. I could ask him to give you one, but I don't know if he would charge. He migh—*" his rambling was interrupted by a sudden jolt that sent him flying backwards. Everyone scrambled to take cover. Adam looked at Hexus, who now had a two-foot-long arrow sticking out of his left shoulder. They were under attack.

10

ADAM WAS FROZEN. He didn't know what to do. Norris unsheathed his sword, a saber with a hilt guard and a curved blade. Hexus summoned fire. Chase readied his fists and Kathrine unslung the new bow she had stolen from the guards and awkwardly knocked an arrow. Even Pormant seemed ready for battle, as he pawed at the mud below his hooves and brayed.

Adam had a sword, but he didn't know what to do with it. He had simply carried it all through the forest. He lifted it with a shaky hand and attempted to seem intimidating, it didn't work.

"Who's there?" Asked a new voice. A dark figure emerged from behind the rocks across the lake. It was a woman. Or at least, the silhouette of one. She had a bow and was already pulling back on another arrow. "Answer me, or my next shot won't be so off target."

Norris sighed and put down his weapon. Adam looked at him confused.

"Erika, it's me. Norris, I'm with Hexus."

"What?" Said the voice. She emerged from the shadows of the trees, set by the sunrise.

She was beautiful, in a warrior princess kind of way. She had short auburn colored hair that was cut at the shoulders. Her shoulder had a leather pad on it, probably as armor, and was strapped around her chest via a leather strap. Her forearms were also covered in these battle pads. She wore a short silk dress that was cut at the knees and a dagger was strapped to her belt, which had a flowing middle part that lead from her waist to a little beneath her knees. A quiver was strapped to her back. Perched on rock next to her, was a bright white owl with glowing yellow eyes. How did Adam not notice it before? She smiled revealing two rows of perfect teeth. Adam could clearly see that her golden eyes matched the owls.

"Wow." She said. "It really is you guys." She descended from the rock and everyone put their weapons down. Hexus smiled, almost in a daze.

"Hey, Erica..." he said, with droopy eyes. He held the arrow that Erika had shot in his hands, a small bleeding cut was left in his shoulder. She walked around the lake and squeezed Hexus and Norris with a hug.

"I thought you two were dead. We all did." She giggled. And Hexus's cheeks turned red. First with flattery, as he obviously liked this woman, which was a bit weird, since he was thirteen and if Adam had to guess, Erika was in her early twenties, but then Hexus's cheeks went red with embarrassment as Norris explained to Erika what happened in Iolcus. How Hexus got arrested after stealing food, how he was thrown in prison and then how he met Adam. He described how Norris broke them out and they fled the city in a hurry.

"We got what we needed," he patted Pormant's bags. "But we're sorry we took so long."

"It was nearly a week." She said while stroking Pormant's mane, "but I'm glad you're back. Come on, the others will want to meet you."

The owl put Adam on edge. It's piercing eyes seemed to look straight through him, as it glided from branch to branch in the thick forest, attacking the occasional rodent at any opportunity.

They followed Erika through several hundred yards of forest.

"So," She nudged Adam. Her voice was almost hypnotic. "Norris told me you survived a gorgon attack?" He didn't realize it was a question until she waited about a minute for an answer. They lead the group as Adam's friends followed behind him.

"Yes," he said. "I broke my shoulder. But then it healed—*"

"Almost over night, correct?" She finished Adam's sentence. He stared at her.

"Yes. Yes it did. Does that happen to you?"

"It happens to all of us." She said, proudly. Adam took back his thoughts of a healing factor being his special power. He was a bit disappointed, but he was intrigued.

"Oh," he said.

"Look at Hexus's arm. It's almost completely closed from that arrow I shot at him." She turned, "sorry again for that."

"It's fine!" Hexus said almost immediately, and entranced.

She returned her attention to Adam.

"You know, my brother and I survived a gorgon attack."

"Hexus told me you guys had all been attacked by something that drove you away from your homes."

Her expression darkened. "Yeah," She said glumly. "The gorgons destroyed my village about a month ago. But then Norris and Eric found me. And my brother and I have been traveling with them ever since."

Eric. This marked another time that Adam heard the name, but he still had zero idea as to who this man was. Apparently the dreams had told him and Norris to gather 11 people. Thought Adam still didn't know why and who even gave these dreams in the first place.

"I'm sure you have many questions." Erika said, as if reading his thoughts, "you're life is changing, and so quickly as well. But I hope that my friends and I can help you."

"Well, you can start by telling me who the hell Eric is, and why you guys need me to find this destination of yours."

Erika grew a smile. "We needed 11 people. The people that gave us the dreams said that. We don't know why. But we know that it might be revealed once we got all 11. And since we do now, maybe they'll show us. As for Eric, he's the leader of our group. He's the oldest. He knows what he's doing. He's the best in combat. The best at surviving and the best music player."

That last statement made Adam confused.

"Music player?" He asked, trying to keep a straight face. Sure he liked music, and so did Chase and Kathrine, but after all those things that Erika said about him, Eric was the last person Adam would have thought as a musician.

"You won't see it when you meet him. But he is."

He was grateful that Erika was willing to answer his questions, but he was bothered by the fact that she didn't hold all the answers.

"You said you and you're brother were traveling with Eric and Norris, but Norris said you guys won't accept people who don't have dreams."

She smirked, "it's true, but my brother also has the dreams. We are twins."

"Oh,"

"Yes, although, you might question that once you meet Eleon."

A man that gave tattoos to a thirteen-year-old didn't seem like he would be related to Erika but Adam didn't say that. Erika seemed sweet, and caring almost like a mother should.

"Will my friends be okay? They don't have the dreams."

She kept her gaze fixed on the direction they were headed in. Her white owl glided down from a branch and perched itself on her shoulder. Erika scratched its neck feathers.

"Your friends will be fine. They're the only people you know, and the only people you trust. And when dealing with things as horrific as these dreams, it's good to have a support group. The satyr however, may find it... difficult to be with us."

Adam smiled; he appreciated her words of wisdom. Her statement about Chase worried him, but it wouldn't be any different from how he was treated in Alor.

He stared into the eyes of the bird at her side.

"What of the bird?" He asked. As if it had been insulted, the owl glared at him and flew off to sit on Pormant's back.

Erika giggled, "I've had Ion since I was little. She's a friend."

That didn't really answer his question, but he didn't ask further.

Most of the shock from Adam's past few hours had subsided, but he was still taking in the fact that there were people out here. That there was a whole world that he had no idea about until he met a boy in a prison. There were forests, and mountains, and people and owls. Maybe he could have gone without the owls, but it was still awesome, nonetheless.

They crossed through muddy swamps and hills of green grass for about three hours.

Norris reached into his satchel and talked with Erika. Unfolding the piece of paper, he dragged his finger across certain lines on it.

"We head south from here I imagine." He said, asking for conformation.

"I'm not sure." Erika replied, "Eric never told us what would happen when we found the last dreamer."

"Your right." Norris told her.

Chase and Kathrine got lost in their own minds, looking around in awe at the world before them, the world they had never seen before. Hexus walked with them, trying to land a stick he had found on the forest floor perfectly upright in the palm of his hand.

Adam grew curious. The map Norris was holding must have had lands of all kinds, and Hexus had seen that they had been all overlooking for Adam. The drive to look soon the map overwhelmed him.

Norris recorded the paper and was prepared to return it to his satchel when Adam asked for it.

Norris tossed him the paper. Adam unfolded it and examined the world.

"Is this real?" He asked, astonished.

Norris raised his eyebrow, "what do you mean?"

Adam looked at the map, "all these places, are they real?" He realized the smile that had grown on his face.

Norris looked at Erika and chuckled, "yes. Yes, still real, kid."

Adam counted five large continents, and a thousand islands to the east. The five continents were called, Vulna, the continent they were on now, Sentros, Fàrnörr, Argana, Okoona, and Kayembe. To the far east, was Halanor, a slender island. All lands were bordered by seas and islands. Six large islands in the west made up the Endless Isles and dozens more in the south west made the Shattered Lands. The two seas separating Vulna from Sentros were filled with islands as well, with Volar, Melcikor and Amba to the north and an archipelago to the south.

Mountains and rivers snakes across the lands, from the Endless Isles to Halanor in the Sunrise Sea.

Adam guffawed at the sight. There was so much to look at, so much to see. A question lingered in the back of his mind, "why had the walls been up for so long?" He said aloud.

He returned the map to Norris after sharing it with Kathrine and Chase and thought about what he had just seen. The thought never left his brain for the rest of the trip.

The sun was almost at its summit and Adam realized how tired he was. With a yawn, he crossed over a pair of fallen trees and almost passed out. It was as if his body was giving up on him. He had stayed up all night, he didn't blame his body. Before he could fall asleep completely, Erika walked into an opening in the forest. Wait, no, Adam thought, not and opening, the other side. They had completely crossed the entire forest.

Adam's tired eyes nearly fell out of his head. He was shocked at what he saw.

For miles, more green hills covered the entire land. He saw so many mountains, hills, rivers and lakes that he losses count. But the strangest thing he saw, was the elephant.

A couple yards in front of him, a massive brown, hairy pachyderm slept quietly as a tall man with a beard strapped several bags on it that put Pormant to shame. Next to the elephant, several animals lay in a small makeshift nest. Adam saw a weasel, a red panda, a white tiger, and a dog, all huddled together in the strangest group that Adam had ever seen. Flying above him, Ion, Erika's owl was flying with two more birds. One was another owl much larger than her, and was grey. The other was a small brown sparrow. Feeding the animals was a lanky boy, a little older than Adam. He had long black trusses and a slim face the color of almonds with bright blue eyes and a clean chin free from facial hair. His arms were different, as they were covered in callouses and scratches. On the sides of his face, were two ears almost as big as serving plates. He had a scrawny body, thought it was hard to tell while he was kneeling, giving a skinned animal to the white tiger. His legs were hairy and he wore a brown tunic with no shoes to shield his feet from the rocky ground. By the looks of him, he was a servant. Next to that lot, in front of Adam, several tents were being taken down by several people. Most of them were Adam's age. In the middle of the whole thing, a ring of wooden planks formed benches around an extinguished fire. Next to it, a wooden table was being folded and tied to the elephant by the man with the beard and another tall man with short, scruffy hair.

"Hi guys!" Yelled Hexus, Adam remembered where he was.

All eyes turned towards them and Adam's stomach sank. Multiple pairs of confused eyes turned to him. Hexus ran to the elephant and tried to wrap his hand around its arm in a hug, but he was stuck in a starfish position instead, as he lay on the rising and falling carpet on the elephants shaggy belly.

One man stood forward. He was tall, about six foot, which made Adam more nervous than he already was. His blonde hair was slicked back and he wore a green, hooded robe and a brown tunic underneath. His pants and boots were muddy and strapped to his waist was a large dagger. Strapped to his back, were two swords as-well as a bow and quiver filled with silver arrows. But perhaps the most intimidating thing about this man was not his height, or his many weapons, but the two huge scars that raked from beneath his bearded chin to over his left eyebrow. Without a doubt, Adam knew that he was Eric. The big bad leader of the group.

"Where have you been? And who is this?" He asked Norris.

"We were side tracked, Eric. We had to stay in Alor for a few more days. We got the supplies, but we did create a riot."

"I told you to not bring attention to yourselves!" Said Eric. He was angry and Adam didn't realize he was backing until he bumped into Chase.

"What about the kids?" Eric asked. "Who are you?"

Adam opened his mouth but no sound came out. Some of the animals were waking up and Adam didn't like the look of that tiger. It's blue eyes glimmered scarily.

"He's the last one. He's the one we needed."

Everyone gasped. Except for Eric, who only seemed to glare at Adam more fiercely. He stepped forward.

"And these two?" He pointed towards Kathrine and Chase.

"Associates." Norris said. The kids seemed to be getting closer, one of them wasted no time. He hurried over to Adam with blinding speed, and before they could count to ten, he showered them with questions. Everyone else seemed used to it. The boy was chubby, with curly blonde hair and blue eyes. His nose was round and his lips were thin. He wore a light blue linen shirt and a leather jerkin that had a golden symbol engraved on the chest, that was a symbol of the Endless Isles to the north, his accent was probably from there. He had read about Endless Isles in a book once, of course, only thinking they were legends. He imagined the entire map he had seen in books to be legends, but here he was, in front of people from those legendary places. The boy had brown pants and ankle height leather boots and had a satchel over his shoulder and a short sword at his waist.

The boy studied Adam, them smiled. He was about Adam's age.

"I'm Theodore," he said in an accent, alien to Adam, "Pleasure to meet you. What's your name? Where are you from? Oh wait, I suppose you would be from Alor since you just came from there—*" wow, Theodore rambled more than Hexus., thought Adam. Thankfully, he was interrupted by a girl to his left. "Theo, leave him alone!"

Erika had reminded Adam of a warrior or a princess, but this girl, she reminded Adam of a goddess. She was about his age and height, with long platinum white hair, and her eyes were a beautiful shade of purple. Her skin was flawless and the color of chestnuts and her lips were enticing. She wore a two piece silk dress with a leather skirt over the bottom part of the dress, which Adam thought was a bit weird, but she pulled it off. Her boots were also ankle high and had a crisscross design of laces in the front. She was seriously pretty, and had no problem letting everyone know. On her waist was a dagger and a satchel. She leaned in and kissed Adam on both cheeks. His face turned to boiling water. His eyes widened and he was left speechless. She whistled a beautiful tune and the sparrow Adam had seen before was perched on her shoulder.

She held out her perfectly manicured hand and Adam shook it.

"I'm Raia. Nice to meet you." More and more kids swarmed the group as Adam noticed Norris talking about something serious with Eric. He knew it was serious because they both had stern faces. Eric walked off, which left Norris with a worried and sour face.

Adam was soon surrounded with new people. His mind suddenly went blank and he yawned again. His eyelids felt heavy and he found himself struggling to stay up right.

"Everyone calm yourselves." Said Erika. "He's tired and needs to rest. Let him get on Quartus and he can sleep while we move."

Adam completely agreed with the idea. At least, the sleeping part. He was nearly unconscious. Then, the tall man with the beard picked him up and walked towards the elephant.

11

ADAM HAD NEVER slept in an mammoth before, but he didn't struggle. The tall man brought him to a small howdah that was built on the back of the massive animal. The inside was small, just enough room for maybe five people, but it was cozy. The bottom was feather bedding. A soft, comfortable carpet protecting Adam from the animals bare back. The walls were curtains and the whole thing was basically a tent on a saddle. The corners were wooden shafts holding up the wooden ceiling. He noticed Hexus, Kathrine and Chase join him inside, but he didn't complain.

Adam was set down in the middle and immediately dozed off. Big mistake.

His dream came back.

He found himself standing in the middle of a field. A grey field with an ocean of tall grass. He was alone. The swaying of the wind sang as it passed his ears. The sky was black and filled with stars. He sat up, and the air left his lungs. Far in the distance, spinning in the black abyss around him, was a sphere of blue and green. The world spun so many miles away, and it all seemed so insignificant. Adam did not even know all of this world, and yet it now all seemed so small.

He looked behind him and found himself face to face with a massive castle. It was huge. Several miles tall. It was built into the side of a mountain and had towers and buildings jutting from the cliffs. Twelve statues of what Adam could only guess were warriors lined the main entrance at the base of the mountain on either side of an ivory tiled walkway lead around the mountain. At the summit, higher than the clouds, sat a golden castle that consisted of multiple towers huddled together. They were all beautifully designed, but the real spectacle was the center tower. A tall structure with a domed roof and a was a mix of gold, silver, white and bronze. He remembered the man from his dream saying something about a golden city...

Lighting rumbled in the sky and the earth shook. Adam could see a gold object flying around the top of the palace. A bird?

It circled the dark, stormy sky, as if it were getting ready to attack its prey. Suddenly, it appeared before him. It never flew down to meet him, it simply appeared in front of him, with a flash of the blue and white lightning. Adam was right about one thing, it was a bird, but any other idea that Adam had about it couldn't have been more incorrect. It was a ten-foot-tall, solid gold eagle. Each of its feathers were made of gold and its eyes were blue as diamonds. It didn't seem mechanical, it was a living thing, Adam could see it's chest rise and fall with each breath and it's eyes had an iris and pupil. The deep black pupil surrounded by the bright blue and iris made Adam feel safe somehow.

It twitched it's head, "You found them?" It's voice was belonged to the man from Adam's last dream. But it spoke without opening its golden beak.

He wrinkled his nose, "more accurately, they found me. But yes."

"Good."

"What's going to happen to Alor?" Adam asked. He didn't know why, that horrid city had been terrible to him. But maybe he still held sentiment for it.

"I cannot tell. It is unclear."

"Oh,"

"How are they. The others?"

"Fine, I think. I haven't really met them yet. I fell asleep on their elephant. I didn't know elephants still existed."

"There are plenty, but not where you are. They are native to the south. Hairy ones live in the north." The eagle said, amused.

"So, why did you want them to find me? I have many questions. I am... scared, and confused, and I feel like my head is going to explode."

He felt a little weird confessing all his feelings to a giant bird, but the words poured out of him. He couldn't stop them.

"I'm sure you are. I can tell you that, in time, all your questions will be answered. I cannot tell you much here. He is listening."

"The dragon? He's not here."

"He is, but you cannot see him. He is in your mind. He is in your dreams. In all their dreams. He sent the gorgons after you."

Adam felt a surge of energy flood through him. Any person who could summon and control a pair of gorgons had to be powerful.

"I thought I summoned them with magic."

"The magic was a signal necessary to show that you were still alive."

Adam didn't seem to notice that last bit. Instead he focused on why the dragon wanted shim dead.

"Why?" Adam asked.

"You are valuable to him. You are the only one who can stop his plan."

His plan? Who's plan? And why was Adam the only person who could stop it? He decided to not ask more questions, as it would lead to only more confusion.

"Oh. Ok. So, um, the others said that once they had all of us, they'll know where they are going. Will you tell them?"

The eagles face seemed to turn agitated. "In time, yes. But he will hear you, so I cannot tell you. He has entered all your dreams. But I have an idea. When you wake up, you will be safe, however in your dreams, you are vulnerable. Come with me."

The eagle turned around and gestured for Adam to climb onto its massive back. Adam placed his legs over the birds wings and held onto its mane. The feathers were soft, yet still made of a mineral.

"Where are we going?" Adam asked the bird.

"I will show you something."

The bird flapped it's massive wings and they took off. With a strike of lighting, they launched from the grassy field and flew over the palace. The dream shifted.

Adam still found himself riding the eagle, but now, they were flying over somewhere different. In the valley below, Adam could see a group of people who had set up camp in the mountains. The camp was much bigger than the one he was staying at. For several hundred yards, possibly for miles several hundred tents were set up. Adam was looking at an army.

The bird perched itself on top of one of the tallest rocks on the mountain. It over looked the camp perfectly so that none of the people below saw them. Adam wasn't even sure if they were human. They seemed, ghoulish.

The men were bony, charcoal black skeletons reminiscent of the ones Adam had previously seen, laying dead in the fields of other dreams. Except these were alive. They wore helmets over their dark brown remnants of hair. Small holes poked out so that the soldiers could look out with their sunken, red eyes. They're bodies were withered nearly to the bone and their jaws fell open, showing two rows of yellow, sometimes missing teeth. Others didn't even have lower jaws. Some simply looked like grey humans with everything still intact, others missed some limbs. They rode on skeletal horses, dragon and hairy beasts that resembled bears.

Their chest plates seemed like they had once been used for battle. Scratch marks and arrow holes dotted their chests. Some even still had arrows jutting out of their chests and backs. They scattered around the area, punching each other for no reason, fighting over food or chasing each other around with their rusty swords. It looked like they had all been a part of different armies. Their weapons were mismatched. Some held longswords, while others held different blades. Some held up large, body length, rectangular shields and spears while others simply had smaller, round wooden and metal shields. Some had beards, others had long hair. None of them spoke, instead, they opened their mouths and uttered a guttural scream.

A shiver made its way down Adam's spine.

"Spartoi." Said the bird. "They are fallen warriors who have returned from the underworld."

"Underworld? Returned for what?"

"Combat. They fight for him." The bird nudged it's head at the lead tent. A tall, black tent with white ropes holding it up stood before the army of tents. Then, a figure emerged from it.

A warrior taller than anyone Adam had ever seen stepped out. He was nearly ten feet tall, and covered head to toe in silver armor. Spikes jutted from both of his massive shoulder pads. His helmet had a path of ridges leading down from his scalp. Strapped at his side, was a sword the size of Adam, and on his back, was a black rod. Adam was horrified, then he remembered it was only a dream, and the man couldn't do anything to him.

"That is general Korax, leader of the Spartoi army. He is like a god to them" the eagle said with a dreadful tone.

Adam looked down the mountain. It's base was nothing new, more green hills and fields, except for one thing. A large city sat at the base of the mountain: Alor.

"Wait, is this... real? Like, is this happening right now?"

"Yes. These soldiers are closing in on your location. They have been following the others for weeks. The dragon tells them where to go. It follows you're dreams."

"Wait, so, these soldiers are really outside of Alor as we speak?"

"That is correct."

"What's going to happen?"

"I'm not sure. They will search here. Once they figure out you are not in the city, they will most likely follow you through the forest."

"Bloody hell." Adam fell to his knees. It was a lot to take in.

"Who the hell is this dragon? He can control armies, and monsters."

"He is an old being, ancient in fact. A primordial. Everything will be clear when the time is right. They call him The Great Snake."

A memory jumped into Adam's mind. "This is the thing that Hexus called 'King'." He realized.

The bird nodded.

"Yesssssss," hissed a new voice. Adam recognized the dragon immediately, "it is I. I control all. And soon Adam, I will have you."

Its sinister voice roared in Adam's head, it he saw nothing... The eagle placed its wing over Adam defensively, shielding him from whatever might come next.

From below the large wing, Adam could see the dream ripple. The sky cracked. A massive white scar had appeared in the dark purple sky as if it were made of glass. And out emerged a large raven.

Adam felt the field of tall grass shift back into existence as he examined the new bird. So this being was a shapeshifter as well? Wonderful.

It was the same size as the eagle, about ten feet tall. It's obsidian black feathers glinted in the moonlight it had brought in. It's talons seemed to be made of solid iron. Whenever they touched together, a metallic clang filled Adam's ears. It's beak was also jet black. It's orange eyes seemed to be made of fire. When it landed, Adam could see the grass around him wither and die. Ashes floated off its body.

"Do not allow the words of this old fool to enter your mind. It is all poison." It spoke, with that voice that made it sound like several raspy voices were speaking at once.

"Don't listen to it Adam. Wake up!" The eagle snapped. Adam looked at the raven. It smiled sinisterly. Could birds smile? He didn't like the answer. It was hideous.

"He attempts to turn you from me. Interesting." It said.

It moved so quickly that Adam barely had time to react. The raven wove around the eagle's golden wing and snatched the boy up in its iron talons.

Adam could feel with metal sink into his skin with the pressure. The eagle chased after it, but to no avail. The raven was already too far away.

It dropped Adam up on the top of the castle from before. Ashes still rained from its skin. They stood beside on another, on the domed roof of the tallest tower. Adam tried to look over the horizon, but only saw darkness.

12

THE SKY TREMBLED, and the crow bellowed, "Watch, as this world crumbles. Attempting to escape is pointless Adam. I can see wherever you go." The crow said. The castle under his feet was now in ruins with several of the statues missing their torsos, or heads or other stone body parts.

Adam looked for the eagle. But it had disappeared.

"Why so sad boy? I thought you wanted your city to die. It was torture for you." Cried the crow.

"Who are you? And what do you want with me?" Adam asked, gathering every ounce of courage in his body.

"I am you're father. I left you when you were little because I never loved you. I left all the children. I felt them as a burden." Adam could tell it was lying. It made no attempt to hide it.

"Adam, listen to me! You must wake up. The army! Beware the army!" Yelled the eagle, as it dove onto the crow from the storm clouds above. The rain made it impossible for Adam's eyes to focus on anything.

"The army? My army! It is futile to run. They will spread my word throughout the land. You cannot escape the inevitability of the Red Winter."

The birds were a blur or black and gold. Lighting struck closely behind Adam. Dangerously close. The Eagle stood above the crow with its talons around the black bird's neck.

The bird stared at him with those piercing red eyes.

"Wake up, Adam! Now! You must wake up! Follow the priestess's instructions! Do it!"

"For what? It is a pointless task. Join me Adam, in welcoming a new age. Where men will be inferior to us both."

An explosion rocked the building, rain fell down from the sky as thunder and lightning rattled the earth.

The crow shrieked as the golden eagle dug its golden talons into its hide and picked at it with its golden beak.

Adam felt the rainwater trickle down beneath his feet, and he slipped.

Falling down the side of the dome, he had no idea what to do. The heavy rain fall made it difficult to open his eyes. He kept sliding and eventually fell off. Luckily, the parapet on a lower level was close enough to grasp. He opened his eyes against the force of the rain and noticed the two birds flying around and attacking each other. Thunder clapped in the sky as another explosion came down on the building.

The balcony crumbled and Adam gripped onto the edge of the ruins left by the lighting. The birds still fought, but it was momentarily stopped by the raven noticing the hanging boy.

It dove to catch Adam, but the eagle chased after it.

Both birds grew closer to Adam. His eyes stung but he held on despite the water loosening his grip. He was holding on with all five fingers on only one hand now.

Four.

Three.

The birds cawed and through their talons each intending to kill their prey. Adam, for the raven, and the raven, for the eagle.

The black talons of the black bird were now only inches from Adam's face. Ten, nine, eight, seven, six...

Then, he let go of the balcony. He felt his body grow weightless as he fell into an empty void of nothingness.

He woke up in a panic, sweating and breathing heavily. He was still in the elephant. Hexus and Kathrine slept next to him.

He heard laughing and talking from outside the tent.

The rubbed his eyes and walked out.

Sitting around a table, Chase and the others all talked and laughed about something that Adam didn't know about.

Adam stepped out from the tent and immediately fell on his face. The ground around him was burying many things, including an annoyingly large boulder, which he found out on his way down to the ground.

Raia, the pretty girl from before noticed him and rushed spot see if he was okay. The others just laughed.

"Are you alright?" She asked. Her skin was smooth and her amethyst eyes were caring.

Adam found it difficult to form sentences. He wiped the mud from his face and looked at her.

"I'm... fine, thank you. Where are we?"

"In the middle of no where." Said a tall bearded man. He punched his friend in the arm. "Zethus got us lost."

The man who had been punched was about six feet tall with short, brown hair and a freshly groomed beard. He raised his hands in defense.

"No I did not. Eric told us to head south. So we did."

"I've been asleep all day?" Adam asked.

"Yes, it's nearly sundown." Said Theodore, the plump kid from before. He was right. The sky had turned a brilliant shade of pink.

Zethus held up a half eaten chicken leg.

"Join us." He said.

13

HE HURRIED TOWARDS them "we cannot stay here!" Adam yelled as he ran towards the picnic. He tried to stuff as many things in a bag as possible. Everyone looked at him like he was crazy.

"Calm down, boy." Said a big man with a beard. "What is it?" He asked. Adam stopped what he was doing. He froze with random objects falling from the bag, which was now soggy because Adam had unknowingly dropped a goblet of wine inside. Everyone's eyes were on him.

"I had a dream last night." Adam said. "Maybe you should all sit down."

As they all sat down around a table eating and listening to Adam's words, most of them developed confused faces.

"I don't know what they are, or why they are after us. All I know is that there is an army of corps men, led by a giant man in silver armor. And they're over those hills." Adam pointed east.

Silence grew over the group; the only sound being made was the sound of chewing and Adam's voice telling the others about his dream.

"Maybe, if we can get over those hills to the west it can give us enough time to get away. We can't take them in combat, they outnumber us one-hundred to one."

Everyone stared at him. The ominous silence was deafening. Then, Hexus began to laugh. Adam was confused beyond return.

"We know about the army." Zethus said, as he took a bite from his second piece of bread.

Adam looked down at the fish on his plate, "Aren't you worried?"

They all looked around as if to get each other's opinions. "No, not really." Said Erika.

We keep a steady pace ahead of them." Theodore said.

A young Asian man smiled, "they haven't bothered us either."

Adam tugged at his collar.

"Calm down, your just nervous because of the dream." Norris said.

"He is right." Said Raia, she smiled, revealing two rows of perfect, white teeth. Adam felt like he had been punched in the stomach.

"Try not to stress. Sit. Eat. Enjoy the moment." Erika gestured at his seat. Adam hadn't realized it was empty until now.

"The food is great. Thanks so much again, dear Akio." Theodore smiled at the eastern boy and kissed him on the cheek. The two exchanged a loving look.

Adam loosened his grip on his plate. He had no idea who these people were, but he trusted them. If they said they were safe, Adam trusted that they were safe.

They all ate around the table as they shared stories.

They talked about their old lives and how they had all been gathered by Eric and Norris.

Adam had learned a few names. He already knew about Theodore and Raia. He also knew Erika, Hexus, Zethus and Norris.

A boy with a purple robe and black, curly hair was named Eli, he had almond shaped green eyes.

Sitting next to him, was Eleon, Erika's twin brother.

Erika was right. Adam never would have guessed they were related. Let alone twins. If anything, he would have guessed that Eleon and Zethus were related. Both were around 6'4 with choppy hair and a scruffy, messy beard, only Zethus had shaved his sometime in the past two days. They had biceps the size of cantaloupes and scars on their face. Zethus had a scar on his left cheek that spread down to his neck. Eleon, a scar left one of his eyes permanently shut. That was intimidating. His arms were covered in tattoos and perched on his shoulder was the big black horned owl that Adam had seen last night.

The last person was a girl with long fiery orange hair and green eyes. Her name was Minerva, and she was a person of few words. Adam realized that Eric wasn't joining them. Apparently, he wasn't a people person. He was in his tent, meditating. He had been waiting to meet him.

Norris had changed outfits. Last night he was still wearing the guards uniform he had used to break Adam out of prison. But now, he wore a brown tunic with brown pants and ankle high boots. Wrapped around his shoulders was a dark blue wool hooded cloak. Strapped to his side was his saber.

Something scurried off Norris's shoulder. Adam realized it was a weasel. The long-bodied brown rodent scurried from one end of the table to the other as it stole a chicken wing from Eleon's plate.

"By the way," Adam said, "What is the purpose of the animals everywhere?"

Zethus smiled, "Vàninëll, our friends. We've all had them for a long time. Eleon and Erika have the owls, Ion and Eos. Akio has Tenzir and Rubius, Norris has Bugbush, Raia has Spew, Theo has Pormant, and Beta and Quartus belong to me." He pet the dog next to him. Then he called to the peasant boy, "Get me another goblet of wine, Asius." He yelled.

"Yes, of course, my lord." Asius responded. The peasant boy responded with confidence, not in the timid way Adam expected slaves to answer. He did not respond in a shy or scared way. Far from it, he was confident and friendly as if he was Eleon's lifelong friend. After pouring the giant man another goblet and handing it to him, he went back to tending to the animals.

Adam tried to focus. All these people had strange pets. He didn't know which animal was which, but for the most part he could guess. He knew Quartus was the elephant. Ion and Eos were the owls and Adam assumed Bugbush was the weasel.

"But who cares!" Eleon shouted. He waved an apple at Adam. "What about you, boy? Tell us about yourself." He took a chomp out of the red fruit.

Adam swallowed down the bitter taste in his mouth. He explained what it was like living in Alor. How miserable everyone was, and how hard it was to make a living. He described the gorgon attack that had happened after he had attempted to get rid of his dreams.

Theodore grunted, "Yep, they're attracted to magic. Ugly buggers they are. But I hear you killed them! That true?" Adam nodded. The audience yelled with claps and cheers.

He continued telling them about the dream in the prison after he got arrested for putting the people in danger.

"Wait," Said Akio, "So they threw you in a prison because you got attacked. Your city seems quite terrible." He murmured while eating his bread. Adam told them about their escape and finally how they made their way here. He told them about his dreams, and how confused and scared he was. However, he though his most recent dream could wait.

"I guess it was because the magic that attracted them was my fault."

"But you were attacked." Argued Akio.

"Yes." Adam answered.

"That's terrible," Said Erika, empathetically.

"That's normal." Eleon crossed his arms. "We all have dreams, and were used to them."

"But why do we have them?" Adam asked.

"Listen, kid," Eleon said, "one piece of advice, do not ask questions. We can't answer them. We have the same questions. We can't help you—*"

"But we can be here if you need anything." Erika placed her hand on Adam's shoulder, cutting off her brother.

"I talked to Eric." Said Norris. "He said he might need to talk to you, but for now, you guys can stay with us." He held up a goblet of purple liquid, and everyone cheered.

Adam felt a tap on his shoulder. He tuned to see Kathrine with a worried expression on her face.

"Are you alright?" Adam asked. She kept the worry in her eyes.

"We need to talk." She said. Adam reluctantly stood up, excused himself and followed Kathrine who was already storming off. Before Adam could say anything, as if knowing that he was going to pester her, Kathrine yelled, "And get Chase too!"

Adam sighed. What was it now? She could be mad at anything and stay mad for a long time. But Adam knew better then to ignore her when she says something. He walked to the camp and tapped Chase on the shoulder. After a brief explanation, he followed him.

The camp was in the middle of a clearing with forest all around them. The forest they had just come from was to the south. Or east? Maybe the north. Adam concluded; he had no idea where he was. After all, it was his first time outside his city.

Through a cluster of oak trees, he could see Kathrine sitting at the edge of a small lake. A slight wind left her hip air to flutter at its will. The trees hissed with the softness of the breeze and Adam could feel the moisture from the lake refreshing his face.

"What is this about?" Chase asked. "When did you wake up?"

"'What is this about'?" She mimicked, "It's about the fact that we are hanging out with armed strangers who are trained killers and we are being tracked by and army of dead warriors in Adam's words."

Adam sighed. "I know it looks bad, but we have to trust these people. I do!" Adam looked at Chase to get his opinion, but the idiot was still gnawing on a chicken bone.

"Look, they are just like me. They seem friendly enough too."

"Maybe, but what do you want to do about the army?" She said.

"Can't we worry about that later? It's late and we are far away from them anyways." Chase insisted.

Adam nodded, "Chase has a point. You are stressing over something miles away. Enjoy the moment. Eat some fruit, drink some wine. You'll be fine."

Kathrine stared at the calm lake. "What of your dream? What did you say?"

Adam pursed his lips. "Two birds. A Golden Eagle and a Black Crow. I think I know a little about what is truly going on. The eagle is the one that gives me my dreams, but the Crow is the one that turns them into nightmares. I don't know why the Eagle gives me them, but I know that they mean something."

Kathrine took out a piece of paper from her satchel. Adam realized she had been wearing the silver bracelet that belonged to her mother. Adam had never met Kathrine's mother, but he could imagine that she would be proud of her to have escaped that city. She unfolded the paper in her hands. It was the writings that the priestess had given him. He thought he had lost it during the attack. She held it out in front of her.

"Do you have any ideas what any of this means? Have you seen them in a dream or something? Anything?" Adam took the paper. He read its contents aloud.

> Past the golden apples.
> Past the festivities.
> Past the impenetrable defender.
> Past a fine feast.
> Past the city from which you came.
> Past the walls that forbid exit.

Chase snatched the paper from Adam's hands. He glared at the last two lines. "'The walls? Exit? City which you came?" He murmured, "that must mean Alor. The walls that forbid exit. It has to be!" Adam took the page back. His brain then exploded with possibilities.

"This... this," he struggled to find words to describe his excitement. "These aren't random words these are instructions. It's like a map without pictures. This tells us where we need to go! It's in reverse, so our next stop must be... the fine feast!"

"What does that mean?" Kathrine asked.

"Easy, we are eating right now? That could be the feast."

"No," Adam said. "That wasn't a feast, that was barely a dinner."

Chase scowled, "I thought it was pretty good." He muttered while he rubbed his belly.

"We could wait and see. But, while we are here, I might as well show you this." Adam reached deep into his satchel, which he had taken before leaving the camp site. He took out the silver rod from the previous night. The designs on it seemed to be clearer I. The pink light cast by the twilight sky.

"I had a dream, my first night in the prison. There was a man. And he gave me a sword." Kathrine and Chase listened attentively. "When I went to see my mother, I took this from my chest. The inscriptions on it match the ones on the hilt of the sword in my dream." He stared at the rod.

Imbedded all around it was the words, "avàn vön àyalë". Adam could read it, somehow. It meant "for the eagle". He saw in eagle in his dream. Was he supposed to give the rod to it? The eagle never asked for it, so he decided that wasn't the answer.

"You have seen a sword before, yes? This is no sword, it's just a stick." Chase said as he took the rod. He began to fiddle with it, licking it, staring at it, feeling the words on the sides and putting it to his eye.

"I can see that, Chase!" Adam snapped at the satyr as he took back the rod.

"How can you turn it into a sword then?" Kathrine asked. She crossed her arms.

"I'm not sure b—"

"Then how do you know it's a sword?" Chase cut him off.

"I don't know but maybe—"

"Well then that is wonderful" Chase said.

"Listen to me!" Adam cried. The others flinched. He hadn't meant to yell, but they simply wouldn't let him get the words out of his mouth.

He held up the old piece of paper, "Don't you think this could help us?"

Chase stared at it.

Adam breathed deeply, "We can show this paper to this 'Eric' man and maybe he can help us get there."

"Zethus already said they were headed south." Chase pointed out.

"Yes..." Kathrine began, "but maybe they were meant to find us. Maybe the fates will it to be so."

Chase and Adam looked at her, she just agreed with Adam. He was surprised.

Her arms were now on her hips. "I say we stay with them, if Adam trusts them then," she sighed, "I will trust them."

"Thank you." Adam said.

They then both stared at Chase waiting for his response, he looked surprised.

"I was never against staying." He exclaimed.

"Great, then all of us will stay with them and show them this."

He looked at the paper one last time, before Kathrine attacked him with a hug. He looked up.

"I'm just glad we are all okay. And we are free." She said.

Chase began to chew on a leaf from a nearby tree. He placed his hands on the back of his head, "I suppose, the fates willed that so as well."

He laughed and hugged both Adam and Kathrine together. One thing about satyrs, they were unnaturally strong, so he could easily lift both.

A voice came from the camp site, it was Norris calling them all. As chase let go and Kathrine and Adam pushed the wrinkled off from their shirts they ran out to the clearing where Norris greeted them.

"It'll be dark soon. We'll need to start a fire." Around the camp, the tents were all set up. Adam spotted a purple one, among the other black ones.

"Chase and Adam?" Said Norris, "go find us some firewood. Go with Akio."

Akio was already walking towards them with a leather pouch of water in one hand and an axe in another. Zethus used several tolls to help set up the camp site. He used a shovel and a pickaxe among other things. Erika was shooting at trees and all the animals were already sleeping inside of Quartus's hut. Even the birds were out of the sky and resting inside of the large beast.

After Adam followed Adam and Chase into the woods, he turned back to see Kathrine walking towards the camp. Ready for another night beyond the wall.

14

KATHRINE HAD TO think, that everything she had seen her so far had been impressive. She loved the forest, the lake where she and the two boys talked, and she loved the campsite. It made her feel safe. She stared around at the half-finished site. Akio, Adam and Chase had gone to retrieve firewood. Zethus, Norris and Eleon were working away on the defenses. They had dug a trench around the campsite and set up sharp wooden pikes jutting out from the barrier. It was like a dangerously sharp shield.

Hexus and Theodore were said to be off fishing for food near the lake, with Raia. And Minerva was playing with a plant in the center of the camp, near where the fire would be. She liked how everyone had a job. Well almost everyone...

Out of the corner of her eye, she saw Erika firing arrows at trees. Almost like practicing her aim. Asius was next to her, gathering more arrows for her to launch at the defenseless trees. Kathrine decided to see what she was up to.

Erika was a beautiful woman. If Kathrine had to guess, she was maybe in her mid-twenties and she had an intensity in her eyes, like she could seduce you as easily as she could slit your throat. Kathrine admired a strong woman.

"Why aren't you helping out with the camp?" She asked Erika.

Erika knit her brow, "Minerva and I already worked on the fireplace.

Kathrine remembered the girl playing with the plant on the wooden logs.

Erika pulled an arrow from the X marked on the oak tree she used for target practice. The arrow hit dead center. And judging by the lack of other gashes in the tree, Kathrine assumed that all the shots Erika had shot, she had made. Impressive, especially since Erika was nearly thirty feet away went, she released her grip on the bow string. She walked back to her original spot while loading up the same arrow and pulling at the string. Then she noticed Kathrine.

"I saw the bow you walked in with." She said after greeting Kathrine, "Do you know how to use it?" She asked.

Kathrine laughed, "barely. I took it because it seemed like and easy weapon to use. I was quickly proved wrong."

Erika let go of her arrow again. It struck the tree marked X with a loud *thunk*. The arrow shaft was halfway into the bark and the butt was the only part visible.

"A fine shot m'lady." Asius said with a smile. Erika thanked him.

Erika handed Kathrine her bow, then walked over to a tree branch that held a second bow and a quiver full of silver arrows. Underneath that branch, Erika had set up a torch. She instructed Kathrine to follow her movements, "I'll show you."

Kathrine examined her fingers, and where they held whatever it was that they were holding.

"Grip the bow with the full force of your strong hand and hold the butt of the arrow in between your first two fingers, hook the same fingers around the bowstring." She shook her index finger on the hand she used to hold her bow and placed it lightly on the flat side of the arrow's head.

"Now, you want to hold it up to your target, keep it still, close one eye, and let go."

Thwip! The arrow flew from the bow at blinding speed, then abruptly stopped when it got stuck in the trunk of the oak tree. Asius clapped.

Kathrine tried to follow Erika's rules. She lifted the bow and stared at her target. She focused on the X in the tree. She could feel the wind in her hair and through her fingers as she readied the arrow. She took a deep breath and let go.

The arrow shaft flew with a whistle and hit just above the X. If she were to aim at somebody's chest, the arrow would hit their neck without problem.

"Very impressive, m'lady." Asius told her, handing her another arrow. Kathrine liked the boy's sweet demeanor. He seemed to be one of the worlds happiest servants.

Erika raised her eyebrows. Her black leather padding made her blend into the dark forest as if groaned with her movements. The torch she had set up illuminated her golden eyes with shades of amber and orange.

"Impressive." She said. "Again." She handed Kathrine the quiver.

Kathrine took a handful of arrows and placed them next to her. Erika walked to a tree near the one she had marked X, pulled out a dagger from her belt and began to scratch at the bark with the blade. Soon, Kathrine had a new "X tree" of her own.

"You will shoot here, and I will shoot the old one." She smiled, while retrieving the arrow Kathrine had shot before.

Soon, Kathrine had begun to become used to shooting arrows. She pulled back, aimed and let go easily with seconds. She had never used a bow before today, since Alor did not allow the citizens to have weapons, as king Adameious believed that they could have used them to start a revolution and overthrow him, which they probably would have if they could.

Kathrine scoffed at the thought. If she had the king of fools, as she called him, here at this very moment, she would very much like to place an arrow between his royal eyes, for all the pain he had caused her.

She kept nocking arrows and shooting. While drawing one back, Erika told her, "He is very handsome."

Kathrine blinked as she aimed, "Who?"

"That boy, Adam?" She giggled.

Kathrine flinched so bad that she accidentally let go of her arrow, causing it to fly dozens of feet in the air over the clearing of the forest.

Erika laughed Kathrine could feel the heat from her cheeks. Asius continued to say encouraging things as he handed her another arrow.

"I'm sorry if I said something wrong." Erika said, placing an arm on Kathrine's shoulder.

"No, no, it's fine." She reassured her archery teacher, "it's just, I didn't realize that you knew."

Erika smirked, "knew what? That you like him? Oh please, Raia may be able to make men fall in love with her, but I can read women as well. I have seen the way you look at him."

Kathrine remembered to bring up that comment about Raia later. She didn't trust that girl. But for now she focused on the conversation at hand, and how she could feel her cheeks get hotter by the second.

"Yes. He is handsome." Was all she could manage as she nocked another arrow.

"Are you two together?" She asked. Kathrine mustered all her strength so she would not let go of the arrow she had in hand.

"It's... complicated." She said.

"I understand. Zethus and I were complicated once as well."

Kathrine opened her closed eye in surprise, "Zethus?" She asked.

Erika smiled, "Yes, he is my husband. The one with the shaved beard digging the trenches."

Kathrine nodded her head. "I see. Why were you two complicated?"

"He was fond of me, but I was not sharing the same feelings. Until one day he managed to save my life. I was out of arrows and a group of thieves had me cornered. Zethus defeated them in seconds, and it seems I have looked at him differently ever since that day."

"That does not sound too complicated." Kathrine said.

"Maybe not. But tell me then, why are you and this boy complicated?" She asked.

Kathrine paused, even she did not know how to answer that question.

"I am not entirely sure of his feelings towards me. I know that I l him, but nothing more." She sighed.

Erika pursed her lips. "Sometimes, the things we want to know the most are the ones that can ruin us the most." She said, as she knocked another arrow.

Kathrine gulped, "Are you saying he doesn't like me?"

"I'm saying it is a possibility that the people we love most in life won't always return our feelings, and I know it seems difficult, but the quicker we realize that, the more time we have to continue moving about our own lives."

Kathrine had a bitter taste in her mouth, she didn't like how this woman was right. Especially since she was probably right about something Kathrine had always wished against.

"However, still," Erika began, "you cannot be sure of his feelings before asking him. Be honest with him. Tell it to his face." She said.

Kathrine looked down. Maybe Erika was right, all she must do is talk to Adam honestly, face to face and then a conclusive answer will arise.

Kathrine raised her bow; she hooked her fingers around the string and used her dominant eye to stare straight at the X on the tree. She inhaled sharply and held the breath in her chest, and then let go of the string.

Sharply and silently, the arrow flew quicker than Kathrine's eye could see and imbedded itself in the wore-down bark in the center of the X. Kathrine had shot her first bullseye.

15

ADAM, CHASE AND Akio had been walking for a couple minutes now. They had gathered the firewood they needed for the camp and were returning, each with several logs of firewood strapped to their back.

Adam's legs and arms began to ache, but he didn't want to focus on the pain. It was almost completely dark, except for the torch that Eli held in front of him. The surrounding illumination was barely enough to keep them aware of what lay ahead. Within three feet, the torch light faded until it completely melted into the dark.

The trees made it worse. With the faint light, they ever so lightly looked like giant fingers reaching for something above the surface while the bodies attached to them lay deep beneath the earth in the underworld. It scared Adam deeply.

"Are we even going the right way?" Asked Chase, annoyed. He stood behind Adam, Akio stared ahead before Adam. He waved the torch back and forth but barely noticed anything.

"I hope so," he said with a chuckle.

Adam looked back at Chase with concern. The satyr simply shrugged. At least, Adam thought it was a shrug, it was too dark to be sure.

A howl came from close in front of them. "A wolf," Adam thought, "not good."

"It's lost." Said Akio. "Separated from its family."

"You mean the pack?" Adam asked.

Akio nodded, "yes exactly."

Chase shook his head, "Wait, wait, wait, you can speak with animals? I can as well."

Akio laughed. "All satyrs can speak to animals. You are spirits of nature." He said, "However, I am no satyr, nor any other kind of nature spirit, thus I cannot speak the tongues of animals, but I can sense their emotions." He said.

"When did you realize you could do that?" Adam asked, wondering if he will ever get special powers.

"About the time that the dreams began. Since I was six."

Adam stopped, causing Chase to bump into him.

The dreams that he had started at around six years old as well! What else could this boy tell him?

"What do you see in your —*" his words were cut off when Akio stuck his hand out to stop Adam from walking further. Adam looked at him, he had a stern expression on his face as he stared at the ground. Adam and Chase followed his gaze, and Adam's heart nearly fell out of his chest when he realized what he was seeing. Akio's hands quickly went to his Katana.

From the darkness of the forest, a big, black, furry mass crawled out. It bared its black, blade like claws and gnashed its sharp yellow teeth. A circle of pink could be seen behind the barrier of rotting teeth as it growled and barked at the group. They had found the lost wolf.

It barked once more, loudly and viciously. Adam stepped back, slowly and calmly.

Akio whispered, "it is not angry, it is only scared." He said. He helped up the torch higher and shook it around, causing embers to fly in all directions.

Chase stepped towards the creature with his face low and his hand out.

"Easy, boy. Easy, now. I won't hurt you." He eased the wolf into his hand and slowly stroked its ears and scruff.

The wolf began to pant and whine.

Chase tried to quiet by showing it love. The action made Akio and Adam drop their jaws. He did it so calmly, as if the large wolf were a cub: a small, furry and cuddly creature that wanted more than its mother's milk and a warm bed.

Chase looked at the two frightened boys, "Akio, I want you to see if you can find his pack. Adam you hold the light."

Akio slowly handed Adam the torch, his eyes never leaving the black wolf. He placed his fingers to his head and cautiously closed his eyes.

Adam felt useless, once again.

After several seconds in silence, Akio pointed south.

"I can sense sadness in the direction." Akio said. "The pack probably realized that he was gone."

Chase looked down to the south side of the forest, and then into the wolf's deep green eyes.

Within seconds the wolf was on its way to its pack without hesitation. It licked Chase's hand with care and ran off into the great unknown.

Chase used his dry hand, which was thankfully his dominant one, to shake hands with Akio and pickup his logs of wood. The. They made for the camp.

The whole place seemed like a painting. Lovely really. The whole camp was illuminated with torches as the two big men, Eleon and Zethus dug trenches and stuck wooden stakes into the ground and pointed them away from the camp as a barrier.

A handful of people sat in the middle of the camp, where the fire would soon be, and talked amongst themselves. Kathrine, surprisingly was not talking with the others but on the far edge of the camp, shooting arrows at an X on a tree, with Erika and that peasant boy Asius. The only other missing person was Eric, who Adam suspected was still in his tent. He didn't blame him, Eric had the biggest tent of all. A large purple one with torches on stands at the entrance. The other ones varied in sizes but there were less tents then there were campers, so Adam figured that many of them must sleep inside of the tent on the back of Quartus, the massive fur-covered elephant. He lay close to the other side of the camp, his dirty, brown fur was so clumpy, that it looked more like several thousand braids swaying in the slight breeze instead of millions of individual hairs.

The other animals were all laying around him. Some, like most of the birds, lay in the nests that they made on Quartus's tusks. Others, like the red panda and the weasel were scattered about his shaggy body. And the bigger ones lay in various other places around him.

It was as if, all those animals, knowing that they were much smaller than the elephant, looked at the furry pachyderm as their protector, covering themselves in his fur hoping that it would act as a shield. It was quite wholesome.

Adam, Chase and Akio made their way to the center of the camp, where they dumped all of Chase's firewood in the middle and saved the rest for other days. Hexus looked at the pile of wood for a moment before setting his hands ablaze. He blasted the wood until embers were flying in all directions.

Adam stared at the blaze until he felt a tap on his shoulder.

He turned to see Akio. The boy smiled, his curly hair nearly blocking out his purple eyes.

"I would like to show you something," he said quietly.

"What is it?" Adam asked, but the boy said nothing and turned around. He whistled a quick tune and the red panda that lay on Quartus now ran to Akio, jumping on his shoulders and curling around them.

He turned his small, fluffy head to see Adam and angled it, as if he was confused with this new boy he had never met. The small creature had rust clouded fur with several white striped and black feet. His face was quite adorable. A small black snout with a ring of red around his tiny face, his eyes were both black and were surrounded with white dots. He made a high pitched squeaking noise and returned to resting. The entire animal seemed quite alien to Adam. He had never laid eyes on one before a couple days ago.

"Where is he from?" Adam asked, "I haven't seen any of them." He noted.

Akio laughed as they answered his tent. A small green one with several decorations inside.

"He comes from where I come from."

"Which is where, exactly?" Adam looked around his tent.

"The east. I was born in an island in the sunrise sea called Halanor, and Rubius is native to the Bronze Plains in the Lun-din dynasty, but was brought to Halanor by poachers. I freed him, and we've been together ever since." He said. The creature licked his ear as if to illustrate the point. The boy had curly hair that nearly covered all the back of his neck. He had a soft face with dull lips and a small nose. Two thin, black eyebrows rested above his bright green eyes and he wore a white tunic with grey pants and sandals. Around his neck, a silver chain connected to a long flowing purple cloak with golden designs all over it, mainly grape vines and large cats that looked leopards.

Adam stared around the small tent. It was quite beautiful, and the smell of tea filled his nostrils. The decorations were everywhere you looked. On a small table, an oil lit lamp was burning away, next to it was what looked like an unfinished painting. Pots of steaming tea also filled the table. Eye catching, colorful and well-made paintings of men in armors of white and black and gold and silver were scattered about the ground. They were ancient Halanese warriors called samurai. Adam had read about them before, but he had never seen what they look like. Many plants were seen, but most of them, Adam had never seen in his life. One he did recognize was the large bamboo shoot in the corner of the tent. As soon as Adam had realized it, Rubius had as well. He hopped of Akio's shoulders and onto the ground. His little black legs scurried along the soft floor as he made his way to the large plant and immediately began ripping off leaves with his mouth when he got there.

Adam saw more paintings near the bamboo shoot. More men in foreign armor, some with the eyes of a man and the mouths of demons. Others with the full faces of a demon and the full faces of a man. They were masks, Adam realized. Other paintings included a beautifully made one with a river zigzagging through the middle.

Even aside of the paintings, there was still more to see. There was an iron and wood made chest. On top, was a stand holding up what was probably the most intricately designed sword Adam had ever seen. It was like the swords that were at Akio's side. A katana, he remembered. The blade was slightly curved, and the cross guard was a circle that surrounded the hilt. The hilt was made with fabric and leather and was longer than any hilt Adam had ever seen. It ended with the head of a white dragon instead of a pommel. The dragon was roaring as if it dared anyone to grab it by the sword hilt that was his neck and swing the sword at anyone.

Even the blade was beautiful. From the middle of the blade down to one side, the sword was dull, but from the other, a zig-zagging line that passed through the horizontal middle of the sword became the blade, a weapon so incredibly sharp that it made Adam uncomfortable. Beneath the sword, the sheath that would always cover it lay on the same stand. All white and made from hardened leather, it had gold designs all over it. The main picture in the middle of the sheath, was of a man in the same reed hat Akio had, slicing another man to pieces with it. It was intriguing, violent, but intriguing.

"Look," Said Akio, he lightly touched the blade of the sword. Barely a tap, so little of a touch, that Adam wondered whether he made physical contact with the weapon. But he did, because when he showed Adam his finger, a bead of red liquid began to slowly grow larger on Akio's pointer finger. He was bleeding from just a tap. Adam hated to see what the sword would do if it were to be swung at a limb, or a chest, or a throat. Akio sucked on his finger until the bead of blood was gone and all that was left was a pink gash no larger than a paper cut.

Adam stared in awe. That sword was made for a warrior, so what was a child doing with it?

"Where did you find the sword?" He asked Akio.

Akio's expression darkened, as if the memory brought some hidden scars to the light. "It belonged to my grandfather. It was his gift to me before he passed away. It's called 'GodSlayer'".

Adam curled his lips in sympathy. "I'm so sorry. You must have been young." Adam assumed.

Akio looked up, but he did not look at Adam. He simply stared at the sword with wet eyes. "I was not yet seven. But once he gave it to me," he said, wiping the tears from his face, "I began to practice. I mastered it, as well as several other weapons." He pointed to another wooden chest in the corner of his tent. Just beside it was a long, polished wooden stick about six feet long: A staff.

Akio opened the chest. Different weapons filled it to the brim. A bladed stick on a chain, a staff, three pronged knives called Üli were small and pointy, a bow nearly Adam's height was inside as well, it was called a Halé and finally, an Oyomï, or a blow gun, was the final weapon inside.

"I managed to master most of them before I turned eighteen, including these two." He gestured to the twin katana strapped to his side.

"But enough of this." He said, turning away from the impressive armory, "I did not ask you to come her so I could show you swords and blowguns. I wanted to talk to you about these."

He walked toward a bigger pile of paintings.

Adam looked at them awkwardly. "They are lovely."

"Thank you. I made them myself. But, my proudest work," he held up a painting with many colors of blue and a triangle of white and grey, "is this one." Akio said.

Adam stood shocked and raised his eyebrows as Akio showed him the painting.

They were identical. His dream and this painting were one in the same. Over a large field of grass, that was covered in blood and fire and dead bodies, a massive mountain appeared. The same mountain that had exploded and birthed a multi headed dragon in his dream.

In Akio's painting, the mountain's peak was hidden behind fluffy white clouds and the bottom was drowning in an ocean of grass, but this one held no dead. It was an exact replica of the mountain, but not of the field, or the sky. This one showed thing flying above the mountain, things that looked like demons, and dragons, and...was that a winged horse Adam spotted? They were all engaged in aerial combat and Adam even spotted what looked like a flying boat. That one was confusing.

"You asked me in the woods what I saw in my dreams," he said, "I see this." Adam looked up at him, he left as if all the air in his lungs had been ripped from his chest and forbidden from reentering.

"Do you have any more?" Adam asked him.

Akio smiled.

On several pieces of linen canvases, clay pots and leather cloths, colors and drawings exploded into sight from within a chest on Quartus's back. The wooden chest, with iron covering, was unlocked by Akio and inside were his works of art. This boy was incredibly talented. He saw drawings pictures of more Halanese samurai fighting or befriending dragons. Adam saw that what the Halanese saw as dragons looked more like serpents with mustaches to the people of the West, like himself.

There was one recurring soldier. A warrior of gold and purple with a black mask of the face of a demon. He was always painted with a snow-white tiger with black stripes, a blue nose and blue eyes. It was Akio and his tiger.

Written above and to the right of the drawing were words in Halanese that Adam could not read.

The other canvases, the vases and the cloths all also held artworks, beautiful fields, and a cave with a piles of gold in it. Perched on top of a small ledge in the caves lay a bright lion the color of the sun. It stared at the entrance of the cave as if daring the person about to enter his lair, to touch his precious pile of not only gold but also, emeralds, rubies, diamonds, pearls and other precious gems.

"See Adam?" Akio looked down at him as Adam knelt to observe the works of art, "we truly are special."

Adam looked up at him, and remained speechless.

16

THE SUN WAS down completely now, and they all sat around a campfire continuing to tell stories. Beside Akio, Tenzir the six-foot-long white tiger with royal blue eyes, black stripes and a pink nose curled up, sleeping, and Rubius the red panda had made a nest on Akio's lap. Theodore sat next to him, drinking ale and talking with Akio.

A black hunting dog panted next to Zethus and Pormant, the donkey slept next to Theodore. On the donkeys back, lay Bugbush the weasel and Spew the sparrow. The owls were flying around in the sky without a care in the world. Hexus was now asleep inside of Quartus's tent, but Kathrine had joined them outside and had been formally introduced to the group and the other way around.

They were all wearing the same. Black or grey wool tunics and pants and not much else. Theodore had a black leather jerkin and Raia wore a white, silk dress but those were the only differences. The past few cities have only sold tunics for prices they could afford.

Chase played music on his pipes while Erika played a lyre and Theodore pinched and pulled at strings on a small pandura. Asius banged on a pair of small drums. Adam liked how this group treated their slave. No. Slave was not the right word. Asius was more than a slave, he was a friend to all in the group. Sure, he followed their orders, but they did not treat him like Alor had treated it's servants. He was a hard worker, like all slaves, his masters just saw that and appreciated it. They treated him humanly.

The fire illuminated all their faces with a beautiful shade of red and orange and yellow.

The night was peaceful and in truly was a beautiful moment.

They ate and sang and drank. The smell of cooking fish they had caught and warm bread they had bought filled the air, accompanied by the embers jumping off the burning wood. Without a care in the world, they enjoyed the moment and the night.

Eventually, Norris pulled out a bag and opened it. Adam recognized the smell that waved from it almost instantly.

Norris licked his lips, "they're still good." He said. He reached into the wool sack and pulled out a doughball. He must have gotten it when they went to Alor. The crisp and sweet surface glowed golden brown, and when Norris bit into it, the inside was a bright yellowish color.

He passed the bag to Adam, and he claimed one for himself. Adam then passed it to Theo, then Erika, then Zethus and so on and so forth.

When the bag got to Kathrine, her eyes lit up excitedly. She reached into the bag and slowly pulled out a doughball of her own. She slowly bit into it and enjoyed every second.

Everyone laughed. Except Eleon, he was still feasting on a fish, sinking his teeth into its scaly body. Even so, the man seemed to never laugh. He had not talked to Chase, only looking at him venomously.

After a long while, the fires crackling was the only noise in the air. The instruments had been put down and the singing stopped.

Adam looked around himself, all these people, they were exactly who he needed in his life. But worries still clung themselves to his mind. The army of the dead, was one of them. He didn't want to face them, but he had a feeling that he would have to eventually, regardless of everyone saying that they haven't bothered them. Maybe they simply haven't gotten a chance to battle them, and when they do, Adam thought it was going to be sooner rather than later.

He twiddled his thumbs as his mind raced from place to place. Eventually he landed on a single idea and stuck to it. He thought about it, and he thought about how Kathrine would not be happy.

But he did it anyways.

Adam looked behind him and searched his bag. As he suspected, the crumpled piece of paper that the priestess had given him was still in laying there, buried under tunics and breeches. The white light from the metal rod he found in his mothers house, illuminated everything of the bag.

He took a deep breath and reached in. He felt his fingers touch something solid and cold, and pulled out the rod. Then he took the paper.

Bringing them both out to the welcoming glow and heat of the fire, he noticed Kathrine stop what she was doing and look at him.

Zethus squinted as he tried to focus on the bright white rod, "What's that?" He asked while reaching for it.

Adam handed Norris the rod, "I'm not sure about the rod, but this note was written by one of the priestesses in my city." He pulled it out and I crumpled it. The creases didn't affect the clarity of the message.

Past the golden apples.
Past the festivities.
Past the impenetrable defender.
Past a fine feast.
Past the city from which you came.
Past the walls that forbid exit.

It was as clear as day. He read the message aloud. Theodore widened his eyes, "Well that was quite prophetic." He chuckled and downed his glass of beer. For a boy, he had quite the tolerance for liquor.

Raia pursed her perfect lips, "What does it mean?" She wondered, now holding the rod herself. Norris had passed it down.

Erika put her hand to her chin, and the other held the paper, "maybe it's some kind of written down map of sorts."

Eleon ripped the paper from her hands. "Are you drunk? These are words. I have no use for words." He was about to toss it in the fire before Norris told him to stop. Eleon took another swing of beer. He had less of a tolerance for liquor.

"You're a mad son of a bitch." He yelled. The paper was still intact. Norris read it again. "How could you have use for words when you can barely read.

Eleon burped, "I can read you shit. I just choose not to." Another swig.

"Your drunk, ain't you?" Erika asked. Eleon hiccuped, then burped, then continued drinking. He laughed as some of the gold beer he swallowed poured down his beard and onto his tunic. Norris took the page and stared at its contents.

"Walls that forbid exit mean the walls of your city, or "the city from which you came"." Norris concluded.

"Well that was simple," said Zethus. "Give it here, it may tell us where we need to go next."

He examined the paper next.

Akio was staring heavily at the rod. "This craftsmanship is excellent. This is a hilt. The hilt of a sword."

Minerva laughed, "Where is the rest of it?" She said quietly.

"Inside the rod." Akio said, matter-of-factly.

"It's made with the help of a powerful magic." Raia said, closing her eyes and lightly touching the rod.

"How do you know?" Adam asked.

"I studied magic when I was younger. I know spells and I can sense when magic has been used." She laughed. Adam laughed with her, and Kathrine scoffed.

"Magic from where? Or what?" Erika asked.

Raia seemed uncomfortable, she groaned, "I don't know, I... I can barely recognize it."

"It says a fine feast is next. Anyone know what that is?" Zethus asked.

Theodore stretched, "A fine feast, my friend, is a feast that is fine." He joked. He scratched at his behind as he walked off to bed, waving as he left. "I believe we had just had it."

"Good night my lord, Theodore." Said Asius, and Theo waved at him.

"Theodore has a point." Norris said, "I say we rest now. We can explore more of these matters in the morning, Adam, but for now, get some rest." He put out the fire with a whip of water he commanded and walked off with an oil lamp in hand.

He put everything back in his bag and put it on his back

But before he could help get everything ready for tomorrow morning, he heard his name.

"Adam," said a new voice. It was deep and stern. He turned.

Eric stood at the entrance of his tent, and the fires from his oil lamps made him look like he was glowing.

Everyone stayed silent, even the animals.

"Come with me." Said Eric.

Adam turned to the rest. Most of them had a look on their face that urged him to follow Eric. Almost like they were pleading with him. Despite Adam's reluctance, he stood up and followed Eric into the darkness of his tent.

17

HIS TENT WASN'T anything special. It was big, but then again, they all were. In one corner, was bedding. In the other was a full quiver. The only source of light were the two dimly lit oil lamps being held up outside the tent. Having a flame in a flammable structure seemed like a stupid decision anyways.

The dim glow from the lantern cast a red tint across the room. Eric sat on the pillow and crossed his legs. He stared at Adam. The massive scar on the side of his face was fear casting. It ran from above his right eyebrow all the down to his sternum and maybe even farther if his armor wasn't covering it from view. He wore an olive-green cloak over an iron chainmail shirt and a grey, wool tunic. His crossed legs were covered with grey breeches and his leather boots ran up to his calves. Along the front, where the laces would have been visible, small iron plates covered them up and protected them under its metal surface. His hands had fingerless gloves and a belt was strapped around his waist.

He was lean, that probably made him quick. Adam could see why the rest of the group followed this man, as he looked like he would strangle you if you didn't obey him. He had blond hair, slicked back all the way, and brownish sideburns that eventually turned back to blond as it reached his chin, giving him a dirty-blond goatee.

Adam had waited for this moment, but exactly like before, he didn't know what to do now that he had the chance. So, he just stood and said nothing.

"Who are you?" Asked Eric.

"My name is—*"

"I know what your name is. But that doesn't give me anything. What are you doing here?"

"I thought Norris told you everything?" He asked.

Eric scowled, "And now I want you to tell me, and if I hear two different stories... well then, that's unfortunate. For someone at least."

Adam saw an intricately designed bow with a beautifully designed quiver right next to two short swords and a long sword. A long staff was standing in the other corner.

"I come from Alor," he said meekly.

"That's a start." He said with a stern face. His blond eyebrows curved downwards on his bright blue eyes. "Continue," Eric ordered. Adam found it hard to disobey the man.

"I only had two friends, growing up." He thought that that was a stupid answer, but Eric said nothing of it, so, Adam thought he should continue.

He explained everything that had happened to that point. His escape, his dreams and the attack with the gorgons.

"I found out things about myself that I never knew."

"Like?" Eric awaited a response.

"These dreams mean something. And I can heal quickly. I broke my shoulder and I healed from it in less than two days. Then I followed Hexus because he told me that, out there is a whole group of people with the same dreams and ability. That can't be a coincidence."

Eric pursed his lips, "Who are your parents?"

Adam hesitated, "my... mother was a peasant woman, a... whore, and... I never met my... father." The words "mother" and "father" tasted like rotten fruit in his mouth.

Eric had a stern face. He didn't faze. None of this seemed to have surprised him, like he expected it to happen. Adam wondered what he was thinking, maybe he was going to allow Adam to stay with them, permanently.

Norris said that Eric allowed them to temporarily remain traveling with the, though not forever. Maybe he was going to allow Adam to stay but he would throw out Chase and Kathrine, they didn't have dreams. This group seemed to be a 'dreamers only' kind of group.

Instead, Eric kept his gaze fixed on Adam and asked, "did you have a dream when you slept last night? Don't lie to me."

Adam felt compelled to tell the truth anyways. This man could kill him with ease if he wanted to. If Adam said something wrong, he could find himself with a blade sticking from his heart.

"I... I did." He murmured.

Eric's face seemed to be consumed by the glow from the lamp. "What did you see?"

"A b..bird. Two birds. One was golden, the other one was black. They fought in front of palace. There was also an army. A huge army made of these, ghoul, black, undead looking soldiers called Spartoi. They were closing in on us, and were just outside Alor."

Those last words echoed in his head.

"Hm." Eric looked down and his eyes dashed from one spot of the ground to another.

"Okay, you can go now." Eric said everything without moving himself. His eyes fixed on Adam as if the boy were about to attack him.

"What? That's it?" Adam asked.

The man stayed silent and turned towards the curtain of the wall. He placed his fists together so that the knuckles were touching, his legs were still crossed.

"What about you all? Who are you people? Surely you can know the answer. You were told to find us. Wouldn't you be happy that I'm here? I'm the last member of this group. Now you know where you are going! Let me and my friends stay." He shouted.

Eric sighed, "I never said you couldn't. In fact, from now on, you will travel with us. All of you. You will follow all orders I give you and whenever we find cities or villages or markets that we cross paths with, you don't talk to anyone, and you don't trust anyone. Now. Get. Out." He turned back towards the wall and continued meditating.

Adam grunted, "not until I get answers."

Eric groaned, "alright." He grumbled. Eric turned to face Adam. His facial scars glowed a bright bronze in the candlelight.

"You are special. You are not like any other human being. Your dreams are messages from somebody, and this group is the same. We are on our way to finding out who." He raised his hands. "Satisfied?" He asked.

He began to turn away once more until Adam called him back, "Where are we going next?"

Eric sighed, "get some sleep. We leave in the afternoon."

Adam looked down, and then stood up and walked out.

It was still dark out, and the group nearly all gone to sleep. But Adam saw Raia and Zethus and Asius. They gestured for him to join them.

"So how'd it go?" Zethus asked as Adam found a seat.

"Good, I guess. My friends and I can stay, but I do not think he likes me very much."

"He's like that." Raia said. "Don't take it personally."

"I'm not, but I just wish I knew more."

"We all do kid." Said Zethus, "But we just wait, until we find out."

"What if we don't? What if we never do?" Adam wondered, "what if all of this leads nowhere?"

The question seemed to take a moment entering everyone's mind.

"We don't know." Said Raia, "But that won't happen, right Zethus?"

He clearly had doubts. But it was a good question. Sure, there was someone telling them something, but what if it was just a coincidence. The low probability of that did not stop everyone from wondering. The tension from the question still lingered in the air. Zethus picked up a torch and lit it using two small stones. He and Raia walked off. Presumably, they simply didn't want to think about the question.

Adam was left alone with Asius. He figured this was a good opportunity for making at least one new friend.

"Where are you from, Asius?" Adam asked him.

"I served Norris's and Eric's old tribe. When they left, after an attack on the tribe, they took me with them." He said with low eyes. He hid them behind a curtain of blonde trusses.

"You were a slave?" Adam asked, bluntly, he noticed.

Asius smiled, "I was, but now I am more. Eric and Norris have been good to me. Norris taught me how to read and write, and Eric taught me how to fight." Adam caught the sound of a foreign accent, though it seemed to be lost to years of speaking Adam's language, as it was pretty faint.

Asius smiled, revealing two rows of crooked teeth. He was quite lanky, and about seventeen years old.

"Eric is a good man, do not worry about what he says. With us you are safe now. And tomorrow, you will get a treat."

He laughed, Adam was a little nervous.

"What does that mean?" He asked.

Asius took one last sip of wine, "every time a new person joins us, they fight Zethus, almost as an initiation battle. Tomorrow, that will be you."

Adam began to worry violently. Zethus was a mountain of a man, and Adam was only... Adam.

Asius stood up, "you should sleep, it will be good for you."

18

ADAM HAD NEVER used a sword before. There was no need to. Back in Alor, he was an occasional farm boy, not a guard or soldier. When Zethus handed him the blade, he didn't know what to do with it. He held it awkwardly. The hilt felt too think, and his fingers almost were barely able to wrap all the way around. The blade was nothing more than a thick wooden plank connected to a hilt. Adam swung it violently, testing how much damage the sword could really do.

Zethus jumped back, "Whoa!" He held up his hands in defense, "you can wave it plenty outside." He chuckled.

He pushed the tent curtains out of the way as they stepped out into the afternoon sun. They had been traveling all day and had recently set up camp. The views that Adam had seen during the day had stunned him. They passed through valleys and canyons and mountains and hills. Adam had never seen so much green. His friends did not share his enthusiasm. As Adam, Kathrine and Chase all stared in awe to the beautiful views, Norris had not cared about it.

"You should have seen it twenty years ago. It was greener." He mumbled.

Adam retuned his mind to the present.

The sun was about to begin setting. His friends were out sitting on logs and clapped as Adam exited. Chase cheered his lungs out and Hexus stood up while nearly drowning Eleon in the wine he accidentally knocked over.

The animals had been fed and Asius rushed over to Adam as Norris did the same to Zethus. Asius tied a leather pad around Adam's torso and knees and arms. When he tightened the straps around Adam's back, the air left his lungs quicker than the light leaves a torch when thrown in water. Zethus stepped forward, his body covered in the same pads as Adam. He looked much more terrifying in them, though. He had obviously used a sword before. A real sword too. He has probably skewered countless men before he met Adam. Asius had told him that Zethus used to be a gladiator, who fought men in a grand colosseum for the entertainment of his king. He was a talented and undefeated warrior, and he had the scars to prove it.

He had no shirt on beneath the armor, so his beefy arms and chest were almost completely on display. Covering his arms were dozens of scars, and on his left shoulder, was a tattoo of two crossing spears. Adam remembered Hexus' fire tattoo. He did want one.

"Alright," Norris said, in the middle of Zethus and Adam, "Your objective is to get the other fighter to yield, in any way. First person to yield three times loses. Ready?" He looked at the crowd, they roared with clapping and cheering. "Ready?" He echoed himself, this time talking to Adam and Zethus. Adam, trying his best to look confident over the fact that he was fighting a nearly seven-foot-tall warrior, nodded.

Zethus said nothing, instead, he smirked, and twirled his sword.

"BEGIN!" Norris yelled.

It happened so fast that Adam didn't have time to react. Zethus charged at him as the crowd frantically celebrated. He raised his sword and plunged the edge into Adam's chest. His lungs turned to vapor, and his limbs liquified. He heard a collective "OOH!" From the crowd as the ground zoomed closer to his face. He held his torso and writhed in pain.

The blades of grass made his arms tickle.

"Do you yield?" Zethus asked, twirling his sword a second time.

"I...yield." Adam groaned, with half of his face masked by the earth.

"Good." He extended a hand for Adam to take. He grasped it and Zethus pulled him up.

Adam carefully planted his feet where he stood and took several deep breathes. The crowd went from silent to roaring in seconds.

Norris waved his hand again, and the second match began. Adam saw Zethus bring his sword down in a curved arc, and quickly slides to the right. Zethus felt his sword cut into the ground instead of hitting Adam and slashed it to his right. Adam tried to guard but instead was left thrown into the ground again. He quickly got up again.

Eric was now sitting in the crowd with a fish in his hands. He took a bite.

Adam hated himself for feeling the way he did, but he promised himself that he would impress Eric at that moment. But for what? He had already let him, and his friends stay with the group. There was nothing more for him to do. Regardless, Adam swore he would see a smile on Eric's face before this was over.

Zethus charged at him, his eyes were flaming. Adam's sword was left with a large dent where Zethus had hit. He readied it and dodged as Zethus stabbed. Adam felt his arm bring down his sword without stopping it. Zethus grunted and fell back as Adam slammed his sword into Zethus' face. The crowd roared with cheers once again. This time, they chanted Adam's name. Eric stayed silent, but he had a spectating intrigue in his eyes. Adam smiled and steadied his sword.

Zethus ran to Adam for a second time. Adam slashed his sword towards Zethus' face but hit nothing. Zethus had slid his way underneath Adam and swept his leg. Hooking his toes around Adam's heel, he pulled, and let gravity do the rest of the work. Adam stumbled and fell to the ground. As he tried to get up, Zethus kicked his in his side, sending him sliding even further back.

"I yield." Adam said, as Zethus got closer. Zethus laughed and the crowd echoed it.

Adam pushed himself to his feet, now angry. He dusted the dirt from his arms and looked at Zethus. Norris stood between them, with his arm extended.

His words echoed in Adam's head, "Begin!" He yelled.

Zethus and Adam charged at each other. Adam lost count of the blows he had shared with Zethus. The swords slammed into each other every second. Adam didn't know how he was doing this. Zethus was a seasoned warrior, and Adam was a peasant who had never lifted a weapon. Yet here he stood, dueling with Zethus as if they were both great soldiers. They dodged, ducked, rolled and punched. Adam's movements were fluid and quick. He could anticipate Zethus' moves as Zethus could anticipate his.

As Adam stabbed at Zethus, a tense pain started to flame in his shoulder. Then his knee, and his torso. Zethus moved his sword so quickly, Adam couldn't see it. It peppered him with blows. He dropped his sword and gave into the pain.

The crowd's cheering became little more than distant echoes as Adam nearly passed out. He took a final deep breath as Zethus plunged his foot into Adam's chest, knocking him back twenty or so feet.

Adam rolled onto his back. He felt his muscles tense up. His fingers tingled. Zethus came closer to him, and his chest took in more breathes than he could count. The blades of grass slowly began to sway in the slight breeze that had started. Adam felt small rocks and leaves make their way across his body as the wind began to pick up.

Zethus lifted his sword and asked, "Do you yield?"

His face melted into a confused look as he studied the winds.

Adam suddenly had his vision back. It was clearer than ever, and his pain had left him. The winds began to swirl and circle him like a cyclone. He felt them curl around his fingers and fill his body with energy. His aching body became stronger by the second.

He could hear the claps halt to a stop. Everyone gasped, the winds picked up, they began to run, and the winds picked up. Zethus yelled and Adam was back on the ground. He looked up.

Thirty feet up in the air, surrounded by a cyclone of wind, dirt, leaves and rocks, Zethus screamed. His body twisted and turned in the air as his screams echoed across the valley. Eric dropped his food and Erika yelled.

Zerhus came flying towards the ground as his screams became louder every passing inch. The ground rumbled, and an explosion of dust, dirt and rock erupted some 17 feet away from the campsite. Adam's ears popped and his knees buckled. His spine shivered and he crumpled to the ground. He felt two soft hands press against him while hearing the others run towards Zethus.

His eyes widened and his vision shifted between blindly unfocused to razor sharp.

"Oh, my gods! Are you alright?" Echoed a feminine voice.

"Is he dying?" Asked a male voice, also echoing.

"No! I don't know! Get Norris!" The girl said.

Adam's vision finally focused enough to identify Kathrine. Her light brown hair was thrown over her shoulder and her green eyes shimmered as they examined Adam.

Norris rushed over to them. He studied Adam thoroughly. He placed a hand on Adam's chest.

"He'll be fine. Let him rest."

"Gods! What the hell was that?" Hexus asked with a goblet of wine spilling and shaking in his hand, "you just launched him a thousand feet into the sky."

"It was more like twenty." Zethus said, chuckling. He had his arm around Eleon and walked with a small limp. The leather padding on his body ripped in some places and his lip was bleeding. Otherwise he seemed fine. That was incredible considering what just happened to him.

"Where did you find that, eh?" He asked Adam.

Adam's head finally stopped spinning, "I... I don't know. I think... I think it's like... a reflex." He said the word "reflex" as if it were a question.

"A defense mechanism." Eric said, walking over. "A way to protect yourself from attacks."

Adam sat in the dirt, stunned, "It's never happened before." Adam said. He was a little bothered, that he couldn't blast Mason and his friends when they were bothering him as little kids back in Alor. But he supposed that then, there was no possibility of dying. When Zethus attacked him, his instincts took over completely, as if the man were about to kill him.

"Don't worry. You will learn to control it." Norris told him, "Asius" he asked the servant; Asius snapped to attention, and Norris pointed to his tent, "could you find some of the Mammoth milk that's left."

"Yes m'lord." Asius scurried off.

"I don't think I've ever been beaten by wind before." Zethus laughed, helping Adam up. Eli handed him and Adam a goblet of wine and lifted his to the air, "To Adam. Master of air." They all laughed and drank.

"I don't think "master" is the proper title," Adam chuckled. "I nearly killed him." He said, dazed.

"You still have a little bit of the wind in you." Zethus slapped his shoulder, then widened his eyes, "Little bit of the wind..." he repeated.

"That will be your name," he exclaimed, "To Littlewind!" He lifted the goblet and downed another round of liquor. They clapped and smiled and lifted their cups, as they celebrated Littlewind.

19

THE MAMMOTH MILK tasted foul, but it did help make him comfortable. Adam's body sank deeper and deeper into the bed he lay on, his sense becoming less and less of what they once were. Next to him, on his right, Zethus lay in a bed of his own. Erika tended to his wounds as Asius tended to Adam's. He kept giving him a little bit of the elixir every so often. His body nearly deteriorated with each sip. To his left sat Kathrine.

"What does it taste like?" Kathrine chuckled as she played with his hair. She always liked twirling it around her fingers because she said it was smooth. It was quite long too, nearly reaching his jaw from his scalp. It always fell apart down the middle, and Kathrine liked it.

"Like... sand. Cold sand." He answered her. They both laughed, but Adam winced. Her expression softened.

"That was impressive what you did." She told him.

"I don't even know what I did." Adam said.

"A number of us have great powers, my lord." Asius said, "Lord Hexus can control fire, and Lord Norris, water."

"What can you do?" Adam asked Asius.

Asius shook his head as if it were a silly question, "on nothing. I am not special like you all." He said, laughing.

His sentence made Adam quite sad for him, "what do you mean?"

Asius focused on Adam's bruises, "Well, everything can do something. Before you and lady Kathrine and lord Chase, I was the only ordinary one."

"Does it... bother you?" Kathrine asked, still stroking Adam's hair.

"No, not at all." Asius replied, pouring more of the mammoth's milk in Adams mouth, "I may be just a servant, but I am a servant with a purpose. I tend the animals, clean the clothes, and I treat wounds. Everyone is good to me. I like this life." He smiled and that warmed Adam's heart.

Kathrine smiled back, "I should go. Chase needed me before, I've been delaying her for long enough." She lightly tugged at Adam's hair and giggled.

He smiled at her as she left the tent and he found himself looking down.

"How long have you two been together?" Zethus asked?

The question caught him by surprise, "What? We're not... She's not my..." he found himself lost for words.

Zethus laughed, "You not very good at lying, Littlewind. She likes you, and you like her." He said matter-of-factly.

Erika laughed, "leave the boy alone Zethus." She teased.

Erika stood up and wiped her hands on a piece of cloth and knocked an eyebrow.

"We should try and get you two on Quartus tonight. Neither of you would be able to walk much." She hooked an arm around Zethus's shoulders and stood him up. He groaned and held his side.

"I'm really sorry, Zethus." Adam said, nervously.

"Ha! There's nothing to apologize for, Littlewind. You gave me a good fight. I like that, I was a soldier."

Adam's eyes lit up, "Really?" He asked, intrigued.

"I'll tell you all about it when we're on Quartus, right now I need to go sleep." He told him.

Adam smiled, Zethus truly was a gentle giant, when he wanted to be. He was capable of great things, but part of him did not want to be. He limped as Erika tried to help him walk.

A long while of silence followed that conversation for several moments. He thought about what Zethus had said about Kathrine... he didn't believe it, but maybe she did like him.

"Hello," said a voice.

Raia stood at the entrance of the tent. Her beautiful white hair was tied up in a bun on top of her head and her violet eyes glittered in the torchlight. Her hands had a light pink complexion for some reason and she wore a white chiton with a rope around her waist. As she walked, Spew, her sparrow, buzzed around the whole place, finally landing on Adam's chest.

"He likes you," She smiled, "How are you feeling?" Her cheeks were pools of pink, complementing her dark complexion.

Adam suddenly found it hard to breath, "I'm... better." He managed. She sat down on the bed instead of the chair next to Adam. She smiled at him revealing those blinding teeth again, "you'll be up and out of here in a couple hours."

"Asius said I'll have to wait until tomorrow." Adam told her.

She undid the clip holding her bun together and let her hair fall down to her shoulders. It bounced off the top of her head and landed in perfect waves and curls. She pushed it against her temple with her hands, creating a bush of brown curls. Then bounced back to its original form. It's snow this surface shimmered silver when hit by any light.

"That won't be. You heal quickly, I hear." She said.

Adam nicked an eyebrow. "Hexus told me." She said with a giggle. Adam saw her smile and got an odd feeling in his stomach. His chest and stomach tingled like millions of creatures ran up and down the inside of his body, and the pitter-patter of their paws made it tickle, almost.

He laughed with her.

Raia pursed her lips, then she took Adam's hand, "That was impressive what you did during the spar." She said.

"I think it was pretty scary." He murmured, looking down.

She frowned, "why?"

Adam looked at her. Raia had odd features, with the pink eyes, hands and cheeks slightly pink-ish and hair as white as her teeth, but she was perhaps the most gorgeous person Adam had ever met. All he could think about was Kathrine, and what she would think. He said nothing to Raia and instead dragged his thumb across her hand, slowly stroking the back of her hand. He thought about the sparring match. The power he felt when he blasted Zethus. The intensity he could feel in his blood, and the fire in his chest that made him scared, he thought he was dying. He felt more powerful now than ever before though.

"All the energy pooling up inside of you," he told Raia, she never took her eyes off him, "it feels like you can do anything." She finished her sentence. Adam raised an eyebrow.

"That's... right," he said, "how did you...?"

"When I was younger, I never had a mother or father. I was born into a group of people called Circe's followers. They were a religious people, but we had a secret." She lifted an eyebrow at Adam.

He pursed his lips, "What was it?"

"From a young age they taught me how to use magic. They said it was inside all of us, the goddess of sorcery, Circe, just helped us release it. I was a prodigy of sorts though." She waved her fingers, and from the pinkness of her palm came 5 tendrils of energy shaking as the writhed in all directions. The pink in her eyes became a deep fuchsia and nearly glowed.

"I was always better than the other girls. I learned to do things they couldn't. I learned how to use the Scarlet Spider spell." She said. There was a hint of horror in her words, as if she regretted what she was about to say after that.

"What's that?" Adam whispered.

"You lose yourself. if your not careful. It's one of the most powerful spells on earth. It's exhilarating, you know? Being that strong. Knowing that you could snap your fingers and destroy half of your enemies. But you can feel the flaws within you. The energy, the magic, it's unstable. You learn that with one wrong move, you could end it all, right there and then."

"That was... pretty accurate." Adam said, startled.

She laughed, "Yeah. Let's hope you don't do anything that stupid again for a while, so you don't mess up that face of yours." She smiled on last time, kissed Adam on the cheek and left. Her sparrow followed, fluttering it's brown wings until it vanished behind the tent curtains, and Adam was left alone with his thoughts.

20

THIS WEEK WAS quite eventful, Theodore thought. They got three new members, the army pursuing them had gotten closer of the past few days, and as it turns out, Adam may very well be more powerful than Zethus, throwing him nearly 30 feet away from where they started.

He had never trained with a sword, but Adam was strong in other ways. Theodore had never seen an attack like that. He had seen Hexus turn into a flaming tornado, Eleon could turn release all that energy when he got angry, Raia could teleport and levitate, on top of her phenomenal magical abilities and even Zethus had that beast inside him that he rarely unleashed.

Regardless of him not being as strong as them, he enjoyed his abilities. He wasn't good at controlling them. He would go to sleep as Theodore and wake up as an animal. Other times he would try and control them by focusing on one thing, but he would transform into another thing.

It had come in handy sometimes though. When he was growing up on the streets, he would steel food, with the face of one person, and then, when the store owner chased him, he would change his face back into his eyes. That was only when they caught him, which they rarely achieved. One of Theodore's other abilities was being able to run faster than the naked eye could see.

He and his friend tested the extent once. He could remember it clearly, they had went to the woods outside their village, and using his bow, Malcolm shot an arrow, and no matter how far it went, and how quick it traveled, Theodore always got to its destination before the arrow did. Quite a funny ability, he thought to himself. He had been teased for being overweight all his life, people called him fat, pig and his least favorite, Giant.

He had though the nickname Giant was meant as a compliment, as giants were great beasts that could challenge even the gods themselves, but his tormentors were always referring to his large belly. He never let it get to him though, especially since he eventually got his revenge by throwing them all in a lake while in the body of a bear, and leaving them cold and alone in the forest. They never seemed to tease him after that, mainly because they feared him. After that they called him demon, or beast of Hades, but he never let it bother him after that faithful day in the lake. He had gotten better at his shape changing abilities after that.

He wondered when the next time he could use his powers would be. Maybe tomorrow, maybe the day after, maybe a week after that. Or maybe, never again.

The latter option was extremely low, especially now, since the army had been getting closer over the past two days. Erika had sent her owl over the horizon to watch their position, and when it returned with information, her expression darkened. The bird hooted in her ear and somehow she could understand it perfectly. A three day march and they would be upon us, but it used to be a weeks march.

Luckily the group always moved. They had never stayed in the same place for long. But Theodore knew that sooner or later, they would have to face that army.

The odds were not great, they were not even good. The odds were terrible. They had thousands of soldiers and Theodore's team was nothing more than a band of young adults. Theodore was little younger than an adult as he would be turning 18 in three months. He didn't think that all their abilities combined were enough to stop an army led by an 8 foot tall man in iron armor.

He tried to not think about it. The thought of a great battle with terrible odds against them made him feel sick.

He lay in his tent, not wanting to go to sleep, because of his dreams. Everyone in the group had them, well then again, almost everyone, now that they had allowed to non-dreamers in their camp with that girl Kathrine and the satyr Chase.

Theodore didn't see a point in having a satyr in the group. They needed warriors, not drunken thieves. He wasn't an admirer of satyrs, as many of them made a fool of themselves in the streets of his village. Chase seemed like a kind enough fellow, but Theodore wasn't about to trust him with anything important anytime soon.

Eventually, the rest of the camp was asleep, and Theodore was no exception. Despite his reluctance to sleep, his eyes fell droopy and his lids sagged. Eventually, his tiredness took him over and he passed out.

He immediately wished he hadn't. He didn't recognize this place, as he hadn't seen it in other dreams before. He was in a forest, and it was quiet and dark. The moonlight casting down on him was the only thing in the way of total darkness. Behind him, a forest so thick that it swallowed all light loomed over him like a vast wall. In front of him, a small mountain stood. It was not the mountain he had seen before. That one had a field, and dead bodies and fire. At the base of the mountain, a cave led deep into the earth.

Theo leaned in for a closer look but the dream shifted. He zoomed into the cave without moving his body, and its stone walls were blurs, but he could see numerous paintings on the walls. Or etchings, he figured, because what Akio made were paintings. These were more like scribbles, of beasts and warriors. The soldiers were thin and all black holding black lines that were probably spears, hunting bulls the size of mammoths. As a matter of fact, they hunted mammoths as well. Judging by the look of them, and their low level of detail, Theo guessed that they had been here for several centuries.

When the cave began to widen, a bright gold light flooded through the tunnel. He flashed into a clearing where he found the light source.

The cave opened into a cavern nearly the size of a palace. The top of the cave, where the ceiling would be more mountain, was a circular top that allowed the moonlight to wash into the cavern. It resembled an empty volcano.

The gold light had come from the light reflecting off a massive pile of gold, silver, diamonds, emeralds, and rubies bigger than Quartus, Treasures were littered all over the place. Theo saw golden goblets, rings, and pieces of jewelry. He saw clothes of wool and silk all stained with blood and weapons. Piles of bones were nearly as big as the ones of gold. Theo could see a rib cage, a few leg bones and several skulls. He felt sick.

The most disturbing part of the bones was that they no visible weapon wounds. They were killed by something different than a sword, something more natural. It had eaten much of them, as their flesh had had chunks bitten off.

At that moment, movement at the top of a ridge rising in the middle of the cavern caught Theodore's attention. He looked up and gasped. Yawning and stretching atop the ledge, was 10 foot long lion so golden that it camouflaged with the pile of treasures below its razor sharp claw- tipped paws. It's mane was a golden brown and it's eyes were the brightest blue Theo had ever seen. It's jaws were rows of knife like, white teeth that didn't look like they belonged to a wild animal. They were too perfect, when they should have been brown and rotting.

The beast was easily bigger than any beast Theo had ever seen. He had t seen many lions, as they all lived in the south, but he had seen the pelts that the warriors in his city wore on their backs. They were big, but not as big as this lion. It was a solid 10 feet long and it's tail swayed like a calm whip. Theo feared that is the lion felt troubled, it could crack his tail and immediately he done with its target. It's mane was nearly the size of a full shield and it's jaw could easily crush a full grown man unlucky enough to end up between its rows of teeth.

The creature did not seem to notice Theodore, even when it had looked in his direction.

"You are not really here." Said a voice. Theo turned, scared. Standing behind him was a man, maybe in his forties. He had brown curly hair covered by a silky white hood. His eyes were blue and his skin was pale and brown trusses seemed to burst from his head. He wore a white toga and sandals with white wings on the ankles. His scepter was a long staff with two intertwining snakes, gold and silver. Above their heads were two white wings made of solid silver.

The man laughed, "You can put your claws away, I won't hurt you." He said.

Theo looked down at his palms. He saw one palm, and one paw. From the elbow down, his right arm had become a black, furry bear paw tipped with silver claws. He focused on his original form and watched as his paws narrowed into fingers, and his claws shrunk back into fingernails, the fur seemed to fall out and disappear with the transformation.

"Who... Who are you?" Theo asked the man. His past his scepter to his other hand, "I'm... a stranger, I suppose. To you. You look good."

Theo raised an eyebrow, "What?"

The man rolled his eyes and laughed, "I see you've gotten better with your abilities." He pointed the winged staff to Theo's arm.

"I've practiced. 10 years could make for great improvement." He chuckled.

The man shared his laugh for a split second, then his expression darkened, "I'm sorry... I'm sorry I wasn't there."

Theo was confused, "I'm not sure I understand." He told the man, honestly.

"I'm sure you don't. You were so little, you probably don't remember it." He widened his eyes and signaled to the lion. Spreading his hands out, he then gestured all around him in the cavern.

"What do you think?"

Theo looked around, he had more questions than ever. "What is this place?"

"It's his den." He pointed to the lion on the ridge. "That is the Lion that guard's my lyre. That lyre is important."

"Why?" Theo Said.

The man walked towards the pile of gold, the lion yawned as if the man's conversation with Theo bored him. "You have always had these dreams, and they always turn into nightmares. I know you want to end that. They all do, all your friends. I can help you do that, but we don't have much time."

As if on cue, a deafening roar came from the entrance of the cave. The lion heard it as well, because it immediately got to its feet and roared back at the disembodied cry.

"Quick Theodore! Look at me!" The man said, "I need you to find my lyre. It's gold, and it's here. Go south. Make it here and get the lyre, the. Continue to the city until you find Silen-'

His voice was cut off from a hint of shadow. Theo turned. The lion continued roaring a warning to the beast on the other side of the cave entrance, only... it was no longer on the other side of the cave entrance. From the darkness of the tunnel, tendrils of shadows creeped out like fingers. Two fiery orange eyes could be seen from the darkness. Another pair appeared, then another and another. With an explosion of black feathers and razor sharp beaks, a murder of crows burst from the cave, knocking Theo back.

The black birds swarmed him. The pecked at his face, and body and every other part of him. They ripped his flesh from his bones. He could feel warm blood trickle down from his forehead onto his lips. All Theo could see were wads of black feathers, turning red as they rustled in his blood. Nothing more. His body was entirely covered with them. They ripped his cheeks off and tore into his stomach. They slashed his peck and opened his back. He screamed and felt himself slipping away.

"The lyre! Get the lyre, Theo!" The man's voice was heard, but the man was never seen again. The last thing Theo saw before waking up, was a murder of crows ripping his body to shreds.

21

KATHRINE WAS TIRED of all these magic dreams. She didn't even believe in magic. But as soon as it seemed that she could get comfortable with a family she liked, boom, they must be a group of crazy adventurers who could never stay in the same place twice because some damn army was on their trail.

Were these people even safe to trust considering the army of corpses (according to Adam)? What did they do to anger an army of the dead? If they *were* walking corpses, that would mean *more* magic. The dead do not simply decide to walk one day. And with more magic, comes more horseshit.

She was sent to get Raia and Asius, who were both at a nearby lake. Cutting through the thickness of bushes she thought about Theodore had said. In one of his stupid dreams, he saw a massive cave, and a pile of gold inside. The gold was guarded by a tiger... no, no, a lion, she thought to herself, it was a lion. The man he had seen had told him to find a harp, not a lyre. Then he had told him to head south until he found some man with a name that began with Silent. Eric had confirmed his name being Silenus rather than the former.

She made it to the shore of a small lake on the outskirts of the camp. Crouching in the water, Asius cleaned several tunics using his hands as a brush. Next to him, Beta, Zethus's hunting dog, and Tenzir, Akio's white tiger played in the lake, throwing mud and water all over each other.

"Hello m'lady Kathrine." Said Asius, dressed in his tunic and cloak. Strapped to his side was a thin and long blade with an intricately designed hilt that connected to the pommel via a strand of gold.

"Where's Raia?" Kathrine asked him. Her hair was braided today and the strands she always liked were in front of her face. She wore a brown shirt with the same black pants as yesterday, but Erika had given her a leather skirt to wear over top of it.

"Who's asking?" Said a voice.

Looking into the lake, Kathrine noticed Raia's icy white hair appear from the surface of the lake. Her umber colored skin shined in the morning sun.

"We have to go. Eric said we move in an hour." She said.

Raia raised a silver eyebrow, her purple eyes perfectly complimented them, and Kathrine tried her best not to act jealous of her beauty.. Her purple lips made a frown.

"When did he say that?" Raia asked.

"About 45 minutes ago." Kathrine said.

Raia rolled her eyes. Without warning, she emerged from the water.

Kathrine looked away as fast as she could, but she could feel her cheeks heat up.

A towel in front of Kathrine developed a purple glow and began to float. It glided in Raia's direction and she confirmed that it was alright to look now.

Her silk gown did nothing to hide what was beneath.

"We're both girls, Kathrine." She told Kathrine, "we have nothing to hide from one another." She rolled her ice white hair into a bun and turned to Asius, "Do you see something wrong with a woman's body, Asius?"

The servant boy laughed nervously, "No, not at all m'lady Raia." He placed the final shirt in a reed basket and walked back to the camp. His face was redder than Kathrine's.

"Get dressed," she told Raia, "we leave in ten minutes."

"Wait–" She felt a hand grasp her arm as she turned back to camp. Raia's eyes were sympathetic.

"I just wanted to tell you, it's alright."

Kathrine made a face, "What is?" She took her arm back.

Raia giggled, "About Adam..." at those words, Kathrine's heart stopped.

"I know how you feel about him, but I'm sorry, darling, he doesn't feel the same way." She took Kathrine's hand and covered it with her second one.

Kathrine tried to hold back her anger. "What are you talking about?" She asked. Raia turned her head, "oh come on now, I know you love him. You have for years. You've always hoped he liked you back, but he never did."

"I don't understand. How are you so sure you know this?" So much happened so quickly. Kathrine already didn't like this girl.

"Men are a simple breed. They don't want many things in life. They want food to fill their bellies, wine to fill their cups and some foreign woman to fill their beds at night." Raia said, making objects float around to her will. She removed her silk and strapped her linen dress around her bare body once more. Then, still using her magic, tied the golden belt around her waist.

"And I suppose you would like to be that foreign woman?" Kathrine said, with her arms crossed. It was a mature thought for a girl of Raia's age, but a thought Kathrine could not shake.

Raia twirled her hair and scoffed, "It crossed my mind," she admitted, "Though I suppose he wouldn't be any good. He's been locked up all his life in a city full of women like you." She said, not facing Kathrine.

Kathrine's ears began to heat up. She clenched her fists. "What the hell does that mean?" She exclaimed.

Raia laughed. What was so funny?

"Nothing. But have you two even done *anything* together?" She turned to Kathrine.

"Well...no-"

"Exactly." Raia Said. "I can give him things he had never imagined of, things you never could.

Her fists unclenched. "Like what?"

"Fun." One of her purple irises vanished under a wink and she finished getting ready.

She whistled a tune, a song so high pitched and lovely that it could have made a man cry.

Her sparrow, Spew, Kathrine remembered, fluttered from the woods and carried two gold earrings. Raia clipped them to her ears.

"What makes you think you can—" a roar came from the camp.

Then a yell, an explosion and more yelling could be heard, followed by a second blood curdling roar, and a mammoth's trumpeting.

Raia and Kathrine looked at one another, then back at the forest, and ran.

They sprinted through bushes and trees until they made it to a clearing.

Asius removed his blade from the eye of the cyclops. Its massive hairy body lay dead in the grass. He looked back and saw Eric removing his blade from a cyclops head as well.

"What the hell happened?" She yelled.

The camp was empty except for those four. The tents were ripped, weapons were on the ground and the only thing that was left were several tracks.

"We have to move," Said Eric, "gather everything and place it in the chests then get on Quartus.

"Where are the animals?" Kathrine asked, not entirely sure where the humans were either.

"They will come back later, m'lady. They are animals after all, but they are connected to us. Pormant and Quartus are here. Along with Rubius and now," he looked and smiled at Raia, "Spew."

"What happens with everyone else? And what are these things?"

Raia signaled to the cyclops corpses. They were all dirty and about 20 feet tall. Their chests were incredibly hairy and their hair was made in a ponytail. They were fat, with pudgy arms and leather loin clothes and they smelled of rotting flesh. Their weirdest feature was their eye. In the center of their head, just above their nose, was an eyeball, although now red with blood, from Asius's sword.

"They were kidnapped, by those ugly bastards." Eric said. "Now, we can follow those tracks, but not for long. Now let's go." He sheathed his sword and walked off.

Asius cleaned said blood off said sword and began to clean everything up. He opened the chests along Quartus's side and in no time the only thing left were the cyclops bodies.

Mounting herself on Quartus, she had several thoughts in her head at first. The most burning one: How was she going to get Adam back?

22

CHASE HAD HEARD numerous stories about these creatures. But they were uglier in person.

Their fat, hairy bodies and short, stubby legs were beyond disgusting and when they opened their mouths, the sight of their brown and yellow rotting teeth was sickening. Their smell nearly made Chase pass out on several occasions. Their bloodshot eyes mixed with their multicolored irises were dizzying to look at. Usually multicolored eyes would be lovely, but not in chased of deep green and brown and black. It looked like filth. The ropes hanging him upside down weren't exactly helping him other.

His wrist were bound to his sides and his ankles were bound to everyone else's. It looked like they were a freshly caught batch of fish caught in a net.

Below them, nearly burning Chase's horns, was a cauldron filled with boiling water and what Chase could only hope were animal bits. He hated meat, but it was a better alternative than what it really looked like.

He took in his surroundings. Bound around him was everyone else from camp. Except Eric, Kathrine, Raia and the servant boy Asius. He needed to find out where they were, and if they were safe too.

He felt the heat from the cauldron making his sweat repeatedly. His moist wrists early slipped from his bonds. He twisted his hand around the rope and hung on to them, he knew that if he let go, that water would leave several burns.

Their weapons were off in a corner, being played with by two tall, fat men, each with a hideous eye in their head.

When a larger man walked into the cavern, it occurred to Chase that the two Cyclopes playing soldiers were children, despite being 6 feet tall.

The cave was massive. One large opening in a mountain that had several hundred tunnels. The Cyclopes, as Adam called them, used the tunnels to get from one place to another, and judging by the way they brought in raw animals and cut them up using knives and blades, and the boiling water under Chase, they were in the kitchen. That could only mean one thing.

"Dinner!" Yelled a wild voice. From behind Chase, Theodore screamed as he saw something. The owner of the voice walked around into Chase's view. Gods of Olympus, it was hideous.

Most Cyclopes were ugly beasts, but this one, it was a sin for him to look at Chase.

The creature had a grotesque head, far too big for its stubby, bloated body. In the center of its massive forehead was a single eye the size of two fists, but its pupil was no larger than a pebble. It vibrated within the whites of the eyes, like the monster was high on sugar. It had sunken cheeks and its mouth was full of brown rotting teeth that could be smelled even from 20 feet away. Rotting corpse was all that filled Chase's nostrils. He nearly threw up right then and there, but he held it back.

The cyclops had an olive green high to its skin and a pink tongue that hung from his mouth and wildly swayed back and forth, throwing spit all over. It's black hair, what little there was, was pulled back into a dirty braid that was covered in mud and bones and leaves. Unfortunately, it's loincloth covered more of the front than it did from the back.

The creature looked back at the bigger cyclops. Chase focused on the bigger one as well, as it was better than staring at the beasts ass.

"When will they be ready?" The smaller cyclops asked the bigger one. Maybe the one in front of Chase was a child as well, as it was not as big as the other, rather around 8 feet tall. The other was around 18 feet tall. It had a full beard filled with filth and a leather cap on its bald head. His whole torso was hairy and his legs were far more beefy than his legs. The larger one turned, "Shut up, Gorb. Father said you are not allowed in the kitchen."

Gorb wailed and gestured to Chase, "But they're raw?" He complained, "That's the best part. And look! A goatman *and* a fat boy. Gorb has luck today! Let Gorb eat them, Dronn, please! Just a little off the top!"

Dronn sighed, "Three good Cyclopes died getting us that meat. You won't touch it until it is served."

"Gorb can't wait that long!" Good complained.

Dronn turned, revealing a pure brown eye.

"Take Ick and Ib and go hunt a deer or something." The two young Cyclopes playing with the swords seemed to relish in that idea, they hopped up and down around Gorb, giving the disgusting creature a disgusted look. That look vanished when Dronn turned though, and Gorb saw his opportunity.

Careful to not make any noise, Gorb opened his mouth and leaned towards Chase.

Chase held his breath, and the creature stuck his tongue out. Green slime covered it.

"GORB!" Dronn yelled. He walked over to Gorb, and slapped him upside the head.

"What was that for?" Gorb wailed.

"Leave the food alone. Soon enough they will be eaten. Now go take Ick and Ib to hunt if you want to eat." He pointed to the doorway like a stern parent.

Gorb drooped his shoulders in defeat. He ordered the two smaller creatures to put the swords down and follow him out the door.

Dronn did a double take. He noticed Chase's eyes wide open and stared right into them. Chase stared into his.

"Hello, little goatman." He said in a deep voice. "I'm sorry you have to witness this. But do not worry, it will be for a good cause. Father says he will have many of his friends come tonight. Then you will all be a tasty meal for them."

"Wait, What?" Theodore yelled.

"Don't," cried Akio. "We taste awful!" He said, failing to convince the beast not to eat them."

Dronn rolled his eye, "Nice try, but I have tasted human before. You are delicious. Not unlike sheep."

Chase winced at that sentence.

"Eat Theo first," Hexus yelled, flailing his head back and forth, "He will last you a solid week!"

"When I get out of this I'm going to kill you!" Theodore yelled.

"You cannot kill the small boy if you are dead and he is dead also."

The beast snorted and turn, mooning the group.

Wonderful, Chase thought, more Cyclops ass.

Norris woke up. During the attack on the camp, he was the first person taken out. He was snuck up on and hit atop the head by a wooden club.

Finally realizing that he was tied up and upside down he mumbled to himself, "shit..." he grumbled.

"Welcome." Dronn exclaimed, he spread his hands. "I am Dronn and this is my city. I really wish you could see it, but alas, one cannot see the outside world from within a cyclops' stomach."

23

KATHRINE WAS APPALLED at how large Quartus truly was. She had never actually seen him walk, since she was either in the tent on his back, or, whenever she was off, he was laying around the ground lazily and with good reason as well, as he had dozens of chests and small coffers strapped to and around him. Not to mention the tent. All that weight must have been exhausting.

Kathrine walked next to the beast and examined him. Eric rode atop him, holding reins and staring straight ahead. The beasts head was so large that Eric's legs didn't come close to fully hooking around. It was wider than a horse back.

She had never seen anything like him. A solid 30 feet tall, and covered in thick, shaggy, brown fur, Quartus walked with legs as thick as tree trunks and a trunk that stroked the ground. His long ivory tusks jutted strait down from his maw but curved upwards the closer they got to the ground, sometimes, they would drag along the ground, causing rocks to jump up.

Asius said he was a mammoth, from the far north, and unfortunately, one of the last of his kind.

Asius had told her a story from years before, "Lord Norris and lord Eric were members of a tribe. A tribe of warriors, of barbarians. They had hundreds of mammoths and hundreds of horses." He smiled warily, "they were also abundant in slaves. One day, the Ironfangs started a rebellionwith flaming breathes came into the camp, and destroyed them all. He killed the horses, the hounds and the mammoths, save one.

Lord Eric and lord Norris survived and took me with them. We took a mule, Pormant and one young mammoth, Quartus. We escaped the tragedy with our lives, but we all lost friends that day."

She remembered a tear running down his face. They were the last living memories of this tribe of warriors. Asius had called them, "The children of the hydra".

They followed the tracks left by the Cyclopes. Kathrine had only seen the corpses that Eric and Asius had left behind but she knew that they were ugly creatures. Grotesque and hideous with one eye in the middle of their head. Adam had told her stories, as he always read and she didn't. She didn't see a point to it. And she never learned. She enjoyed stories, but she enjoyed the, much more when they were being told to her. Reading was a waste of time. Time she would much rather use learning how to hunt for food and survive on the streets. It was not a good lifestyle, but it was better than begging. Her mother would not have wanted her to be a beggar.

"Make your own path," Kathrine heard her voice, "Your choices will affect you, and those around you."

Kathrine fingered the bracelet around her wrist. Her mothers bracelet. It was a gold band with etchings on the inside that had Kathrine name, Atticus, her father's name and her mother's name. She hadn't seen the name Vorena in a long while. Kathrine whispered it. She tasted the word. It was sweet, like honey. But the memories were bitter. Three months of sickness. After the first month, her father had died, and after the third, her mother had as well.

She remembered how little she was. How that had effected her. She never liked opening up to people about that again. She shut down when ever people brought it up.

She pushed the thoughts back into the far corners of her brain. She wasn't trying to focus on that, she wanted to focus on getting Adam and Chase back.

"Where are the other animals?" Kathrine asked, noticing that the path they were taking was mostly free of creatures, save Pormant, Quartus, Rubius and Beta.

"Most of them come and go as they please." Said Asius. "They aren't exactly domesticated, m'lady Kathrine." He said. "Some are." He patted Quartus' side, and scratched Rubius' chin, who was resting on his shoulder. He was a lazy creature. Adorable and fluffy, but lazy nonetheless. He seemed quite alien to Kathrine. She knew what a lot of these were, like mammoths and dogs and birds, but she had never heard of an animal called a "red panda."

Beta the hound barked. She had been sniffing the trail they followed for about an hour. She stood in front of everyone, leading the way. Dogs were loyal and friendly beasts, but Kathrine had never taken a fondness to them. She had grown up around the stray cats that filled the lands of the nature spirits in Alor, and realized that they were much different creatures. It was cats she liked better than dogs.

"I think Beta has their scent, m'lord Eric!" Asius shouted to Eric.

Eric ordered them to get on the mammoth's back. She was surprised that they obliged. Who was this man? And who was he to give orders to this lot?

Regardless, she helped tie a rope around Pormant's body and hauled him up to the mammoth's howdah. She was concerned as to what they were going to do that required them to prevent the mule from walking.

When everyone was inside the tent, Beta remained on the ground. She wagged her tail and stared at Eric with patient eyes. Her tongue bounced up and down with each pant and she barked, throwing slobber up from her mouth.

Eric looked back at the dog, "Beta!" He yelled, and the beast stopped panting and stared straight at the path ahead.

"Forward!" Yelled Eric.

Like an arrow shot from a bow, Beta raced forward.

Eric whipped the reins on Quartus, and the mammoth bolted after the dog. Beta launched dirt from the ground with each step, and Quartus trumpeted as he began to pick up speed.

Kathrine felt like she was riding an earthquake. Asius was wrenching and Raia closed her eyes.

Kathrine got the sweet taste of satisfaction from her scared expression.

Although the ride was not exactly smooth, Kathrine wasn't scared. She howled and shouted as the mammoth rushed threw the forest.

Trees, so below Kathrine that they looked like bushes, rushed past her view in a blur of green and yellow.

After ten brief minutes of sprinting past the trees of the forest, the peak of a mountain became clear. A tooth shaped stone of bronze colored stone and shining with silver lights stood solid on the horizon, casting a shadow over the valley that covered its base.

Kathrine marveled at the view. The first mountain she had scene since leaving Alor. The others may have thought the mountain was small, but Kathrine nearly fainted at its beauty. Sliver stone lined the outside until it ended it a pointed faded peak, nearly impossible to see because of the clouds. The base had a massive whole that seemed like it was created by explosives, or a large fist. Kathrine noticed the plethora of other holes on the sides the mountain and figured they must be tunnels, or at least one tunnel with several entrances and exits.

After letting the animals take refuge in a nearby field with Asius as a guard, Kathrine, Raia, Eric and Beta all faced the mountain. Beta sniffed the air, and Eric and Kathrine nocked arrows. Raia's hands flared to life with a light purple mist.

Kathrine looked at her with heavy eyes. She remembered Erika's comment about Raia's control over men. She was beautiful, annoyingly so, with her ice white hair, deep purple eyes that seemed almost hypnotic and her dark complexion that Rene led the color of tree nuts, but she couldn't guess how a man could fall for her fictional personality. She was enticed with trying to seduce Adam. Kathrine wasn't going to let her do it, of course. But part of her could help but wonder what would happen if Adam fell for it. She had no idea how Adam felt about her, and the whole debate in her head made her want to punch the stone wall, or Raia, or Adam himself.

Raia calmly added more light to her magic, causing a bright pink light to illuminate the dark cave. The trio stayed silent, and the only sound that was heard was the loud panting Beta did. Her clawed paws lightly scraped along the cave floor, adding more sound. Stalactites and stalagmites riddled the cave, making them look like fangs within a massive mouth.

A bellow came from within the cave, Eric froze and urged the girls to do the same. They hid behind a stalactite and said nothing. Eric called to Beta, who calmly pranced towards them and curled up next to Kathrine. She resisted the urge to say anything as the dog curled up on her back and threw her legs in the air, with a goofy look on her face. Her golden eyes glimmered and her canines were yellow. Her tongue hung from her mouth. Kathrine scratched her belly to keep her from barking and then payed attention to the potential threat that lay deeper within the cave.

Two voices seemed to be in an argument, they were deep and raspy, and their words were spoken in between belches.

"We got them all!" Said the first voice, in defense.

"Then what killed Hagrid, Thumb and Happy?" The second one asked, much more commandingly.

"Perhaps it was the Forest Father!" The first exclaimed, sounding much more juvenile than the second.

A sound like a slap echoed in the tunnel, and the first voice wailed, "OW!"

"You imbecile! How many times do I have to tell you that the Forest Father is a myth made up by your grandmother?"

"He is not! Gorb saw him! He told me!"

Another slap, another wail, "Gorb is mad. Now enough of this, you better pray to the gods that you got them all, cause if you didn't, what happened to Hagrid, Thumb and Happy could happen to you."

Kathrine heard the second beast walk off and the first begin to swell up in tears. She remembered the three dead Cyclopes that were left at the old camp. They had a family, and that family is now wondering where they were.

The first voice, the boy beast, began to walk and murmur under his breath. Kathrine could hear sadness in his voice, and the faint slap of tears hitting the rock beneath them.

"Stupid dinner. We could have had deer, or bear, like we always did. But we had to disturb the stupid humans. Poor humans, the Forest Father likes them. I said we shouldn't." He grumbled, louder and louder.

Kathrine gasped, not louder, closer.

Loud thumps shook water from the stalagmite points as the beast got closer. Finally, the beast showed himself. No bigger than Zethus, a creature with a lean, muscular body slowly walked by the team with tears in his eye. His eye was a large circle the color of beach water in the center of his head. He had a flat, side nose and bottom canines that poked up from his bottom jaw above his lips. His oily black hair was pulled back into a braid, held together by bands of reed and animal fur. He had pointed ears, a hairy body, a leather loincloth and a slight green tint to his skin. He had no facial hair, and was shorter than the corpses of Hagrid, Thumb and Happy, implying that he was no more than a child.

Beta sniffed the air again, and Raia stuck her hands out. A purple bubble formed around the three as the Cyclops turned to face them. A look of confusion washed over him as he looked at the team.

Beta barked, but the Cyclops did not react. Raia's bubble was a cloaking spell.

A pink crack popped in the bubble above Kathrine's head, as if the bubble were made of glass, then another. Raia had a bead of sweat trickle down from her brow. The spell was fading, and Raia was straining. More cracks made their way down the bubble, and the cyclops didn't move.

The beasts blue eyes darted from place to place, inspecting the corner where the crouched.

BOOM! The bubble shattered and the beast shrieked in horror. Beta barked and Raia fell to the ground.

Eric nocked an arrow, and aimed at the beasts head.

"Stop!" Kathrine threw herself at the bow. Eric let the bowstring go. The arrow whistled through the air, hitting a stalagmite over the cyclops' head.

The beast shouted and curled up into a ball.

"He is just a boy!" She said to Eric. Eric nocked an arrow.

"Not for long. He will grow up. He's one of them." He aimed again. Kathrine put her hand on his arm. She urged for him to stop.

In the middle of the cave, the little cyclops trembled and sobbed.

Kathrine slowly walked over to him, careful not to startle him. She reached her hand out.

He yelled when she put her hands on him, and pushed himself away.

"Wait," She said, "I won't hurt you." She whispered.

This plan was ridiculously terrible. As Eric helped Raia up and Beta panted, Kathrine held her hand open for the cyclops. His baby blue eye was red from crying. He looked terrified. Kathrine took pity. He was a boy. A boy who didn't wish to hurt her, but knew he would have to. His jaw quivered and his knees trembled.

"You... Who are you?" He stammered.

"My name is Kathrine. I am looking for my friends."

The words resonated with the cyclops. He knew where they were, Kathrine thought.

"What's your name?" Kathrine said quietly. Her hand was still out. The creature looked at them with caution. He examined her fingers. He studied her cuticles, and all to make sure that they wouldn't end up around his neck.

"B...Boo." Said Boo.

Kathrine stayed calm and tried to keep Boo from doing something irrational.

"Kathrine!" Eric yelled at her. "What the hell are you doing?"

Kathrine ignored his words and kept her hands up. Boo remained terrified of Kathrine. His body was turned away from her and his face was in distress.

Beta calmly walked over to Boo and began to lick his hands, then his face. Boo squealed, then he calmed down, his hands eventually slowly moving across Beta's back.

"Dog! Dog! Hello dog." He said simply. A small smile made its way to his face and curled up the corners of his mouth, revealing more pointed yellow teeth. He kept looking up at Eric, Kathrine and Raia, especially Eric.

He was clearly scared and that Kathrine felt terrible. He was so young.

Judging by his behavior, probably not much different from a human baby. He was nearly 7 feet tall, but she had seen the corpses in the field.

Those were nearly double, almost 14 feet tall.

Boo began to get a little more comfortable. He took Kathrine's hand, albeit, with some reluctance. When she didn't hurt him, he smiled.

"I like your dog." He said. "It is a good dog."

She smiled. The poor creature is nothing more then a peaceful boy who liked dogs. Probably pointed as a monster by others.

"Her name is Beta." Kathrine said.

"Beta!" Boo laughed.

"Kathrine!" Eric and Raia hissed, "we need to go now. More are coming and Raia can't drain herself like that."

"K...Ka-Kathrine." Boo said, slowly and carefully.

Shit. She couldn't decide what to do. Boo was sweet and adorable and kind. She couldn't leave him, especially how she knew how this was going to go. An idea crossed her mind.

"Boo?" She asked, looking down at the crouching creature.

He looked up, and his blue eye glimmered with curiosity.

"Could you lead us to our friends?" She asked.

Boo stood up, putting his rear in the end and still petting Beta, who closed her eyes and curled up at his leg.

Boo stood up straight. He looked at Eric with discomfort.

Kathrine called his attention, "He won't hurt you. I will be here if you get scared."

Boo nodded. Then told the group to follow him as he walked deeper into the mountain.

24

MINERVA TRIED TO keep herself from falling unconscious, but being held upside down, as steaming air came from the bowl of boiling water below her provided quite a challenge.

She focused on her bracelet as much as she could, but the conditions made it impossible. She was sweating terribly and could feel her restrained slipping from her arms and feet.

Everyone talked amongst themselves, arguing what to do. She said nothing. She didn't like talking to people, it made her worried. All the attention on her made want to throw up.

She wondered if she could use the steam from the boiling water to make her bracelet expand. After all, it was a vine: a plant. She was good with plants. Better so than with humans. Humans were too complicated, she liked the simplicity that plants brought. Dirt, water and sunlight were all you needed to satisfy a plant. Humans needed food, and attention, and love but not to much love or it will scare them, and not to much food because it will make them fat and so on and so forth.

That's why she loved her abilities. Ever since she was a little girl living in Sicily, she had been able to control plants. Make them grow, make them twist and twirl, and even make things like Peat explode. She had gotten good at certain things. Toxins that she released from mushrooms had the ability to knock a person out cold and she could even change the thickness and textures of plants. Her bracelet, although a vine that could be found around any forest floor was able to turn into weapons like a whip or blade among others.

Unfortunately, the Cyclopes had taken her satchel, which had almost all those things, save her bracelet. The ones that had eaten the mushrooms sat in the corner of the cave entranced in the terrible high that the plants had brought. They slouched, motionless and laughing at absolutely anything. Minerva knew the feeling, she was a child when she discovered the mushrooms, and a child loved put things It their mouth.

The ones that had the Peat Bombs had been popping them outside. She hear the cracking of tree bark just beyond her reach as the Peat Bombs exploded against the trunk of the trees. Loud bellows barely resembling laughter came from the same place, Fortunately, without Minerva's influence, the Peat bombs only made a small pop rather than a full explosion. She could clear this whole mountain with only a couple of the plants.

Chase the satyr kept bickering with Norris over what to do.

The ugly cyclops in front of them, named Dronn was laughing, he said sweaty raw human meat is quite possibly the best meet the gods had ever created. The thought made her gag.

Lucky for them, that meant the pot of boiling water was not going to be used to cook them, not entirely.

Clouds of steam curled up around Minerva's face like snakes of smoke. She cloud see her fiery orange hair hang upside down She could hear the many explosions of the bubbles in the pot of water, and the hissing that came from the small amounts of water that fell from the pot and onto the flames that heated the pot. The tongues of fire swallowed the small drops water and made steam from them.

The sweat trickling down her arm had made the vine around her wrist big enough to function. She focused on it, and the endless possibilities it held. She wanted a solid, thin and sharp vine that she could use as a blade. She spread out the water throughout the vine. She felt it elongate and stretch,

Dronn yelled, "Quite your yapping!" He shouted. It echoed through the cavern.

It broke Minerva's concentration, causing the vine to fall into the pot below. The ensuing splash caused her to jump.

She shouted. And Dronn laughed.

"You'll spoil your meat!" The cyclops grumbled. He removed everyone from the hook holding their restraints and placed them of a slab of stone the size of a wagon. He removed them from each other and one at a time, carefully placed them side by side. They were still restrained, and Hexus grunted, "get me out of here!" He screamed. His hands glowed red hot, and sparks would occasionally fly off but they never caught fire. Minerva figured his fire abilities were like hers, in the sense that, he had to focus in order to activate. But gods, if he wasn't terrible at it.

Not to mention the humidity in the cave. It would have been useful for her, if she could focus, or Norris, if he wasn't half unconscious, but for a person with fire-based abilities, humidity was obviously not his ally. She heard him yell and shout but couldn't do anything. If she was able to, she would have yelled at him to not move and focus. But, she couldn't. She was born unable to speak, growing up only able to use noises like sighs, gasps and facial expressions and grunts. She could understand others, and even thought in the Common Language, but her lips could not form words.

Hexus was going to kill himself, he struggled and squirmed so much that he nearly fell off the slab. That would be a face-first fall nearly ten feet down.

Luckily Chase called his attention, "if you fall you, you die!" He simplified. Hexus stopped his squirming.

Minervas only weapons were gone, her magic didn't work, and she was bound and tripped on a giant slab. Things couldn't get much worse.

Things got much worse.

Dronn, with his eye-watering, disgusting stench constantly drifting through the air, walked into a chamber so massive, a palace could fit in it. The ceiling was almost 50 feet off the ground and was fully made of a reflective marble, blue, silver, white. Judging by the structure of the cavern, Minerva figured it was a natural formed cave in the side of the mountain.

The walls were lined with thousands of vines, bushes and even trees that stuck out the the walls like arrows stick out from a target.

In the center of the cavern were about 24 fully grown Cyclopes. They sat at a long banquet table big enough to serve Quartus on with room to spare.The creatures ranged in size from 6 feet tall to around 30 feet tall. The biggest dwarfed them all. Sitting just ten feet under the ceiling, the biggest of the Cyclopes was frightening more than he was disgusting.

Forked and braided, a beard red as rust grew from his chin. He had no mustache to accompany it, and his head was bald with several tattoos and scars on it. Bulls horns jutted from his head. His single eye was the color of mud and two massive tusks poked out from his bottom lip. He wore a cloak made entirely made of animal skins. Dozens of sheep, cows and deer had fallen victim to his tunic. And now, Minervas nose was added to the list. The foul smell that hung in the air made her want to cry.

"What's this?" One of the Cyclopes said, slowly and banging on the table with his massive fists. The others joined in, and soon, what sounded like a stampede of mammoths was the only thing Minerva could hear. That and the excited yelling of the other Cyclopes.

"Fresh meat!" One said, melodically.

"Pass 'me here!" A second ordered.

"Goatman!" Yelled a third. It was Gorb. The hideous cyclops that annoyed Dronn in the kitchen.

The others chimed in with Gorbs chant. "Goat! Man! Goat! Man!" They yelled.

Chase was now squirming in his binds, trying to free himself from what must have been hell on earth for him.

"Goat! Man! Goat! Man!" The beasts chanted. The biggest one, who sat at the end of the table smiled silently and squinted at Chase.

"Quiet." He told his brethren. His command fell upon deaf ears, however, as the beasts continued about their chant, "Goat! Man! Goat! Man!"

He grimaced, "QUIET!" He roared. The command echoed throughout the cavern. The Cyclopes, like hushed children, all stopped their chanting. Minerva's ears rang. Although she could not form words, noises were not strangers to her. She groaned.

The horned cyclops stood up. "Welcome everyone." His voice was deep and raspy. "I am honored to let you all inside my humble home."

"We live here, Po." Said a smaller cyclops, with annoyance. Po stared at him with his mud colored eyes and snapped his green fingers. The two Cyclopes next to him stood up quickly and walked over to the smaller one. One at a time, they raised they're hands and punched the smaller one so hard that yellow, rotted teeth fell out. They sat back down as if nothing had happened.

"Now... if anybody else wishes to so rudely interrupt me, now is the time." Po grumbled.

He looked around, pleased. "Nobody? Ah, very well. As I was saying, welcome everyone! I am Polyphemus! King of all cyclopes. As we all know, today is the anniversary of my sons Ick and Ib."

He signaled to two young Cyclopes, one had black hair, the other, red. They smiled and showed disgusting rotting teeth. "Unfortunately, three of my other sons Hagrid, Thumb and Happy were killed today by those wretched monkeys that call themselves humans. All that death, just to bring us this."

He signaled to Minerva and her friends. "A little small if I may say so myself, but there is no doubt that they will taste amazing. I ask you my brothers and sisters, to pray to the gods so that may grant them a place in Elysium, the eternal paradise."

He raised a horn full of a brown liquid. The others followed, "For the fallen!" They all yelled in unison as they poured some of their ale out on the ground and drank the rest.

There was more food at the banquet. The dead bodies of deer, sheep, cows and pigs were all placed on stone slabs that matched the one she and her friends lay on. Some were skinned, other still had fur, none were cooked.

As Dronn looked down at her, a shiver made its way up her spine. He grinned.

"My king!" He said. Dronn placed his hands around Minervas legs. He pulled, and held her upside down like a prized hunting prize. Blood rushed to her brain again. She nearly fainted.

She counted exactly 24 Cyclopes, all of them staring at her and hoping to get a bite.

Polyphemus studied her as he sat at the end of the table.

"Please, try it." Dronn said, as if he had cooked her, "They are best raw."

The giant scoffed, "we eat all things raw, Dronn."

That reply gave him a frown. He let go of Minerva, sending her body to fall into the stone slab. She shrieked, and Hexus yelled, "Minerva! Ahh! You son of a bitch!" He told Dronn.

Minerva writhed, and tried to open her eyes, nothing was broken, but her arm would be bruised for a while. She opened her eyes and saw Polyphemus. He pointed a rotting and disgusting claw-like fingernail to Hexus and smirked.

"Bring me him." He ordered.

Dronn smiled. He picked up a still squirming Hexus and brought him over to Polyphemus. Hexus fit in the giants palm perfectly.

"Hmm." The cyclops sighed, "You are a dinner well deserved. I lost three of my sons to you and now... you will know my vengeance."

Hexus shook, and yelled. "Put me down, you bastard! I'll burn your arse straight to a crisp! I'll bring the whole cave down! Then you have to eat anything raw anymore!"

Polyphemus laughed, and the other giants joined in. Ignoring the boys threats, the giant opened his mouth.

Hexus squirmed some more and cursed some more.

At that moment, everything was a blur.

A shape with the rough outline of a hound pounced over Minerva and on Dronn, pinning him to the ground. His screams became gargles as the creature bit into his neck.

Minerva could hear the gasps of Cyclopes, cheers from her friends and the screaming of Dronn as he was savagely attacked by the mystery beast.

"What is this?" Polyphemus yelled, "Kill them all, you bastards!" Hexus was still in his hand, except he was free of his binds, and an arrow stuck out from Polyphemus's chest. "Kathrine!" She thought. She saw purple mist remove her binds: Raia.

The battle grew. Roars of Cyclopes echoed through the chamber as arrows and explosions riddles everything. The food that had filled the table was now flying through midair.

Hexus, Akio and Eleon flew from place to place, Eleon blasting Cyclopes with red mist and Hexus setting off explosions with fire. Akio sliced each way with a hidden blade he had.

The banquet was a war scene. One by one, the creatures fell from either arrows or fire.

Minerva turned and saw all her friends hold off an army of Cyclopes. Beta helped wherever she could, pouncing on incoming beasts and viciously mauling them.

She heard swords clang, and screaming from Cyclopes.

Across Kathrine, a tall, younger giant held off several of his larger brethren.

"You are a traitor!" Said the little Cyclops's opponent. The smaller one was an ally of her friends. He was protecting them.

"You are a monster!" The younger one said. They held each other's fist in the air, trying to keep the others hands from slamming on their skulls.

A punch in the gut made the younger cyclops double over, with air quickly leaving his lungs.

The bigger cyclops raised his fists, ready to bring them down on top of the younger one.

Minerva saw an opening. She called upon the vines on the cavern walls. She called upon the trees, and the bushes.

Moving like a whip, the vines flew. It looked like a green tentacle bursting from the wall, she made a pulling motion, and the stone ground cracked and shook and opened, making way for the incoming vine. Like pulling a rope from a swamp.

The green arm twirled and flailed as it flew to its target. The cyclops screamed as its body touched the vine, but the noise had been gone as quickly as it came. As if it were nothing but a fly, the vine threw the beast across the cavern and into the wall.

"YES!" Yelled the younger cyclops, "I thank you Forest Father!" He yelled, being to no one visible.

Minerva ran to him. She was cautious, but the creature did not harm her. He looked at her with the bluest eye Minerva had ever seen.

He did a double take between her and the vine, then he stood up.

"F...Forest .... Mother?" He murmured, cautious for the battle around him. Minerva was clueless as to what he talked of.

His eye sparkled with curiosity. Minerva just smiled and laughed.

His expression turned grim, and he jumped in front of her, knocking her to the ground below.

She heard a bellow behind her and turned, still on the ground, to see the younger cyclops wrestling with an older, bearded one.

They threw fists, feet and grunts left and right, probably braking bone after bone with each hit.

The younger one, with his blue eye yelled at her, "Go! You must leave!"

Minerva stared at the blue eyed cyclops for one final moment. He had saved her life and she didn't even know his name. He was a traitor to his kind. But Minerva knew he would become a friend to them. Her feet moved before she did. One after another they pushed against the rocky ground, taking her further and further away from the battle behind her.

25

"BEYOND THE CITY from which you came" was Alor. That made sense. "Beyond the walls that forbid exit." Again, the walls around Alor, which had been up for a century. That also made sense.

So, judging by the next line in that note the priestess had written them, "a fine feast" was next.

Kathrine looked all around her. Although it made her gag, the food being launched up and falling onto the floor, like deer, cattle and pigs, would make a fine feast for a cyclops. So far, the priestess was accurate. Although her prediction had been in reverse, it had been true. When they got out of the cave, they would need to find an "impenetrable defender" of some kind. Theodore had mentioned a lion guarding a lyre, but that was a concern for later.

Kathrine was transported back to the problem at hand, roaring Cyclopes and a screaming Hexus.

The giants stomped around his and barked their fangs. Hexus said nothing, instead he lit his hands ablaze and garbled back at the monster.

"DIE!" Said Polyphemus, raising his massive fist.

"Grrarglablah!" Yelled Hexus, flailing his tongue about. His hands blazed to life as he, Akio and Eleon took the big beast.

Those two were a destructive duo. She sniffed, and smelled death. The rotting corpses of the animals sent a horrid odor in the air.

She remembered Boo leading them here, saying "you will now we are close when you smell it". He did not lie.

He led them down the dark tunnel, barely lit by Raias magic. Kathrine could feel the gravel crunch beneath her feet. Beta trotted by her, panting and sniffing.

Eric, per usual, said nothing and kept a grim expression on his face. The scars on his face were illuminated by Raias magic.

Raias ice white hair flowed behind her. She said nothing to Kathrine, and Kathrine wished nothing more than to plunge an arrow through her eyes. She kept her glance forward, ducking whenever they heard a noise...

Until the smell hit her. Rotting meat filled her nostrils, and Beta sneezed. The poor creature was bred to have a keen sense of smell. 10 times stronger than any humans.

Boo pointed straight ahead, "That is where dinner is." Then proceeded walking forward. He crushed gravel below his feet, and having some small stones seemed to attack him in return, as they bit into his feet and stayed there, drawing little blood all over his calloused heel.

"Get ready." Said Eric. Those were the last words Kathrine heard before Beta barked and sprinted forward. As if it were planned, Eric raced after her, with an arrow already nocked. He threw up gravel with each step.

Raia followed him, and so did Boo. Finally, Kathrine raced into the cavern, where dozens of Cyclopes were feasting on animals, and for dessert? Her friends.

Beta had already mauled the first to a horrifying level. He lay squirming and screaming in a puddle of his own blood, holding his neck hard and grimacing.

And so, the battle began. Hexus and Eleon were already off, destroying as much as they could. Adam and Chase joined them. Adam had found a wooden branch and Chase held his fists up as if one of his punches could knock out the 12-foot behemoths that were Cyclopes. Eric jumped from creature to creature, firing arrows, and never missing his target. When he ran out, two short swords at his sides were unsheathed and swung. He used them so smoothly, again, never missing a target. She understood why the group feared him, as he moved as quickly and as quietly as the wind. He was fast, and strong, and skilled. He pulled his mask up over his mouth and nose, pulled his hood up over his head and continued his fighting.

After he was freed, Norris had run off to retrieve the teams weapons. Swords clanged as they hit the ground, then clanged again as everyone reached for theirs. Eleon picked up his hammer and mace and smiled, evilly. Then he turned around, and let out the loudest war cry Kathrine had ever heard.

Adam tossed aside his stick and picked up his sword, he swung using the moves Zethus had shown him.

Kathrine lined up shot after shot and was holding her quite impressively, at least she thought so. She missed some of her targets, and made others. Erika locked eyes with her, also wielding a bow. Her husband, Zethus spun and thrusted with a spear behind her.

Boo roared as he threw punches with his own kind. He fought viciously. She could tell by the way that the older one had treated him in the cave that he obviously loathed them. But she knew, part of him was reluctant to do this. Mainly from the sad face he made as he locked eyes with another cyclops.

Kathrine felt a hand on her arm. She turned. It was Adam.

"Thank you!" He said. He pulled her in deep for a hug and squeezed. When he pulled back, she studied his face. He had dirt covering most of it and a small gash over his left eye, which created a small river of blood down his eyes, nose and dropped off his chin. Somehow it didn't make her wince.

His sword was wet with blood. The red water glinted in the light when he shifted it.

This was not her ideal romantic moment with Adam, but it was still better than arguing with Raia over him when he was not around.

Polyphemus bellowed. Hexus pledged him with fireballs as if her were a catapult. His arms moved in full circles, launching fireballs when the arc reached the top, and remaking them at the bottom. Eleon flared with red energy. Clouds of red mist flared around him. A black bear, the size of a cyclops roared and threw its claws about, Kathrine imagined it was Theodore, using his skin shifting abilities.

Norris and Eric moved as a duo, Norris with his Sabre and Eric with his short swords. Raia launched balls of pink energy alongside Minerva, who was...gardening? Along the end he of the cavern, where the walls met the floor, a small row of dirt had formed. Minerva planted small green and black spheres one by one in it. And then sat cross legged in front of it.

Planting flowers in a battle and never saying a word? ... that girl was very odd. Kathrine made sure to keep an eye on her.

She launched more arrows. Pulling back on the string was the easy part, keeping the arrow level with the target was the hardest bit. The Cyclopes ran from place to place, attacking all those who threatened their king.

Their king! Kathrine thought. That's it!

She stuck her fingers in her mouth and blew, and a loud whistle came out. Beta raced to her side, and jumped on any cyclops that got too close, to Kathrine. That allowed the perfect cover. Kathrine licked her pointer and middle fingers. She reached into her quiver and pulled out her last arrow. He fingers passed over the bowstring as she slipped into the end of the arrow. Her hand pulled back. She anchored her strongest eye at the tail of the arrow and relaxed her bow arm. The world seemed to slow down. She remembered the words that Erika had told her: keep it still, and let go.

Her eyes focused. Polyphemus swung his thick hands up and down trying to crush a Hexus, Akio or Eleon.

Her fingers went straight. The arrow flew from her bow, and made a straight line from Kathrine, to her target.

It whistled threw the air, getting closer to Po's eye.

Finally, it dug straight into his pupil. Kathrine had hit her mark. The cyclops king threw himself back in pain.

"I AM BLINDED!" He yelled, as if announcing it would make any difference. In his enraged panic, he stood up, revealing meaty, stubby legs. His massive body fell from place to place, until finally, he collapsed on the ground, his eye, though closed, leaking and creating a lake of blood.

The others yelled, even Boo, and Kathrine immediately regretted her decision.

There was no time for that, though, as several more explosions shook the cavern. Dust rained down from above and the Cyclopes continued to gather around their king.

Minerva urged for them to move, and everyone except the giants began to flood the scene.

Boo hesitated. Kathrine didn't want to see him die, not yet. He was kind, and gentle and young.

"Come with us!" She yelled to Boo, immediately thinking it was a stupid decision.

The blue-eyed beast looked at her with hurt eyes, then turned his sadness onto his people, who yelled in anger at their fallen king.

Kathrine saw his chest move up and down as he took a deep breath, he muttered something along the lines of, "For the forest" and turned to Kathrine.

She began to run to the exit, which was covered in a cloud of dust already. She shielded her eyes from the falling rock and began to cough. Footsteps gathered behind her, closer, and closer.

Suddenly, an invisible force wrapped itself around her waist and lifted her off the ground. She felt Boo pull her closer and safer as he rushed through the cave. The ceiling came down in the cavern, and soon followed the ceiling of the tunnel. Stalagmites came crashing down as if the cave were closing its mouth, and its razor-sharp teeth tried to feast of Boo and Kathrine.

She saw an explosion of dust behind her and Boo. Rumbling filled her ears. Her friends were nowhere to be seen, hopefully already outside and safe.

The cloud of dust rushed towards her, hissing and roaring. Boo ran. He threw up rocks as he pushed his feet back. The dust drew closer. Boo kept running. Light came from the other direction, and the end of the cavern was a steep drop.

She closed her eyes, and suddenly felt like she was floating. She forced herself to open her eyes again and looked around her. Boo had jumped from the cavern, and the cloud of dust sealed the tunnel behind them with a loud BOOM!

The cyclops landed and crushed the grass beneath his feet. He panted, catching his breath. She still hung as his side, also breathing deeply,

"Dog!" Yelled Boo. His arm unhooked his arm from around her waist, and let her fall. She grunted, But was unhurt.

Boo sat in the dirt, petting Beta, who closed her eyes and licked his face. He laughed, and she found herself joining in as she lay in the grass, still catching her breath.

A voice called to her. She looked up, the others surrounded her.

Taking her hand, Erika raised an eyebrow, "That was an impressive shot!" She said, hoisting her up.

Kathrine got to her feet, and dusted herself off, her leather clothes that Erika had given her shook as the slapped it to clean it off. Small clouds of dust came off her clothes with each slap. The rest of the group cheered, except Adam.

He stood in between Norris and Akio, with his arms crossed and his sword sheathed. He didn't need to say anything, his gaze said enough.

"Eric went to get Quartus, so we must leave soon." Norris told her.

"Raia went with him." Hexus pointed out.

Good, she thought, off with her.

The group eyed the creature behind Kathrine, who had forgotten that the creature was there.

"What will we do with Blueye?" Chase called him. She liked the name.

Boo looked up from petting Beta, who was wagging her tail, excitedly.

Minerva stepped forward, and seemed to have a silent conversation with each other, solely spoken through eye contact.

She put her hand out, and Boo placed his head in its warmth.

"I guess he stays." Kathrine said.

"I do not see a problem." Chase said, somewhat reluctantly, "as long as he doesn't eat me."

26

ADAM DRANK HIS wine. He did everything possible to keep it down. It tasted bitter and made him gag. The others laughed at him.

"We see the problem, Littlewind." Zethus said with a chuckle.

"We don't have access to the best brewers in the world, or any brewers for that matter, so we make our own." Erika explained. Adam nearly doubled over. His mouth tasted of sand.

He found something that that hellhole Alor did better than these people: wine. Sure, it was mainly Diocles who made the wine, and the other satyrs as well, but it was far better than what he currently held in his hand.

Chase drank water, and Theodore stayed with his mug of ale. He still seemed shaken from his dream, despite having it almost a week ago.

They had been traveling for days south, down to where Theo Said they would find the lyre of a man he saw in his dream.

The cave was still about two days walk from where they were now, and where they were now didn't seem any different to where they had been a million times before.

A field, with no flowers and tall green grass that flowed in waves with the wind. They were on a hill, and the dim lights of a village glowed beneath them. A small town called Oakshire.

The tents were built, the defenses drawn and the fire lit. They sat around the fire, cooking a deer they killed by impaling it on a stick and turning it over the fire. Boo ate a raw deer while Minerva sat on his shoulders. Those two had proved to be inseparable. However reluctant they were about letting Boo in the group was gone by now. The cyclops was a kind, gentle and loyal friend to them now. Chase was still shaken by him every so often, but that didn't effect anything.

Eric sat with them, surprisingly. He never said a word and kept a dark expression, which was a little less surprising. Adam still knew very little about these people, but most of all, Eric.

He was a mystery. Even the people he had been leading for over a year, like Erika, Eleon and Zethus didn't know him. The only person who could speak at all on his past was Norris, and he stayed with sealed lips.

Adam was curious to see what stories a man like Eric could tell. How he learned to fight, or how he got those terrifying scars were only two. Norris had said he had a past he would rather not relive. That was all Adam knew.

The thoughts came to him as the others talked of their pasts, Raia was raised by a cult of sorceresses, Akio had trained under his grandfather, who had given him his curved blade, Godslayer and Eleon had been a gladiator fighter. Zethus was a soldier who lived in The Great East in a city called East-End and Erika grew up as a smart child, not knowing why her brother wanted to live his life inside an arena despite not being forced to. He went willingly? Odd, but then again, he had that war-like flare to him that suggested that he enjoyed fighting. Hexus was the son of a blacksmith from a kingdom to the east called The Crimson Kingdom.

"What about you?" Chase asked Eric. The camp went silent. Eric took his blue eyes off the deer he was eating and flared at Chase. Chase frowned, like he regretted his question.

He said nothing, instead taking another bite of the deer.

Nobody objected, they believed that if they did, Eric would skewer them with his blades.

"Where did you learn to fight like that?" Adam asked stupidly. What was he doing? Eric had already terrified every question out of Chase, so what chance did he have of getting Eric to open up.

He never lost sight of his deer. "My father." He said, after a long while.

"Was he a warrior?"

"Yes. A damn good one as well." He said, monotone.

"Where is he now?"

Eric stood up, and calmly walked over to Adam. Chase backed away until he no longer sat on the bench. Adam heard several gasps and sighs.

The flames illuminated his face with a golden glow. His dark blue eye danced in contrast with his light blue eye that was scarred over. The three scars across his face made his left side a ruin. His lip had scarred over, leaving the impression that he only had half of his lips and his nose had been almost missing its left nostril. His left eye missed part of an eyelid and the scars ended around the top of his forehead. The scars looked like so precisely, that they resembled cuts from a knife ra5er than an attack.

"Do these scars scare you?" He asked, calmly. Nobody made a move.

Adam saw no point in lying. "Yes." He said, glaring back at Eric. Eric leaned in closer.

"Then stop asking questions, 'for you end up with one of your own." His leather vest squelched as he stood back up. Adam felt sweat run down the back of his neck.

Eric turned from Adam. "We still have two days to go. We leave at dawn. Get some sleep." He turned back to Adam, "now."

Adam stood up, again defying Eric. He didn't frighten him, much. Sure, he was tall, and grizzled and knew how to use a sword better than Adam knew how to use a fork, but he was nothing but a bully. Adam had dealt with bullies.

"We should get horses. That way we could get to the cave faster!" He said.

"HORSE!" Boo yelled, agreeing with Adam. Chase jumped. Minerva laughed.

Eric stopped in his tracks, and Raia held her forehead. Kathrine rolled her eyes and shook her head, while Chase chuckled.

"And where would we find horses?" Eric asked, unamused.

"That village probably has some. We could go there once all the lights are out and... uh... borrow some." He saved himself from saying the word *steal*.

"That's not a bad idea." Norris said. Adam smiled proudly.

"What if they don't have any?" Kathrine asked.

"It's worth an attempt." Adam said. "If I'm wrong then we walk to the lion but, if not, we gained horses."

"What about Quartus, and Pormant and Boo?" Akio asked.

"Pormant can run." Theo said. "Just take off all that stuff and put it on Quartus."

"Quartus can run as well." Asius said. "With or without the chests and coffers and bags. He's quick and strong." He patted the beasts feet.

"Boo can run as well!" Boo raised his bloody hands. The deer corpse was no more than antlers.

"Then it's settled, Quartus runs with Asius, Pormant with Theo and Boo with Minerva. The rest of us are on horses."

"Quartus can keep up with horses?" Chase asked.

"We'll have to wait and see." Adam said, staring at the city at the base of the hill.

For two hours they had been waiting for all the lights in the village to go out. Finally, the last torchlight was extinguished.

Adam, Akio, Raia and Eric craft out from their hiding spots. Shrubs and boulders did good jobs at concealing people in the dead of night if necessary.

"Split up, search for the horses." Eric said, not turning to face any of them. His hands were firmly gripping his sword hilts. The chirping of crickets was accompanied by the howl of the wind.

They stopped on the villages premises and the gravel crunched beneath their feet. Adam held his sword, dented and chipped with one hand and Akio followed him with a nocked arrow in a longbow and Raia's hands flared with her pink magic.

The wooden houses lined the gravel streets on either side. In the distance, fields of wheat and other grains. Everything was silent, except for the distant whinnying of horses. This village had stables, stables that held horses. Adam smiled at Eric, who glared at him.

They followed the sounds of the horses throughout the village, which wasn't hard, as it was not very big.

One of the buildings, like the armory, held a lot of equipment that they could use. Eric found a quiver full of arrows, Adam found a sword that was not dented or chipped and Raia found a dagger. Akio stood guard.

Almost an hour passed until they found the stables.

A wooden building the size of a house, had two gate doors locked closed by a metal bar. Raia used her magic to unclog it. She raised her hands and the bar glowed pink. It floated up I up in the air and fell back onto the ground.

Adam and Eli opened the gates, revealing 2 dozen well equipped horses.

Some snorted, others whinnied, and others stayed silent.

They moved as fast as they could.

They all grabbed as many horses as they could. Adam held the reins of three while he tried to mount a fourth. He threw himself onto the saddle, slipping off every time. Raia, Akio and Eric were already mounted. He decided to run.

They raced up the hill, where everyone was still sleeping and the horses still made their noises.

After tying the reins to the dining benches, they finally were able to calm down.

Akio hopped off his steed. "Well done, Littlewind." It sounded queer when Akio said his nickname. They were the same age.

Regardless, he took the compliment, "thank you. Good thing we pulled it off."

"Good thing you didn't do anything to make it all go to shit." Eric said, bitterly.

Adam scowled at him. Nothing made that man smile. He was left alone, tending to the horses. They had taken grain, and anything else they could find in the farms.

Adam thought about that village. How they would wake up in the morning and realize that they had no horses, or crops. He wondered if the whole world was like this. Poor, and without help from other places. He hadn't really seen any other cities since Alor. In fact, any people at all was a rarity. Ever since Alor, the only people he had seen or interacted with were only the people in this group. He wondered why Alor had those walls up for a century if there was an outside world. This world was strange, and dangerous. The Cyclopes made sure to make Adam realize that.

He noticed something about the nature as well. He had never seen a flower in person, and even now, outside of Alor's walls, a flower was still something his eyes have never witnessed. Forests were full of trees and grass and nothing more. Most of the time, the ground was nothing but rocks and twigs, making even grass a rarity. Nature was dying. He could tell, and he wasn't even a nature spirit. Chase was a Satyr. He had a connection to nature. Of course he felt it dying. That young girl Minerva also had a connection of some sort to nature, being able to control plants. That's why she al ways played around with plants, Adam realized, she tried to keep nature alive. He wondered why she never spoke. Maybe she was scared to. Perhaps, but the true answer eluted him.

He jumped as voice behind him spoke, "Impressive."

Raia giggled. Her perfect white teeth shined in the light of her magic.

"Oh...hi." Adam said, stupidly.

"Hi." She waved her hand jokingly. "That was a smart plan you know, getting the horses."

"Thank you..." he didn't know what to say.

"So..."

"So..." this was the worlds worst conversation.

"Tell me..." Raia began. Adam sighed with relief that he didn't have to start the conversation. "What was Alor like?" She asked. He raised his eyebrows. It was an odd question, but he wasn't about to shut down in front of someone this beautiful.

"It was...." He paused, "terrible."

"Really?" She laughed.

He found himself going on and on about life in that city. It had its good parts, but it was terrible most of the time. Poverty, disease and other horrible things were common in that city. They talked, and laughed and slowly Adam found himself drifting to sleep.

27

A fortnight ago

GROWLS AND GUTTURAL grunts filled Korax's ears. At least, they would... if he had any. The sides of his face had nothing but two deep holes where his ears once were.

Even without them, he could clearly hear the Spartoi fighting over whatever it was they were fighting over.

Most likely food, even though they didn't need to eat. They were dead for damn sake. They didn't need to sleep, they didn't need to rest or drink, but they all fought over the most comfortable spot on a rock, or the ground, or water, and often tore each other to bits over the remains of an animal.

They were idiotic creatures. He hated them dearly. But they knew how to fight, so he kept them around. He watched them as they passed him. Some held dented, rusted swords, others walked without any weapons. He would have loved an army that had the military intelligence to form actual ranks of infantry, ranged and cavalry, but alas, The Great Snake gave him these creatures. They were sprawled before him in the valley below. Thousands of them walked in different groups of different numbers. A few hundred in this group, several thousand in the other and a dozen more of here. It was an unorganized mess.

They varied in size and shape. The Freshs were men that had died within the fortnight, The Dryys had been dead for about 2 months, Decayers for several months to a year and Rotts were essentially walking skeletons that had been dead for over 2 years. Their skin was all but gone, leaving only bone as what remained. That is what Pontarius had said, as he resurrected them with his Shadowmagic.

Korax was a member of the Greymen, like Pontarius. He was the king of the Spartoi, and the Greymen and the Kobaloi. But the title was about the only thing he gained aside from his life. He had been itching for a fight since The Great Snake had brought him back to the land of the living, about a year ago, but he was put in charge of the great snake's greatest army: the great children. All "offspring" of his majesty, and they were simply a group of rotting corpses and short, vicious imp like creatures.

Some of the Spartoi rode hellhounds, massive, shaggy haired, black wolves the size of bears with fiery red eyes and teeth like knives, others rode their skeletal dragons, which had rotting skin for wing membrane, leaving them unable to fly, but still had the ability to spit fire, and others rode horses with skin so rotted, it fell off, leaving the bone underneath visible.

"They passed through here, my liege. There is a large opening on the western side of the walls." Xuthos said, next to him.

Korax's pieces of iron armor clinked against his chain mail cloak beneath and clashed loudly against one another as he moved. He wore an iron gorges connected to an iron chest plate and iron shoulder guards via long iron chains. His iron gauntlets covered his hands and his legs were protected by leg guards and iron boots. All of it was placed over a chain mail shirt.

He leaned back from his sword. It was called the Red Blade. The blade was ruby red, hence its name, and so long that it could slice a man clean in half. The hilt was a black rod ending in a pommel in the shape of a diamond and the cross guard was a jet-black trident with the red blade serving as the middle prong.

He watched it disappear into its black, leather scabbard. His spear, Widowmaker was strapped to his back, and he placed his helm on his head. Its small eyeholes became the only source of light as he put it on. He looked down at his general, who stood nearly three feet below him. Korax was a mountain of a man in a suit of armor, or at least he used to be. Now he was a mountain of a beast in a suit of armor. He used to be a real king. An eight-foot warrior feared throughout the land as the Iron Man. He slaughtered armies, and destroyed his enemies, only to be killed in combat over three hundred years ago. He remembered the hot, desolate pits of Tartarus. The fires that engulfed the underworld in all directions. He had suffered in purgatory for what seemed like an eternity. He remembered his death, as the flaming catapult ammunition zoomed towards him, and his body grew hotter. Seconds later, his body was engulfed in flames, and half of his face had peeled off. The iron armor he always wore became fused to his body and he lay there in the battlefield, dead and alone. His vast army had died with him, and now they stood sprawled out before him in the form of Rotts. It hurt him to see his valiant men reduced to walking corpses. He had some living men in his ranks, but they were few and far between, and most of them were sick from being around corpses for so long. That caused them to die and be resurrected into more mindless Freshs and Dryys.

He was revived by The Great Snake nearly three centuries later, called upon to fulfill The Great Snake's wishes.

He hated his new appearance. Once a handsome man with a square jaw, blue eyes and a full head of thick, dark hair, he was now a hideous creature with half of his face melted off, revealing the skull beneath. He had no nose, and the little skin he still had was rotten and as grey as a stormy sky. His eyes glowed red and his teeth were permanently showing, as he no longer had lips.

He had his helm on most of the time to conceal his hideous visage.

He realized what Xuthos had told him.

"Good. Ransack the city." He said, "Tell the people about their savior, and kill them if they wish not to follow us. But give them the option. And tell Pontarius to bring the dead back as soon as they are gone."

"Yes, of course, my liege." Said Xuthos. Xuthos was another Greyman. He had skin as grey as stone and as thin as a leaf, so some of his bones and even insides were slightly visible. His cheeks were sunken, and his eye sockets were empty, save for small red dots in the middle that were his pupils. Korax envied him his nose and his ice white hair, even if it was barely there, and only circling his head rather than covering the whole top.

He was dressed his iron armor. His black and yellow cloak swayed in the wind over top his armor. Chain mail covered his black and yellow tunic and a chain mail quilt covered his pants. Strapped to his side, was his sword, Nightmare, and a cursed blade. Its black smoke illuminated Xuthos' waist. In his back was strapped a bow and quiver. The wood on the bow was as black as the crow that was perched on his shoulder. He walked off, his cape billowing in the wind.

"Sh-shall I inform Lord Pontarius of thy command?" Asked Kobos. He was a hideous creature. A hunchbacked, green-skinned Kobalos less then half the size of a man, with pointed ears, oily strands of black hair and pointed, yellow, rotting teeth. His right arm was a stub and his left foot was clubbed. He shivered and shook with each step. His eyes were a pale white, but the creature had excellent eyesight, regardless and his nose poked out from his face, and resembled a beak.

Kobaloi were normally ugly, but they were also foolish. Although he was uglier than the rest, Kobos was vastly more intelligent than them, and so held a higher rank as alchemist apprentice. The other kobaloi were simply foot soldiers.

"Yes." Korax said in a metallic voice that echoed in his helm. With that command, the kobalos waddled off.

They stood on a cliff, overlooking the city of Alor. Apparently, the team of Resisters had been here. They had been awaiting further orders from either The Great Snake or the second king. Finally, less than an hour ago, a messenger bird had come bearing a message from the second king with only a single word: Advance.

The sky was a dark in the dead of night and the moon shined in the sky. No stars were visible. Hills and plains were all that could be seen for miles and that was it. There was a forest to the west and a few rivers scattered but other than that, there was nothing here. A massive city with towering walls, in the middle of nowhere. It was a desert of dark green fields.

Stheno and Euryale had died here. The first city that Korax had seen in his year of life, and it was the grave sight of two of his closest allies.

The Spartoi closed in around the city and Korax heard a cough behind him.

"You called for me, my king?" Said Pontarius.

Korax turned.

Pontarius had locks of long black hair on the back of his neck but lacked any on his head. A triangular hole sat in the middle of his face in place of a nose. He had lost it in death, being killed in Korax' service over 500 years ago.

His face was sunken with the same red eyes as Korax and Xuthos and a hint of bone showing on his jaw and a thin, pointed beard on his chin.

He wore his white robe, with a belt of various elixirs and potions around his waist. Kobos came waddling behind him, limping on his walking stick.

"Go with Xuthos. Spread the word of The Great Snake. Give the people the option of following us or death. Kill them if they refuse our lord, then bring them back." Korax ordered.

Pontarius pinched the bridge of his nose with skeletal fingers. His nails were yellow and rotting and his teeth were few.

"If only if were as simple as snapping my fingers," he flailed his hands about and then hid the, under his sleeves again, "Necromancy takes time, my liege. And equipment. Equipment that I do not have at my immediate disposal."

Korax despised the stubborn Alchemist, "then find the equipment." He ordered, "Stheno and Euryale noticed this city because of its magic.

It must have some magical artifacts. Find them, and use them. Am I understood? I need the corpses fresh. They are the easiest to control."

Pontarius scowled, "Understood, my liege."

Korax heard his chain mail sway together as he descended his cliff. His steed rested at the base. The chimera that the Great Snake has gifted him was a beauty of a beast. Its body was that of a lion and its back legs were covered in dragon scales. The tail was a snapping venomous serpent that hissed with joy as Korax approached. The beast had two heads. One of a razor toothed goat with black eyes and curved horns that nearly made a ring around its ears and sprouted from the shoulders of the main head: a maned lion with horns jutting from the creature's head. Acid dripped from its goat maw. Leathery wings flapped with excitement on the creatures back. It sank its lion fangs into the body of a deer it had recently killed, staining its mouth red. All that was left of its meal were blood-soaked bones.

It roared at his presence. Korax smiled beneath his helm. He threw an armored leg above the creatures back and pulled at its main lightly.

The Chimera roared and flapped its wings, and a cloud of dust flew upward. The Spartoi howled as they saw their king in the air. His shining armor reflecting the moons light.

"Forward my soldiers. For you serve The Great Snake." He bellowed, unsheathing and raising his blood red sword.

A combination of Spartoi gargles and Kobaloi screeches filled the air.

A flash of grey and white past by him. Xuthos, now on his hippogriff, hovered next to him. The steed was smaller than the one Korax rode. It had a combination of white feathers and white fur. Its back legs were the hooves of a horse, while its front were the claws of an eagle. It's face was an odd combination of both. It looked like a feathery horse with a beak. Feathery, white eagles' wings sprouted from its shoulders.

"Your words rally them, sir." He spoke through his iron mask.

"Perfect. Advance." Korax told him.

The hippogriff cawed and glided downward to the frontlines.

His Chimera glided upwards. The massive city was enclosed behind a stone wall so tall, it took the Chimera several flaps of its wings to reach the top.

The Chimera finally landed on the top of the wall. Almost 100 feet above the ground, the wall was bare. There were no watchtowers, or archer ridges, no way up or down. It was simply a collection of massive vertical stone slabs together. Vines swung from the top, and moss grew all around. The houses were thousands of splotches of brown in a sea of green grass. Several orange circles of fire burned below him. A massive group of people were gathered at the base of a huge castle on the far end of the city.

He grunted under his mask. The Chimera flew downward to see what it was that they were gathered around. His eyes widened at what he saw.

In a brick courtyard, with massive stakes in front of them, hundreds of people stood chanting and yelling.

"Burn them! Burn them!" They cried.

Korax's eyes moved through the crowd. He saw the cause of all their excitement

At the base of the castle, the several stakes that were drawn into the ground, held bodies.

It seemed queer how there were hundreds of people but thousands of houses, not enough people to fill those houses. Then he remembered the hole in their wall. Some escaped, he realized.

The people hadn't noticed him yet, they still chanted for the burning of whoever was decorating those stakes.

The first two were adorned with the hanging bodies of the two gorgons that attacked the city. They were already dead, wish bloody gashes all over their bodies and arrows jutting from their backs, but the people had still tied nooses around their necks and had beaten them bloody. They threw rocks and filth at the bodies, yelling "Burn them!" And cheering when a flying arrow had pierced the creatures face, sinking it in. Korax growled.

The second, like the first, was bloody beyond recognition. The townspeople had shot arrows at it as well, so many that it resembled a porcupine. The common folk wore tunics of brown wool, with ropes as belts, but the city guards were much more decorated. They wore red under armor with silver armor and chain mail.

A man in white and gold stepped forward. He was fat, with a round face and small features. His hair was all black and he resembled a large baby. He was dressed in a white robe with gold designs and a crown sat atop his head. He was most likely the king of this wretched place.

"Hear this, people!" He chanted. "These beasts are harm to us no more! For our brave soldiers have vanquished the bastards!" He lifted a lit torch.

The people roared with cheers.

"And now!" The king yelled with his hands up, "They will burn, along with the woman who brought them here!" The guards hoisted the hanged body of a third person. An old woman with bony limbs and a noose around her neck. Her breaths were heavy, and her face was wrinkled and covered with warts. Her purple cloak swayed in the wind.

The men pulled her up. She twitched, and shook to be free, but to no avail. It was a burden for her to breath, with only choking noises coming out instead. Her eyes danced from place to place, examining the last sight of her life. Her feet flailed around, unable to find ground. Her face became purple and bloated as she kept struggling, until finally, she was still.

The people cheered. The king waddled over to the stakes and plunged his torch into the bodies of the three victims.

The bodies were set ablaze and the townspeople erupted with satisfied yelling. Korax roared with outrage. The words of The Great Snake were lost to these people. They already burned the bodies of two of his children. Korax had made up his mind.

They laughed at the deaths of his friends...Korax was furious.

The Chimera glided to the event.

The crackling of the fire was extinguished with a gust of the chimeras leathery wings. Good, Korax thought, I hate fire.

Screams and shouts were heard. The people panicked when they saw him. The king dropped his torch, and the city guards raised their spears. Korax's army walked through the hole in the wall. They all slouched and groaned. Everyone screamed. The Chimera landed on the brick courtyard with a clink of its claws. Its goat mouth dripped with acid and it's lion mouth smoked. It roared.

Korax jumped off his steed and felt something poke his side. He looked down. Dozens of guards had tried to stab him with spears and swords, but they simply hit the iron armor and bent or shattered upon impact. Arrows bounced off him and everyone yelled, "demons!"

Korax swatted at the guards. They went flying. His armor was now dripping with blood.

"Do not panic, people of Alor!" He said. Nobody heard the command, instead they shrieked in horror. Korax scowled. He raised his hand.

The Chimera let out a blood curdling roar, a shout so ear pericing that everyone looked to him with horror, just as he liked it. Everyone heard that. They were still and they were silent.

"I am Ithacus Korax! King of the Spartoi, Kobaloi and Greymen. We serve The Great Snake! We serve the father of the two gorgons you just burned." The townspeople shivered. "This bodes I'll for you all, but there is a solution. Pledge your life to the new Snake god, and your blood will not be spilled, but turn him away, and you blood will soak this ground. You all have two simple options: join us, or die."

Silence spread in the group for a moment. Then the king stepped forward.

"You are a demon" he scowled.

Korax rolled his eyes, "No, fair king. I am no demon. I serve my god loyally, and the people who escaped this city and put a hole in your borders. They caused your own people to flee, they are the ones who wish to destroy The Great Snake and his vision for a new world. You have already seen a fraction of their power!" He signaled to the hole in their Great Wall.

"We wish to save you! The Great Snake wishes to save you! All of you!" He cried.

More silence.

"False man!" A woman yelled from the crowd.

Korax grumbled, "That was a grave mistake." He unsheathed his long red sword.

"Monster!"

"Kill the metal man!"

"Burn the Iron Beast!" He smiled at that name.

"Kill them all! Kill them all!" The people shouted.

Women shrieked and children screamed.

Korax widened his eyes. He raised his sword. He heard the sound of squelching meat as he plunged the sword from the king's stomach. The royal gasped and coughed blood.

"That was exactly what I was thinking!" He looked at Xuthos who had already unsheathed his blades and stood attentively.

Korax repeated the people's order. "Spartoi!" He them all!"

With that order, the Spartoi and Kobaloi roared and ran to the people. They fled to their houses, but at the lead of Korax's Chimera, they were set ablaze by the dragons.

Korax heard the yelling of men and women as he prepared to add more soldiers to his vast army.

28

Present

ADAM BEGAN TO lose all feeling in his legs.

They had been riding for a full day, and in the hours since they mounted the horses they never got off. His legs began to tingle. He didn't say anything, everyone else seemed to be comfortable. Eric led the group on a blood red mare, next was Norris on a white stallion with brown spots like freckles all over its body. The twins Erika and Eleon followed, then Hexus and Akio and Theodore on Pormant, then Raia. Adam was flanked by Kathrine and Boo, who was carrying Minerva, those two were inseparable. He carried her on her shoulders, and stared at every little thing that he passed with his massive baby blue eye.

Kathrine rode a small pony barely big enough to keep her legs off the ground. Chase held the reins on his horse, a large mare with a short mane and a coat the color of honey.

Adam held his waist, still somewhat noxious, and trying his best not to fall off.

He felt a smack on his head, "Wake up!" Chase nudged him. "We are nearly there."

"We have been "nearly there" for three hours now." Adam complained, letting go of his waist. "My insides feel like rubble."

"Quite your whining." Chase said, amused.

"Let's see how good your laughing after you have my supper all over your face."

"You didn't have supper." Chase corrected.

Adam frowned. They hadn't eaten since yesterday morning. They were running short on food and supplies. Adam hoped another city was up ahead. He hoped it had an inn, with a warm bed and a warmer meal. He hoped for a library. He wanted to hide himself in the words of tales long past, from a bygone era. He wanted to read of beasts, and monsters, and the heroes who vanquished them or how he could vanquish them himself if given the chance. Kathrine had done a great job in the cyclops cave, Adam wanted a hero moment like that. So did Chase, Adam knew it, ever since he was a boy, Chase had always told him how he wants to be a hero.

But they needed something to save in order to be a hero. Until then, they were going to be more regular folk.

Or were they? Adam knew deep down inside himself that he felt bad for Chase and Kathrine. During his fight with Eleon, Adam had summoned the wind, or at least, people told him. He had his eyes closed the entire time, but he remembered opening them and seeing Zethus nearly thirty feet in the air, flailing his arms. That meant he had abilities, as did the others, except Chase and Katherine.

"We need food." Said Adam, "I need food." He rephrased.

"I'm sure a city will show itself soon enough, my lord." Asius said, riding on top of Quartus a few feet behind them.

"You don't have to call me that, Asius." Adam told him, laughing.

"Nonsense, I am at your service, my lord."

Adam scoffed at that. He had never had a servant. He remembered most of his friends were servants to the richer people of Iolcus. He had never really wanted one. He felt that it stripped a person of their dignity to follow every command given to them by a person that was not their parent. He felt odd ordering Asius, who was a boy of seventeen, a whole 2 years older than Adam, to do anything.

He shrugged off the comment.

Chase turned to look over his shoulder, "Asius do we have any food left?" He asked.

Asius shook his head, "none, my lord. A few files of clover elixir are all that is left."

That was not good at all. Mammoth milk was medicine.

"You couldn't have stolen a chicken or two while you were stealing horses?" Kathrine asked Adam.

"It never occurred to me." He told her.

Even when she looked like all hell had fallen on her, she was still beautiful. Her green eyes glimmered in the sunlight, and her chocolate colored hair fell over her shoulder in a braid, as always. A bow and a quiver were strapped to her back. He would've smiled, if he didn't feel sick.

His stomach roared in anger. He tried to hush it, but his stomach wouldn't listen to his commands.

The cawing of an eagle pulled his eyes to the sky.

Adam had plenty of time to think on the way to their destination. He pictured his dream, and the massive raven that attacked the golden eagle. It's fiery orange eyes still stared at him when he closed his eyes. He remembered what Theodore had seen, the thousand crows picking and tearing away at his flesh. He remembered that the crow first showed itself as a dragon, a serpentine dragon. The gorgons had called for a creature called "The Great Snake". He felt a connection.

"Adam?" A voice called. Kathrine had asked him a question.

He blinked quickly, "Are you okay?" She said.

"What?" He was discombobulated, "Yes. Yes I am." He finally answered. His brain throbbed and his stomach growled, his muscles fell weak. He felt useless. He felt like a burden that Chase and Kathrine had to lug around them and keep from dying. He was nearly useless in the battle against the Cyclopes. Minerva and Kathrine had been the true heroes. They were treated as such. Adam felt the group giving them more and more respect with each new event. First the escape from Alor, where Adam had become friends with Hexus, then the initiation training with Zethus and discovering his powers, finally the battle of the Cyclopes and Kathrine killing Polyphemus. The people were starting to like them.

He felt Chase was a different story. He was not as engaged with the group as Adam and Kathrine. Sure, some of the group had treated him with slight hostility, like Norris or Eleon or Eric, but Chase did not have to distance himself from the team. This world was dangerous, and it seemed like it was out to get this group, but that meant that they were greater in numbers, and distancing yourself from the group of trained warriors, like Chase was doing, was perhaps not the wisest of decisions.

Despite all those moments, Adam knew he still knew nothing about the group. Where did they come from? Why was Eric their leader? What about these dreams was important? Why was there a damn army on their trail?

That last question, he had never even asked. Zethus was good at telling stories, and most times, he would tell the story of a group of heroes who tried to retrieve a magical fleece granted with the ability to heal anything or anyone. He told them of the people who opposed them.

Adam remembered his dream with the eagle. The bird had shown him the army of the dead that had been following them. They were called, Spartoi. Those were the ones that opposed Eric and his group, he thought, forgetting that he was now a member of that group.

Adam shivered. He shut his eyes, and the flaming pupils of the raven flared to life again. His head began to spin.

He jumped backwards, falling off his horse.

Images flashed in his brain. A battle. Thunderclouds. A garden. That same garden on fire. A mindless party filled with people kissing and lusting after one another. A lions den with mountains of gold. A great island in the ocean. A cave with a mouth of fire. Flames. A deep endless pit. A war on an island. The explosion of a mountain. A voice echoed in his ears, "Salvation or destruction." It bellowed, deep yet feminine, and familiar.

The ground hit his back so hard that his eyes flew open.

"Adam!" Kathrine yelled. She stared down at him, holding his head up.

He breathed hard. "The. . . Garden. . . The par. . . The. . . Mountain." He mumbled. Chase's voice echoed and Adam's vision doubled.

"Wake up, my friend! Open your eyes, Adam!" He shook Adam's shoulders, awkwardly, while still steering the horse.

A slap was heard. "Ow!" Chase yelled.

"Don't shake him!" Kathrine yelled with distain.

Adam huffed and puffed, but no matter how deep his breathes were, they were never deep enough. He eventually regained his senses. He blinked fast and stared at the people around him. The only sound he heard was the light thudding of horse hooves hitting the ground.

Theodore, Raia, Norris and the twins had all gathered around him.

"He's winded." Said Eric.

"He's tired, and hungry." Chase corrected.

Eleon growled at him, "no one asked you, goat." He barked.

Chase scowled, But remained silent. Norris felt his head.

"He is drained. The cyclopes fight tied close with his release of powers must have caused extreme fatigue." Get him inside Quartus.

Adam could barely understand him, but at least he was able to rest and regain his strength.

Kathrine sat next to him inside Quartus. Chase was left outside on his mare. The beast stood up, and continued walking. Adam could hear Beta chasing flocks of birds and Boo yelling after her, "Dog!" He bellowed, "Come here, Dog!" Minerva laughed and snorted. A cool breeze rustled the curtain walls, and when they flew high enough, you could see mountains and plains and forests for thousands of miles.

"It's beautiful isn't it?" Kathrine said.

He did not look at it, instead focusing on subsiding the horrible pain in his head, "Yes." He said through his teeth.

"Why does this happen?" She stroked his hair.

"I...don't know. Norris said I was drained."

"Do you feel tired?" She asked him.

"A little." He didn't. He felt like a stone brick had hit him in the head. He felt like he wanted to fight. He felt like a thousand flames flared inside him. He felt dangerous, yet simultaneously in danger.

Dangerous and bed-bound? He scoffed at his own dullness. He was obviously just exhausted from a lack of food and sleep.

Kathrine pursed her lips, "maybe you should drink some of the glowing water they have."

She looked over to her left and opened a chest with several medicinal objects inside. Cloths for cuts, braces for broken bones and mammoth milk for pains. Although it was all they had, Adam was grateful that they were not lacking in medical equipment. Kathrine pulled out a vial. The small bottle white from the contents inside.

She broke the lid open, and poured a bit into Adam's mouth. It still tasted fowl, like rotting fruit over a cake of sand, but it did help the pain in his head.

"Get some rest. You'll need it when we make it to the lion's den."

He scoffed, "which will be when exactly?"

She smiled and stood up, ready to take her leave.

He took her arm, "Kathrine?" He asked.

She looked back at him with her emerald green eyes.

"I... wanted to thank you." He told her. She smiled at him.

After she went out to Quartus's head with Asius, Adam refused to fall asleep. If he drifted off, the raven-dragon-shadow creature would flare to life again. It's black mass made up of ash colored scaled and feathers, and its eyes were made of pure fire.

Try as he might, the weight on his eyes became too great to resist. His eyes shut closed.

When he woke up he was panicking. He looked around him. There was no difference. He was still in Quartus. He was still on his way to the lion's den. He did not worry because of his dream, he was worried that he had, in fact, no dream. It was a rare occurrence, but it happened.

He threw on the nearest set of clothes he saw: a tunic, a belt and leather sandals below dirt colored pants. He threw open the curtain walls and squinted. The sun flared in his eyes. When his eyes adjusted, he saw a man sitting at the base of the mammoth's body. Snoring came from next to him and Adam saw Minerva patting a sleeping Boo.

He thought about the vision. The dreams became worse, when they did happen. They took the form of vision during the day, and nightmares during the night. The visions that came during the day were more often and more violent than the dreams. The others had told him that they did not have dreams either, instead, they were being replaced with visions.

He tried to make sense of all of them, or any of them, no answers came to him.

He knew the lion's den with the mountain of gold had to be the one they were close to, but it's importance was still a mystery to Adam.

The man sharpening his blade turned around, Norris smiled.

"You're awake. Good." He sheathed the Saber.

"Where is everyone else?" Adam asked, scratching his head. It was beautiful outside. The sun placed a shining blanket of gold light across the grass and the clouds were less grey than usual. The horses grazed in a nearby field as others lay sleeping around Quartus. They snorted and whinnied.

Norris pointed before them. Adam squinted, and when his vision adjusted, he saw a village. Short, cobblestone columns making up buildings and smoke billowing from several of them. Towers jutted from the ground and noise came from it. The silhouettes of people scrambled from place to place. Wooden houses and merchant huts were surrounded by people.

"They went to get some supper in the village. Applewood it's called. I offered to stay with you." Norris said, "they fed the horses and Boo and went to find more equipment."

"Thank you." Adam said, descending from the mammoth. He couldn't think straight. He knew the city had a bed to sleep in, and food to eat, and those thoughts flooded his brain.

"Let's go." He ordered to Norris.

The village was even more incredible up close. People of all kinds walked amongst each other. Some carried wagons, others held their children and others held their loved ones by the hand, smiling and laughing as they sandal crunched over the gravel paths. Children played and danced in the streets as singers performed with string instruments and their voices on the sides on the streets, with an empty mug in front of them for satisfied listeners to fill with coppers or silvers or golds.

An audience of smiles greeted Adam. He smiled back. Cobblestone roads and gravel walkways were buzzing with people and horses and dogs and cats. They searched for a half hour before finding a tavern.

A group of old men had challenged them in a gambling game. Norris had won easily and had gifted Adam a small clay chip. Adam had tasted meat so good or ale so refreshing or bread so filling. About an hour in, they reunited with the group. Kathrine and Chase were glad to see Adam better.

"There's an inn not too far from the library." Chase said. Adam could not decide whether he wished to see the inn or the library first.

"We aren't staying long." Eric said, grimly.

They had all new clothes, bought from the market. Adam kept his clothes. Their weapons were left back at the camp, along with the animals. Adam had been reluctant to leave them but Norris assured him that they were special creatures. Able to take care of themselves. Boo and Minerva were with them as well, as they thought bringing a six foot cyclops into a city of people was perhaps a mistake.

"Eric, we're tired. If there is an inn, best we take it." Argued Norris.

"People talk of a cave holding thousands of treasures not to far from here. They fear the beast that guards it. It must be the lion Theodore talked of." Eric seemed concerned.

"Then we make our move in the morning, when we are rested." Zethus said. "We have enough money for one night."

Eric scowled, "Very well." He finally said, clearly reluctant.

The team rejoiced like a group of gleeful kids.

Buying the room and getting comfortable was simple, the inn keepers had given the two largest rooms, one for the women and another for the men, and they had all visited the bathhouses and Adam even bought clothes for tomorrow, along with a new sword and chest plate, but it was falling asleep that caused problems for Adam.

He couldn't get his own mind off of his visions, and their quest to find whatever it was that they were finding for these "dream givers", whoever they were.

Adam shuffled through conversations with the men like gambling chips. Adam had kept one made of clay Norris had given him in the tavern, and flipped it between his fingers, sometimes losing the infrared dotted design behind his fingernail, and other times being able to count them.

"You were a soldier, no Zethus? From the Great West?" Eleon had been saying.

Zethus fidgeted with a small charm on his necklace: a red amulet with a golden outline. He seemed smaller without his armor, which he constantly wore. Adam was still reluctant to get on his bad side. Zethus was a big fellow, although also a kind and caring one. "I was." He said, plainly.

Hexus knit an eyebrow, "How was it?" He asked.

Zethus frowned, "Hell." He mumbled. "You travelled for weeks, through mud, mountains and waters all to kill thousands of men you had no quarrel with. War was the bane of every man fighting it." He found himself saying. The other men were uncomfortable, but no one tried to stop him.

"It just seemed like more senseless violence to satisfy the needs of a king who gave no damn for us, and who we gave no damns for. Its... it was always the innocents who suffered the most. Sure, the soldiers fought and died and killed, but we never saw our loved ones die. It was the innocents who saw their families die. We killed dozens of farmers, or smiths, or woodworkers all because they happened to be from the different side of a border than us? We told ourselves that we were following orders, we always asked ourselves why we did it. Then we remembered our families. Our parents, children, wives, lovers, brothers, sisters. We fight for the ones we love." He said.

A long while of silence past, nobody dared to even breath. Adam looked up and saw a single tear making its way down Hexus's face. His face was plain, as if he had just seen horror in its truest form.

After another mug of ale had been finished, Eleon burped, breaking the silence. "The beautiful whores." Eleon said, much less poetically.

They shared a laugh. Eleon reached into his sack and pulled out a pipe with a ball of dried weeds. He sprinkled the weeds into the pipe and pushed them down with a thumb. Hexus had sparked a flame on his finger to light it and they passed the pipe around, each one taking deep breaths with their lips around the tip. Adam breathed in the relaxing fumes, and coughed hysterically. The green weeds glowed red-hot like embers inside the bowl. Smoke billowed in the air. Eric stayed silent and motionless on his bed, he wore no shirt, revealing dozens of cuts and scars and bruises across his chest and abs.

"I remember my first woman." Said Norris. "Her name was Elissa. She had the body of a goddess, and skills like no other." He showed the figures of her body with a wave of his veiny hands, and winked at his last statement. He was horribly drunk. They all laughed.

"May Lee." Said Akio. "We were young, and we were drunk. She could have taken any man at that party, but she chose me." He closed his eyes and took another breath of the weed. Be brought a skinny hand up and ruffled up his black hair. Theodore nudged him on the arm, a look of shock on his face, and Akio smiled him, then kissed his cheek.

"How many women have you been with, Littlewind?" Zethus asked, blowing a cloud of smoke into the air and handing off the pipe to Theodore.

Adam shook his head, confused, "what?" The question was a jumble of words to him.

"Women." He repeated, laughing. The other chimed in, chuckling.

"How many have you slept with?"

Adam felt his cheeks turn hot. He was still unfamiliar with the body of a woman. He had always wondered who his first partner would be, and he sometimes secretly thought of Kathrine as being his first love. The question was normal amongst men, he knew that, but he hoped he would not have been asked it. He had never bedded any woman, for better or worse. He did not know whether it was because he was unattractive or simply because he never got the chance.

"I've never slept with a woman." He told them, defeated.

Hexus howled, slapping his knee. Eleon chuckled and Theo snickered.

Eleon brushed ale from his beard with a stroke of his meaty arm, "That is tragic to hear."

Zethus looked at Adam. His shaved beard began to grow back into a light stubble around his neck, chin and upper lip, adding a darker color to his amber colored skin, "pity. You're a handsome lad. I'm sure any woman would give you a great night."

"Aye!" Norris stood up. His cream-colored tunic was wet with spilled ale and the buckle of his belt was undone, revealing his lower torso, "there must a brothel in this city."

He slurred his words heavily, that made Adam laugh along with everyone else.

"Come, Littlewind! I'll show you your woman for tonight!" He pulled out a sack of gold pieces. "Perhaps four gold pieces for an hour?"

Zethus stood up, immediately dwarfing everyone around him, "do not pressure the boy. His first time should be with the one he loves, not some common whore."

Hearing those words made Adam feel queer. His heart pounded rapidly in his chest the banging on war drums and he felt streams of sweat form on his neck. His mouth dried up like the leaves they smoked, and his stomach tingled from the inside, like a thousand butterflies flew within him. He had heard the words "common whore" a thousand times growing up. The people in his city called his mother that, because that is what she was. One may have thought a prostitute would end her ways after conceiving a child but alas, Adam grew up with a mother that bedded a hundred men every month.

He felt disgusted by the thought of his mother. So many times, he had wanted to hurt her, to make her go through the same pain that he had endured at her hands. He through the mental image of her away.

He thought about whatever whore he would bed tonight, and him getting her pregnant and conceiving a child. He knew it was not common, but his father had done it, why could he not? The bastard son of a bastard son. He had never known his father, but he knew his mother never loved him, from the way she talked of him.

He pushed the thought aside. He would already be on the other side of the country should a woman come to him with a child she claimed was his. He shivered at the thought. What a horrible life that child would have, he realized. It would not be fit for a child to grow up without a father. Adam knew the pain of growing up with a prostitute mother and no father. The mother of his children will not be a common whore, he promised himself that.

As Zethus said, the one he loves should be the one he beds, but a problem lay with that statement: Adam knew not if he loved someone. Yes, he had imagined growing old with Kathrine, but did he love her? He debated it with himself. "Love" is a strong term, and it was often thrown around as if it did not hold the power it does.

Adam thought, to tell someone that you love them is to trust them with your every existence. It is to promise them your undying loyalty for a thousand centuries. It is to join the universe you live in with the one they live in and share every part of your existence with one another. Love making was as filled with as much affection as a kiss, or a hug. Hell, even a look in the eyes could mean love, if it is with the right person. No person should sleep with another for simple pleasure.

Eleon grunted, wiping more ale from his beer, "why not? All our first times was with a common whore. He should practice first and then give the woman he loves the time of her life." He winked with his good eye.

Adam gulped. Akio winced at that statement.

Eleon and Norris got closer to him, "come, Littlewind! She'll show you, whoever she is."

They stepped out of the inn and into the darkness of the night. Torch lights were set up along the roadsides and the buildings. Eleon and Norris sloshed around drunkenly, swaying their mugs back and forth and chanting a song about a soldier who defeated all of wife's suitors that had come to her after a long war he had fought.

The brothel had been a walk of fifteen minutes, and throughout the city, people sitting or standing outside taverns had stared at him and his drunken companions singing their song. They stood in front of the buildings, drinking ale and smoking weeds and knit eyebrows and laughed at Eleon and Norris. The brothel was a stone building with a tile roof and wooden rimmed windows and doors. Lights shined onto the rock roadway and the clanking of cups and laughter of men and yells of pleasure were heard inside.

The door was a wooden gate barely taller than Adam, so Norris and Eleon both had to bow their head in order to pass.

They banged their cups together and laughed hysterically as they walked to the bar.

The walls had smaller rooms within them that led back into the main room and bar, so the whole building was shaped like a flower from above, and the pleasure rooms were in the "pedals", while the bar was in the center. The walls blocking off the pleasure rooms were nothing more than curtains of red silk swaying back and forth, and unfortunately that left little to the imagination as to what lay behind them.

Eleon walked to the front table and slammed four gold coins in the middle, causing the other men's drinks to fall over. They grimaced at him, but all were too drunk to care. Norris immediately found comfort in two women who walked up to him.

"Let me get your youngest worker." He said to the man at the front of the table. The man wore a brown wool tunic with a black leather vest thrown over top. His face seemed to be a mismatch of different people, with one eye being as brown as his shaggy hair, and the other being as golden as the coins Eleon had given him. His beard was braided into two prongs and his left ear was missing part of its lobe, as well as a ring finger from his right hand.

He took the coins from Eleon and examined them on his palm, "Hmm," he grimaced, and shut his brown eye to further study the coins.

The man opened his mouth to speak, and inside, Adam saw two rows of the most disgusting teeth he had ever seen. Some were brown with filth and others were solid gold with some silver thrown in. He was missing his bottom front teeth, "Laura!" He shouted in an ugly, raspy voice, revealing more of his foul teeth.

From behind him, a large double curtain of red silk was pulled back and out came a young girl.

She was about Adam's age, give or take a year or two, with long blonde hair and blue eyes to match him. Her cheeks were plump, and her lips were thick. Her nose was small and dotted with freckles. She wore a silk robe that was almost see-through. Her eyes darted from man to man, seeming frightened by Norris and Eleon, but for some reason, finding comfort in Adams gaze.

The queer feeling in Adam's stomach had doubled upon seeing Laura. She was by no means ugly, but he didn't know if he felt comfortable with going through with this.

Eleon gasped, "Gods! She's perfect! We'll take her for an hour!"

"We?" Adam said, suddenly disgusted.

"We?" The bartender repeated, "You paid for one man. Who will it be?"

"I!" Yelled Norris, turning away from his girls for a moment. He burped and then cleared his throat. A finger was thrown at Adam, "I mean... him!" Said Norris, burping between syllables.

"Very well." Said the bartender, still glowering at Eleon and Norris, "Laura you know what to do." He barked.

Laura nodded, and took Adam's hand without hesitation. She led him past the double red curtain, where there were more women drinking and laughing while sitting on the laps of their clients. A drunken man in the corner played a flute and some of the men sang.

Adam held Laura's hand tighter, so that he would not lose her.

They walked into another room, which was empty save for a single bed. The bedding was animal fur with feather-stuffed pillows, like at the inn.

Laura took a burning candle and lit the rest with its flame, so that they're flickering light was the only thing protecting them from complete darkness. The room soon smelt of a combination of roses and smoke.

Adam took a deep breath, "so? Um, how old are you?"

Laura took off her dress, "fourteen."

Adam flinched-fourteen?" He asked. She nodded.

She was naked now, and her curvy body glowed in the faint light of the candles.

She pushed Adam onto the bed and began to undo the strings on his shirt, he felt sweat dampening his clothes. His heart pounded.

"Th-that's a little young for this life, don't you think?" He asked her.

She giggled, straddling his legs, "don't worry about that." She bit her lip and knit an eyebrow.

Adam swallowed back his reluctance. His shirt was off, and Laura dragged her soft hands up and down his torso. She began to make her way down to his pants before taking his face and pulling him into a kiss.

He froze, stunned. He felt his lips lock with hers, but he felt nothing more from it. "Perhaps it's the weeds I smoked," he thought to himself, perhaps that's why I feel nothing.

But he had not even inhaled much. He was not invested in this. It hurt him to say it, because Laura was very attractive, but regardless of what she looked like, she was a stranger. He did not love her, and although she kissed him and rubbed his body, she did not love him.

Laura continued to kiss him and stroke his chest. She pulled away, "time for some real fun." She whispered to him. Her hands had locked with the waist lined of his pants before he put his hands on her.

"Wait," he said. She looked at him, confused, and still holding his pants.

"What if we... what if we took it slower?" He asked. Adam felt like an idiot saying this to a girl who had been bedding men for a living, but a big part of him was very reluctant to continue.

"What are you talking about?" Laura asked him. Her blue eyes stared at him in annoyance.

Adam stared at the eyes, they were lovely indeed, but they were not the ones he loved. He did not love Laura, no matter how skilled she could have been with him. He looked down at his body, which was now wet with sweat.

Laura rolled her eyes, "you don't like me?" She stood up.

Adam stammered, "no, no. I like you!" He lied, "it's just, I... I am—"

"Not ready?" She crossed her arms.

He sighed. She threw her hands up and let them fall to her thighs with a slap.

"Well then." She said, putting her silk robe back on, "It seems as though you wasted my time. you can leave now." She stormed out of the pleasure room.

Adam chewed his lip, and stared at his shirt, sprawled out on the floor.

Eleon and Norris had already somehow managed to find their way back to the inn by the time Adam had finished his 'night' with Laura. That was a whole four gold pieces that Eleon had wasted on him, only for him to give them up for refusing to bed Laura, but it was better than making love with a person you didn't love.

He walked up to the wooden door that led into their room. Inside was quiet, not a soul awake.

He pushed the door open and examined the inside. The oak planks making up the door creaked as they moved forward, causing some people to shift in their sleep but remain asleep. He stared at the inside and the faint light being let off by a candle on the wall. He pushed the door all the way open.

"How was it?" Zethus said, sitting at the foot of a bed, with his elbows resting on his knees.

Adam flinched, then breathed, "it was... good." He couldn't tell these men that he wasted their gold on a prostitute only to never use her skills.

"Don't lie to me, Littlewind." He chuckled, "we both know you didn't sleep with her."

Adam let his hands fall to their original spot, "How?" He asked, as cautious and frightened as a lost wolf cub.

"If you had slept with her, you would be sleeping with her." He crossed his large arms, revealing several scars from wounds that had at one point been deep cuts.

Adam sighed.

Zethus chuckled again, "get some rest. It's late, and we will be on our way in the morning. If the others asked, you returned at dawn. They will still be asleep by then."

Adam half-smiled. He appreciated Zethus's act of kindness.

After a while Adam lay in an empty bed with the furs covering his body up to the neck. His head lay in the feather stuffed pillow, sinking into its unchallenged softness, until his eyes could stay open, no longer.

29

"WHERE ARE WE now?" Adam asked the Eagle, annoyed.

It's ruby red eyes seemed to glow with confusion, it tilted its head to the side.

"We are going to the army. The Spartoi." He said.

Adam remembered the Spartoi. They were disgusting creatures made of grey flesh and black blood that had been the dead bodies of the damned that had returned to life.

"How is that possible?" Adam asked. Thinking of a way that the dead could walk again.

"There are many possible things that you may find impossible." The Eagle responded. It gazed at the sky and suddenly, Adam rode on its back as it flew over the vast valley. It's massive golden wings sliced through the air, leaving streaks of white in the sky. It made no noise as it flew, and clouds passed them by as quickly as blades of grass would while traveling on horse.

Adam squinted at the horizon, but try as he might, nothing came into view.

"You received my sword, yes. The one I gave you." The Eagle asked.

"Yes," Adam told it, "There were strange markings on it. Lettering, in a language that I have never seen before."

"The Old Tongue of the Gods. There are few left that can read it."

"Then why could I?" Adam looked down at the bird.

"It is written in your blood, boy. There is still you must learn, even about youself."

Adam knit an eyebrow.

"You have had many questions. It is time you know the answers to some."

Adam held onto the birds back, without saying a word, he was curious as to what he would see.

He felt the wind travel through his hair like it was a maze, and he felt the softness of the birds golden feathers rub against his fingers as he held on to them.

"Tell me, Adam, what do you see?" Asked the Eagle.

Adam looked again at the horizon. This time, the clouds blocking his view had split, almost like someone had cut the mist with a sword.

The picture of a grove filled his eyes. For hundreds of miles, the valley was covered with beautiful trees as green as the grass that covered the ground. Thousands of other trees dotted the land, adding vibrant colors to the green ocean. Trees of white, red, pink, yellow and gold all shined brightly, as if gold nuggets grew from their branches. Adam looked closer, the gold nuggets were not nuggets at all. The trees all had dozens of golden apple dangling from their branches. Some had fallen onto the ground, and littered the ground with spots of shining light. He remembered the last line of the priestess's message.

Past the golden apples.

Past the festivities.

Past the impenetrable defender.

Past a fine feast.

Past the city from which you came.

Past the walls that forbid exit.

They had learned, after the battle of the cyclops cave that the vision the priestess was in reverse. The "impenetrable defender" they needed to best was the lion with an impenetrable hide Theodore had seen in his dream. Adam knew this was where their journey would take them.

"I see a forest. With golden apples, too." Adam told the Eagle.

The bird nodded, "Good." It said. "The garden of Hesperides is an ancient forest of these beautiful trees, and for thousands of years, men have come to it, seeking aid from the gods." He said.

Adam flinched, "Gods?" He asked again.

The word was a stranger on his tongue. The people of Alor no longer worshipped the gods. Most people thought they were fairy tales to tell the children. Adam had never been brought up with the religious beliefs of several deities controlling every aspect of celestial existence. He knew of nobody who truly worshipped the gods, save for, Zethus and Chase.

Some of the satyrs and nymphs back home had believed in the gods, and how they were spirits sent by the gods down to earth to care for it and all its creatures in the shape of human animal hybrids. Satyrs always use to say that the satyr represented the perfect form of a human, simultaneously in touch with humanity and nature. They said that is why the people hated them so much, because they simply reminded them of their imperfections.

"Yes. The gods." Said the Eagle. "Different people have different names for all of us. Others simply believe that we are all one god. We created this world, we created its inhabitants, but we never intended for things to become so lost."

Adam raised an eyebrow, "lost?"

"Humanity has lost its way. Slowly yet surely, day by day, they destroy the only home they have, the only home we had ever given them."

"How?" Adam asked, feeling the wind leave his eyes unable to open.

"They refuse to believe in the gods. And the prayers of men are the only thing that we use to get our power. We use our power to keep the universe in balance. Without our power, we cannot control that which threatens you all."

"And what exactly is that?"

"The Great Snake." Said the Eagle, sorrow in his voice.

Adam frowned, "What is he?" He had heard the name many times before, but still sounded as if he had heard it for the first time.

"He is an evil more ancient than your world. A beast from an age long past, the cosmic embodiment of absolute destruction, and he is coming."

Adam felt his spine shiver. That was enough to make anyone terrified.

"How do I know you are telling the truth?" Adam asked.

"I would speak no lie to you, nor anyone else." The Eagle insisted.

Adam saw the statement as truth enough. They flew, passing everything and nothing. The garden of golden apples was gone, and all that lay below them was a valley of splotchy colors. Adam saw the blurred colors of fields or mountains or lakes or cities, all of them so fuzzy that Adam could tell what it was they flew over. This was not real, he knew that much, so perhaps everything they passed was an illusion.

"Big illusion", he thought.

"Centuries ago, The Great Snake rose once." The Eagle said, in a grim tone, "he was created by the Primordials, in a last effort to rid the world of the new gods once and for all. He razed mountains, and cities and thousands of warriors. He came close to destroying me, but I defeated him. I threw a mountain on him. The same mountain you see in your dreams."

Adam raised an eyebrow, "You threw a mountain on him?"

The Eagle chuckled, "Yes, boy. It may sound queer to you now, but you will learn that there is little that can truly be called, "impossible" in this world." He said the word as if he had never said it before, as if it had no effect on him, and he could turn the impossible, possible.

"What about the dead bodies? And the giant at the peak?" Adam asked the bird, remembering his dream about the mountain.

"The bodies are of soldiers. You will battle him Adam. A great battle between your army and his. At the base of the mountain, in The Shimmering Sea."

Adam was still learning so much about the world he had no idea he lived in, and he knew that there was much he had still to learn. All of his new friends were from faraway lands. From the North, South, East and West there were millions of people he had no idea of. He was glad the stories he had heard in his youth had turned out to be lies, like the outside world being overrun by beasts, or being a wasteland. It was not, it was beautiful, and full of gorgeous animals and creatures. Adam had never seen a mammoth, or a tiger or an owl before he met the others. To him they were all stories from books he had read from the city library. He remembered the thousands of old books they had there, and the thousands of times he had been there searching for a method to rid himself of his nightmares or find an explanation to them. All those searches were in vain though, and he never found anything.

He thought about that mountain. He knew it had to have meant something. If it meant nothing, then why would he have the same dream again and again? He sometimes saw it as a gateway, or a path, or a landmark that showed him where to find a buried treasure or something. Of all the things he imagined the mountain as, a prison was never one of them.

"He has remained there, only because we deem in so. We gods have used our power to keep him weak, and imprisoned. But now, we are the ones who grow weak. We need humanities prayers, something we no longer receive. Now, he grows stronger by the day."

"You said I am to fight him? Is that what these people are? And army?" Adam asked.

The Eagle flapped its large, gold wings, thrusting a refreshing gust of colder wind into Adam's face, "Yes and no. You are the beginning. You all will be the ones to raise the army, just as The Great Snake raised his."

"The dead soldiers..." Adam realized; he began to think what more could be connected.

"Smart boy." The Eagle Said. "We will speak more in time, but now, it is time I show you something."

They glided downward, and Adam felt a falling sensation throughout his whole body. From the deep, endless smoke of the day came the never-stopping darkness of night. The stars were balls of light that only sparkled in the sky, and the wind howled as if it were its own entity. A faint noise was heard, like shattered glass mixed with the yell of a man. More cry's and shouts filled the air. They were violent and loud and bloodcurdling. They filled the air, each one adding more horror to the quire of screams that came before them. At one point they seemed random, coming from here, then there, then there and then from there.

Adam saw the silhouettes of black creature's buzz from spot to spot, eventually realizing that they were ravens. Their eyes were red as blood, as were their feather. They resembled ravens of immense size.

"Nightcrows," The Eagle said.

Terrifying, they were, but Adam feared more what they followed. A fly buzzed past his eye, then a second by his ear, and a third and fourth. Flies and ravens...? Adam thought. Then he realized.

"The army of the dead." He whispered.

The Eagle said nothing, instead gliding above the dead soldiers in silence. They were still nowhere to be seen, shrouded in the flawless cloak of the dark night, and the only things hinting to their existence were the animals that followed them and their shrieks, resembling humans getting burned alive or enduring some other form of horrendous torture.

When they finally came into view, Adam valued the darkness that had shrouded them. Thousands of rotting corpses twitched and limped their way forward in groups of varying size. Some had dozens, other hundreds and others had no more than five, but they all behaved the same. They spoke in gurgles, shrieks and growls that sounded like a creaky door. Some wore their rotting armor Adam had seen before in his last dream, others wore commoners' clothes like tunics and dresses, all soaked with dark pools of blood.

Some rode skeletal horses, others rode skeletal dragons or massive bear-like creatures. Adam had never seen them before, neither in person nor in a book. Their teeth drowned in pools of drool within their massive jaws, about the size of two human heads, and their red eyes created constellations in the ground beneath Adam and the Eagle. F

"Look at them. What do you see? What is different from your last sight of them?" Asked the Eagle, still flying towards the front of the army,

Adam studied the walking corpses. Although some were corpses, there were some that resembled men more than skeletons. Right there was a blacksmith, with a leather glove holding a hammer in one hand and a red hot, extremely dented, and over there was an old woman he had seen in Alor, always sewing on the road sides. And there was the baker Adam had stole from... and the old men who had threatened him and Chase, and the guards that had defended from the Gorgon attack.

The more he looked at the more he recognized people. The man in the cloak who had run into him during the Gorgon attack, and another old man who always smoked his pipe on his window ledge. His whisky hair was flowing in the wind, so he was freshly dead. They all were. Unless they weren't. This had to be some sick dream, another nightmare brought on by The Great Snake. He was imagining this. The army had followed them, but it had left Alor. They were innocents who had done nothing wrong.

Adam's heart stopped. Twitching and gurgling along with the choir of other cracks and growls was a woman with a head of dark brown hair so curly that it popped out around her head like a cloak. Her face was pale and bony, with sunken eyes and red pupils in the center. She wore a silk dress with a thin string acting as a belt. The white of her dress was stained red with her blood in the center of her chest. The hole that had brought that blood was large enough to fit a hand in.

He looked at her for as long as he could.

"That's my mother..." he murmured.

"Yes. I'm sorry, Adam." The Eagle sounded sincere.

"I always wanted to hurt her. I always wanted to do something bad to her." He stammered. The abusive his mother had given him had been nothing like the warm embrace that a mother should have. He remembered her cold hands, and her sharp nails, digging into his arm as he screamed to get away from her, when he was younger. The scar left by the time she had attacked him with a piece of shattered glass remained on the left side of his chin. He told himself that she was an evil person, that she deserved it, but part of him knew that she didn't. Years of a terrible life behind walls of stone preventing a better one had led her to be a bitter and angry person. Her violent nature was not her, not truly. When Adam's father had left him before he was even born, his mother snapped. He imagined she was a gentle person at one point, but all the troubles in her life had changed that.

Seeing her now, in this state made Adam feel odd. He had no idea how to feel. She had had a terrible life, only for it end as a mindless soldier for an army of the dead.

They kept flying, and Adam lost sight of his mother. His insides turned, as if excited to see what was next. It made Adam sick, even in a dream.

The Eagle glided past legions and legions of dead soldiers and men, all of them shrieking along the way.

When they made it to the front of the line, Adam gasped.

20 men in grey and black armor rode skeletal horses. Three more men were riding steeds at the front of the army, flanked by the first 20, 10 on each side. In the center was the tall man in iron armor from Adam's last dream. His silver armor glinted orange in the light of the torch that the man to his left carried. Strapped to his side was a six-foot sword easily capable of ripping off limbs, tucked away in its scabbard, and a long black rod strapped to his back. He was terrifying, but his steed was more so. Half the size of Quartus, the beast had the body of a lion, but two heads, one of a maned lion and the other of a goat, jutting from in between its shoulder blades. It's tail flailed behind it, as if it were its own entity. It took Adam a moment to realize that it was its own entity. Ending in a hissing mouth with long fangs, the beasts tail was a snapping viper, and huge leathery bag wings jutted from its shoulder blades, covering the armored man as if protecting its rider.

To their left, rode a shorter, more normal sized man. His face was covered with an iron mask that showed nothing but his red pupils with a group of feathers gathered on the top of his neck. His armor was black with a flowing cape of ripped black and gold cloth. A short sword was strapped to his left and a dagger to his right and he held a torch in his left hand while holding the reins of his steed with his right. His steed resembled a horse in some ways and an eagle in others. It had an equine body with feathery front haunches and an eagles talons for front feet, but a horses hooves on its back legs. It's tail was a whip of thousands of long feathers, and it's mouth was a golden beak. It's ears resembled the ears on Eleon's owl Eos, like cropped groups of feathers.

It's sunken eyes glowed golden in the darkness and its feathers shined in the torchlight, revealing its large, white wings.

To the right of the tall man, rode a man on a red horse. He wore a long white toga with a red star sewn in above his heart. His skin was a pale grey and his hands were bony and withered. His hair was long and barely there, but the bit that was there was white as snow.

The Eagle flew above the group and Adam got a better look at the armored men. They all resembled living shadows, black as night and silent save for the crunching noise their steeds made as they stepped along the dark grass. The man in the toga was sunken eyes and a bony face, with a hole for a nose, and no lips, leaving his teeth exposed. To his right, hidden from Adam's previous angle, was a small green creature riding what looked like a wolf. The beasts fur was black as night, with deep green eyes and no pupils. Its fur was a deep red color around the open wound in its side. The beast had its ribs exposed on the left side of its body. It's mouth dropped saliva from several rotting, yellow teeth. The green creature riding it was a small one, about the size of a child. It's back was hunched forward, and it's left foot was curved into its ankle. It's right hand held the wolf's fur and its right hand was nothing more than a stump. Its face looked squashed in from the top and bottom and it's pointed ears poked out from the sides of its head. It's face was a collection of hideous features, a hooked nose, beady eyes and rotting teeth and it's hair was thin, again, barely there and looked wet.

"They're all dead." Adam said, dismounting the Eagle. He knew the Spartoi were living corpses, but to see so many at one time was heart stopping.

They had landed on a ridge overlooking the army. The Eagle stood next to Adam, observing the army in front of him as Adam did. It's ruby eyes seemed to make a light of their own.

"Yes." Said the Eagle.

"How? How are they dead, and still breath?"

"The Spartoi have been brought back from the underworld. The ones at the front have been revived by he who calls himself The Great Snake and the rest were resurrected by the man in the white toga soon after their death.

Adam looked at his feet. Death was sad, but it was necessary and sometimes even better than other things. These people had been stripped of their right to a peaceful after life, instead being forced to walk around the earth, in their own rotting bodies, following a man they knew not. The thought was quite pitiful, but it lingered in Adam's mind for moments.

"Why do they want to find us?" Adam asked the bird.

It sighed, "The Great Snake seems it so. They must find you and..."

It stopped. Adam pressed his eyebrows together in frustration.

"And...what? Find us and do what?" Adam asked.

"And kill you." The bird said, bitterly.

Adam flinched, he stumbled back, "Wh—Why? What would we add? He must command an army of a hundred thousand right here." He gestured to the army.

"No. They wish to end your existence entirely. They do not wish to add you to an army, so much as leave your bodies to rot on their own. You, Adam, are the only ones who can stop The Great Snake's plans."

Adam flinched, "plans? Only ones?" He repeated.

The Eagle nodded sternly, "Yes. I told you that long ago, the beast had attacked earth, but the power of the gods had stopped him." It said.

Adam raised his eyebrows, "You crushed him under a mountain for thousands of years." He remembered.

"And those thousands of years have come and past. He now rises." It was clear that the Eagle was in distress. His eyes evoked fear in

Adam's soul. "He plans to complete his mission given to him by the Primordials. He wishes to destroy this world. He is the embodiment of evil. For centuries the gods have watched over this world in many forms. We can do that no longer." Though a noble decision, Adam could see the Eagle was not happy enforcing it. "That responsibility must be carried by you all now. We are no longer capable of stopping this creature, so you must be."

It was much to understand in suck little time, but Adam made an effort. He and his friends were to be the next generation of gods? He could not fully understand the Eagles request. He wondered why them. He wondered why it was only this specific group of people who had the responsibility of saving this world. They were the only ones with the dreams, and they were gathered by Eric. Adam had received some answers, but he still had more.

"Worry not, boy." Said the Eagle. He had a reassuring glint in his ruby red eyes, "I will explain everything when you find me."

Adam looked at the golden bird, who was watching the army pass them by with an ever so attentive look.

"Find you? Where?" The Eagle said. "When you find my sons lyre in the lions den, give it to Silenus in the shadow city to the south, and ask him to lead you to the garden of Hesperides." Adam made sure to remember that name.

Adam gasped, "the garden is real?" He asked with excitement. The forest with shimmering golden apples dangling from the branches was the most beautiful thing Adam had seen.

"It is as real as the army you see before you." That sentence had shot Adam's excitement with an arrow. "This is The Great Snake's army. He raised it to help in his cause, and you must do the same."

"Where will I find an army?"

"It is a large world." Was the Eagles only reply

Adam stared at the passing corpses that dotted the valley below. They limped and twitched their way forward.

"Come. Let me show you something." Said the Eagle. He lowered his back for Adam to climb onto him. Adam gripped its soft feathers and the eagle pushed upwards with a thrust of its massive wings. They were off, flying over and away from the great army, instead, flying over top of the golden garden. The smoke cleared and the sky was black in night. The trees reached nearly 20 feet in the air, with green vines swinging from the branches, and moss growing on the trunks.

Far on the horizon, a tree the size of half a mountain. Vines hung from it, creating a wall of foliage reaching down to its roots, which stuck up in some parts past even the canopies of the smaller trees below. It's trunk was as thick as a tower and it's leaves glowed with thousands and thousands of shining apples.

"Silenus will lead you here." Said the Eagle. "Here you must find the black dragon. He will help you."

Adam looked at the eagle with visible confusion. "The black dragon is evil you said it yourself."

"I said that The Great Snake was evil. And that was no lie. The Great Snake and the black dragon are different beings."

Adam nodded in agreement. "The black dragon is here. With my daughter."

Adam pictured a black dragon protecting and Eagle chick. A smile spread across his lips.

"No." The Eagle Said. "She does not look like that." He chuckled as well. "Silenus will bring you here. When you give the lyre, tell him to bring you to the golden apples, but avoid his flowers. Please, Adam. Avoid the flowers."

Adam obliged whiteout thinking. What flowers? Why did this bird always speak in riddles?

The Eagle began to descend towards the center tree.

"The Heart Tree." It said. The tree was so massively large, Adam got vertigo simply looking at it. Flocks of birds filled the few notches of sky that the canopy of the tree could not. Red birds, green birds, blue birds, small birds, large birds, birds with feathers of a thousand different colors. It was truly spectacular. This entire garden was the most beautiful thing Adam had seen.

The Eagle flapped its wings harder. Vines and leaves from the trees flew backwards. They landed and Adam got off the bird. They had landed on the roots of the heart tree. Adam looked up, and the vines and leaves of the massive tree and the flocks of chirping birds blocked out the entire sky.

"Here is where you will find him." Said the Eagle.

"The black dragon?" Adam asked.

The eagle nodded, "along with my daughter and the dream giver."

Adam widened his eyes, "I thought that was you." He said. He felt everything around him. The sweet breeze rustling his hair, the fallen leaves mad apple cores brushing up against his feet, and the cold comfort of the shadow of the heart tree looming over them, as if protecting them.

"Partly yes. But there is another, there are many others." The Eagle seemed concerned for something. He cocked his head around nervously and lowered his neck. His talons began to appear behind the curtain of golden feathers that had once hid them and his beak opened ever so slightly.

Adam frowned, "is something wrong?" He asked.

The eagle raised his wing, "he is here." The bird whispered.

"The Great Snake?" Adam asked, worried.

"Adam, wake up or—" he was interrupted by an explosion.

Through the canopies of numerous trees, by the northern end of the garden, a plume of fire raged upwards, as if it came from a volcano. A second followed, then a third and fourth, each one larger and louder than the last. Stone and tree trunks burst open as easily as raw chicken bones and fire raged across the forest as hundreds of trees were set ablaze every second.

He told the Eagle to lower its back but it did not so much as look at him, instead focusing on the exploding part of the valley.

Adam pulled at the birds feathers, but they returned to their natural state as the explosions blasted in the distance, getting less and less distant with each passing explosions.

From the deep darkness of the forest, a low hiss came out almost as a whisper.

"You are not welcome here!" Yelled the Eagle.

The Great Snake let out a laugh that sounded like a broken hiss. "Has that ever stopped me before? Why do you waste your words, bird?" He said. Another explosion shook the ground.

It took the form of a massive viper. Orange eyes blazed to life within their sockets, making his serpentine face glow in an orange light. Scales as black and shiny as ink covered his entire body. His oily black body coiled and curled around the place, and where he dragged his belly, the grass below withered and turned brown and died.

"Listen to me, boy. This bird speaks of the gods. But where have the gods been your entire life? You lived in torture, for all fifteen years of your life. The bastard of a whore, you had no place in this world, and yet they decided to put you in here."

"Adam do not listen to his words. His lips bring poison."

Adam stumbled back, tripping over a small root he had not seen before. His heart threw itself against the walls of his rib cage. He looked to the forest, where the fires still raged, killing everything.

The snake turned to the chaos, "you see where it will bring you? The Eagle talks of destiny? But what is your destiny of concern to him? He has abandoned you. They have all abandoned you!"

Adam covered his ears, terrified. His head began to throb.

"Listen, boy!" The Great Snake bellowed, his fangs bared now, "the gods have left this earth to rot! I plan to free it! To give it a new future! The Red Winter will liberate us all! This!" He turned to the explosions and fire behind him, "this is what yours "gods" bring."

The eagle had heard enough. It opened its massive golden wings and threw its talons onto the snake's body.

The serpent dodged and lunged at the bird, with its fangs bared. The long fangs pierced the eagle's side and it shrieked. Thick, golden blood poured from the wound, creating a golden mirror in the ground.

"Wake up, Adam!" Cried the bird, violently flapping its wings in a futile attempt to break free from the viper's grasp. The snake coiled its body around the eagle, his eyes flaring with mere energy every second.

"Stay, child!" It said, "and I will show what a new world can be." It bit into the Eagle again.

Adam had to wake up, but he had no idea how. He shut his eyes and focused on the sounds of death around him. The trees creaked and gowns as their trunks exploded into splinters. The leaves hissed as they turned into embers and the branches let out roars of pain in the cracking noise of them falling apart. Adam looked up, within the far away canopy of the heart tree, red lights danced. The flames consumed the leaves and apples from the trees and their vines turned to whips of fire.

The blazing red lights roared all around him. He cloaked his eyes and focused on the little silence around him. He tried to wake up, by remembering where his body was and where it was headed, and then, his eyes shot open, and he was staring at the wooden ceiling of the inn.

30

"RED WINTER?" NORRIS asked, finally sober from his previous drunken state.

"That is what The Great Snake called it!" Adam argued. "The end of this world, and the beginning of a new one?"

Hexus shivered, "How does he do it?" He asked, clutching his arm in fear.

Adam looked at the ground and shut his eyes, reluctant to share such ill news with his companions, "the army of the dead following us. That is The Great Snakes army, and the mountain we see in our dreams is where we will fight his army."

"Fight his army?" Chase said, scared.

"Spartoi. Undead monsters. Mindless creatures. I heard their howls, and they were like...gargles. All of them were almost... hungry."

With that, the room went silent.

"You said that you saw at least a hundred thousand corpses walking in that army. How the hell will we do anything?" Hexus threw his arms up.

"We need armies, and when we get to where we are headed, we will get an army. The gods will provide one."

"The gods?" Asked Norris, as if the word were a curse. "The gods don't give a damn about those who suffer to live. To them we are less than a horse's shit. I promise you boy, the gods seldom listen to prayers or messages that humans give them."

Adam frowned, "The Eagle said he was a god." He said.

"What?" Hexus Asked.

"He said it is words like that, that strengthen the divide between the gods and mortals."

"It is their own fault; they know not about the struggles here on the earth." Norris said.

Adam sighed. These men were not believers in the gods. Their entire lives had been built on struggle. No god could allow things to be so terrible. Adam had seen a beautiful world since leaving Alor, but his sight was narrowed by his inexperience. He knew now, war, poverty, disease, starvation all existed, things he hoped were only found in Alor. Alas, they were common around the lands they have passed, and will continue to be common around the lands they will pass. He remembered Norris' words days ago, when Adam had seen the world, "it used to be greener". This world was once beautiful, but something happened, the humans stopped believing in the gods, and their power faded, causing things like war, poverty, disease and starvation to be common in the lands they have passed.

Eric stared at air, his scars hidden from Adam's view. "We need to move."

"Agreed." Theo Said, throwing his satchel over his shoulder, "you said that the lions den has a lyre? And we need to give that lyre to who?"

"Silenus." Chase said.

"Nobody asked you, goat." Eleon grumbled, holding his head from last night.

Chase stood up, a stern look on his face. "Perhaps not, but if anyone else wishes to give us any useful information about who Silenus is and why he will help us then be my damn guess, but until then, you lot will have to listen to me."

Eleon growled beneath his breath, defeated. Adam smiled, and Norris laughed. Eleon had been a thorn in the side of Chase for as long as they had known him. Never once had he shown any respect to the satyr, instead he showed him the same amount of hatred as those men in Alor. It was satisfying to see him be put in his place.

They packed their equipment, having already used fresh water provided by the innkeeper to clean themselves up. Breakfast had been brought to hem little more than an hour ago and Akio, Asius and Zethus had already went to tend to the animals with Boo and Minerva.

Eric splashed more cold water onto his face and dried it with a cloth hanging off the side of the bucket. He wore no shirt, revealing more scars up and down his torso. He took Norris' waterskin and poured som into his mouth.

"Very well, goat." He said, pouring more water down his bare back, "What is it that you know about this Silenus?" He gestured with the waterskin.

Chase puffed out his chest and studied everyone looking at him. He cleared his throat, "Well... the elders in my village used to tell stories of Silenus."

Eleon guffawed, "So were looking for a story!"

Adam frowned, "we come from a place where the very existence of people beyond our walls were stories. I used to think the warriors of the east were stories until I met Akio." Adam argued. He had seen all of these things for the first time, once believing that they were nothing more than stories. Still, with the only evidence of Silenus they have being a story from Chase's childhood, it left them all quite unsure.

"He is a satyr." Chase finished, sheathing a dagger he had bought before. He wore a light brown tunic with a leather vest and no pants. His horns curled above his head and his belt held the dagger.

"My friend, Diocles, used to tell me that Silenus was a soldier for the army of Dionysus, the god of wine."

Norris chuckled, "I've never had the gods to thank for a damn thing but there," he raised a finger to the sky, "there is a god I can respect."

Eleon scoffed, "one who uses a bunch of drunken animals for troops. Sad." He stood up and walked out of the tent, intentionally bumping into Chase on the way out.

"Forget him, Chase." Adam reassured him.

Chase looked around, angered by Eleon, "he raised the young god and taught him many things, about nature and its inhabitants. When the god took his seat at Olympus, the old satyr grew sad and disappeared. It is said he lives somewhere in the south, in a city called-" he said words in a language nobody understood.

"What the hell is that?" Hexus said.

"In Senewa it means "shadow city"." He said.

"Senewa?" Theo Asked, visibly confused.

"It's the native tongue of the satyrs." Chase explained.

Adam remembered his dream. "The Eagle said something about a shadow city. He said Silenus would be there." He clapped his hands in victory.

"Wonderful!" Yelled Hexus, "we know where he is."

"Except we don't." Norris said, pinching the bridge of his nose, "we know he is in a place called "the shadow city" but we have no idea what the hell the shadow city is, or where it is."

"Actually," Theodore began, "maybe we do. In my dream, the young man who told me about the lions den told me that its home was now a shadow." He twirled his golden trusses between his fingers, "he said the lions home was now a ruin." He looked up at the rest of the group.

Hexus put a finger to his chin, so an impenetrable lion who lives in an abandoned city?"

"Nemea." Norris whispered to Eric.

Eric scowled at the air, "I know." He put his green tunic on, followed by his dark green cloak and weapons.

"We leave now." He said, throwing open the door.

Everyone followed him.

Norris wore a dark woolen tunic with a woolen cloak and his leather boots. His Saber was strapped to his side. Theodore had a sand colored shirt with a dark brown colored leather vest over top and dirt colored pants with sandals on his feet. A short sword was sheathed on his hip. Hexus had a knee length, red colored, woolen tunic and his leather gorget that curved over his shoulder and sandals. Adam wore the same clothes he wore to sleep last night, a woolen tunic with woolen pants and sandals.

On the edge of the city, the women already sat ready on their horses with Eleon, Akio, Zethus and Asius. Boo sat, petting Tenzir the white tiger with caution while Minerva sat on his shoulders.

Kathrine reared her steed, and her mare threw up dust with each stepped as it clipped over to Adam.

"Morning," She said, smiling down at him.

He looked up at her, she wore a woolen shirt tightly woven and a long dress below, covering her from the waist down and giving the impression that her mare wore a coat of its own. The horse was a beautiful milk color with a blanket of furs covering the saddle. It's reins ran across its white face and it's tail wagged away flies and mosquitoes. Kathrine still had her hazel colored hair braided with golden rings twisted in and two strands of hair hung freely on either side of her face.

He smiled back at her, "you look happy." He told her. Her green eyes sparkled like emeralds.

Kathrine held her mares reins with her right hand, and with her left, the black leather reins of a colt rested in her palm, "I had a good rest." She tugged lightly at the reins and the colt walked over to Adam. Its fur was the color of bronze and its mane was black as night. He threw one leg over it and held onto the reins.

It was his first time ever riding a horse on his own, and he had only ridden with Chase before. Eric rode before them on his white horse, his green cloak billowed in the slight breeze.

"South of here is the lions cave, and south of that is the shadow city that Chase talked about!" He shouted to the group. "We follow Silenus from that point on and we make it to wherever it is we go." He turned his horse around and rode forward, alone. The others followed. Most were on horses, Asius rode Quartus and Theodore rode Pormant the mule, while Minerva was on Boo's shoulders.

The buzzing of the people in the village was overtaken by the group making small talk within themselves. Hexus repeated why Adam had said in the inn to Boo and Minerva and Eleon rode with Zethus, making expressions of frustration and anger. He was most likely talking about Chase, but Zethus only looked forward with a hopeless look on his face read, "what can we do with this lad?".

Erika rode with Raia and Theodore talking about gods know what and Norris and Akio rode with Chase, trying to learn more about the satyr language "Senewa" and Chase laughed whenever either of them pronounced something incorrectly.

Adam had grown up with dozens of satyrs of nymphs, and so he understood Senewa and spoke a broken version of it. Kathrine was better than he was and Chase was fluent in it. Although Chase did not like it when people called him "goat", it would seem as though he and Norris had taking an admiration for each other. Or at least a respect.

All around them, the animals walked. The birds flew all around them, fluttering or flapping their wings and Beta the hunting dog chased Rubius the red panda back and forth. Tenzir, with more class than the other animals, rested on one of Quartus' tusks and astonishingly, the mammoth did nothing to stop it. Bugbush, Norris's weasel, scurried from place to place around them, avoiding the hooves of horses and the stomps of a mammoth.

A queer feeling took hold of Adam. As trees and fields and rivers and lakes passed them by, Adam thought about the people he rode with. They were as lost as he was. Until recently, they had all been strangers, and now, they rode side by side, to a future none of them knew. They all shared dreams of death and destruction and they were all targets of The Great Snake because of it. The gods were leading them to Olympus, and these dreams were more like messages.

"Where did you go last night?" Kathrine asked.

Adam felt his grip tighten on his horses reins, "What do you mean?"

Kathrine scoffed, "I know you left the inn with Norris and Eleon last night. I saw you."

Adam sighed. Kathrine raised an eyebrow, "it is not a big inn, you know?"

"I know." Adam said. He could not tell her the truth, about the brothel, about Laura. Even is Adam never bedded her, he had entered a whorehouse prepared to bed a whore.

"We got a few more mugs from the tavern. Norris and Eleon were drunk."

"Oh.." Kathrine said, "were you not?"

"No." Adam laughed, "I hadn't had that much to drink."

"Ohh..." She said awkwardly.

Adam sighed, "I had a dream last night." He said.

Kathrine said nothing, instead choosing to look at him, concerned.

"I saw the army following us."

"The army of the dead?"

"Yes... they... they made it past Alor..." he contemplated telling her about the massacre.

"I saw my mother..." he said.

A look of simultaneous dread and shock washed over her, curving the corners of her mouth down.

"Adam... I'm..."

"I know... it's ok..."

"What about the rest of the city..."

He hesitated. She couldn't know. They both hated it, but the thought of innocent people being killed in the way they were was too much to fathom.

"I didn't see anyone else I recognized. The king once told me some of them made it to 'the golden city' whatever that means."

She looked down... "what else did you see?"

"A garden. With golden apples on the trees. That's where we need to go. After we get to this lion, and pass the satyr Chase says will help us, the Satyr will take us to the garden. From there... who knows?"

"We're almost there..." She said, happily.

He smiled.

Adam heard nothing but the faint sounds of jingling reins and the putter patter of horse hooves stepping into the ground. Most of the trip had been in silence, fat chance that Kathrine believed his story, but he didn't want to say another word to her.

Valleys of green past by, and the mountains on the horizon turned the circular sun and made it a triangle. Somehow, the mountains never seemed to get closer. Adam figured they must be, they had been moving south for hours, but the mountains were just jagged triangles in the distance.

They had seen animals in the distance more than once, but they never bothered them, and the smell of rain water was heavy.

Night had fallen by the time they made it to the cave holding the lion. Norris had explained how the lion had ravaged the city of Nemea for years. People gave it gold and riches, but what is that of concern to a beast?

"Stop here." Theodore said, dismounting Pormant. He had helped in leading the group since he had seen the lion in his dream.

The group all dismounted their steeds as Asius tended to them. The boy was a hard worker, rushing from place to place to tether the reins to a spike.

Adam looked around him, I front of them was the mouth of a cave that lead deep into a small mountain a small bit higher than 30 feet, a hole of rock with so little light, that Adam stood in the mouth and thought he was closing his eyes.

A field of green surrounded it, and in the moist grass was a constellation of small indentations in the shape of lion paws.

"Must have gone hunting." Akio said, bending down to examine the prints.

Behind the small mountain with the cave, a city lay in the valley, so dark, Adam felt as if the night sky was reflecting off of a lake.

After the encounter with the Cyclopes, Adam was reluctant to enter the cave, but Eric had ordered only a small party enter, while a second party find Silenus in the city.

Adam entered the cave with Eric, Eleon, Erika, Zethus, Theodore and Norris. Asius stayed with the animals along with Boo and Minerva and Kathrine entered the city with Eli, Chase, Hexus and Raia.

The city had no lights, Adam wondered if there were even people living in it. It is called the "shadow city" for a reason, Adam thought.

They set their belongings outside the cave with Asius. Adam put his sack down and rummaged through it looking for something he might need.

A sword was sheathed at his side, but her still had the rod that the Eagle had given him during escape from Alor.

Adam felt a hand on his shoulder. Kathrine looked at him, her green eyes somehow adding light to the darkness of the night.

"Be careful." She whispered. She pulled him in close for a hug, and pulled away after a minute. Her group, armed and ready, had called for her, and she disappeared into the night.

Adam took a breath. He stared down at his shaking hands. The silver rod glowed a bright white.

Adam knew it was a sword, the Eagle had shown him in his dream, and the rod felt like a hilt of some kind, but Adam still had no idea how to summon the blade from the rounded stick.

Norris sheathed his saber, "You find out how to work it, yet?" He asked.

"No, not yet." Adam said, turning it in his hand.

Adam tucked it away in his sack and threw it over his shoulder. He gripped the hilt of the sword he actually had and pulled it from its sheath.

The blade felt lopsided, heavier on one side then on the other. The hilt felt too thick and large for Adam's hand. He couldn't hold it properly and the pommel bothered his hands if he tried to take it with both. Too big for one hand but to small for both.

"How do you know it's even a sword?" Asked Erika.

"I don't know. I just feel like it is."

"We better hope that's worth something." Eleon said, hooking his mace and hammer to his back

The darkness of the cave was frightened away by the flickering of the torchlight that Eric brought forward. He led the group, walking ahead of everyone with his right hand cautiously on the pommel of his sword.

Zethus followed, his red armor glinting and dancing in the flickering light, as he leaned forward, with his spear pointed at any and all threats. Eleon held up his massive weapons. Norris, who was behind him, handed him a dagger and the small blade shined orange.

Norris had his curved saber away from its sheath, his brown eyes danced from corner to corner attentively.

Adam was second to last, holding his sword with two uncomfortable hands and squinting to see for any threats.

Theodore had a short sword in his right hand and his left was covered in black fur and ended with claws in place of fingers.

Lastly was Erika, carrying her own torch and a spear glinting with the torchlight.

As they descended deeper into the darkness, silence became the dominant noise. The crackling of the flames became a faded popping as if in the distance, and not even the sound of their shoes on the stone became as deafening loud as the silence. No one breathed, or said a word, in fear of alerting the lion. Their eyes could not see past the bubble of light the flames allowed, which was only a few feet. The torch light flickered on the wall, showing their path was a deep corridor, then it crawled forward, into a bigger area.

A cavern bigger than they could see opened in front of them. The walls were pure stone, as was the ground and there was no ceiling, instead, an empty space where a ceiling would be, allowed the faint light of the stars and moon to shine through.

Adam looked around them. Theodore's dream had not lied, he thought.

A few feet in front of them, at the base of a tall ledge, was a mountain of gold.

It shimmered when put in the light of the torch, and diamonds, rubies, emeralds, gold, silver, opal, amethyst and other treasures danced around, blindingly.

"It is supposed to be on that ledge." Theo whispered, pointing upwards.

The group followed his finger. A tall ledge loomed above treasure mound so tall, the torchlight could not show its peak.

"Find the lyre. Quickly." Eric murmured, stepping forward and inch.

Adam looked to the ground, to see where he was stepping. The bloody bones of men, women and children littered the floor, clutching the remains of crushed urns, weapons and toys. Adam felt hot tears flood into salty puddles in his eyes.

Adam examined the odd weapons dotting the floor: swords dented out of shape, spears snapped in half, shields torn to bent shreds and hammers and axes all crushed and cracked.

A loud and uncomfortable ˜crack˜ filled Adam's ears. He flinched and swung his sword backwards, nearly decapitating Theodore, who's foot stood in the middle of a human rib cage. His face was pale as paper and he had rivers of tears on either cheek.

"It's a girl..." he stammered, crying.

Shuffling came from the pile of treasures behind them, and a figure in black emerged from the pile.

"Alert!" Norris whispered.

His cloak billowed and he raised his saber as the lion roared, throwing a claw at his stomach.

Norris shouted, as his body flew deeper into the cave and disappeared in the darkness.

31

THE PEBBLE SKIPPED along the stone walkway when Kathrine kicked it. It hopped inches at a time with a hypnotic, *click* *click* *click*. The houses they past were empty and silent. Cobwebs grew on the windows and the wood had rotted on the doors. The bricks were chipped and cracked and the only noise heard was the low hum of the breeze. The city truly was a shadow.

Hexus walked next to her, making flame appear and disappear in his hand with snaps of his fingers. He had been telling her about his old life, how he lived in the Scarlet Nation, across the shimmering sea and in the scarlet kingdom. He was an odd boy, with iris' as red as blood and a smile so big it made Kathrine smile along with him.

He was the youngest of the group, no older than 13, and he acted it as well. He was full of energy and always had to be fidgeting with something. He was cute, as a younger brother would be.

"My mother was a farmer," he was saying, fire still flickering on and off in his fingers, "but my uncle was a blacksmith. He made weapons with fire and hammers and he taught me all I know."

Kathrine chuckled, her quiver was slung over her shoulder, and her bow fit in her palm perfectly.

"He sounds like a good man." Kathrine, laughing.

He stared at his flaming finger, "he was. What about you? What do your parent do?"

Kathrine frowned at her bracelet. The voice of her mother echoed in her ears. "I love you" She said. "I know you will do great things." Her father told her.

"My parents died when I was younger." She told Hexus, keeping a slight smile as best she could. She was upset about her parents, but Hexus was still a child, he had no reason to be frowning over her parents.

"My father did too. I never met him, and my mother never really spoke of him." Hexus said, joining Kathrine in the immortal activity of kicking rocks.

"I don't know his name."

"Vorena, and Atticus." Kathrine said after a pause.

"Those were their names?" He asked. She nodded. "Lovely names."

Kathrine smiled. She fingered the gold band on her wrist. She missed her mother, the kind loving person she was. Her parents were good people. Good people who did not deserve their death. Slowly withering away within weeks. It was slow, and painful.

Kathrine he scoffed at thought of people "deserving" death. Everyone faced it, yet so few people deserve it. All the terrible people, like the killers and rapists always died quickly, while it was the killed and raped were the ones who died in agony. Kathrine thought it sick. How dare people still believe in divine beings. The way the world worked left little to imagine that there was a man or woman controlling everything. She figured the gods didn't care. They seldom did, and when they did, it was because a human had disgraced them.

Kathrine had heard the stories Adam told her. The only reason the human disgraces the god is because the gods never gave the human anything to give grace to. Death reined supreme over everything, and everyone, not gods, and yet people prayed to the gods, asking for mercy and aid. Those prayers fell upon deaf ears. Why would the gods give a horses shit about humans, when humans seldom gave a horses shit for each other?

Kathrine wondered what the gods did, or if they even existed. Maybe the humans prayed to the wrong gods, and everything was terrible because they were angry. Maybe the gods were just stories past down for centuries. Had anyone ever met a god? Or spoked to one in the flesh?

"Over here." Akio yelled.

To their left, was a drop not to steep. They rushed her to see what Akio had seen, and extinguished their torches less they be spotted.

"Over there," Akio pointed, his sword clanging against his armor as he lowered himself onto the ground. "Past the statue."

Kathrine squinted in the darkness. Through the cover of night, hundreds of houses and buildings stood silently, as if waiting for inhabitants. The house they had seen so far were all uninhabited, and they looked like they had been empty for months. In the middle of the dead houses was a statue that was half destroyed. The figure of a human was simple to make out, but it lacked a face or arms, all of which had fallen off due to months of neglect. Spouts jutted from its fingers and a small point in the middle of its flat white face, but no water came out, leaving the fountain beneath it dry as dust.

Far beyond the destroyed fountain, a light blazed. The flickering light of a torch, or multiple shone in the distance, illuminating nothing more than more dead houses.

"Shh, do you hear that?" Kathrine asked the group.

Kathrine listened to the noise. It was a collective shout, like lost souls screaming from the pits of damnation, or.... Gods forbid...

"A party?" Hexus Asked.

Kathrine dreaded the word. She had been to parties, and she had not enjoyed them. Parties meant whine, or ale or beer. Neither one affected people in good ways, and no drunk person was fun to be around.

Kathrine sighed. "Is that where we need to go? Is that where Silenus is?"

Raia knit an eyebrow, "doesn't Adam's note say something about a party?"

Kathrine remembered the message that the priestess had wrote.

Past the golden apples.
Past the festivities.
Past the impenetrable defender.
Past a fine feast.
Past the city from which you came.
Past the walls that forbid exit.

The lion that the other team was confronting was the impenetrable defender, Kathrine knew, and the other obstacles had already been past. "The festivities" was the only one left before the garden of golden apples Adam had mentioned. This had to be where Silenus was.

"Good. We could get a drink before we find him." Said Chase.

Kathrine rolled her eyes.

Akio stood up and unsheathed a knife from his side. He put a finger to his lip and signaled for them to follow. Chase pulled a knife, Hexus' and Raia's hands flared with fire and magic respectively and Kathrine nocked and arrow in her bow.

Akio led the way, sliding down the hill, creating a cloud of dust in his wake. The rest followed.

The dusty ground crunched beneath their steps, and created clouds of dust reaching their knees. As they drew closer to the party, the sounds of sloshing liquid and laughing filled the air.

Chase sniffed, "it smells like honeywine and roses." He said, curiously. Kathrine sometimes forgot that a satyrs senses were far superior to those of humans.

"Odd combination," Kathrine whispered. "Can you hear anything specifically?" She asked Chase.

He closed his eyes, focusing. "No." He said, frustrated. "Just laughs and people singing in Senewa."

"Definitely satyrs then." Akio said, holding the blade up to his eyes as if to guard his face.

They crept around corners, staying pinned to walls so as to not get spotted. The cheers and laughter and music grew closer with every step, and Kathrine felt her finger clinging onto her bowstring tighter with each passing second.

Akio stuck to the outside wall of a brick house, with a sidewalk parallel to their front, a street perpendicular to them on the left and the party behind them, past the corner.

Akio peeked around the edge of the house, and his black hair turned gold in the revealing light.

"Guards," he whispered.

"How many?" Asked Kathrine.

"Only two. With Spears." Akio said, clutching his knife tighter. "There are people all around them thought,"

"People?"

"Satyrs... and women with pointed ears..."

"Nymphs..." Chase said.

"Should we go?" Hexus Asked, holding a flame.

"They might know where to find Silenus." Raia argued.

"Doubt it..." Akio said, turning around the corner once more, "they're all drunk off their ass."

Chase scoffed, "I'm one of them. I'll go. I'll find Silenus, and the information we need, and then we leave."

"It's not safe," Kathrine said. "I'm coming with you."

He rolled his eyes, "for what? It's perfectly fine."

He was probably right, but Kathrine had a knot in her stomach, like she knew something was going to go wrong. Situations like these rarely went well for them, she had realized. She gripped his arm tightly and he looked at her.

"Fine. Come on then."

Everyone took a deep breath. Kathrine looked around her. Raia looked at her dismissively.

Kathrine scowled. She saw no reason for Raia's hatred for her. She did not even know if it was hatred Raia felt, but she knew that Raia wanted Adam and Kathrine couldn't let that happen.

They stood up straight and turned the corner.

Chase greeted the guards in Senewa with a wave of his hands.

They looked in their direction.

The light of the party was nearly blinding after Kathrine eyes had adjusted to the darkness of the city. Torch posts were set up all around the front of a large stone building with some lighting braziers. Tables were scattered throughout the front, all of them occupied by fat satyrs, skinny satyrs, old satyrs and young satyrs. All of them were drunk and most had a nymph on their lap, laughing as they told their jokes.

The guards at the front looked identical. They were tall, dark haired satyrs with skin as black as night. Their eyes were gold and their horns curled above their heads. They wore rings on their ears and golden jewelry all over their well-built arms and their necks. Each held long spears with shafts made of wood, and their dark leg fur swayed with the flickering flames.

The one of the right remained straight faced as Chase and Kathrine approached. The one on the left thrust his spear forward and yelled something in Senewa. Kathrine could not understand.

"Put down your damn bow!" Chase translated, holding out both hands in pleading.

Kathrine put her nocked arrow back in her quiver and lowered her bow. The satyr straightened again.

Chase regained his footing. He greeted the satyrs in Senewa once more, before proceeding to ask where they could find Silenus.

The two guards looked at each other, pleasantly surprised, Kathrine read. One of them said something in Senewa, and the other laughed.

The one on the right reached over his waist, and Kathrine found herself reaching for an arrow in her quiver.

The satyr on the left grunted, and her hand froze. The satyr to the left retrieved the wineskin strapped to his shoulder, and dangling over his waist. He uncapped it and pushed it forward, demanding for a drink. The contends inside sloshed around.

"What the hell is this?" Kathrine said.

The satyr with the wineskin said in Senewa, "drink to enter."

Kathrine rolled her eyes. She plunged a hand into her quiver and nocked it quicker than the guards could react.

The second guard raised his spear frantically, nearly knocking over a brazier and launching embers everywhere. The light got the attention of the other satyrs and nymphs.

Kathrine stood still in the doorway, her nocked arrow now aimed st the satyrs forehead.

"Hold! Hold!" Chase yelled. "Nobody needs to die! Kathrine put the damn bow down!" He cried.

Kathrine kept her bow up. She was not about to let some random people poison her friends and her.

Footsteps came from behind her. The rest of the group had exposed themselves, seeing that Kathrine had drawn her weapon, they thought a fight would brake out.

Raia's and Hexus' hands flared with their powers, while Akio had his entire sword unsheathed. The other satyrs and nymphs watched the conflict with excitement.

"Gods..." Chase muttered. He turned to the guards. He said in Senewa, "we only want to find Silenus. Tell us where to find him and we will leave, with no bloodshed."

The first guard thrust the wineskin outwards again. Chase took it. "We drink to enter."

"How do you know it's not poison?" Akio asked, his sword still drawn and pointed at the guards.

"It doesn't smell like poison. Silenus is inside, and we need to enter if we are to make it to the garden soon." Chase raised the wineskin to his mouth. The top half of the tip disappeared behind his lips as he drank it, and reappeared as he handed it to Kathrine.

"Are you sure about this?" She asked him.

Chase wiped his mouth, "just drink it. It taste like honeywine."

Kathrine was not concerned for the taste, it was the effects that worried her. What kind of security would hand out free liquor to people seeking to enter their establishment, unless the liquor was another form of security.

Kathrine downed the drink. Chase lied. Piss was a more accurate description of the taste rather than honeywine. It burned as it travelled down her throat, but she swallowed it regardless.

Akio downed some, then Raia, then Hexus.

The guards stepped aside, taking the wineskin back and dunking into a barrel full of their honeywine to refill it. Bubbles floated to the surface of the barrel as the group entered.

The door was a wooden plank blocking off a massive party. Music blasted form every corner of the house, and hives of dancing people filled the room. The light covered their faces, but the paint covering their bodies glowed in shades of pink, green, blue and orange, among others. Kathrine looked around. Her eyes fired from one corner to another, trying to find where the music was coming from. She hadn't heard any when she was outside, and yet inside, it was as loud as can be, and it came from everywhere.

Her eyes watered. Smoke from pipes filled her eyes with a stinging pain. She felt a hand on her arm. Chase stepped forward.

"We find Silenus and the information we need and we get out." He coughed between words.

"Gladly." Kathrine looked behind her. Akio, Hexus and Raia were all gone. They had been following her only a moment ago!

The room was a maze of people, at least 200 all dancing and drinking. Kathrine couldn't stand up straight. The pink and orange and green an blue figures bumped into her, singing and shouting in excitement. Some people were kissing, although Kathrine would not call it that. They were more intensely rubbing onto each other, with their black hands covering the colored, glowing paint on their bodies one bit at a time.

Chase took her hand, "don't let go!" He shouted over the music. Strings, winds and percussion instruments all rang in her head.

She could see Chase less and less the deeper they walked into the party. Her sight of the things around her blurred, and she saw nothing but a blob holding her hand. The people around her had voices like swords, that cut through her head with piercing pain. She kept her eyes from closing the best she could. The color of their makeup made her head spin.

"Over here," Chase yelled to her. Her eyes opened fully after hearing his voice.

They made it to the other side of the building, opposite from where they came. Another doorway led further into the building, guarded by two more satyrs.

Chase walked over to the first, he whispered something in Senewa in the satyrs ear, and he nodded. He looked the same as the ones outside, with a black complexion and gold eyes and jewelry. His horns curled into rings directly above his head. His Conrad looked the same save for a thick beard growing on his chin.

They pulled back the red curtain leading into the further rooms and a blinding light made Kathrine wince.

The music still played in her head, but it faded as she left the main room. The smaller room behind the curtain was round, with stone columns lined along the wall of hold up the ceiling. She didn't know the shape of the previous one, because she could not see in the dark. The smell of wine wafted in the air, and Kathrine couldn't help but inhale. The other room had stunk of that piss, honeywine. Torches were lit along the columns on the walls, and a pile of fruits and gold as big as Quartus lay in the middle. The floor was marble and the ceiling was quartz.

Nymphs wearing beautiful white dresses and thin gold bands on their heads pranced around. They danced, or sang, or just sat in the corner and looked pretty, drinking wine. In the middle of the room, behind the pile of fruits and treasures was a throne of leather and wool. It resembled a sack really, but the look of the person sitting in it, and the row of guards that flanked it gave it the look of a throne.

Sitting in the sack-throne was the fattest satyr Kathrine had ever seen, and she had seen countless fat satyrs. Like Chubbz, a young satyr back in Alor who was always teased for his weight. He never got insulted, thought, and took his nickname with pride. This satyr was not Chubbz, however. He was fatter. His gut stuck out like a bubble and his curly beard sat atop his bare chest, and swirling up his long ears into a tree of curly auburn hair. He had curved horns above his head and his legs were up in the air, with hooves pointing to Kathrine. His bushy eyebrows shielded soft, lazy purple eyes and his beard swirled around fat lips and under chubby cheeks. In one beefy hand, he held a mug, in the other, a nymph lady, wearing nothing but a see-through silk dress.

His fat wrists and fingers were decorated with dozens of bracelets and rings and his beard hid many of the gold chains hiding under his chins.

A look of curiosity took his face.

Chase began to speak in Senewa, "hello, are you—" he began to say

"Hold ye tongue, I speak the language of men." Said the fat satyr, with one hand in the air.

Chase bit his lip, annoyed. "Right. Listen we need to find a fellow named Silenus, do you where he might be?" Chase said, seemingly losing patience already.

The fat satyr looked at his nymph companion, his arm curled around her, "looks like they want me, sweet!" He said, with an echoing wheeze of a laugh.

Kathrine raised an eyebrow, "your Silenus? You helped the gods?" She asked with a snicker. It felt disrespectful, but she felt as if she were not looking at much, just a fat man with a penchant for drinking and lusting.

Silenus looked at them, insulted. His arm came away from the nymph as it pushed her aside. She contained her laughter.

"What's that of concern to ye?" He said, poison in his voice.

"We need your help." Chase said, trying to calm down another potential fight. Silenus had about a dozen of the gold satyrs at his command, outnumbering them 10 to 1. Should a fight break out, Katherine and Chase would surely lose.

Silenus leaned forward, his hooves finally touched the ground. He took a random mango from the pile of fruits before him and took a wet chomp, drenching his beard and chin in the process. His ears twitched and flicked the air, he was listening.

"We need you to find the garden of the golden apples." Chase said, bluntly.

As Kathrine expected of the oaf before them, Silenus guffawed.

"Ye want me to do what?" He shouted, his mouth full of yellow sludge that was once mango.

Kathrine rolled her eyes, "the garden. We were told you could help us."

"Who exactly told ye that?" He asked, taking a swig from his mug.

Kathrine thought about her answer. They had learned from Adam, who had learned from a dream. But who did the dream come from?

"A... man told us." She regretted saying anything.

Silenus chuckled, "a man?"

"In a dream." Chase said.

The satyr seemed to accept that answer. Silenus sighed, "damn those divine bastards! I lived me life perfectly before those wee shits mucked it all up." He examined his mango with gusto. "Forget ye pointless quest, children." He said flatly, "join us. I know this fella wants to." He snapped his fingers at several nymphs who all circled Chase. They danced around him, sensually, rubbing his chest methodically and staring into his eyes. They giggled as he reddened.

Kathrine kicked one of them, she squealed, and pranced off.

"We don't want to join you party. We need to leave, and find this damned garden. And you are going to help us!" She stabbed a finger at him.

Silenus had a burning hatred in his eyes, "and if I don't?"

Kathrine had no answer to that. She never imagined how difficult it would be to convince this fool of anything, frankly, she never imagined what she might have encountered in the shadow city.

"Fine." Chase said, "can you at least help us find out friends?"

Silenus chuckled, "too late for that, kid. They're off celebrating."

Kathrine knit her brow, "celebrating what?"

"Why, the end of the bloody world of course!" Silenus said, happily and matter-of-factly.

Kathrine winced at that. "What are you talking about?"

Silenus chuckled as if his statement needed no explanation, "What's to explain?" He said. "This world is going no where. The gods have abandoned us, ye both know that. I choose to let me followers drown their sorrows with wine and love. Me children have no need to experience the pain of this world once it comes crumbling down on all of us. Instead, I numb them. I give 'em this sanctuary and allow 'em to forget life's biggest problem."

"And what is that?" Chase asked.

"Death." Said Silenus. "We all have to leave the world at one point. Whether it be today, tomorrow or in 50 years, it comes for us all. Weak, strong, poor, rich, old, young. In here, there is no pain for that, there is only love. And the love amongst my followers is stronger than any."

Kathrine scrunched her nose, "they are your prisoners. They are no followers."

Even as her words left her mouth she could not help feeling as if she were lying. She knew at least part of what he spoke was true. She had never had the gods to thank for anything. She grew up an orphan, with such little opportunities that she looked to stealing for a lifestyle. Yes, Adam's mother had taken her in, but at the cost of her son. Adam's mother was kind to her, but she was not a kind person.

Kathrine's life was full of strife and struggle, and she was a child! And now she found out that there was a world outside the one she knew. She grew up in a terrible city with people who were always mean to each other because the lives they led made them bitter. Satyrs and nymphs were thrown out of regular society, and people stayed homeless, hungry and begging. What gods would allow that to happen?

Kathrine looked up. The nymphs and satyrs I this building and partying like this lived in peace with other people. They were happy, blissfully unaware of any problems that the world might bring, like the end of Said world. Kathrine could see why Silenus wanted people to forget their troubles.

He stroked his beard with sausage-like fingers. "Why say that? Ye chose to follow me. Ye chose to drink the lotus water."

Kathrine remembered the honeywine at the entrance. "That was..."

"Call it...a convincing tool." He said with a wave of his hand. "It can be very difficult to let go of your worldly possessions. But believe me... once you are with us...your worries will be gone.

"Wait I.. I don't understand." Chase said.

"No...there is no need to my child." He snapped at more nymphs, "take 'em."

"What are you doing?" Kathrine asked.

Responding to their captors orders, six nymphs stood up from around the room and closed in around Chase. They slipped a flower in his mouth and he smiled as he unproblematically ate it. Kathrine opened her mouth to speak, but she was silenced by a flower of her own.

The flavor exploded in her mouth, it tasted familiar... like the doughballs back in Alor. It was warm, and smooth, and she loved the taste. She chewed and swallowed and immediately took a deep breath.

"Worry not, child." Silenus chuckled, "for ya finally delivered from the gods cruelty." A wheeze filled her ears as she walked out into the party. The music filled her ears again.

Kathrine began to feel loose, like she no longer had control of her own body. The world slowed to a crawl. Her vision doubled. Her knees buckled. She tried to stay up, but her body betrayed her. She knew there was something in the flower... but she...couldn't...think.... straight anymore...

Chase was gone. She looked up. People were kissing, drinking and loving out it the middle of everything. Her bow was no longer on her back, and her quiver had disappeared. Colors danced in her eyes and lights flashed in her mind. Her head felt light and her sensations of reluctance evaporated, and her limbs took a mind of their own, as Silenus laughed. She accepted the feelings of peace and found herself smiling as the music blasted in her head.

32

AS MORE AND more shouts filled the cave, Adam's fingers grew tighter on his awkward sword. Norris was launched nearly 30 feet, to the wall of the cave, he grunted and his sword changed against the stone. Eric unsheathed his sword and swung in the air, where the lion would have been, but he cut air.

Adam missed Hexus, who could have lit the cave up in seconds. They were all blinded by darkness and the only indication to where the lion was were the terrified shouts of the rest of the group.

"Where are you, you bastard?" Eleon shouted, his hammer and mace smashing into stone.

Zethus swung his spear, grunting and Erika followed the shouts with a torch. Theodore roared in the body of a bear, and Norris was still not heard.

A roar came from 10 feet before Adam, he stumbled back and accidentally stepped on something soft.

Norris grunted, "get off me!" He ordered. Adam jumped, and the lion pounced. Norris' unconscious body disappeared beneath a cloud of black shadow, and he screamed as the lion pressed its claws into his flesh.

Adam raised his sword, ready to bring it down on Norris' attacker. When his blade hit the beast, a hard clang noise rang through the cave. Adam lifted his sword again only to notice it was lighter than before.

He tried to touch the blade, but there was none. His hand passed through air.

He grunted as a kick from the large cat launched him backwards.

"The impenetrable defender!" The name echoed in his head. It's hide can't be pierced! He realized.

Norris drenched the beast in cold water, making it roar in discomfort. He froze the water and slashed at the ice, but it was him who screamed as the beast broke free.

Norris screamed more and Adam saw a ball of orange jump to him. Erika raced to help her friend, throwing her torch forward as the saw the beast.

Finally some light. As the torch touched the lions fur, it exploded into flames. Fire roared all around the beasts body and it crackled as the lion roared. It did not seem hurt, instead, hits mane stayed flaming and its eyes glowed blue like diamonds. Adam finally got a good scale to its size. The lion was massive, bigger than a horse, and twice as bulkier.

Adam reached into his pack, the silver rod was still in there. It glowed brighter than ever, lighting up the entire cavern.

Eleon charged at the beast but to no avail. The feline reared its claws and swiped, launching Eleon backwards into Zethus. Eric dodged. He ran towards the flaming cat, a sword in each hand. He vaulted off Zethus' body and jumped onto the beast, blades drawn. Adam saw the problem immediately.

"Don't!" He yelled to Eric. Eric landed next to the lion, and stabbed at it with both swords. The blades caught fire as they hit the lion's mane and Eric roared. They did nothing on the beast's skin. His swords did nothing. He accepted that and dropped them. They clattered as they hit the stone. The cat swiped, but Eric flipped over the beasts paws and grunted, catching his breath.

"What can kill this thing?" Eleon said, getting up.

Theodore bolted forward, his paws banging against the ground and his roars challenging the lions for dominance.

The black bear charged and rammed into the lion with enough force to knock it over. The mane was extinguished, leaving Adam's rod as the only light source, still, the lion was unhurt.

Theodore stood on his back legs and roared.

The lion charged, tackling the bear with all fours and biting into it with its massive fangs. Theodore growled, taking his claws across the lions golden fur, not leaving any marks, as if they were made of wool. Blood trickled down the bears black fur and the lion threw him to the side.

Adam held his rod, trembling. The lion looked in his direction.

"Adam!" Yelled Erika, "get the lyre! We need to leave."

Adam turned, the pile of treasure was glinting blindingly in the light of his rod.

He rummaged through everything, throwing gold coins to the side, and tossing chalices and pieces of armor to the side. Finally, in the corner of his eye. A silver object sparkled. He looked over, and the lyre shimmered. A pair of stags antlers jutting out of a turtle shell with strings in the middle.

"I found it!" He shouted.

The lion roared, as if he understood the meaning of Adam's statement.

Adam turned, holding up the rod. If it was a sword, he would need to figure out how to make the blade come out in less then 10 seconds.

The lion charged, roaring. Adam slapped and hit the rod, but still nothing happened. He turned his back to the lion, crawling through the gold pile towards the lyre.

He felt the weight of the lion shift the pile as it landed behind him. He screamed, and turned. The rod burned blindingly bright, Adam had to close his eyes. The lion was on top of him.

The roaring abruptly stopped. Adam opened his eyes. The lion still had fury in its eyes. But its body stood frozen, stuck in a pouncing position. It's growl turned into a gurgle in its throat and its blue eyes disappeared behind closed eyelids as it stopped breathing.

Adam felt warm water on his hand. His fingers still cling to the rod, but the rod was no longer a rod. The from point facing the lion, a slim silver blade appeared, thin as paper. The rod had grown a cross guard, in the shape of a gold eagle with its wings spread, its eyes red rubies, and the pommel that had appeared was a silver sphere. Just like the one Adam saw in his dreams. Blood trickled down from the wound the blade had made in the lion and covered Adam's hand in red water.

He stayed panting and breathing shakily as the weight of the lion eventually over came him.

The cat would have nearly crushed him if he hadn't move out of the way. The lion crumpled onto its pile of treasures, staining the coins red.

Zethus and Erika came rushing.

"You alright, Littlewind?" Zethus asked, lifting him.

"I'm fine... I just..."

"Don't know how to react." Zethus finished.

"You were right," Erika stated, admiring Adam's sword, "it was a sword all along." She fingered the blade and eyed it down, examining the craftsmanship."

"What kinda of a sword becomes a stick?" Eleon Asked, holding his shoulders.

"Powerful magic." Eric stated. "Forged with magic."

"That must be why it was able to pierce the hide." Erika said.

Eric took the blade and stroked its blade with a gloved hand. "Adamant." He whispered.

"Adam-What?" Eleon Asked.

"Adamant. People call it Eversteel, or Skystone." Norris said.

"Whatever the name, it's a powerful metal. Forged from gods know what."

"Maybe it was the gods." Zethus said.

"Foolish horseshit." Eleon muttered. Zethus rolled his eyes.

Most scoffed at that, Eric stayed silent, observing the blade. Adam received it when Eric thane it back, but his hands trembled. Adam wasn't going to fully deny Zethus' theory, even the Eagle told him the gods were real, but deep down, he wondered if they were up there, cheering at their successes or laughing at their failures. Faith is an odd thing, he thought. There are people who place their lives solely in the hands of a being they cannot prove nor disprove the existence of, but believe in nonetheless. Adam did not understand it, but he didn't want to garage those who did.

Adam panted the thoughts away. His name trembled, and the splatter of blood dripping from his hand echoed through the cavern as it hit the ground.

Everyone collected their things. Norris flowed the water back into the leather pouch on his hip and the others looted what they could from the treasure pile. Spoils of war.

Adam laughed at that. This lion was a great beast that had terrorized this city and killed countless people, and it had been killed by this team of young runways. This team truly was incredible. Eleon had taken Adam's blade for an idea he had, and stayed in the cave.

"Look at them all." Zethus said. "Innocents. Never given the proper burial rights." He was on the brink of tears. Adam realized this was not the first time Zethus had seen an innocent corpse. He had probably grown up seeing his loved ones die.

"Until now." Norris said. He left to get a spade from camp and returned not too long after. They exited the cave and t was still dark out. Everyone held a body in their hands, except for Eleon, who still held Adam's blade inside for gods know what.

After digging enough graves for the bodies, they gently placed the skeletons in them and buried them with dirt and gold.

"Payment for the ferryman..." Zethus said.

They stood around the graves, silently mourning them. They did not their names, nor the lives they lived, nor their age, or race, or their faces, but none of that mattered. Zethus had said that everyone deserves tears on their graves. They left the cave after that. Adam liked that.

Eleon had left with a cape made of the lions hide. It's head curved over its head as if the lion had eaten him and his head stuck out of its mouth, and its arms had become flat pieces of furs tied around his neck.

They walked through the dead city. Buildings were in ruin and empty. Cobwebs covered everything the spiders could weave them through, and the ground was dust and gravel crunching beneath their feet. Roofs had caved in, and houses had massive holes in the walls. There was no living thing in sight. The city was dark and lifeless. The only source of light was Adam's sword, which had retreated into its rod form. The cross-guard, pommel, and blade all disappeared. He held the rod upright, and it turned the cover of night that sheltered the city bright as day.

He walked alone with Zethus, and the soldiers' tall spear glinted in the light as he used it as a cane. Everyone walked before them, with the two, Adam and Zethus, trailing behind them. It seemed queer for Adam to think of Zethus the way he did.

Zethus was clearly a powerful soldier, one who was skilled in fighting and killing, but the way he acted was far from that.

Norris, though a bit immature and unpredictable, showed that he was a warrior by the way he acted. Eric was obvious. Eric had the mark of a soldier. His face was left a ruin during a past fight, and he had learned of the world's intention to chew up and shit out anybody who crossed its path. Anyone...He was a quiet person, one who had seen the horrors of war, and knows its effects on people. Those years had turned him into a bitter soul, with good reason. He still had love for people, like Norris, who Adam imagined was his best friend...his only friend.

Zethus, however, was a kind person. He was intelligent and gentle when he wanted to be, and he never cursed the gods like the others did. Everyone seemed to have a distant for the gods... except Zethus. Adam felt it queer that this man... this man who was no more than a stranger only two weeks ago, had acted like a friend the entire time.

Adam took a long look at him, he had a facial scar, and his arms were covered in scratches and dirt and redness. His beard, which was once a stubble that darkened his upper lip, chin and neck now began to grow thicker and darker, hiding part of his scar.

It was hard to believe that he had the same terrible nightmares that Adam did. He was plagued with the same problems, but he did not act the same way. Adam always saw him with a smile on his face. In fact, back at the inn, when Hexus had asked him about his life as a soldier, Adam had seen him at his most vulnerable.

"What's on your mind, Littlewind?" Zethus asked.

Adam looked up at him, he was a tall man. "I was just thinking about... the dreams..."

Zethus frowned, he needed no explanation. "I know they are not a pretty sight. And you are but a child... I cannot imagine what it must be like to see those at your age."

Adam did not see himself as a child, he was 16 now, almost a man, although Zethus was in his early 30s. Adam had grown up with the dreams since he was young, the nightmares always kept him up at night, and he dreaded whenever the sun came down. He could not go to his mother, because she was either busy with a client or didn't care.

When she moved in with them, Kathrine stayed with him. She had had bad dreams before, but normal ones, that everyone had. Dreams about falling from a great height or leaving your house naked, not about a bloody war in front of a flaming mountain.

"I'm used to them..." he said, solemnly.

"It's still not right. These dreams mean something... our future, no? You say there will be a battle where we see the mountain."

Adam sighed, "That is what the Eagle told me. Against "The Great Snake". Whatever the hell that is."

"We'll find out." He slapped Adam's shoulder. Adam smiled.

Zethus was a good man. He did not deserve to have seen all things he did. No soldier did, really.

"Do you miss it?" Adam said. Zethus looked at him.

"What?"

"Your life as a soldier... in the Great-West."

No sound but crushed gravel.

"Sometimes. I remember what good memories I had. My family, my friends."

More gravel.

"I think of the things I did, no other men, and I say "no... that is not what this life was meant for"." He sighed, "but I did them. I pray that I forget those things, but I wake up every morning with the memory fresh in my head, as if I had gone to sleep the previous night with their blood still fresh on my hands. I think I am a murderer, but I suppose there is a difference between a murderer and a soldier."

"What is it?"

"Murderers enjoy killing." He said.

Adam patted his armor, trying to make him smile again, "you saved countless men women and children."

Zethus chuckled, but there was no humor or joy in it, "at the expense of how many innocent men women and children. Soldiers are not always men. Kings can get desperate, and little boys can think themselves heroes. You do not think about it when you slash for sword, or throw your spear, or fire your arrow, but when you look down, after you survive the battle.... And you see the people who you killed, it sometimes makes you wish you never won the battle at all."

Adam frowned... he couldn't help but agree with Zethus. He knew war was horrible, but he saw it as necessary... there is a war coming... he knew that. The war against The Great Snake, to prevent the Red Winter, the Eagle said so. Adam knew many people would need to die in order for them to win, but he didn't want to accept it.

He wished for a library. He hadn't read anything since before he had left Alor. He wanted to bury himself in the papers of a book and the soft leather of the covers. He wanted to drown himself in the tales of ages past and read about the adventures of beloved heroes.

He figured he was on one of those journeys right now... chasing a mysterious goal for the hope of all. The Eagle called this Great Snake "the cosmic embodiment of absolute destruction". Adam knew heroes had to kill monsters to achieve their goals. Monsters placed there by the gods. Adam thought...

"Why do you believe in the gods?" He was curious. He had grown up with the faith of the gods crumbling and thinning everyday. No one truly believed in the gods, Adam didn't know what they did believe in.

Zethus chuckled, this time, as if the question amused him. "I believe in them because I chose to. This world could not have possibly been brought to life on its own. If there are no gods to believe in... what is there to believe in?"

Adam paused at that.

"The gods have a plan for us all, regardless of what their names are, or the number of gods, or their domains, they exist. They must." He said.

Adam paused again. If there were gods, did that mean there was an Underworld as well? The thought sent a shiver down his spine.

"Love." Adam said abruptly.

Zethus knit an eyebrow, "What?" He asked, chuckling.

"You could believe in love." Adam said. He felt stupid saying it. Gods and love were two different things. But he felt nothing else to say.

Zethus smiled, "Yes. I suppose you could."

"Here!" Norris yelled, from far ahead.

Adam and Zethus rushed forward. Around a corner and straight ahead, was a light the color of the sun. They heard festive yells and cries of laughter.

"Past the festivities." Adam whispered to himself.

"Silenus must be here..." Norris concluded.

"Ready yourselves." Eric ordered.

The shuffling of leather and the clang of iron was evident. Adam stammered, "no don't." He whispered, worried.

"What?" Eric paused.

Adam took the lyre out of from his satchel to his side. "Perhaps..." he stuttered, "we should enter... one at a time."

"The others were probably in there, how do we know they still are?" Asked Theo.

"How do we know if this is even the right place?" Eleon Said.

"There is no where else to go." Norris said. The light bickering quickly turned into arguing. Adam got their attention by standing up right, his hands still clutching the silver rod. They all looked at him.

Adam took a deep breath, "I'll go alone." He told them. No one seemed to argue with that, and so he turned and continued forward.

The building was made of stone bricks and little more. A red curtain passed for a door and outside it dozens of cheering satyrs and nymphs drank and sang, happily. The entrance was guarded by two dark satyrs in gold jewelry, holding spears. Beneath the curtain, shadows and lights danced around to music that was not playing.

He entered easily enough, showing the guards his lyre and passing through the space made for him, after drinking a cup of honeywine they gave him, but it was the inside that made him uncomfortable.

All around him, with now blaring music, people coated in glowing slimes, drank, sang and loved. The shouts of pleasured women and laughing men filled his ears, while the smells of honeywine and dried weeds filled his nose.

He tried his best to maneuver any way he could through the crowd, but to little avail. Where had the music come from? There was none playing outside, but there was a performance playing inside. And invisible one. No matter where he looked, he could not find the maker of the string sounds, wind sounds and percussion sounds. He shook the queer feeling out of head, but it refused to leave.

Adam felt tears in his eyes and clutched the lyre tighter. He turned, in front of him, a well built man was kissing a nymph while another rubbed him up and down. He found a glass in his mouth at one point, deciding to drink the contents inside. He found a pipe another moment and inhaled deeply. The fumes filled his already cloudy eyes with more water.

"Adam..." said a voice, sensually. Adam looked forward. Raia stood only a few feet before him, her purple eyes glowing in the dark.

"Oh my goodness! Your okay! Good. We need to go." He urged her to come with him.

"Why?" She asked, staring into his eyes. "What's the point anymore? The Great Snake will win in the end, and there is nothing you or I or anyone else can do about it."

Her perfect teeth nearly shined in the lights and her arms made their way to Adam's neck.

"What are you talking about?" Adam was confused. How had Raia given up so easily? Something about the party threw him off.

Her hands moved up and down his cheeks and her eyes never lost sight of his.

"I don't.... don't understand." He said in a small voice.

One of her fingers was placed over his lips.

"Shh." She said. "Let me show you."

She leaned in. Her finger was away from her mouth and her lips got closer. Adam felt her lips lock with his and he shut his eyes, letting go of the lyre.

33

To HELL WITH magic, or wind abilities or skin changing powers, Chase needed none of that to tell that something was wrong.

As the nymphs giggled all around him, rubbing their hands all over him, a feeling of caution took over where pleasure should have been. His palms were wet with sweat and his breaths were short and heavy.

"We are going to make you very...very happy." One nymph Said, looking down at him with seductive eyes.

He wanted to move but they would not allow him, they giggled as he struggled and began to pour honeywine on his chest, laughing.

"What are you doing?" He asked, straining.

"Sweetening things up." One nymph said, with a smile of white teeth.

The voice his head came back. "Leave. Leave." It said. It had only appeared after Silenus sent the nymphs after him... it had only been telling him to leave. At times he would smile and laugh along with the nymphs, only for the feelings of dread and worry to return. If he were Diocles, or Chubbz, he would have liked this, but the feeling of dread and the voice in his head got in the way of pleasure. He had two nymphs on either hand holding them down, two on his hooves and another next to him, rubbing the honeywine all over his torso. His stomach and chest shined wet.

The girls began undressing and Chase almost felt as if he should look away. They crawled on top of him and smiled, laughing as if he had not looked worried.

He shook his head. This was not right. He had to get out of here. He had come here for a reason, and with certain people, but who? He remembered Silenus was important, but his memories were nothing more than faint images thanks to that damned honeywine and flower that the nymphs had fed him. He though long and hard. He remembered a lyre, a small harp of sorts and how they needed to give it to Silenus. But he didn't have it. It was coming! He realized that other people were bringing it.

"Yes, Yes... remember young satyrs." Said the voice in his head.

There was a garden, of golden trees...no, not trees, apples! They need to get there, to the south of Vulna! He remembered the map Adam had showed them. He remembered their destination and their journey. He needed to leave.

"Wait," he told the nymph straddling him, "this is not right."

She bit her lip, "oh you want to take control?"

Chase thought of an idea, "Yes... yes I have." He smiled.

The other nymphs let go of his hands and waited for his orders, smiling and undressing.

"You!" He pointed to one with a head of curly black hair and a bronze complexion, "I want you with her." He pointed to the nymph next to her, who had long blonde hair.

The one straddling him smiled, "what should I do?"

He stroked her face, "go with them." He smiled.

He barely waited for her to get off him before he shot up. The nymphs frowned with disappointment as he left them in the room.

He walked into the common room, the colors of the dancing people flashed in his eyes. He held his head to keep it from falling off his shoulders.

"Get out. Leave. Get out." Said the voice. "Find Silenus and leave." It told him.

Silenus... he needed to find Silenus.

Kathrine had never felt more alive. Dancing around with more people, and listening to the music blaring in her eyes, she had left all of her worries behind. She felt excited and energetic. A rush of positive emotions washed over her. Kathrine felt herself let go of all reality. And she loved it! Her body bounced on its own, and her heart rumbled in her chest. She had smoked, and she drank. At the entrance, the honeywine was nothing more than cold piss, now it tasted like the nectar of the gods. She looked for Adam, wondering if he was here yet. She wanted to be with him. She wanted to hug and kiss him. She wanted to tell him how she felt about him.

She made her way through the party, a huge smile on her face. The waves of people jumping and celebrating grew by the minute. She was in the middle of it all, about to be crushed on all sides by drunken strangers.

Her bow had left her back a while ago, and her quiver had disappeared as well. Her braid had nearly come undone, and she felt hot. The clothes she wore didn't help with the heat. She was sweating all over, and her mouth needed something other than honeywine, anything but honeywine. And yet all she craved was the honeywine. There was no water, or food, just honeywine and more of those edible flowers. She felt tired and yet, energetic, she felt exited and exhausted all at once.

She knew she was doing something wrong, but it was as if she didn't care.

"What's happening to me?" She asked herself, laughing. Her eyes barely opened and her smile never hindered. She didn't care for right or wrong anymore, she had already forgotten how long ago she had entered the party, an hour? Two hours? A day? A week?

She needed to leave, but her body kept her pleased. She was a prisoner in her own body, and she liked it.

She took hold of a random nymph she saw, having the time of her life.

"What day is it?" She yelled over the music.

"What?" Yelled the nymph. Her nose and cheeks and lips and forehead were all covered in glowing paint and judging by her glowing hands, she had placed it on her face herself.

Her lips resembled glowworms dancing together as she spoke! "I do t know what you saying!"

Kathrine laughed, "Your so funny!" She told the nymph. What was she doing? How was this funny? She had no idea what she was doing.

"Oh my gods!" Said the nymph kissing her on the cheek.

"Wait, Wait!" Kathrine asked, laughing, "what's happening to me?" She couldn't help but smile at her own ignorance.

"What do you mean?" Asked the nymph.

"Why do I feel like this. I feel like…" Kathrine tried to form words.

"Like your floating?" Asked the nymph.

"Yes!" Kathrine exclaimed, delighted.

"Yes! That's the magic!" Said the nymph.

Kathrine shook her head, "magic?" She asked.

"Yes!" Replied the nymph. "Silenus puts magic in our wine, it helps us forget!"

Kathrine raised an eyebrow, "Forget what?" She asked.

"I can't remember." The nymph replied. They both shared a laugh. Odd reply, Kathrine thought.

They left each other as quickly as she had complimented her, Kathrine had already forgotten her face.

Chase made his way through the party. He pushed and shoved his way past drunken satyrs and nymphs and ignored the flashing lights.

He needed to find the lyre. He needed to present it to Silenus, and finally leave this place. Finding Hexus, Eli, Raia and Kathrine would present a problem as well, but he was going to take care of that.

Out of the corner of his eye spotted a flash of white. He turned and saw Raia dancing with a young man. The young man had paint on his face and blond hair.

"Raia!" Chase yelled. She didn't answer. "Raia!" He called louder. She paid him no attention, instead she focused on her partner. She leaned in and kissed him lightly on the lips, and then they kissed. They wrapped their arms around each other and held tightly one another.

Chase grunted in frustration. "Raia we need to leave! Why won't you listen to me! RAIA!" He walked to her. People unwillingly bumped into him from all sides, drunken and singing.

He took Raia by the arm, but she did not so much as look at him. She kept her eyes closed and her arms around the shoulders of her boy. Chase pushed him back. He stumbled.

Chase gasped. With a face covered in paint and the smell of honeywine and weeds all over him, Adam resembled s different person.

"What?" Chase yelled confused. "What are you doing here?" He took Adam by the shoulders and shook him violently. He simply laughed.

"Enough of that!" Raia snapped at him, taking Adam back and locking her lips with his again.

Chase suckled in air, then coughed, as it was mostly smoke from the weeds.

"Where is the lyre!" Chase yelled to him. Adam said nothing. "We need to leave!" He yelled. No one reacted.

"Please!" Said the voice in his head. "Please leave!" It was deep and booming, like a man urging him that something bad was going to happen. He took its council. He left Adam and Raia to their... comfort.

He turned, seeing more spinning colors and trying to ignore them. He pushed through more people, trying to find the exit. If Adam was here, that meant the others were as well. It meant that they had found the lyre and were waiting outside, or they were somewhere in the party. He hoped it was the former, but he knew it was most likely the latter. Why would Adam have entered if it wasn't with the lyre.

He needed to find somebody familiar. He need to find the lyre. Racing past people, and doing his best to not give into the weeds and drinks, despite the dozens that were waved before him, he finally found it. Or rather... someone else had.

Across the room, a man with glowing paint all over his body waved his orange colored arm in the air. "I've got a new instrument!" He cried several times. No one heard him, but if they had, no one cared. Chase pushed through the crowd to find the man, but he disappeared behind a wave of bobbing heads of glowing paint. Chase followed.

The people seemed to be getting tighter by the second. He felt sweaty hands slap him on the shoulders and pull him towards more alcohol and weeds, but he resisted. Chase had no idea how... but he resisted. The voice in his head kept calling, this time yelling his name with its commands. "Run. Go. Leave, Chase. Find the lyre and give it to Silenus. He will lead you to the golden garden." It said. Its words echoed in his head, and the world slowed down. He readied himself. His body built up speed, and he lost all patience. He knocked people over, and heard their grunts as they hit the ground. He didn't care. He pushed and shoved and felt heat building up in himself. He was angry now. He was frustrated with the crowdedness of this stupid party and he was angry at Silenus for trying to tempt him with it. He was angry at himself for nearly falling into it. He told himself he would never abide by the rules the people had set upon him in Alor. He was not one of the other satyrs that they hated. He had nearly become one, he was about to prove all of their cruel hides right.

"No." He said. "Not today."

He finally made it to the boy. The orange of his arms had peeled off around the fingers and filled the strings with paint. Chase reached for it. His fingers curled around the lyre and he pulled it away. The boy had a sour reaction to the horrid noise his fingers had made against the lyre strings as chase pulled it away.

"What the hell do you think your doing?" He asked in a fury. Chase glared at him, he had more important things to do. The orange boy ignored his previous anger and went back to drinking and dancing the second Chase turned away.

He made his way across the party, pushing and shoving some more. A boy with dark skin and red eyes raced past him, yelling repeatedly, "I've got hot hands!"

"Hexus." Chase said. He was gone by the time Chase had realized. That was three people he knew, he still needed to find Akio, and if they were in here, Norris, Erika and the others.

He saw the golden guards of Silenus' room from across the room. Their armor glinted and glowed in the dark, and Chase kept his gaze fixed on it.

When he finally made it, the guards tried to stop him, but he raced through the linen curtains.

Silenus still sat on his throne, as two nymphs danced in front of him. He laughed, and Chase took a deep breath.

"Enough of this, Silenus." He bellowed. All head in the room turned to him.

"I see ya are finished with Viola and her friends already." Laughed Silenus. "They must be disappointed."

Chase grunted. He tossed the orange lyre to Silenus. The fat satyr looked at it. For a moment, his face said nothing, then his eyes widened with shock.

"Ye killed it? Ye killed the beast." He said.

Chase nodded, "we've done you well. Now I hope you can return the offer."

He scratched his beard. With a dismissive wave of his hand, his guards and nymphs walked out, the nymphs giggling.

"Take us...to the garden." Chase said.

The room was empty save for them two, and the lyre in between them, slowly rocking back and forth on its turtle shell. Diocles had told him about a legend, a young Hermes, the god of messengers, killed a tortoise and a stag and combined the two to make the first instrument: the lyre. It was a strange instrument, but it made beautiful noises. Chase loved making music, he wished he had a chance to do so back at camp. He brought his flute, pipes and a drum, but he seldom used it.

Silenus considered the idea, as if wondering what would happen if he did lead them there.

"Why d'ya trust the gods, boy?" Silenus Said.

Chase felt as if someone had stabbed him in the stomach. It was the gods! Up until know, gods sending them messages had been nothing but speculation amongst the group, but Adam's most recent dream, added to the knowledge that this satyr presented confirmed the theory. Chase almost laughed. For so long, he had grown up in a city that abandoned the religion of the 12 gods. Now here he was, chasing the gods.

"What have they done fo' ya?? Fo' any of us? They abandoned us. They left a broken world in our hands and expected us to keep it together." He said.

Chase understood now. "The problems aren't because of any god. Blame us. The people down here on this earth, stopped believing in them. I've been locked away for all my life in a world that no longer worshipped ANY god! It was these dreams the gods send us that led me out of there." He remembered their escape from the city. Norris and Hexus had realized Adam from prison and they came to find them. Hexus had used his own made bombs to blow a whole in the Great walls Chase had looked up to for all his life? When he saw the dust clear, and a massive whole in the middle of the wall, he was astonished.

"They are just stone." He realized. They were not magic, or created with some incredible substance. They were just stone. "It was the dreams of the gods that led us to you. It was them who gave friends other than Adam and Kathrine and any other satyr." He thought of Eriks and Norris and Hexus and Zethus. Although they did not like satyrs, and Chase did not like them, Eleon and Eric gave him a place as well. Eric had allowed him in the group, and Eleon had simply not killed him yet.

"These gods gave me better fortune then any human ever has. That's why I trust them." He said.

Silenus sighed, "I understand it must have been difficult for you, being with people who loathed you. I wish I was there when it happened, but you must understand that the path they lead you on is not much better."

He sat forward, and his eyes were small with pity. "Your friends will die, and you will watch them. A war is coming boy, and you must learn to fight it. It was the gods who made war, and hate and death."

"Death existed long before the gods. As did war." Chase said.

Another sigh from the old satyr, "you are a stubborn son of a bitch, boy. Pack your things. We take our leave for the garden."

Chase wanted to jump.. his heart beat in his chest like and echo. He need to find the others, and get them here.

"Lift your magic." Chase told him. Silenus froze.

"What?"

"I want you to lift your magic, and its hold on these people. Free them of your grasp."

Silenus grunted. "I agreed to none of that."

Chase said nothing. He glared at Silenus, and the old satyr sucked his teeth. He formed a triangle with his hands and broke it.

"There." He said, grunting as he finally pushed himself upwards.

The voice in Chases head returned.

"Well done, boy." It said. He smiled.

Katherine still could not find anything. Her senses began to return to her. She could finally think somewhat clearly and the music began to fade. Her vision came back to her as two images became one again. Kathrine stood upright. The people around her stirred. Groans and moans filled the common room and she realized where she was. She hadn't found anyone, but it was easier now. Torches began to get lit around the common room, and light was finally granted. The party was filled with nearly 200 people. They crowded the whole building, laying on couches sleeping on the floor or simply standing up. She looked around. Her head throbbed and it screamed in pain at the most minuscule of sounds.

From across the room she spotted him. Adam stood, frozen, facing away from her. Her heart pounded in her chest and she sighed in relief.

"Adam!" She called. "Adam!" More people around her began to stir, realizing where they were and what they were doing here. Kathrine got closer to Adam.

Her heart sank as a pair of dark, hazelnut colored hands rubbed Adam's neck and hair, covered in jewelry and tipped with beautiful purple nails. From in front of Adam, a white silk gown glowed in the torchlight. Kathrine made her way around them, and saw the rest of the silk dress, more hazelnut skin, more jewelry and ice white hair.

"R...Raia." The name tasted of poison.

Her purple eyes flicked open. Her eyelashes fluttered Adam's face as they continued to kiss. She pulled away, giggling.

"Oh I'm sorry." She said, evidently not sorry, "I didn't realize you were here." The bitch! She was going to do it regardless of her presence. Kathrine witnessing this was just a treat for Kathrine.

Adam's eyes opened, but his hands stayed wrapped around Raia's waist. When his blue eyes met with Kathrine's, he stared.

"Kathrine!" He said, startled. His hands vanished from Raia's waist. His face flushed and Kathrine was left with an open jaw. He looked around frantically, "I was just trying to...um" he failed to come up with an answer. Raia traded her bottom lip with her thumb, holding in a smile. Kathrine knew her theories about Raia, and yet she had done nothing, because she knew Adam would never end up falling for her tricks of seduction. Raia visited him when he was injured and was there when they first met the group. Was it that simple to fool a man? Kathrine didn't want to believe Adam would do this to her. Although, how could she have expected less? She was a street rat. She took his place as his mother's favorite child. She always managed to prove Adam weak and incapable of handling his own problems. She had made him feel like less of a man. But had she? Back in Alor, things were never like this. She never had to worry about another girl. In her mind, she always saw them together, growing old watching their children play in a future hopefully better than the present. Evidently...he did not.

Her heart shattered. She felt a heavy feeling in her chest. She shut her eyes, and never opened it. If she opened them, and continued seeing what she saw, that would mean it were real. She want it to be real, she didn't want to believe this. Her feet took her away from it, quicker and quicker. Tears grew in her eyes and anger built up in her chest.

"Kathrine, Wait." Adam said. She didn't want to hear him. She didn't want to look at him. She didn't want to think of him, and yet the sight of Adam and Raia had seared its way into the endless echoing chambers of her dismembered mind.

Silenus was slow. Very slow. He hobbled on, limping. His legs were thin, yet they managed to hold up his fat body.

"Gimme a minute." He said, straining as he leaned forward. Judging from his physique, Chase guessed he hadn't stood up since he had sat down on that sac thrown, and that seemed to be a while ago.

"So..." Silenus began. "You want to die, lad? Is that it? You want to kill ye' self?"

"What are you talking about?" Chase asked.

"Well, I'll take ya to the garden, but don't say I didn't warn ya. Places like these, sacred to the gods... well... let's just say that it don't turn out well for most people who visit em. The gods are cruel beings. They're not like people, they don't feel remorse or mercy. All they're cruel acts are just in their eyes. They burn cities, kill mortals and add a wee plague to torture the world for a few years, and then have mortals pray to them."

Chase stood silently. Kathrine's bow was in his hand and her quiver in the other. Eli's equipment was strapped to his back. Silenus poorer the rest of his flagon in his mouth after throwing away the mug.

"Surely that can't be true. The gods must have some benevolence."

"Benevolence for 'em selves maybe, but for humanity? No a smidge."

Chase convinced himself it was a lie. The gods had to have some care for their creations. The way things were now Chase could find it easy to believe, yet a sliver of his soul knew that everything he had done so far, everything Kathrine and Adam have done, and everything that had happened to the world, it was for a reason...

"Well then." Silenus Said, picking up the lyre. "I suppose it's time we march to our graves, but don't be angry when I yell "I told you so" to ye grave, eh?" He said, swaying and hiccupping.

Chase rolled his eyes, "You alright?"

Silenus burped, "I may be a wee bit fluthered. But no matter. I still know the way."

They found the others outside, among the scattering members of the party. They looked around, confused. Some cried, others were throwing up on the ground. Hexus was one of them, vomiting as Zethus patted his back.

"Right then." Silenus Said, putting his beefy arms on his large waist, "off we go."

34

Now HE WAS angry. Adam had tried to talk to Kathrine for days. She wouldn't dare even look at him. They had passed a city called Birchfeild about three days ago. Two days after they got Silenus to show them the way. Adam had seen nothing but fields, prairies, mountains, rivers and lakes ever since. And now... on the horizon, were... more mountains. He checked the map he got in Oakshire. The Golden Kingdom was a large place, around 600 miles from east to west and almost double from north to south. The capital was not far from where they currently were, about a two days walk from their current position, but they weren't headed to the capital. Athenia was a lovely place, Norris had said so, but it was a distraction at the same time. The garden was north from a city to the south called Agradon. They would surely reach it by tomorrow, granted there be no distractions.

"Fat chance of that" Adam thought to himself. His horse snorted a reply Adam did not understand. He rubbed its mane. His legs and butt felt sore from riding so much, but they were so close. He was not going to complain now. They had fought off some bandits yesterday. Chase had received a new sword and Adam had gotten a new scar. Across his chest, where one of the bandits had slashed their scimitar. It stretched from his left shoulder down to the top of his belly button. It had not yet fully healed since the incident, but most of it had faded into a light scar.

Adam loved his healing abilities. Chase or Asius never healed that quickly, if they got hurt at all. And Kathrine... he had not seen.

She had not come to him when he mounted Quartus in the medical tent on the mammoth's back. He had drank more of the Mammoth's milk and gagged his mind out. Still, Kathrine did not care. When he lay on the field, hi blood trickling down onto the brown grass, coloring it red, she did not face him. And when he had requested her presence by asking Hexus to find her, she had left the poor boy empty handed.

He had not meant for Kathrine to see him and Raia. He had not meant for Raia to find him, and he surely did not mean to kiss her. His brain was in another realm, the weeds and the liquor had made sure of it, but the spell that Silenus had casted on the honeywine at the entrance had truly been the cause of his drunkenness.

He had recovered from that, and later talked to her about it. She seemed to have understood, and even said she apologized to Kathrine, but Adam had no way of confirming that, since she always turned him away. Considering Kathrine had not liked Raia long before she kissed Adam, Adam concluded that Raia was lying.

He looked down at the scars on his feet that the Gorgons had left when they attacked him. Kathrine had cared then, she had enjoyed him in Alor. She had loved him and he had loved her, but neither of them knew of the others feelings. Now, after that all of that had gone to shit, he realized how she felt about him.

The clopping of horse hooves on the brown grass and the stomping of Quartus's feet made crunching noises in the dry grass.

Adam rode his brown mare next to Asius on Quartus, and on his right side was Theodore, riding on Pormant, and playing with the weasel and red panda that scurried alongside the donkey's hooves.

Chase rode next to Eric, who rode an ice white stallion, nearly 7 feet tall, with Silenus on its back.

"Oh if I could ever find a woman better than you, oh oh ohhh!" Sang Silenus, with his hands bounded. They would have gagged him, but then he wouldn't be able to show the way to the garden.

Erika laughed and Hexus tried to sing along.

"Silence the goat before I kill him." Eleon growled. Adam scowled at him. His face was wet with sweat that had kept fallen from his forehead ever since he got the lion-skin cloak. Adam envied it at night, as it most leaky kept Eleon warm during the cold, but it seemed to be a burden during the hot days. Adam found himself sweating in nothing but his tunic and breeches, both of which constantly stuck to his wet body.

Silenus kept on singing, "I wouldn't know what to dooo!" Or at least tried to. His bounded wrists were loose enough to pluck the strings on the lyre, which were sounds much lovelier than his voice.

"I'll strangle the bastard! I swear." Eleon Said through his teeth.

"If you kill him, he can't take us to the garden." Zethus said, which went without saying.

Eleon snorted. He rode his tall dark brown stallion, who's coat shimmered in the light of the burning sun. Its mane was a well trimmed row of black running down its back and its black tail flew like a whip behind it. Eleon had cut a whole on the lions's back, making room for his mace and hammer. "There is no damn garden." He mumbled.

"What?" Erika asked,

"There is no damned garden, for shit's sake!" He yelled.

Everyone froze on their horses. Hexus's pony stopped from its trot to a walk. The jingle of reins echoed around the party.

"Always the angry one." Zethus muttered.

"Don't you say that you son of a bitch. You exactly what I do. These dreams are a curse no more than that. They have no meaning, or deeper purpose, they have nothing!"

"You don't know that." said Norris.

"I know the gods have nothing to do with it."

"I thought you didn't believe in the gods." Chase snickered.

Eleon growled, "ill strangle you, you shit. Don't think your any better than us just 'cause you got this sack of shit out his den." He pointed his chin at Silenus.

"I do not think I'm better then all of you, just you, Eleon."

Norris and Hexus laughed. Eleon flared, "You think your funny?"

"Certainly. Why else would they all be laughing?" Chase replied, resting his head on the hand of his new sword.

Zethus dismounted his stallion. The horse snorted.

"Get off your horse, goat. Let's see if you can prove that."

Chase scoffed, "you don't scare me."

"Get. Off. Your. Horse." Eleon snarled through gritted teeth.

"Eleon, enough with this shit!" Yelled Erika, "get back on your horse."

"No one was talking to you, little sister. Know your place." He pointed his mace at her. She raised an eyebrow. "You should know yours." She said, bitterly.

"I'm tired of this son of a bitch! Always with something to say." Eleon said, pointing his chin at Chase. "I want to see if he is good with his swords as he is with his words."

All the horses stopped. Eli chuckled, Theo gasped, Asius had a worried look on his face and Eric said nothing.

"My lords," Said Asius, "Perhaps combat is not a reasonable—"

"Shut your damn mouth, servant. 'Fore I shove my foot down your throat." Eleon told Asius. Asius shrunk into Quartus' fur.

"Eleon enough." Zethus said, dismounting his horse. "Why do you feel the need to torment the poor fellow?"

"Now you want to ride his dick. Is that it? He's a damn animal, Zethus. Why do you take his side?"

"I'm not on his si—"

"Don't lie to me you, you fool. You take me for an idiot?" Eleon Said.

"Are you drunk?" Zethus asked.

Eleon snickered, "No I'm not bloody drunk, you bitch. I'm just tired. Tired of him." He pointed to Chase again.

"GET OFF THAT DAMN HORSE BEFORE I THROW YOU OFF!" He yelled.

Zethus held him back. Chase ignored him. Adam felt his hand drawing closer and closer to the rod on his side. He had been practicing how to release and retract the blade, and he could almost do it at will now. He had been practicing how to use the blade as well, and he was ready to defend Chase at any moment, but he knew he was not match for Eleon.

Adam squinted his eyes, was he hallucinating? From the top of Eleons shoulders, steam flowed in the air. It swayed from left to right with a red color. More red steam sizzled from his feet, then his arms, then his head.

Zethus yelled as he jumped backwards, startled. He looked down at his steaming hands, red with blood. Eleons armor was burning up.

"The hell?" He looked at Eleon. Red flashing lightning crackled around Eleons feet like angry spider legs. His eye flashed red and his teeth were borne.

"So that's what you do?" Adam wanted to say. He had seen Hexus' control over flames, and Norris' control over water, and he had seen Theodore change his shape and Raia use magic. Zethus had immense strength and Eric had better fighting skills than any regular man. Even Adam had some sort of control over wind or something along those lines. He had not been able to summon his powers since his fight with Zethus. Adam figured Eleon could heat up his body and summon red lightning just as the rest were able to do what they were capable of.

More red steam flew off Eleon. His eyes flashed with red lightning. The red crackles crawled up his arms like glowing legs and lit his weapons up with red flashes.

Eleon yelled a wild war cry, wordless and loud. It echoed through the valley. The earth rumbled and everything seemed to have exploded. A flash of red and white propelled Adam off his horse. The animals cried and everyone yelled as they flew backwards in the explosion. Horses whinnied, and Beta the dog barked wildly. Rocks skipped along the dirt and patches of steaming grass flew high into the air. He heard the boom in his ear, but it fell to the sound of ringing in his head. He felt solid ground once more.

Adam opened his eyes, and he wished he had kept them closed. Thirty feet in front of him, surrounded by a mess of upside-down horses and thrown supplies, was Eleon, standing over Chase. His red mace was held above over his head, and he brought it down hard. Chase was horrified and Adam yelled. The ringing stopped.

Zethus came out of nowhere. He grabbed Eleons mace before the spikes touched Chase. Red flashes blinded him. Grunts and yells filled his ears. He managed to push himself upwards. His rod had already become a sword. Adam charged forward.

He made it about twenty feet away from a wrestling Zethus and Eleon before a pain hit him in his ribs. He flew sideways, and his sword clanged on the rocks.

"Don't." Said Eric, standing above him. His woolen mask was covering his nose and mouth. Adam never noticed how dusty and clouded it had become, like a building had collapsed on them. He looked at his cut hands, white and caked with dust with rivers of bright red blood zigzagging across his palms.

Adam felt a hand take his collar and pull him to his feet. He coughed.

"Don't try to stop it." Eric said. "They will stop it themselves."

The cloud of dust made his eyes water. Adam wiped the stinging tears from his eyes.

Zethus threw a jab at Eleon with his golden spear, and Eleon blocked it with his mace, while swinging another attack with his hammer. His hammer clanged against Zethus' shield. They both bled from their mouths and cuts all over their bodies. They fought like warriors. Skilled warriors. No strike was unnecessary, and their movements were smooth and natural. They were as swift as serpents, and as quick as cats. The sound of metal striking metal echoed, accompanied by wild yelling and hardened grunting.

"Enough of this!" Erika's voice cried. "You'll kill everyone."

That seemed to be a distraction enough. Eleon looked behind him, which gave Zethus the perfect opening. He brought his leg up and pushed it towards Eleon. Eleon coughed as Zethus' leg kicked him back, catching him off guard. He crashed through the field of dead grass around him, his lightning crackling and his voice shouting, as he fell back nearly thirty feet. Zethus rushed forward. He placed a foot on Eleons breastplate and held a spear to his throat.

"Enough." Zethus said, panting.

From around the battle, the heads of more people poked out. They surrounded the two warriors and sounds of disapproval left their mouths.

Eleon lay smoking in a field, his weapons fallen at his sides, and the entire team holding weapons to his face. The look he gave nearly made Adam smile.

"Two horses." Akio said, "two horses were killed." He patted a crying Hexus on the back. The poor boy felt sorry for the animals. Zethus finished tying the restraints of Eleons wrists. He sat angrily, in the dirt. His clothes were stained with mud and grass and his face was caked with white dust.

Zethus looked down at his work. Eleon scowled at the ground, not looking at him. Zethus stared regretfully at Eleon.

"You know wasn't my choice—"

"Piss off." Eleon spat. His beard dripped with fresh blood.

Chase leaned on a tree, "I never liked him." He said, clutching his sore arm.

"Me neither." Adam said, his arms crossed.

They both had small scratches and wounds on their faces and bodies. The explosion had sent them both flying and had made a mess of their formation. Norris and Erika were still out looking for all the supplies, which had flown farther than anything. Akio tended to everyone's wounds and put the two horses out of their misery. They had broken their legs, and the bone stuck out of the ankles. They whinnied in agonizing pain, until Akio had stuck a short knife if their hearts, and the animals could finally rest.

Adam felt his sore elbow up and down. He had hit it against the ground in the blast. He watched Eleon. The tall man sat, his knees close to his chest, looking down and breathing heavily. His hands were bound behind his back and his eye was closed.

"The big man looks angry." Boo said behind him. Adam looked back. The cyclops had grown inseparable from Minerva who constantly sat atop his shoulders. The beasts big blue eye never left sight of her. He was with her at all times and called her the "forest mother" whatever that meant. He guarded her from harm and became a monster if any one tried to hurt her. He was her guardian.

Adam saw the relationship as odd. Suddenly, Minerva gets captured by a group of Cyclopes and then befriends one. Adam realized he had never heard her voice. Maybe she just didn't like to speak, or didn't like to speak to him.

The valley turned pink in the light of the dusk sun. The sky was an orange color, with a pink sky become more and more vibrant the further it was from the sun.

Norris and Erika had returned with most of the missing supplies, which unfortunately did not include Adam's bag. He had lost in in the battle. His rod was still strapped to his belt, but his clothes and the paper that the priestess had given him were gone. The thought made him frown. The camp had been set up around a blazing fire. A ring of stones gave it a barrier and lit the entire place. The tents had been made and the defenses had been drawn. They sat around the fire, like they always did. Adam looked around him. The people smiled and laughed and for a long while, it felt as if all was good. Adam wondered how people like this could stay together. They all came from different parts of the world, and not one of them was the same.

Erika was the daughter of a noblemen whereas Adam had grown up poor. He never got an education, and it was Diocles the satyr who had taught him and Chase how to read and write. Erika had tutors in her large home who taught her how to cook and dance, while others taught her how to fight and survive.

She was rich. He was poor. Yet now, sitting here and surrounded by the same smiling people, Adam realized they were nothing more than equal. "The dreams," he thought. "It's the dreams that keep them together."

The belief in the meaning of the dreams kept them close to one another. They ate together, and sang together and laughed and joked together.

Eleon lay with his hands bonded, next to Quartus, far from the group. He didn't say anything, and sat facing away from them.

Beta and Tenzir growled at him. Although the blast caused by Eleon had killed two horses and sent all of their supplies flying away, most of he other animals seemed unhurt. Beta and Tenzir had no wounds and the birds flew gleefully in the air. Eos, Eleons owl, sat perched atop his shoulder, his body facing away from them, but his head never turning away from them for an instant. It's yellow eyes glowed in the dark that shrouded the rest of his body. And it's talons made sharp, clinking noises against the metal of Eleons armor.

Adam stood. Chase looked up at him, "where the hell are you going?" Adam didn't answer. He walked closer and closer to Eleon. Eos screeched and Adam nearly fell back. Beta barked and Eli came to his side.

"Let him be." Akio said.

Adam regained his balance. He continued further, and with each step he took, Eos' feathers ruffled like a blooming flower. Adam raised his hands in defense. The owl sent out another ear-piercing shriek.

"If you come any closer, he'll rip your eyes out." Eleon murmured, still dressed in shadow and facing away from him.

Adam believed him. "I was wondering if you...wanted food."

For a time, Eleon said nothing, and Eos stood on his shoulders frozen. The owl resembled a statue of feathers, as if it were dead. Finally, Eleon chuckled, "am I your prisoner now? Is that it." He laughed humorlessly.

"You placed yourself in your own chains." Why did Adam feel the need to speak?

"Tell your goat friend to know his place." Eleon grunted.

Adam flared his nostrils, "if it wasn't for him, we would still be in the shadow city. You ought to show him a little respect."

Eleon scoffed at the sentence. He was an arrogant shit, wasn't he?

Adam stared at him. Shadow covered all around him like a pool of darkness. He sat there in the middle, pathetic, alone and beaten. Adam saw no point in showing him any more time. He turned, leaving him to his punishment.

The voice had left. Chase hadn't heard it since they left the shadow city. He remembered the way it commanded him. It was so sure of its orders, so hopeful for their escape. "Why me?" He asked himself, "why was everyone else affected. Why was I the only one able to resist."

The answer eluded him. He figured this must be how Adam felt. How all of these people felt. They all suffered with these dreams for so long and always wondered what they meant, some living their lives without an answer.

"Until today." He said to himself. Less than a two-day ride south of here, was the golden garden. What is that voice was the same as the dreams, or at least from the same source? He would soon find out at the garden. He knew that much.

He had been seeing maps all day. It seemed as if every time he blinked another land mass had appeared on the map. He had begun to keep track of where they had been and predicting where they might be in time.

The oil lamp flickered dimly, brightly coloring the map. Hills of green, mountains of stone lay spread over hundreds of miles. He counted the seas, and the mountains ranges, and even the islands in the Shattered lands to the east, of which there were thousands.

Chase traced his finger across the hundreds of names of cities and countries and continents.

"A..ash...Ashbagbah." He said slowly. The light of the burning candle made the letters dance and shift in light and dark. Chase could read, but these words avoided his eyes this time. It took him a moment to pronounce a name, and even then, he was not certain if he had pronounced them all correctly.

"O...okoo...Okoona." He slowly stammered.

He looked to the north east, past the Lun-Din dynasty, Ashbagbah and west of the Lands of the Mountain Men. A mountainous, green filled place lay there, above a city called Canatorë and a river called Thermivor.

"Ron...Ron" he could not manage in the flickering light.

"Rondoran." Said a voice behind him.

He looked up. His tent was still empty. Chase turned to see the entrance. Zethus stood, a knife in one hand and a small wooden figure in the other. His feet were bare, and his arms were scarred and scratched. Behind him, his hunting dog barked with glee, as she feasted on a fresh kill: a squirrel. Beta gobbled it down and wagged her tail in the air.

Chase frowned! "Oh, I didn't realize..."

"It's fine. Really." Zethus laughed. "Silenus stopped singing not to long ago, so your voice was all I heard."

Chase had forgotten about Silenus. "Right. Sorry I'll keep things down." Chase said. For such a large man, Zethus was a kind fellow with a heart of gold. Put off the people chase had spoken. Two at this camp, sethus was the most likable. Chase did not mind the soldier's company, but it did strike him as queer.

"What are you..."

"I want to apologize." He said, putting his wooden figure-hand on his chest. He wore a large woolen tunic with long woolen breaches and a linen vest over his shoulders.

"For what, you've done nothing wrong." Chase felt out the need to explain his saving from Eleon. Zethus did not need reminding of another fight.

"I'm here to apologize for Eleon." He said. Chase let go of his previous thoughts. Odd that one man would have to apologize for another's mistakes. Chase did not stop him.

"He can be thickheaded sometimes."

Sometimes? Chase wanted to ask sarcastically. He simply nodded silently.

He stared at the ground, where blades of grass danced in the wind around his hooves. He looked forward, still at the ground, where blades of grass danced around Zethus' feet. Chase pursed his lips.

Was his appearance really cause for so much trouble? He didn't want to think so, but he had seen the others like him in the shadow city party. He didn't want to become like them. Those were the ones who fit the stereotype. They were drunkards, and thieves and cheats. He wasn't like them. Right?

"People believe what they want." Zethus said, "whether or not what they believe in is right."

"Beliefs are always right in the people who believe them." Chase said. He appreciated Zethus' efforts. "The cruel do not see themselves as cruel and the kind never see themselves as kind."

At that, Zethus let his arms drop. His eyes met the ground.

"I've met satyrs." He said, still looking down. Chase looked up. His black, scruffy beard had almost completely grown back now, and it lay like a shadow over his neck.

"All the ones I've met were drunkards, and thieves." He looked up and smiled, "but I have not met all satyrs."

Chase laughed. Truly, Zethus was Eleon's opposite. He was kind and caring and gentle. Eleon was rude, and angry and rough.

"Your horse was one of the two killed, no?" Zethus asked. Chase felt a queer feeling in his stomach, as if he had been punched. He nodded solemnly. Nature spirits had a unique connection to all living things, and animals were stronger than others. It hurt them to see animals die, literally as it did emotionally.

Chase had felt his connection with animals as soon as he saw Erika in the woods with her owl, Ios. Some of the animals that these people had, Tenzir, Beta, Spew, they had an energy not like the others. Rubius, and Quartus and Pormant and Bugbush had a connection to Chase, but not so much as the others. Some of the animals were more than just animals.

"You'll take mine tomorrow." Zethus said. "It's the big brown one, with the long black mane." He said.

Chase laughed, "thank you."

Zethus smiled approvingly. He raised his pointer finger, "one day." He said. "We can all go to Rondaran. After all of this is over, I'll take us." He smiled and stretched his hands.

Chase raised his eyebrows, "then let the gods be finished with it." Chase said. Zethus chuckled at that.

"You're a good lad, Chase." He smiled and walked off, Beta trailing his heels, taking her mysterious energy with her.

Chase turned and walked back into his tent.

Chase curled his lip. "Good lad." Zethus had called him. He remembered Diocles calling him the same thing. Chase wondered where he was now. Adam had said that the army of the dead had destroyed Alor, but he had also said he had no memory of seeing the nature spirits with the new forces. He had seen his mother, and the baker that had chased them weeks ago, but no satyr and no nymph. Perhaps that meant there was hope, hope that his family were not all gone.

"You have a new family now." He thought. These people were his family. Many of them might have been strangers, but after the battle of the Cyclopes cave and the fight with Zethus and Eleon, Chase trusted all of them, except of course Eleon.

The leader, Eric, was also nothing more than a name. Chase rarely saw him after they set up camp. Eric never ate with them or sang or told jokes. Chase had seen his face before though. His strong jaw and thin, long, ruined nose. His small lips and his cold, dead eyes that had seen things unimaginable to those who have not. He figured a man with memories like his seldom told jokes. And to think! Erika had said he was the best musician out of them all. Odd.

Chase dragged his finger across his map. His eyes flew from the mountains in Sentros to rivers in Kayembe and islands near Okoona and the snowy tundra of Farnörr and the cities that covered them all.

"One day." He heard his voice say, "one day, I'll see them all."

35

"ABOUT A THREE days ride." Creaked Xuthos.

Korax smiled below his helm. They were close, oh so very close. His advisor stood ready for commands and attentive. Korax liked that.

"Good." He said. His deep voice echoed in his helm. His hands clutched the hilt of his sword hard.

"How many soldiers are there." Korax asked.

"Soldiers"? False names for these hideous creatures.

"Nearly six thousand, sire." Xuthos Said.

"What is your command, my lord?" Asked Pontarius. His assistant, Kobos, chittered next to him.

Korax stared at the map before him. The golden kingdom was not a large place, the smallest of the three kingdoms of the south, but the continent of Vulna was. They could pass the golden mountains to the west, and thought unlikely, sailing west across the shimmering sea was not impossible. They could make to Kayembe in less than a week. Argana was nearer still.

"No," he thought, "sailing would need a boat, and where could they get a boat?" He was frustrated. More than frustrated, he was angry. These rebels were nothing more than a group of damned children!

"Children." He repeated aloud. The Great Snake had naked them the "false warriors."

"Sire?" Xuthos said, firmly, "we have reason to believe their leader may be older."

Korax held the hilt of his great sword even tighter than before. He snarled beneath his helm and heard the concerned whimpering of Kobos. Pontarius sighed and Xuthos straitened himself with a rattle of his armor.

"What bloody difference does it make?" He snarled. "They continue to evade us time and again." He slammed the war table hard, causing the small wooden figures that represented his forces to fall over and off the table. Kobos hurried over to return them to their spots. His armored hand came away from the map. He knew the false warriors were heading south, but now they were playing no more than cat and mouse. Korax's army had begun moving at night, to gain distance on the children, but somehow, they have managed to delay their defeat, time and again. Korax dragged his iron claw across the table, and the wood growled and cracked in response. He needed to get in front of them. Cutting off their route and attacking from behind while the others closed in from in front. They could surround them and kill them all, but they needed a location.

He grunted and felt everyone behind him jump. "Get the priestess."

Pontarius exited. He three open the curtain and let it fall back into place behind him, as he vanished into the darkness. The alchemist had used necromancy on the priestess, and her corpse stood up as they were leaving Alor. The withered old bat had done nothing to deserve it, but she had abilities neither Pontarius nor Kobos had mastered. It was her bloody fault that the children had escaped the city, and by the god, Korax would make her pay for that mistake.

"The troops continue south, my lord." Xuthos said, "Perhaps we should join them."

As their king, Korax led them forward, through forest and lake. He had ridden his chimera at the head of the army with his loyal guards at his side. The Warriors Black. The fifty or so men were Greymen, resurrected by The Great Snake. They wore all black. Cloaks, pants, boots, hoods, scarves all so dark that they vanished into shadow at the slightest disappearance of any light, with the only thing visible through the darkness were their silver masks, staring with eyes like the night sky. They rode on their black stallions and wielded black swords and spoke no words.

"That is an army," Korax thought. "One thousand of these and I could take the world." The thought was pleasuring. They fought like no man and were more loyal than anyone else Korax commanded. He could send a group of no more than ten ahead to cut off the path the children were taking and cut them off while Korax attacked from the rear.

"Call for the warriors, stop the army."

At that moment, Pontarius entered the war tent. His torch cracked as it lit up the dark tent. Xuthos left to tend to his duties.

"She is here, sire." He said, hiding his withered hand behind his back. His white toga was long and woolen, with orange light from the torch w in waves of color across his chest. Next to him, the priestess stood silent. She was a horror to the eyes.

Her eyes were the color of curdled milk, in direct contrast to her charred body, which had left half of her chin no more than black bone and burned skin shutting one eye. A torn purple robe flowed over her hunched back and her grey, bony hands ended in long, white fingernails, longer than her actual fingers. Around her neck was a line of reddened skin that had trails of dried blood snaking from it down her chest, from where her noose had left its mark. Her cheeks were almost as sunken as her eyes and her thin lips were in a permanent frown. She groaned and stretched her hands. Her fingers cracked and popped.

Korax sighed, "bring the bitch here."

Pontarius pushed her forward, she stumbled and looked up to Korax. Korax looked down on her, taking a deep breath.

"I need the elixir." He croaked. She reached into her cloak.

"It.... is.... not.... yet.....ready..." her voice was a slow, burdened wheeze. From her sleeve she pulled a small vile of glowing blue liquid. Korax took it and shook it gently. The liquid sloshed inside, and light blue bubbles rose to the surface.

"How much more time must you have?" He asked the hag, handing the vile back to her.

"No...longer...than...a...day." She said, taking the vile and hiding it in her sleeve once again.

He scoffed, "a day." He repeated, in disbelief. They did not have a day to waste with this. They needed a host, and the only suitable one was with the children. The Great Snake had said it, and they followed his word.

The Great Snake was a divine being, the savior of the world. The King of Crows, the Dragon Prince, Father of all monsters, the Storm King. He had many names, but they were all one entity. He saw a future molded by him and deemed it more worthy to exist than the one that was. He had showed Korax, when Korax had died. It was beautiful, and he saw what stood in the way. He pledged his new life to The Great Snake and had vowed to destroy those who stood in the path of his future. The perfect future molded with the blood and bones of those who refused to believe. Korax would like to see that future.

Korax had lived a feared warrior but had died with no dignity. He was unbeatable in combat, until he was beaten in war. The memories of his old life were comforting and kind while the ones of the underworld were visions of poison and death. He had stared into the voids of hell, and it had stared back at him, forever searing its horrifying image into the confines of his mind.

He turned his head to the hag and his chain mail rattled. "Very well. Conjure away witch." He waved his hand at her dismissively. She turned away from him.

Korax rested his arms on the war table and stared at the figurines that dotted the map of Vulna. These wooden toys no larger than his finger, had defeated him.

The entrance to the war tent flew open. Korax felt the gust and saw it knock over figurines.

He turned, "What is it?"

"A reward my lord." Xuthos said, "for all your divine work in bringing the King of Crows' dreams of a new world a reality. Truly, he had blessed us." He stood proudly, with his iron helm beneath his right arm, its plume still waving from the speed Xuthos had used to arrive at the tent.

Korax tilted his head, "a reward."

Xuthos smiled, revealing two rows of yellow rotting teeth, both of which missed several teeth. He snickered, and handed Korax a small sack, made for traveling.

Korax took it. The leather groaned and cracked as his hand took it, and Korax noticed it's almost charred appearance. He curled his fingers around the mouth and opened it.

"Dirty clothes?" He grumbled. Xuthos would not be one to play games. He was loyal to a fault, but this... was this a trick?

"It belongs to one of the children." Xuthos told him, his voice excited and mouth twitching.

Korax took a deep breath. He turned the bag over and let the contents fall onto the floor. Clothes slapped the ground, before Korax heard the sound of ripping paper. He grimaced at the pile. Xuthos knelt and moved a shirt, revealing a torn piece of parchment.

Xuthos picked it up. It was stained with blood, splashed with water and torn down the middle almost in half. The message was still readable.

Xuthos took it with both hands and with a loud and clear voice said, "Past the golden apples. Past the festivities. Past the impenetrable defender. Past a fine feast. Past the city from which you came. Past the walls that forbid exit." He looked up and stared at his king with confused eyes.

Korax stood silent. Golden apples...

The witch woman stiffened at the reading of the parchment.

Korax glanced at her with intrigue. "How do we know it belongs to the children."

Xuthos smiled, "the clothes that were found with it had cuts."

Korax sighed, "cuts?"

"Cuts that match the slash of the Iron Lion. In the shadow city."

Korax raised his head. His fingers lay on the pommel of his sword, tightly grasping it. They had passed the shadow city not yet a week ago.

Trailing the children was no challenge, the same could not be said for anticipating where they were headed. Until now. He looked at his map. For the past fortnight, they had been trailing south. The first line in the paper told of the golden apples.

"The garden of Hesperides." Pontarius concluded. "It is not shown on any maps."

"What do you know of this, witch?" Korax asked the hag.

She faced the ground, her hood waving over her head. She laced her hideous fingers and groaned.

"I.... had.... a.... vision.......my.... lord." She said in that raspy whisper of a voice. "Their.... mission.... lead.... them......to.....the.....garden."

"Yessss." Korax hissed. "They march for the garden."

He remembered the last time he had been there, denied entrance at the gate and forced to march around to attack the great city of Athenia. Now was not that time, and Korax had no intention of being denied anything.

"Ready a team. We ride in the morrow. We'll cut them off at the entrance."

"What of the guards, my lord?" Xuthos asked.

"What of them? I will be leading the team myself. I will do with them as I please."

Xuthos turned to find the team. Korax smiled.

"Your word will soon be as true and as known as the world itself, my king." He whispered to The Great Snake. His testament will be here soon, his judgment will is near and it will not be merciful. Korax saw it now. These children die, and their plans may finally come to pass.

"Cities will burn! Countries, entire lands will fall! Kings will burn, seated on their false thrones, and those who do not believe will be condemned to an eternity in the deepest pits of hell. Armies and generals will be wiped clean from the face of the earth, and from the very center of its being, the world will burn, and from the ashes, his new world will arise. Beautiful and true. This world will finally know peace." The sun crawled up the eastern horizon, washing the lands in a golden light, and Korax laughed, as the sun rose on the first day of a new world.

36

A RIVER OF sweetness dripped onto his tongue, and his insides danced as the wine trailed through his body. He wished he would be drunk already, that way Silenus' music might have entertained him. Now though, the satyrs' songs did nothing but ring in his annoyed ears and bring more wine to Norris' lips. He shook the skin in his hand, and the faint splashing of less than a sip of wine was heard.

"We're out." He grumbled, taking the last of it and tossing the wine over his shoulder.

"Atsa shame!" Silenus said. The satyr sat behind him, riding the same horse, his hands bounded. His long curly hair tickled Norris' neck and his singing was deafening. Norris tried to focus on something else, anything else. Alas, when he closed his eyes and shut his mind off, he only saw Silenus singing.

"I know how Eleon feels." He thought.

Eleon had been bounded and left inside Quartus. Asius had been reluctant to continue the voyage on Quartus, but Norris had reassured him that everything was alright.

Silenus continued singing. He wanted to gag him, but they needed the satyrs voice for directions. The wind blew north, against them, and the days had grown colder in the past week. The sun shined in the sky, occasionally taking refuge behind a cloud or two. They walked through the morning dew, leaving muddy tracks in the ground with faint squishes behind them. The hooves of Norris' steed had been caked in mud; the red fur painted brown.

It whinnied, and Norris stroked it neck.

"We're almost there." He told the tired horse.

It snorted in acceptance. Norris sat up straight and jabbed an elbow at Silenus, "how far away is the garden?"

The satyr chuckled, "Your eager aren't ya? You don't need to worry; we'll make it there in a couple hours."

That was an answer Norris liked. He smacked his lips, the sweet taste of wine still lingered on his tongue. He wished for more. He hated the taste of water. He had more than enough to drink, but it was the water he used to fight. His saber had shattered in the lion's den, so his leather pouches were all he depended on for weapons.

He couldn't remember where he learned the magic, especially since his old tribe was very opposed to it. They forbade him from using it, and he obliged. Instead, they followed the laws of sword and axe and shield. Magic was work of the gods. And the gods were not welcome with them. He remembered his old life, before the dreams meant something. Before he had known anyone other than Eric and Asius. Norris sometimes wondered if Eric remembered that life, though he figured that there would be much that Eric would want to forget. The Children of The Hydra they called themselves. Norris and Eric's father had always told them that they were 'noble warriors who kneeled to no ruler but the Dragonskin' but Norris knew better. They were barbarians. Savage warriors who knelt to no laws of men either.

The men he had grown up with, the men he had looked up to, they were savages. They killed, pillaged, plundered and raped all they wanted, and slavery was a common practice, used against the children of captured concubines.

Höthör Dragonskin wanted no one taking his throne. His children were all loyal to him, and never dared usurping him. But the children he had bore with his many, many concubines posed him a threat. If they were born disfigured or small, they would be left to the elements. If the mountain lions didn't kill it, the weather would. The infant would freeze in a matter of hours and everyone was powerless to stop it. Those born healthy and strong were made as slaves, like Asius. Eric and Norris had been blinded by Höthörs title as their 'father'. Norris had always known he wasn't his true father. Norris had skin the color of hazelnut and coarse black hair, whereas Höthör was white as snow with fiery orange hair. Eric was not his child either. They were the children of gods know who. Neither of them had parents, and so Höthör had become one.

Fire. He remembered. Fire. Heat. Flames. That night echoed in his mind, playing repeatedly a thousand times a second. He heard the screams of men and women. The wails of horses and mammoths. He saw himself tossing an unconscious Eric over the back of a young mammoth, Quartus. Asius was at the reins. Gods, they were strong then. Strong of mind and of will! Asius was the child of a whore, but he had the determination of a Child of The Hydra. They had left then. They had fled the death. The Night of Fire marked the end of The Children of The Hydra, and all that was left of their legacy was ashes and bones... after that, wine had never tasted so good, and the whimsy of drunkenness was a safe haven. When he was drunk, the shadows of his past could not pass the light of his intoxication. He was free.

Silenus' loud songs had transported him to the present again. The satyr howled with glee as everyone let out a collective sigh. Except Hexus, the young boy clapped his hands to the rhythm.

They had not packed enough wine for this trip.

The valley stretched out before them. The grasslands were a motley of green and orange with splotches of golden and evening red poured over from the sun. It was not yet noon and the chirping of birds filled the air. Petrichor emanating from the drying grass and filled Norris' nostrils. They had stopped to feed the horses less than two hours ago, and now, Norris regretted not eating then. His stomach growled and his mouth was dry and tasted sour.

"What is this garden place anyway?" Hexus asked. He rode on a large white mare with Zethus walking next to him, holding the reins. No one had an answer.

Norris cleared his dry throat, "it's sacred to the gods." He said. It had been an age since he last spoke the word "gods". The word tasted queer.

"It was raised by Hera, the queen of the gods. Ladon guards it."

"Ladon?" Chase asked.

"A monstrous hundred headed dragon. Black as night and big enough to encircle the trunk of the heart tree twice over."

"Heart tree?"

"The biggest tree in the garden, in the center."

Adam sighed, "I saw a black dragon in my dreams. The Eagle told me to find it."

Silenus scoffed, "Don't listen to that Eagle fella. If I'm anything to go off of-"

"-you're not."

"-I should tell you that those magic twats want nothing more than to further their own agenda." He pursed his lips. "You know... I once served the royal shits themselves." Norris could feel the heat of his breath on the back of his neck.

"All they did was prevent me from having any fun. I wasn't allowed to curse or drink... Hell I could barely have lady friend over. They were all 'bad influences for the children." He waved his hands mockingly, "which was a lie, they all loved the children."

"Children?" Zethus asked. "What children would be allowed in the house of the gods?"

"Well at the time, Dionysus was little more than a baby and the twins Apollo and Artemis were about your age, girl." He nodded at Akio.

"I'm a boy." Akio protested.

"Whatever." He shook his head.

Akio rolled his eyes.

Hexus made an odd sound, "Wait. So, if you were there when Dionysus was a baby, how old are you?"

Silenus looked at his fat fingers, "one three...forty-two...." He mumbled. "I lost count after one thousand and fifty-three." He grumbled.

Zethus laughed. Theo and Hexus joined in and Akio laughed as well.

Norris sighed. He thought of nothing else but getting more wine.

The hours had passed, and the afternoon sun stared them with a bright gleam. The horses had been rubbed down and fed, and they stopped for an hour or so.

Hexus brought a flaming finger to the edge of Norris' redweed filled pipe. He inhaled the smoke, held it in, and finally blew out. The puff of smoke danced in the wind before vanishing into the air. The white clouds sprouted from the sky like forests of wool and green plains stretched out for miles.

Eli stirred the rabbit stew cooking over the fire as everyone else sat around doing whatever they wanted. He had gone hunting earlier.

Theodore had an ale, Hexus was building something with metal and wood next to Norris and Erika practiced her archery with Kathrine. Adam and Chase were nowhere to be seen, neither were Raia and Asius. Minerva played with the animals in the company of her towering protector Boo. Norris though it odd, how he had constantly heard stories to stay away from beasts like Boo and animals like Chase, but now, he travelled with two of them, and they were both opposite to everyone else's assumptions. Zethus took a wooden knife to a block of wood in the shape of a man, in front of Norris. He dragged the blade up and down the figurine's arms and legs, giving it more detailed features. It was the first time that Eric sat with them since they had left the hidden woods. They had always travelled during the day and rested at night. They never took breaks during the day, so when they did have breaks, the tents were always drawn, and Eric always sat in his, doing gods know what. They had woken up early this morning. The goal was to sleep in the garden, assuming they would even reach it before nightfall.

Norris could not help but stare at him. He had been a good man. A noble man. He always did the right things and fought for those he loved. He was a changed man now. After the Night of Fire, the Eric that Norris had known had died, and this one had taken his place. He was a bitter man. He never smiled or laughed, and the sound of his voice was seldom heard. He spoke with his bow and his arrows were his words. He was a beast in a man's skin. The way he fought was not normal. It was not orthodox, it was not...human.

The idea was not impossible. Everyone here was able to do things no human could. They healed quicker and they were faster and stronger than other people. They were something else, but exactly what... no one knew.

Norris inhaled deeply again. He looked at Zethus. The soldier carved away on his figurine and stuck his tongue out as he examined his work.

"You know, the titan Prometheus made people the same way." Hexus said, "he carved them out of wood and gave them life."

Zethus chuckled, "Prometheus sculpted us out of clay. He molded us as mirror images of the gods. It was Athena that gave us life. She breathed life into the figures, and the first man and woman were born."

Hexus slurped on the rabbit stew that Akio had given him, "oh." He said, while blowing on the stew.

Zethus extended a hand. "here" he said. Hexus took it. When Hexus pulled back, he saw the little wooden figure in his hands. The wooden man stood ready for battle, with a sword in one hand and a shield in the other.

Hexus examined it. Zethus smiled at the boy, "keep it."

He sat back and pulled a second figurine from his pack.

Hexus smiled and immediately began pitting the wooden figuring against imaginary foes, complete with fighting noises, grunts and groans.

Norris sometimes forgot that Hexus was only a child. He was no older than thirteen. Although many people would have considered him grown, Norris saw him as little more than a kid. He was strong of will and stubborn as an ox, but he was also immature and childish. Norris vowed to remember that as Hexus's battle noises showered him with spit.

"Not like that, boy." Zethus said. He waved the figuring out of the air. The wooden soldier fell to Hexus's knees.

Zethus laughed, "you pray to it. A relic for the gods." He helled his figurine up, a small wooden tree, so detailed that Norris would have guessed it to be made of clay.

"Pray to the gods?" Hexus said, as if the idea was alien to him.

Norris could not help but chuckle, "the man has gone soft in the head!" He exclaimed, taking another puff of smoke. He blew it out in rings.

Zethus knit an eyebrow, "you shouldn't mock the gods."

Norris pretended to not hear the comment.

From within Quartus's tent, a deep laugh echoed. Eleon stuck his head out from behind the tent, his body facing away from them, and his face covered in shadow.

"Why.... Do you pray?" He asked. His voice was a hollow wheeze, barely heard. Everyone froze. Faces of distain and discomfort appeared seemingly without end.

"Tell me Zethus." Eleon continued, "do you think they will answer? Do you think they will help you? The gods have been deaf to the prayers of man for centuries. Your prayers will not change that." He spat the word 'your' as if it were a curse.

Zethus closed his eyes and put the wooden tree to his forehead, "forgive him, lord Zeus, for he knows not what he speaks of."

"I know damn well what I say!" Eleon yelled in response. "Your more naïve than a child for thinking that the gods will answer."

"The gods have blessed us on this trip-"

"Blessed us? "Blessed us" he says!" Eleon mocked. "They've blessed us with a journey that has no end. They have blessed us with low food and almost no water. I haven't eaten, all-pissing-day!" Wads of spit flew from his beaded lips as he shouted. Hexus had wide eyes and a quivering

"Your scaring the poor boy!" Norris told him.

A labored wheeze came out where a laugh should have been, "of course I am. I tell you all the truth and you believe me to be mad!" His laughs became soft sobs, truly, he had lost his mind. "I just want some food." He said, gasping and sniffing. Eric stopped sharpening his blade, hiding it behind his sheathe.

Eric stared at the silhouette, "give him some." He told Eli. He had a reluctant look on his face.

Akio climbed onto the resting mammoth's furry body and served Eleon a bowl of the rabbit stew.

"How will I eat this without my hands?" He asked, smirking.

"I won't cut you lose." Akio said.

"But I can't eat...without my hands." Eleon protested, slowly.

Norris blew out smoke, "pour it in his mouth." He told Akio

Eleon shook so suddenly and violently that Quartus woke up, startled. Hexus rushed over to immediately sooth the worried beast.

"Pour it into my mouth, and I'll bite your hand off."

"Then starve for all I care." Eric sighed. He pulled his leather gloves over his hands and stood up.

"Cut me loose so I can eat!" Eleon said, louder.

"We are not going to free you." Eric said simply.

"I must eat. Untie me so I can eat. I'm not your prisoner dammit!"

"I am not going to free you—"

"Then kill me for shits sake!" Eleon's scream echoed through the valley. The camp went silent. Akio had dropped the rabbit stew, and the brown soup seeped into the grass. Theodore had spilled his ale and Hexus looked up from Quartus's head. Norris had nearly dropped his pipe. The squawks of startled birds filled the sky above them.

Eleon breathed heavily, Eric sighed.

He stared at the ground for a moment and continued forward. "Find the others," he said, not facing the crowd, "we leave in an hour."

"yessir." Hexus said quietly.

Eric paused at the name, then continued forward.

"Kill me you son of a bitch! KILL ME!" Eleon kept shouting as Eric walked off. Norris's ears began to hurt from the violent screams.

"Curse you! Coward! Kill me!"

Eleon's screams echoed in Norris's ears. For miles and miles, all that was heard

Past the thicket of trees surrounding the camp, a lake shimmered in the afternoon sunlight. Asius strained tunics and breeches, hoses and shirts, in the water while Raia splashed gleefully in the middle of the lake.

A flash of brown appeared next to him. Norris looked down and Hexus ran past him, yelling wildly.

A wave of water splashed over his face and he closed his eyes, sputtering.

"Jump in!" Norris heard Hexus say, from the lake.

He wiped the water from his eyelids, "We're leaving soon, get dressed."

"We leave in one hour. We have time. And the water is great." Raia said, pushing her white hair back.

Norris stared at the water. His bored reflection stared back, shaking and moving with the ripples of Hexus's endless splashes. He had not seen himself in a long time. His beard had grown bushy and thick on his chin and neck, and his black coarse hair and mustache were decorated with small streaks of white and grey. His blue eyes looked more like dirty Lapis Lazuli now, more than the sapphires they resembled in his youth. His dark skin was dry, his eyes sunken and his hair unkempt and almost wild. Norris was on the brink of thirty now, but he looked closer to death much more than any older person he had ever met.

A streak of light rushed across the water. Norris stared at the surface blankly. The lights shimmered. They flickered in and out of existence with every ripple in the water. Norris stepped closer; his leather boots pushed against his feet as the water pushed against them. His cloak became heavy with the water it soaked in, but he did not look back to see it. His eyes stayed fixed on the surface of the water. There was something under the surface. Something he did not see. The light returned. They shimmered in colors of turquoise and blue and orange and gold.

Norris squinted. The lights took solid form. The rippling silhouettes of buildings and streets glistened under the surface. Thousands more buildings flashed to life, all made of quartz and stone with tile rooves and shining stones that Norris had never seen. The streets were a shingle of shining white and red pebbles and blue and green and turquoise seashells. The streets were lined with sidewalks made of the same glowing stone as the houses. Lamps lined the streets, as busy inhabitants of the city buzzed around as if with all the time in the world. In the distance, a dozen massive towers made up a cluster of skyscrapers.

Norris looked at the people walking on the sidewalks and the carriages they road on the streets. He stared at one man, who did not look like a man. His skull twisted into a twirl around the back of his neck. He was hairless with pink, almost reddish skin. His legs were a swirling mass of tentacles and his long, almost boneless arms ended in meaty hands with three long, sausage-like fingers. The man turned around. A beard of more wriggling tentacles covered the lower half of his face. His massive eyes were black as ink with no whites and he had no nose: a Cephaloid.

Norris gasped. He looked away from the creature and saw another.

This one had long, white silky hair and a flowing beard. His ears were pointed, and his eyes shined a beautiful green. Sprouting from his forehead were a pair of lobster's claws, snapping and grabbing at nothing. He had a round belly, with pudgy arms and chubby hands. The lower part of his body made Norris blink. He had scaly, green horse legs where his legs should be and a long fish's tail where his butt should be. Scales glistened all around the tail and legs and fins sprouted wherever they could, on the ergots and behind the forearms of the horse legs and along the fish spine. The end of the tail split into several fins, all connected by a turquoise membrane.

"An Icthyocentaur?" Norris whispered. He felt his body grow heavy.

"Look, boy." Said a deep voice in his head. He leaned forward. "Look at your old home. There is much I wish to show you." He fell.

He felt the water splash all around him as he fell in. The lake swallowed him whole and he hadn't even noticed.

Schools of fish swirled around him. Yellow, blue, red, orange, green. The rainbow of fish passed him by as he sank closer to the city below him. He heard a dolphin trills and click. He saw manta rays swim next to him, with billowing bodies, as if they were capes in the wind. Sea turtles chirped and mermaids sang. Carriages were massive hermit-crab shells decorated with hundreds of gems and pearls and driven by turtles with reins, or they were closed off caravans made of a pearl-like stone, carved in the shape of waves and decorated with flowing strands of colored seaweed, and pulled by sunfishes. Their massive fins cast large shadows over the gravel. Horse-fish hybrids, called Hippocampi chittered as their riders pulled on their reins.

All around him, the beautiful city shimmered. The lake had disappeared, his friends were gone. He was swimming in the sea. The underwater city glistened in the sunlight shining through the surface.

"Norris?" said the voice. Norris breathed in. He could breathe! He could see clearly, and he could hear normally. Was this a dream? He hadn't gone to sleep...but perhaps he had. Perhaps the entire encounter with Eleon in the camp was all an illusion of sleep.

"You can see all of this. It will all be clear to you, but you must reach the garden." Said the voice. It was deep and commanding, but familiar. He had heard it before, but he did not know when or where. Perhaps one of his many dreams.

"It is in the garden?" Norris spoke aloud. The voice said nothing.

"Where is this?" Norris asked. The voice had called it his "old home", and it did seem familiar, but would he not remember a life beneath the waves? If the memories were in his mind, they now eluded him.

"Norris." Said another voice, different then the first and more familiar. "Norris get up!" it pleaded with him, childish and high-pitched.

Norris felt water push against his body as he floated away from the city. The buzzing streets and bright lights became specks of color on the sea floor as he flew to the surface.

"Norris!" Hexus said again as Norris finally broke the surface. Water washed his face and he opened his eyes. Hexus stared at him with confused scarlet eyes.

"Where are we?" Norris asked, sputtering. He looked around. The trees parted slightly in the canopies to allow streams of sunlight to flow down from the sky.

"You fell in the lake. We though you drowned." Hexus told him.

I can breathe underwater, he wanted to tell him. The words did not come out. The vision had left him speechless.

"We're leaving now." Hexus said, a towel around his shoulders.

Norris stood up, the lake lightly splashed around him and slapped at his cape. His sleeves dripped and his clothes were heavy. He spat water from his mouth and noticed his feet. A few feet in front of him, the water ran up and down the sloped shore. Norris stood in the middle of the lake and the water did not reach past his ankles, yet, the city seemed so real.

37

For MILES AND miles, the garden shimmered in the moonlight. The golden apples resembled a thousand shining suns, all glowing in the darkness of night. The canopies of the trees fused together as if it were all tresses on the head of a massive woodland being. Oak, birch, spruce, ash, weeping willow, and walnut trees, all with different color leaves and trunks danced in the wind together. All of them had dozens of the shining suns that were the golden apples. Some also grew kumquats and hazelnuts and apricots and other nuts and fruits.

Adam gawked at the view. The hooves of their horses thundered on the grass as they galloped away. Eric and Zethus had undone their reins and let them free.

"We've taken the poor creatures far enough." Zethus said. The other animals stayed with them. Quartus stomped around the field, and Tenzir licked his white paws with a pink tongue. Beta wagged her tail and barked at the fireflies that occasionally flickered in and out of sight. Her jaw snapped closed as she tried to swallow the glowing bugs. Hexus stood on the edge of the hill next to Minerva, with his hands out, explaining something inaudible. She giggled and he stood proud and smiled. Boo slapped his hands in the air, also trying to catch fireflies as everyone else readied their equipment.

Zethus walked towards him, his pteryges slapping at his leather greaves. His armor was on in full. His breastplate and gorget shined crimson red and his shoulder plates clanked with the movement of his arms. He held a vest made of boiled leather, leather arm and leg guards and a chainmail byrnie, and proudly smiled as he presented it to Adam.

"You can't walk in there naked." He said, pushing the armor into Adam's hands. The chainmail and arm and leg pads fell to the ground. The vest was surprisingly heavy, considering its small size. Adam realized he only wore his woolen tunic; the same one he wore when he had left Alor. His other clothes had ben lost in the explosion Eleon had caused. "Thank you." He said. He was confused. He did not see the threats that this garden posed. Regardless, he didn't complain. His old armor was worn out leather, so he was more than happy to receive anything but.

It was all heavier than he had presumed. He easily slipped into the byrnie and strapped the boiled leather over it. The vest hugged his ribs tightly, almost squeezing the air out of his lungs. The leather pads did the same to his wrists and legs. He strapped a leather belt around his waist and sheathed a sword in a leather scabbard strapped to his side. The adamant rod-blade he had used in the lion's cave had refused to reveal itself every time he had tried to summon it. Fortunately, Zethus had been training with him and Chase for the past few weeks. He had gotten used to the oversized hilt, wielding it with both hands, and his arms had become familiar with the weight of the steel weapon. He kept the rod-blade with him, though, putting it in Chase's satchel.

The satyr walked up to him, a sword at his side. He wore leather armor of his own, though he seemed much less comfortable in it.

"Protected by a dead cow." He said with a frown.

Adam laughed, "it's either a cow or you walk in there naked." He said.

Chase scowled. After a moment of struggling with his belt, he turned behind him. The garden, though beautiful, glowed more ominously. The thoughts of needing to wear armor to enter the forest rattled Adam, and he figured Chase would feel the same.

Akio climbed down from the rope ladder hanging off Quartus. His cloak waved in the breeze and his reed hat shook lightly as it struggled to be untied around the boy's head.

"Eleon is tied tight." He said. The name brought frowns around the group. Erika sighed, Zethus comforted her and Hexus exhaled deeply as he scratched the back of his head. Chase groaned for a moment, brief enough to not be noticed by anyone else but long enough for Adam to realize that the name clearly brought him physical discomfort.

After finishing readying their weapons and armor, the group began to descend the hill. Adam fiddled nervously with the pommel of his sword. Ahead of him, Kathrine's hazel hair bounced up and down with each of her steps. She had not talked to him since the incident in Silenus's lair. He had attempted to speak with her multiple times, alas, to no avail. She had been around Erika the most. Her archery had been getting better. She could pull back her bowstring almost as quickly as she could fire the arrows, and her accuracy was eye-catching.

Adam felt a nudge on his left arm, "Go talk with her." Chase told him. Adam felt his fingers tremble with anxiety. A nervous chill ran up his spine and his stomach jumped at the idea.

He cursed himself. His pace quickened until he was next to her.

"Kathrine." He called to her. She did not look back. A strand of hair jumped away from her face as she blew a quick breath against it.

"Kathrine, please... listen to me." Adam did not know why he said that. He had nothing to say to her more than an apology. He could not say 'sorry' once more, especially since she had shown no interest in it the previous dozen times. He thought about something to tell her, something new, something she would love to hear.

"We might die." The words fell out of his mouth, and his stupidity allowed them to. Kathrine's face looked horrified; her green eyes wide. He needed to save himself, "I don't know what might happen in the next few hours." *Good!* He thought, "I want us to go back to the way things were."

"Adam, enough." She said, holding up a hand. She froze, he followed suit. He was nervous for the words that might come next.

"Look around you. We aren't in Alor anymore. We aren't alone in this world; we know that now. You can control the wind and I wield a bow." Her eyes looked at the ground, somber and filled with sadness. Adam sighed as the rest of the group continued forward. "Things will never be the same again. We walk towards the rest of our lives, and perhaps some things should be left in the past." She finally met his eyes, the emeralds that were her irises darkened as she looked away again quickly. Her footsteps faded away as she followed the rest of the group down the hill.

Adam stood alone on the field. Waves of wind sailed through the grass, tingling his ankles lightly. He stared at his feet, then his hands. The hands that had launched Zethus in the air. It had seemed so long ago that they were no more than regular hands, without abilities... without danger.

Kathrine's words echoed in his mind. *We walk towards the rest of our lives,* she said, *things will never be the same again.* He looked up, the garden seemed to stare at him with a million shining eyes, all glinting with disappointment.

Chase walked up to him, "Well," he said, pursing his lips and raising his eyebrows, "I suppose... we should get going." He said awkwardly. Adam sighed. He had tried. He had tried and she turned him away. Kathrine sounded sincere. She wanted to leave him in the past. The garden they had all worked so hard to reach was before them now, and past that, Adam would know the answers to everything; the dreams, these people and maybe more things he had never considered. The thoughts would be overwhelming, but he felt it queer that they did not. He had not yet come to terms with his curse, and the danger they were in. The forest unsettled him, but if he turned around, he would be met with an army of the dead. Now, staring at the vast ocean of glimmering trees, he did not know which one he preferred.

Yet, the thoughts of Kathrine forgetting about him worried Adam more than a forest or walking corpses. The answers he had always wanted were close, but the help he had always had, was gone.

"Adam, get over here." Chase's voice called to him. He realized he was still alone, at the top of the hill while the rest of the group had already reached the base. They stood at the entrance of the garden, and the dancing flames of their torches shined orange light around them. He rushed to their side, and their nervous shuffling became clear to him. Eric crouched beneath a thicket of bushes before them, all glistening in the moonlight as if they were wet. Gasps and sobs filled his ears. Minerva covered her mouth in shock, looking up at the trees at something Adam could not see. Hexus looked away entirely, keeling over as if he would vomit. The buzzing of flies surrounded Adam as he noticed Zethus muttering a prayer with his hands to the sky. Adam looked at what they saw, and he clenched his jaw and sucked in a sharp breath.

Bodies. Several bodies. Men wearing gold armor were hung up in the trees, sharp branches jutting from their rib cages. Rivers of deep red blood dripped from the impaled corpses, pooling beneath their floating feet. Their mouths gaped as flies buzzed around them, bathing in their blood and indulging in the fresh slaughter. The smell finally hit Adam, and he gagged. Their limp, discolored bodies were covered in slashes and cuts, some even had arrows jutting from various places. Adam counted ten in total, four on the ground, laying in blood, and six in the trees, watering the corpses below with a shower of red. Their swords and shields lay around them in a mess. Some had pale skin, others dark. Their eyes remained open, and Adam could feel his heart quicken as he stared into the endless black voids of a dead man's pupils. Eyes seemed different in death. They seemed... alive, still, while the rest of the being had expired.

Eric reached out and touched the blood dripping from the thicket of bushes, "fresh." He said flatly, "very fresh." He wiped his bloody finger on the grass.

"Their swords," Norris said, "They are clean."

"Who gives a damn." Theodore cried, "Let's move before we end up like them."

"Maybe if we go forward, we *will* end up like them." Akio said, gulping.

"The swords are clean." Norris finished. Eric examined the grass leading into the forest, the ground around the bodies and the bodies impaled in the tree branches. This was no work of a bear of wolf.

"This was an ambush." Eric said, glaring at the massacre. "These men guarded the entrance to the forest, when they were attacked. Look at the arrows in them, the arrowheads pierce their backs. They were not attacked from the front." He raised and pointed behind the group; in the direction they had come from. Then he turned and pointed into the woods, "They were attacked from behind."

38

THE BURIALS WERE quick. Zethus had always carried a spare spade with him, and it always became useful when the team set up the defenses for the night. Lately, however, the shovel had been used for burials more than anything. The human remains in the cyclops cave, the lifeless bodies in the lion's den, and now, the ten guards at the entrance of the garden. Adam had attended more funerals in the past fortnight then his whole life. He did not know the names of the slain, but he felt it unimportant to know their names, just that their lives had been stolen from them far too early. That was enough.

Everyone stood silently, looking over the dirt piles that were the graves. They had never managed to get the guards named, but their unfamiliar faces had not caused Zethus to lose respect for them. Their swords laid flat on the top of the piles, their blades clean and shining in the moonlight.

Zethus kept his eyes shut and his hands closed on his golden pendant. He prayed a silent prayer and when he was done, pulled his shovel out from the ground.

"Farewell my friends," Zethus crouched over the graves, lightly patting the ground, "you fall for the glory of Ares, may your service be ever repaid in the fields of Elysium."

A wheeze emanated from on top of Quartus's howdah, and Adam sighed.

"They're not your friends." Eleon said, staring at the night sky. His hands were bound behind his back around the support beam of the howdah, and his wrists were red from all his restlessness. Adam stared at him, his mace and hammer were somewhere in the chests and coffers dangling off the mammoth's sides, Adam felt it a stupid idea to let his weapons so close to him. Eleon had not been right of mind as of late, and Adam figured that he considered it their fault. Eos hooted at the group, his talons curling around the roof of the howdah. The owl's yellow eyes bore a hole in Adam's soul and he felt a tingle run up his spine as the bird's feathers ruffled. Erika's white owl, Ion hissed back.

"We move forward into the forest," Eric said, ignoring Eleon and slinging his bow over his shoulder. Everyone had removed their weapons and held them to the graves out of respect for the dead; "a common practice for fallen soldiers in The Great West", Zethus had told them. There was no time for the requiem, also a common practice in The Great West. Adam felt bad because of it. He wanted to give the soldiers their full honors, and his guilt piled up in his throat as he saw Zethus's grim expression as they walked into the forest.

The forest was not as thick as Adam had expected. The stars had been replaced by glowing, golden apples and the night sky melted into a canopy of dark leaves, all rustling and hissing in the wind. The different colored trunks sprouted from the rust colored dirt. The soft pathway snaked into the darkness, shining orange red in the flickering light of the torches and Hexus's fire. For the most part, the trip was silent, save for Silenus's directions.

The road forked occasionally, and the massive Heart Tree was not visible through the thick canopy, so following its direction was not possible. After a few hours of walking through the forest, the golden sunlight of day began to creep through the leaves, lighting up the pathway. The torches were extinguished, and the group set up camp in a clearing.

The shingle of dirt made patches in the green grass and the hissing of running water ran through the camp. Zethus set up the defenses, Asius fed and tended to the animals, and Akio and Erika were cooking luncheon over a fire with metal pots. Sparkrocks sat next to the fire, lightly smoking. The salty smell of pork sausages filled the camp, and Adam was glad that they had raided the outlaws before entering the garden.

"Adam," a voice said. Adam turned, seeing Zethus walk up to him, wooden pails and waterskins hanging over his waist and clunking against one another in his hands. He tossed a pail and skin at Adam, he caught them. Boo the cyclops followed behind him, Minerva on his shoulders.

"There's a river not far from here, we need water." Zethus said.

The rushing water of the stream foamed on the rocks, ferns and cattails swayed in the breeze and Adam hummed along to the music of croaking frogs and chirping birds. Logs and twigs swam in the stream and small waterfalls splashed and hissed. They followed the river for a short while until they found where it pooled into; small pond filled with small animals and beautiful plants, a small waterfall leading the stream into the pond. Cherry blossom trees hung over the pond, all holding golden apples, dropping pink leaves into the water. Rocks and vines hung from the branches and mossy rocks sat in the underbrush. Glowing insects and pixie like creatures with the wings of a butterfly fluttered all around them.

"Fairies." Zethus chuckled. Boo guffawed, holding a finger out for the creatures to perch on. The fairy landed on his finger, occasionally fluttering its wings quicker than the blink of an eye. It was a curious little creature with a plump golden body resembling a caterpillar's cocoon with four small nubs acting as limbs. It had big white eyes and two small *mandibles*, bubbling lightly. Its four, thin wings buzzed excitedly as it fluttered away. More creatures came from the depths of the forest. Mushroom headed creatures with plump bodies and small black eyes played around the water. The mossy boulders shifter, revealing turtle-like creatures with large lazy eyes and turquoise skin like leather. The boulders acted as shells, with moss and plants sprouting from the top.

"What the hell..." Adam muttered, lost for words.

Minerva silently and lightly tapped Boo on his round shoulder, and the cyclops lowered. She jumped off his shoulders, her red hair bouncing. She lowered herself near the pond, kneeling by the water. She reached he hand out, and the forest creatures curiously walked over. The mushroom creatures giggled, and the fairies fluttered about the silent girl.

Minerva laughed. Boo laughed dumbly, "Forest... mother..." he said quietly, petting a rock turtle.

"She has a connection to them." Zethus said, smiling.

Adam scoffed, "How is that?"

"Hell, if I know. The world works in odd ways, and if she managed to befriend a cyclops, nature spirits should be simpler." He knelt by the pond, pooling the clean water into his pail. Adam knelt beside him, looking around at more creatures coming from the forest. Walking green twigs and living shrubs waddled over, followed by more flying fairies and flower creatures.

Adam did not imagine fairies looking like this. In the stories Diocles told him in Alor, fairies and pixies were tiny people with beautiful wings and magic. These were no more than animals, queer-looking, but natural. He felt no magic, but he felt calm, at peace. He feared that. As of late, he had not been calm without something happening afterwards, and the thought of the dead men at the entrance lingered in his mind. The man who had died later than the others, his horrified eyes telling a story of fear. Adam remembered it all. They stared at the bodies on the branches when one of them gasped suddenly. Everyone jumped, and Erika sobbed loudly.

"Shadows..." The man said... "Living shadows...." Then he was gone.

They buried him after that.

A quiet coo brought Adam back to the present. A mushroom creature rested its stubby, fingerless hands on his knees. It stared up at him with big black eyes. Adam smiled. It was quite cute, and it was no larger than a baby. It cooed again. Adam laughed. Chase would like it here, so would Kathrine. He sighed at the thought of her.

"It's the girl, isn't it?" Zethus said, chuckling.

Adam flinched, "What?"

"The girl... Kathrine? That's what's got you down?"

"I... don't... I can't-"

"Ehh... don't worry about it, Littlewind. Feeling wrong because of a woman doesn't make you any less a man." He said, smiling. "It just means you care."

Adam did care. He cared that Kathrine did not care anymore. He wanted to talk to her, to have her scold him for being stupid the way she always did. She was so much to him, and he could not bare the thought of losing her completely.

"You love her, don't you?" Zethus dunked a waterskin in the pond, and bubbles piled up on the surface.

"Wh... what I--"

Zethus laughed at Adam's stuttering. "Don't try to cover it up. Men often try to hide any feelings they may have for a woman, for fear of humiliation. That's why a whorehouse is never out of business, you don't need to love a whore for her to give you a hell of a night, just coin. A real man worries not for what others think of his love. Real men... are not afraid of love."

Adam thought for a moment, "Love is... a strong thing to call it."

"What else would you call it? Infatuation? No... infatuation means you want nothing more than to bed her. One night, with her in your bed, will satisfy everything you have inside you." He dunked another waterskin, Adam scooped water with the pail. Adam felt a bead of sweat ball on his brow. Bedding Kathrine was a strange thought.

"I've seen the way you look at her, bedding is something far from your thoughts." Zethus said, waiting for the skin to fill up, "so that means, you love her."

"My father used to tell me that children my age cannot know what love is." That sentence made Adam feel queer. He spoke of Diocles, the kind satyr who had raised both him and Chase. Adam had a mother, the terrible woman she was, but he had never known his father, his real father. Diocles took care of him and taught him things all fathers should teach their kids. He taught Adam how to fight, how to have fun and how to shave. Adam had drunk with him, and they had shared many lovely afternoons together, the closest thing to a family Adam ever had.

"How old are you, boy?" Zethus chuckled again, settigna side a full skin.

"Fifteen."

"To hell with that. To hell with all of that. You do not need age, nor wisdom to know what love is. Love is a feeling. Do you need age or wisdom to feel anger, or happiness? No! Or course not! You may not know *why* it is that you love someone, or when you started, but the feeling... a feeling of joy that you get when you see someone, that is always familiar."

Adam laughed. Zethus was wiser than he let on, and all things that he said made him think. Perhaps he did love Kathrine. He hated to be apart from her and he hated having to think of his old memories of her rather than make new memories *with* her.

"Do you know what the thing about love is?" Zethus asked, wrapping an arm around Adam's shoulders.

"No... I- I do not."

"Everyone always thinks about love as a thing they need something from. They always ask, *what could this person give me if I marry them,* but if you truly love someone, you should ask what *you* can give *them*. See love is not about taking and thanking, it is about giving and caring."

Adam smiled. Zethus hugged him with one arm. Adam figured Zethus would know about love like that. He and Erika were always together, and Adam knew Zethus would always protect her. The thought that Adam was close to Zethus while Kathrine was close to Erika was comforting. Though, he supposed that his revelation was all for naught. Kathrine did not want him in her life anymore, she said it to him herself.

A twig snapped in the woods across the pond. Zethus bolted to his feet, his sword singing as he pulled it from its scabbard. The animals croaked and groaned and scattered into the woods. The mushroom creature resting on Adam's leg brayed and fled into the underbrush, the lazy turtle rocks waddled away, and Boo turned to face the woods behind them. Adam, Zethus, Minerva and Boo all stared into the woods where the animals croaked at.

Adam had not brought his sword with him but held up a rock with his right hand. His rod grew heavy on his waist. Minerva climbed up onto Boo's shoulders and trembled while looking at the woods.

Clicking and chittering came from the darkness between the trunks. A loud and violent croaking sound erupted from the shadows, and the source burst out.

Gaunt, dead-looking human-like creatures burst from the thicket, clawing and swinging at the air with sharp nails and clean swords. They splashed through the pond, screeching and shrieking. They resembled corpses, thin, grey colored skin, and gold armor glinting in the sunlight. Adam counted four, with more bursting from the forest.

"BACK!" Zethus yelled at the others, holding a large hand out. He swung his blade, cleanly slicing two of the creatures in half by the waist. There were ten in total now. The two legless wights swung their grey arms at Adam, shrieking and screaming. Adam kicked at them and fell back on his butt.

Boo roared as he ripped apart two more of the creatures, rotten flesh and grey bones flying all over. Minerva screamed as she fell off Boo's shoulders. The cyclops turned around, "LEAVE, FOREST MOTHER! IT IS NOT SAFE HERE!"

The silent girl did as her protector said and fled into the woods behind them. Boo roared again, picking another creature up and ripping out its entrails. Despite its missing guts, the creature continued to shriek until Boo stepped on its skull, crushing it.

Zethus hacked at another, and then a third and a fourth. They did not stop coming. The ones that had been slashed in half kept squirming, shaking around in the grass determined to kill the man that had halved it. Two halved monsters crawled up Zethus's pant, tearing up the wool and knocking over the pails of water. He slashed at them with his sword, knocking the heads off the creatures.

Adam yelled as two more clawed at his legs, screaming as their sharp claws dug into his leg. He swung his rock hand, slamming the stone square in between the eyes of the first creature, and brought it back down on the skull of the first. He swung his stone up and down on the creature's head repeatedly, until its skull was no more than a pile of black sludge. He panted looking at the black puddle and gasped when the first creature jumped back up again. He swung his stone again, but to no avail. The creature was unfazed. Adam stared into the beast's eyes and cold, red glowing pupils in the swirling black pits that were the sockets stared back.

Adam reached for his rod on his belt, feeling it grow hotter by the second. He closed his eyes and swung the rod, expecting the same result the stone had. The creature's shriek was abruptly cut off by the bite of metal in the beast's neck. Adam opened his eyes; he heard flesh tear and saw the beasts head slowly roll off its shoulders. The creature's body went limp and it dropped onto Adam's legs. He hurried to get it off.

Adam stared down at the decapitated heads, the ones that Zethus had cut off growled and screeched in the dirt, their respective bodies crawling around on all fours nearby.

Screeches erupted from the pond, and three more undead beasts twitched and convulsed in the water. Adam yelled as the creatures bolted forward, swinging their clean swords and screeching their blood curdling shriek.

The trees near the pond opened, and from the darkness came the largest creature Adam had ever seen. Something so large, so terrifying. birds in the distance flew into the sky at the sound of an earth rumbling bellow. The roar shook the leaves of the trees next to Adam, and wood and plants exploded from the dirt, flying towards Adam.

He felt a large body shelter him, and Boo yelled as the trees burst to make way for the massive creature. Another roar came from the forest and Zethus and Boo fled behind boulders, sheltering themselves from the onslaught of splinters.

Adam saw the creatures in the pond through a space between Boo's arm and the boulder, turning to see the new, giant beast. The three monsters were destroyed in seconds, the first falling beneath the massive, clawed foot of the giant beast and the other two getting ripped apart by a pair of massive jaws, or two pairs, or was it three? Adam shut his eyes; he was far to terrified.

Silence fell, and the massive creature loomed over the three of them, casting a large black shadow over the pond. Adam heard his breathing, far too loud for the beast to not hear them.

"Come out now, little ones." Said a voice, deep and gruff.

Boo peaked over the boulder, and his large, round blue eye lit up. "Black Dragon..." he slowly said with a smile.

Adam crept fingers over the rock and held his head up over the boulder, finally seeing the creature in all its glory.

Facing the group with massive golden eyes and a large black body. It was larger than even Quartus and its body was covered in oily black scales. Its strong legs were thicker than the tree trunks and a dozen snake-like heads with long necks and snapping jaws swirled around a thick main head, its expression solemn. Spikes ran down its dozen necks and sharp teeth poked from its jaws. Two dragon heads chewed on the remains of one of the pond creatures, while two more snapped at a dangling body in the mouth of a third. Most queer of all, from behind the legs of the dragon, a little girl near seven years of age appeared.

"Do not be afraid now, boy. Save your fear for later." Said the main head of the dragon, its yellow slit-pupiled eyes never leaving Adam's.

"The Black Dragon..." Adam said, remembering Silenus's words.

"Hello, children. I am Ladon."

39

ADAM WAS FROZEN in the grass. Zethus still held up his blade to the dragon, breathing heavily. The beast was huge, dwarfing even some of the trees, its thousand heads swirling and snapping.

"Put your sword down boy." The dragon said. Adam doubted his eyes. He doubted his ears as well, was this all a dream?

"You are awake now, I assure you." The girl said.

The little girl was no older than seven, surely. She had long brown hair, half of it tied up in a bun and pale skin. Her eyes glimmered a pretty blue and when she smiled, she revealed crooked teeth. Her nose was small, and she wore an all-white toga.

"Who the hell are you?" Adam asked, his arms shaking.

"Put down your sword," the dragon said.

Adam had forgotten that he still had his sword. He remembered what Silenus said about the dragon. He called the blade back into its rod, surprised that he could do that now.

The little girl walked over the pond, picking up the dropped skins and pails, filling up the empty ones with water. "I would assume you need these." She handed them to Zethus. He took them, still panting.

The dragon looked up with its main head, as if hearing something that Adam could not. "There isn't much time. You must follow us, where are the others?" The dragon lowered its head to be face to face with Adam. The dragon's head was larger than the horse Adam rode to the garden on. His piercing eyes never blinked.

"They... they're upriver... by our campsite." Adam stammered.

Ladon sniffed the air, some of his head growled. "Very well. Forward everyone." The girl hopped up onto the dragon back and disappeared in the maze of heads.

Zethus held his arms out, "Wait, what is going on." He asked.

"This is the dragon Silenus told us about." Adam told him.

"I know that. But who are you?" He jabbed two fingers at the girl.

The girl stuck her head out from behind the dragon. She rolled her blue eyes and climbed off, wiggling her legs to get a hold of the ground. A small dragons head came down beneath her feet, giving her a foot hold and lowering her down to the ground. She walked over to them with bare, pale feet.

The girl stuck a thumb at her chest, "My name is Hebe, daughter of Zeus and Hera and goddess of youth." She curtsied sarcastically and gave a look that showed she was tired of explaining her titles.

Adams eyes widened, "Goddess?" He repeated. The words seemed to lie to his ears. "But you're a little girl..." He chuckled.

Hebe laughed, "My gods, the goddess of youth, A LITTLE GIRL?" She shouted, taunting Adam with endless amounts of sarcasm.

Zethus chuckled. Adam realized that of course the goddess of youth would be a little girl. He had heard stories of gods presenting themselves to mortals as different creatures or people, for is a human bared witness to their true form, their very mind would become nothing more than ashes in their skull

Hebe crossed her chubby little arms, "Now... can we go?"

Zethus held up a head of one of the creatures he had decapitated. It snapped at him with ruined teeth. Adam widened his eyes at the sight of the creature. He remembered his dream with the Eagle showing him the vast army of the dead. Seeing the creature now, it was more terrifying than his nightmare. The thought of thousands more sent a shiver up Adam's spine.

"It's a Spartus. Part of the army that has been following us." Adam told Zethus. Zethus put the snapping head beneath his arm and tied a rope to the legs of the body. He dragged it behind him, "The others must see what we saw." He told Adam, crushing the other skull beneath his boot. The second body went limp.

"A rogue?" Hebe looked at Ladon.

The dragon groaned, "No," He said, "this is Astos. There is Halus, and Mavor, and Ryden and Cedrick."

Adam examined the bodies... the rivers of dried blood that snaked across the golden armor worn by the creatures.

Adam's eyes widened, "The guards. These were the guards at the entrance of the garden."

Zethus lowered his gaze, "Shit..." he muttered, dropping the body in his arms.

"They were killed and brought back to attack you all." Ladon said, "They were meant to escort you to us, but when we heard word of their deaths, we looked for you ourselves." The dragon's expression darkened.

"Should we bury them again?" Adam asked, thinking of Zethus.

"No." Zethus said, surprising Adam. He picked the rope up again and began dragging the body behind him, walking upriver, "They'll only come back again."

"The man is right. We leave them here and make our way to the Heart Tree, at once." The dragon stepped forward, revealing more of his massive oily black body. Heads hissed as the dragon walked by. Everyone followed, Boo running along after giving the dead bodies one last dismissive kick like an angry child.

Adam ran up to Hebe, she walked by the shore of the stream, balancing on the rocks on the edge. Adam stood before her.

"What is this? Why are we here? What does all this mean? The dreams, the army, this garden, why all of it? Why any of it?" He felt somewhat embarrassed asking it all at the same time, but the words flooded out of him. He could not stop it and he did not want to. He had nearly died several times since leaving Alor and he wanted to know for what. He wanted to get the answers he always wanted, that all of them had always wanted. Alor was a pile of rubble now, and his mother, and everyone he had ever known was dead, all walking along with this massive army.

"I know you have questions, and soon enough they will all be answered, but for now all you must know is this; this forest is called the Garden of Hesperides. Its sacred to the goddess Hera, and it holds a gateway."

Adam now had more questions, "a gateway to what?" Hebe laughed as if the answer were obvious.

"Olympus, silly. The home of the gods. They need you all there, so they used the dreams to bring you here. You needed to leave Alor so they used the dreams to lead you out. The dreams led you to the lyre which you needed to convince Silenus to lead you here." She held up her hands.

Adam stood dumbfounded. He supposed it all made sense.

He shook his head to save the thoughts for late, "What do the gods need us for?"

Hebe frowned, "Don't know, they wouldn't say," she said dismissively.

Adam scowled. The gods were real... that was something he never would have thought real. He suddenly felt a wave of anger wash over him. If the gods were real, why the hell have they let the world become so bad. Alor was a hell. The massive stone walls prevented anybody from leaving, even though there was a world beyond those walls. What god would allow that? Adam balled his hands into fists and yelled as he punched a tree. Splinters flew and his knuckles bled, but he felt no pain, only anger.

"That was unnecessary." Hebe raised an unimpressed eyebrow.

"I don't care." Adam told her.

Ladon sighed, "Your answers will soon be given to you, but for now, you must calm yourself."

The rest of the trip was silent.

When they made it to the camp, almost everyone stood petrified in the shadow of the massive dragon. It took minutes to become accustom to, but eventually everyone accepted it. They had been getting ready to run into the forest after a terrified Minerva raced into the camp, tipping them off. She was relieved to see Boo alive, and the others were happy to see Zethus and Adam once again.

Silenus guffawed looking at the dragon, "How are you, ya scaly bastard?" He wheezed.

Ladon groaned, "You have completed your task, Silenus. Well done."

The satyr sighed, "Always so formal."

They sat around the smoking pile of ashes that were once logs. The pork sausages and boiled potatoes were served to everyone except for Chase and Silenus, who ate only the potatoes.

After they were finished, Zethus called attention to the Spartus. He got the body from where he had hidden it from dinner and dropped it in the middle of the camp, still writhing and growling.

"What the hell is that?" Norris asked, rummaging through the new skins and pails. He pulled out his own skin and took a long drink. He spat the water out when he realized it wasn't wine.

"This is what's following us. An army of these things."

"Spartoi." Norris said, returning the skin to Zethus. "I've seen them in my dreams. I'm off to sleep. Call me when you have wine in those skins."

Zethus scoffed, "call me over when you find an alehouse in the middle of the forest."

Norris scoffed back.

"We're close now." Eric stopped fletching his arrows, placing the remaining ones in his quiver and slinging it over his back. "We sleep here and follow the dragon to what it is we need to see in the morrow."

Raia came rushing behind everyone, Adam was not happy to see her. Surprisingly, she did nothing to him, or anyone. She kept her bright purple eyes fixed on the twitching body.

"We need to leave now." Her expression was unlike anything Adam had ever seen on her face. She was scared.

"What are you taking about?" Theodore asked. Akio did not wait for a response, immediately slinging a pack over his shoulder.

"I've seen this magic before. Black Necromancy."

"The hell?" Hexus asked.

"Necromancers have the ability to speak to the dead, those who practice Black Necromancy make the dead do evil things. Its reckless and dangerous. My people have a legend about a necromancer who lived with us a century ago. He was one of us, a follower of Hecate, but he thought himself more powerful than the goddess of magic, so he invented the ability to raise the dead and bending them to his will. He nearly destroyed our entire city with only a couple dozen. We see thousands of these in our dreams, and I fear the idea of what they could do."

"What was the necromancers name?" Hexus asked.

"Pontarius." Raia said, her expression darkened further. She turned her back on the creature, packing her things and joining Akio in readying to leave. Hexus and Theodore began to pack as well.

"The bastard doesn't even have a head, how is it still alive?" Silenus asked. The Spartus growled in response. Everyone jumped.

"The necromancy attacks the heart and brain," Raia said, "Destroy either of those, or it dies."

"My sword did nothing but piss it off." Zethus complained.

"My sword did." Adam said. Felling uncomfortable when all eyes turned to him.

"Adamant." Eric said, staring at the Spartus. He looked over at Zethus and Adam, "Give me your swords."

Zethus unsheathed his, and Adam took the rod from his belt. The blade appeared in a beam of light and Eric held it in his hand. Eric stabbed the creature through the chest with Zethus's blade, and it did nothing but cause the creature to wail loudly. Adam covered his ears. Chase flinched. Eric pulled out the first sword and thrusted in Adam's. The creature went silent, and the beast was still.

Hexus laughed, but there was no humor in it so much as fear, "So... Adams is the only sword that can kill these things?"

Erika sighed, "We don't know that."

Theo scoffed, "Yes we do! Nobody has another weapon made of that shit!"

Akio gulped and stepped forward, "My grandfather's sword, Godslayer is made of this also."

Theodore threw his arms up in defeat.

Chase crossed his arms, "Wonderful, so while we are all torn apart by these things, Adam and Akio will be untouchable." Everyone shook their heads. Worry spread across the camp, and Adam felt he was somehow responsible for it. Akio was not pleased with it either.

Eric handed Adam his blade back, "keep that with you boy, lest you head come apart from your body."

Zethus threw his sword in his scabbard again, "Raia." He called to her. She turned. "Do you know any magic capable of killing these things." She shook her head, her silver hair bouncing around her. More sighs.

Hebe clapped her hands, "If we make it to the Heart Tree before tomorrow night, we can make it out of the forest before the Spartoi catch us."

Raia stared daggers at her, "A few things, girl;" He said, coldly, "First of all the Spartoi are already here. Why they haven't killed us yet, I can't tell you, but as we clearly saw at the entrance of the garden these creatures fear nothing. They already caught up with us. Second, what in the hell would a tree do against an army of these things, and third, how do we even know we can trust you?"

Ladon growled quietly, but loud enough for Raia to step away from Hebe.

"Listen here, girl." She spat the name out in a taunting voice, "If the Spartoi had already caught up with you, you would all be dead, and I don't see any of you with arrows in your back or knives in your throats! Second, this tree is about the only thing that could stand between you and death and third, you have no other choice! You know you have to get to the Heart Tree, but you have no clue how to get there, so tell me, what is it that you can do?" She widened her blue eyes as if daring

Raia to say something. Raia stared at her, wanting to say something, but being betrayed by her tongue.

Adam tried to contain his laughter, Norris and Hexus did not. They howled loudly; tears even ran down Norris's eyes. From the corner of Adam's eyes, he could see Kathrine sitting on a long, the faintest smile tugged at the corner of her lips. Then she laughed

40

THE TREE WAS bigger than anything Kathrine could have ever imagined. The morning sky was almost completely blocked out by the canopy of leaves all casting a massive shadow over the clearing. Vines and leaves dangled from the thousand branches and millions of shining golden apples all sparkled in the crown of the tree like golden stars. The massive trunk was so huge that other trees sprouted from it like a thousand, leaf-covered arms. It was covered in a thick coat of soft, green moss all over and flocks of thousands of birds flew from branch to branch. The roots jutted from the ground, all furry with moss and all the size of buildings. Holes and spaces between the massive roots were big enough to house a hundred people and small mushrooms covered the bark.

Kathrine stared at it all in awe. The Heart Tree was bigger than the walls of Alor, and nearly three times as thick. The sight was beautiful. Dozens of creatures greeted them. Kathrine had never seen such queer looking animals. Small pudgy things with mushroom atop their heads like hats, and mossy rock-turtles with leathery skin and drooping faces. Butterflies and firebugs and ladybugs and dragonflies fluttered around them, hurrying from place to place along with cocoon shaped creatures.

"Fairies." Adam called them; his hands covered with dozens of the small, beautiful creatures. They all glowed bright colors in the shade of the Heart Tree. Walking twigs and rose-headed critters emerged from the underbrush. Walking shrubs and beings of living moss played in the grass and the smell or rain was potent. Small streams ran in from the forest and waterfalled into dozens of small ponds, all teeming with more of the nature creatures.

This... was the most beautiful thing Kathrine had ever seen.

They set up camp at the base of the roots. Chase did not even bother to set up a tent.

"I could live like this for a while," he said, throwing himself onto a blanket of green moss. Kathrine laughed. Everyone seemed happy here. Akio sat cross legged in the field; his limbs covered in playing creatures while a mushroom nibbled at his reed hat. Minerva danced along with the hummingbirds and butterflies, laughing when she saw Boo covered in ladybugs. The friendly cyclops guffawed. Theodore took pandouris from a coffer on Quartus and began to play a tune, smiling when Erika sang along.

"This is a wonderful day, beautiful in every way!" She sang in her beautiful voice. Zehtus banged on some drums while Asius blew into his pipes and Silenus took his lyre. The satyr had lost his restrains a while ago, but the red marks on his wrists from the chafing was clear. Kathrine felt guilty for seeing him tied up in the first place, but her negative feelings soon left her be as Silenus pulled at his lyre.

She laid in the field, feeling the blades of smooth grass kiss her arms. Everyone seemed at peace. Ladon slithered around the trunk of the Heart Tree and Hebe greeted the nature spirits. Even the animals played around in the field with the nature spirits. Beta wagged her tail and barked at a shrub while Rubius hopped around with the mushrooms. Quartus lay on his side in the grass, his howdah had been put to the side, along with Eleon and all their supplies. Everyone was happy, save Raia.

Kathrine had loved seeing her scolded by a girl less than half her age. She had never thought to see something so satisfying. Raia had been silent the whole walk to the clearing. Kathrine had thought about her words to her at that lake so long ago. She said she was going to take Adam. Kathrine had tried to convince herself that she did not care, but it is always difficult to bury a lie. When she saw Adam with Raia in Silenus's lair, her heart seemed to shrivel and fade away into dust. She had not liked Raia since the moment she kissed Adam on the cheek when they first met, and the kiss her and Adam had shared was enough to make Kathrine hate her.

She did not want to hate. Hate was an ugly thing, but perhaps it was necessary sometimes. She was not angry with Adam, he was drunk and the herbsmoke had done away with his mind, but that had not made her feel any better. Kathrine wanted to forget about it. She wanted to forget about him. *I'll never face that which I ignore*, she always told herself. She said it to Erika when the two had been walking.

Erika walked near the end of the group towards the clearing, a hand on Pormant's reins. Kathrine had decided to follow along. They walked along; Kathrine finished up her pork sausage.

"The further you run away from your problems, the further you run from solutions." Erika had told her after the conversation had come up. Kathrine had said. Kathrine hated when other people had the ability to prove her wrong. Growing up with fools like Chase and Adam, she had always been the sensible one while the other two were off thinking of gods know what.

"I would very much like to forget about that night," she said to Erika.

Erika nibbled on her potato, blowing on it occasionally to cool it down, "many people do, but if we forget our past, we forget the lessons we can learn from it."

Kathrine tilted her head, confused, "What lesson?"

"Forgiveness." Erika said.

"But I forgave him." Kathrine took a large bite of sausage. She grew up stealing scraps or eating Adam's mother's horrid cooking, so Akio's meals were always delicious and appreciated.

"Maybe you did, but does he know that?" Erika said, taking abite from her potato.

Kathrine widened her eyes. She had not talked to Adam in so long. She never realized that she had never made it clear to him that she was not angry. She had told him that she wanted to keep him in the past. Kathrine had never realized how that could have made him feel.

Even now, lying in the grass field, the guilt washed over her. She looked up, and saw Adam sitting with Chase, admiring the view of above.

She cursed herself silently, then walked over to the two.

Chase noticed her first and gave an awkward goodbye to Adam, hurrying away to join the music circle. Adam turned to her, a queer look spreading across his face.

Kathrine opened her mouth to speak, but a voice from above spoke first.

"Everyone up here!" Eric yelled, at the top of the highest root. Everyone followed his voice. She looked to Adam, and he only shrugged.

When Kathrine made it to the top, she thought her eyes lied to her. At the top of the root, leading in the trunk of the tree, a cave in the bark lead into a cavern of wood and leaves. Hexus was about to light his fire when a voice from above called down, "no need for fire here." At that, thousands of glowing lights appeared on the wooden walls.

"Fireflies," Zethus said, gold shimmering in his eyes.

The ceiling remained dark, save for two spots of glowing white. The source of the voice lowered. Hovering above the group, thirty feet in the air, a billowing cloak danced in shades of purple and blue. It floated down before them, stopping to hover three feet off the ground. Kathrine stared at his face. He was attractive. A boy no older than she, his skin was black, with strong cheekbones and a long face. His eyes glowed hot-white and he covered his face with a purple hood, casting a shadow down to his top lip. Kathrine saw no body beneath the vast cloak, bigger than any one she had seen before. Long and dark, made of dark silk and embroided with golden swirls. He had no sleeves nor visible legs.

"Who the hell are you?" Theo asked.

"Morpheus, son of Hypnos." Said the boy. His voice was far too deep to be that of a boy of his age. It was smooth like silk, but commanding and assertive.

"The god of dreams." Zethus announced. Morpheus nodded. Adam gasped, "The dream giver. The Egle told me about you." He said.

Kathrine needed to hold her head. Everything in the last day felt like it had not yet happened. She felt as though this was all a dream. She felt as though she would soon wake up in the middle of the forest again, so many miles from the Heart Tree again. It had all happened so quickly. They had not even set up their tents for the past night when Hebe and Ladon had found them. Those two were a concern in and of themselves.

Kathrine had never believed in the gods. She always thought they had either abandoned their creation, humanity, or had been the creations *of* humanity. Life in Alor was far too terrible for anyone to believe that divine beings were looking down on them, protecting them from danger. Sometimes Kathrine had looked to the great walls of Alor and saw a prison wall rather than a shield.

Now she was in a sacred garden, trying to *find* the gods of Olympus she had heard so much about. The irony was baffling. She did not know if she wanted to return to Alor. It had its troubles, poverty, violence, segregation, but she figured it was better than dying with these people she had known for little over a month. It seemed so long ago that Hexus had blown that hole in the walls and her and Adam rushed out, seeing mountains and rivers and oceans for the first time. It was simpler.

No, she told herself, *your place is here now. These people may be new, but they are your friends now.* They had come so far for this moment, and it had all started when Chase suggested they go see the priestess again. She did not always believe in the gods, but she believed in destiny, and she was facing it right now.

"What is all this?" Zethus said. Kathrine returned to the present.

Morpheus looked at them all, fireflies floating around him, "you have many questions, and the time has come for them to be answered."

Little sunlight made it into the vast cavern, but the fireflies allowed plenty of light. Some of them sat on the mossy ground, cushioned by plants and mushrooms, others sat on the branches of the large branches that sprouted from the walls. They were the size of horses and thick enough to hold them.

Morpheus floated in the middle, his eyes closed, shadow washing his whole face. "Danger is brewing in the bowels on the earth, and it will affect all peoples, from the furthest of the Exile Isles of the eastern coast of Halanor"

Those names were unfamiliar to Kathrine, but she thought she would study the nearest map when they left the tree cavern.

"What kind of danger?" Adam asked, all the way up on a tree branch.

"An antient and restless force, older than all of humanity. Older than I even."

"The Great Snake..." Hexus whispered. The quiet name echoed off the walls and hung over the group like a dead animal. Kathrine had come to see the title as a bad omen.

No one spoke. No one needed to speak. The name was enough to evoke dread in everyone. This creature had an army perusing them and had killed everyone in their dreams ten times over.

"It has many names," Morpheus finally said, "The King of Crows, the Dragon Prince, the Lord Serpent. But it has only one true name: Typhon."

The name sounded familiar to Kathrine, though ever so slightly. A faint story in the back of her memory she could not quite reach.

"He's real?" Erika asked, suddenly terrified. Kathrine had never seen her scared, and she hoped to never see it again. Erika was a strong woman and she was brave and smart. To see someone like that quiver before a name... Kathrine's skin grew goosebumps.

"What do you mean _he's real?_" Theodore asked, "what is he?"

Akio sighed, his expression dark, "A million years past, the Titans had been defeated by the Olympians in their war. Seeing her firstborn children die, Gaia, one of the eldest living beings in the world, and the earth itself birthed a terrible creature. She named it Typhon. It was meant to be the bane of the Olympians, meant to be the destroyer of their dynasty and the savior of the Titans.

"The monster had been unleashed on the earth, and its power was devastating. Its steps threw up mountains and its roars shook the sky. He had sent the Olympians to Kayembe in fear. The gods took the forms of cattle and fled as far south as they possibly could. But now Zeus. The king of the gods stayed and fought with the beast, nearly dying several times in the process. After a battle that lasted ten years, Typhon had been defeated, crushed beneath a mountain the king of the gods brought down on him. It is said that the volcanic eruptions from the mountain are breathes of fire from the beast, trying to destroy the rock that holds him prisoner."

The group was silent again. Kathrine pinched the bridge of her nose. She thought of the worst. "So, this... *Dragon Prince*... is he finally awake. You said it yourself, he's leading the army." She said.

"He leads not the army," Morpheus said, "he only wills them."

"That is not much better." Norris said, skipping small, flat pebbles against the mossy bark of the floor.

"How?" Eric said. "He has been beneath that mountain for thousands of centuries, why is he rising now?"

"Humanity." Morpheus said. All eyes turned to him, "The gods have used their power to keep the beast imprisoned. But their power relies on the prayers of humanity, the fewer prayers they get..."

"...the weaker they become." Theodore said.

Kathrine frowned. She had never thought she would feel guilty for denying the gods, but seeing it now, it made her uncomfortable. It was sickening to think that in some cruel way, humanity was the only one to blame for its own destruction.

"He is not at his full strength now," Morpheus continued, "he is only powerful enough to will things as he desires from the pits of the underworld. But that will not last forever, in time, he will rise, and this world will know the true meaning of chaos."

Hexus whimpered. Norris sighed, "Well that sounds all well and good, but what does this have to do with us?" Sounds and looks of agreement all shined in the light of the fireflies.

"The time has come for new gods to replace the Olympians, as they did to the Titans and the Titans to the Primordial Ones."

Laughs came from the darkness, "So you mean to tell us…" said Zethus, "that we will be the new gods?"

Nobody quite knew what to say to that. The thought was beyond the thoughts of any normal human person. Kathrine had heard stories of men trying to hold the power of gods. Kings and conquerors of old, and every single one of them, fell before the might of something they could not control, despite their ambition.

"You were all chosen for a reason." His eyes opened, the glowing white lights glared at Kathrine, "well most of you were chosen." Kathrine felt more eyes on her, and a scowl tugged at the corners of her face. Morpheus turned his head to scowl at Chase as well.

Chase and Kathrine; the two out of the entire group who did not have the dreams. She had not seen it as a problem until now. Clearly, Morpheus thought otherwise.

Morpheus turned back around and shit his eyes once more, his smooth voice returning, "you are a special lot. Some of you posses the strengths of the gods, and others, must learn to control their powers." He looked at Adam. Kathrine felt her nails dig into her palm and she balled her hands into fists.

"The dreams are meant to be messages between you all and the other gods." Morpheus said, "they order me what to send you, and I make you see it in your dreams, but Typhon always enters those dreams. He corrupts them, turns them into nightmares."

"That's why we always the terrible things, like the bodies, and the fire… and… the mountain!" He sat up, a look of surprising glee on his face, "The mountain we see in our dreams! It must be the same mountain that Zeus buried Tyohon beneath."

"Akio," Eric said, "In your story, where is the mountain?"

Akio shook his head, "It could be in a thousand different places. The story was told in my village, but Halanor has no volcanoes."

"The Eagle in my dream told me he had crushed a beast with a mountain, in the Shimmering Sea." Adam said, "Does that mean…"

"The Eagle is the symbol of Zeus, king of the gods." Morpheus said.

Adam gaped. His expression was somewhere between horrified and intrigued. Kathrine had never expected this. A month ago, they were fleeing a baker for robbing him of doughballs. Now, they were to become the new gods.

We? It was wrong. *They* were to become new gods, while Kathrine remained a mortal. She didn't have the dreams, after all. Her and Chase would stay on earth and age and die while all the rest lived for eternity in the kingdom of the clouds. The thought made her feel... lonely.

"Well, what about me?" Theodore asked Morpheus, "I don't see an Eagle. My guy was a man, without a beard and kind of young-looking."

"Hermes, the messenger of the gods. The lyre was his and so it was he who sent the message to retrieve it."

"What makes them different?" Eric asked, "What makes Adam see Zeus and Theodore see Hermes?"

"The different gods appear to whom they choose, I cannot say their will, for it is not my place, but I can say that each of you have a connection to the person you see in your dreams."

Connection. The word made Kathrine feel worse. These people were truly meant to be amazing. They were to be beautiful things, capable of endless wonders, all because of their connection to the people they see in their dreams.

Kathrine sighed at the thought of her destiny again. She said she faced it here and now, but perhaps her destiny was to die with men.

"You," Morpheus said. No one said anything. Kathrine looked up and noticed every pair of eyes on her. She suddenly felt cold and nervous

"Have you heard of the Prophecy of the Three Kings?"

She frowned. She had never heard of any prophecy before. She shook her head in confusion.

Morpheus grinned, "Recite it to me." He said. More eyes seemed to stare at her, and she felt their weight on her goose bumped skin. She tried her best to understand what was going on. She had never heard of a prophecy, but she compelled herself to remember, nonetheless. Alas, she reached for something that was not there. Then, the words passed her head. They were quicker than lightning was brighter than flames. She caught few words, *Red winter, great battle, hands, Atlas, sea* and *light.* They burned themselves into her mind for half a second before they disappeared, and the face of a young, handsome man disappearing with it. He had curly blonde hair and piercing smoky green eyes. He had a square jaw with full lips and a long nose.

She screamed. Heavy breathes sent gasps around the group, and Erika rushed up to check on her. Her heart rushed in her chest and sweat rolled down her head.

"It seems you are not yet ready," Morpheus said, sounding disappointed. Kathrine held her head, none of the eyes had left her.

"Ready for what?" Eric asked, his hard gaze now cautiously on Morpheus. Morpheus remained silent. Norris stood. Erika joined him.

"What the hell was that?" Erika asked.

"Is she okay?" Hexus asked. More concerned murmurs filled the cavern, all echoing off the bark as Morpheus stayed silent.

Finally, the god spoke, "Everything comes in its own time. The prophecy has been lost to time for centuries, forgotten by this world. The only one who can remember it is the Oracle." He eyed Kathrine with white glowing eyes at that. The prophecy states that three kings will oppose the gods, plunging the world into an endless war the likes of which it has never seen. They call it the war of ---"

"Red Winter..." Kathrine and Adam said at once. She looked at him. His wet, blonde hair fell over his crystal blue eyes.

"You know it?" Morpheus said.

"I saw it in a dream..." Adam said, "I told the others about it."

Kathrine nodded, "I saw it too... in that... vision." She was still shaken by it. She needed to find what it meant, but she knew her answers were not going to be found here. She finally knew how Adam felt, and that annoyed her. He always did enjoy saying, *I told you so,* regardless of how seldom he said it.

"The Red Winter will come, but for it to come there must be a third king. The third prophesied destroyer of the old world."

"Who is that third king?" Adam asked.

"I know not his name, but I know he is the giant you have all seen in your dream."

Zethus laughed, "Volar." He said.

Everyone looked up. Norris clapped, "Volar!" He repeated. Kathrine frowned.

"What is a Volar?"

"The largest Island in the Shimmering Sea, and at its center... a volcano." Asius said. Everyone rustled in realization.

"My army and his army..." Adam said, thinking with his eyes shut. "In my dream with the Eagle, he said I would do battle with Korax. Korax and the Great Snake. Their army will fight my own, in the middle of the Shimmering Sea."

"You begin to see the true image." Morpheus said.

"So, the mountain we all see in our dreams," Akio began,

"Is where the Great Snake resides." Theodore said, snapping his stout fingers.

"The third king eludes us, there is an army on our doorstep and the island of Volar is thousands of miles away." Hexus said, throwing his hands up.

"Yes, we have many problems," Morpheus said, "But we must make it to Olympus, and there we may be able to put this all in the past. You all, you all sitting in this tree, you are the future of this world. You never asked for it, it was thrust upon you, and for that I am sorry, but now is no time for anger. Now is the time for action. Rest well and arm yourselves on the morrow, for soon enough, we walk to the castle of the gods."

41

"WE LEAVE IN the morrow." Morpheus announced. It echoed through the field. Chase felt the chill of night hit him as he left the Heart Tree's cavern. His arm hairs stood straight and he carefully lowered himself to the grass, hanging on to branches and shrubs on the way down. He was greeted by the nature spirit creatures. They all cooed and played near the streams of water and in the grass.

He looked up. His smile melted into a frown as he locked eyes with Eleon. The man's amber eye stared at him, while the scar on his right eye glowed golden in the light of the fireflies. He was tied to a post, his arms behind his back. The lionskin cloak still drooped over his shoulders, and the mane swayed in the breeze around his head. Chase turned. Everyone slowly descended the roots, ready to sleep for tomorrow. No one saw him.

He walked over to Eleon, who was now staring directly at the grass. He stood there silently, watching the man. His beard was covered in dried blood and spit. His face was scratched, and his skin was dry. His clothes had stains of food and blood on it and his breathes were short and far between. They sounded like brief snorts. Eos, his horned owl squawked.

"Are you going to keep staring or are you going to say something, you little prick?" Eleon barked.

"You stink of sweat and piss." Chase said coldly. He felt no pity for the man. He deserved his punishment. Eleon had nearly killed them all just because Chase had set him off. Regardless of that, Eleon had not been likeable before that. He was a hulking, ill-mannered drunken fool.

Eleon just laughed, "you seem so brave with me lying beneath you. Make no mistake, animal, when I get out of these bonds, I will come for you first, then that fat goat Silenus and your friends will come soon after."

Chase scowled. He was terrified, but he was not going to give Eleon the satisfaction of his fear. He contained his fear with a deep breath, putting on a mask of courage. "You would hurt your sister?"

Eleon scoffed, "No. I will free her. You lie to her, and I will show her the truth."

"What truth?"

"You are not like us."

Eleon's owl hissed.

He kneeled before him and stared him in the eye.

"Why do you hate me so much." Chase asked. He had realized that often happens with the people in Alor as well. Many people hated the satyrs, but when asked why, they had nothing to say. Most thought them thieves, drunks and animals, but nobody had ever said thief or drunk in person. Odd.

As expected, Eleon said nothing. Chase straitened himself. He crossed his arms, "I asked you something." He said.

Eleon growled.

Chase lowered his face, trying to catch Eleon's eye. A wad of spit hit him in the face instead. He scrambled to wipe the slobber from his cheek with the back of his hand.

Eleon smiled with yellow teeth. "You're an animal." *Animal.* Chase had not heard Eleon call him anything different. He turned and walked to the camp; tents were already being set up.

Eleon's wheezes mockingly punched him in the ears over and over. He turned the laughs away. He had no reason to hear them. Eleon was the drunkard and the fool. He accused Chase of being the things he himself was. That was a funny thing. Chase did not need Eleon to accept him. He had made a name for himself in this group. He had saved them in the lair of Silenus, and he had fought of the raiders with them. He ate with them and sang with them and traveled with them. He was more a part of their group than Eleon was, and the thought made him smile.

42

ZEUS. THE NAME echoed in Adam's brain. He knew not whether he wanted to kneel before the god of punch him in the nose. He asked why he could not do both. Fury boiled in his blood. He wanted to hit something. He wanted to walk up to Olympus itself and curse the gods in front of everything.

Fifteen years of misery and abuse, all for what? The past month had been more eventful than his entire life, and all because he needed to become a god? The word *god* did not match with his name. The words had never been conceived in the same sentence.

He thought about it. He thought about becoming a god. It was inconceivable. It was a thought so extraordinarily wild, that he felt as though he had dreamt it. He had no way of knowing how the next few days would play out, but he knew few things for certain.

The army had caught up with them now, and it will be soon that they make their first attack against the group. *Or second,* Adam thought. If they had struggled at the ambush in the oasis, Adam was reluctant to see what a full assault could do. He feared their leader as well. They were controlled by that beast of a man Adam had seen in his dream. Korax was his name, completely clad in iron and taller than even Zethus. Adam had seen his sword, the six-foot blood-red blade and the heavy obsidian-black hilt. That giant man had taken Alor in less than a day, and he was close to them now.

The mountain that he had always seen in his dreams was the volcano that trapped Typhon, he knew that much as well. He could connect some things to what Morpheus said. Korax led the army, and Typhon led Korax, but did Typhon answer to anything else? Adam knew not, and he did not want to.

Morpheus's words had been echoing in his head all night. He repeated them himself, for fear that he might be dreaming it all.

"The future of this world..." he said, "home of the gods... my army and his... Volar... Shimmering Sea... my army and his... third king.... Third king... my army and his... third king"

He groaned. So much had happened in that tree. Kathrine had a vision, and she had seen part of an ancient prophecy. Morpheus said something about and oracle and looked at Kathrine when he said it. Adam was not happy with it. To receive the answers he desired, he only raised more questions.

He had no army. He had a few friends all armed with blades that cannot kill these devils, and he was told to do battle with them at the base of a volcano he had never been to before, in the middle of a sea he had not known of until a few days ago. He needed air.

Crickets and fireflies danced in the field outside his tent. The massive Heart Tree loomed down on them, a thousand feet high. Its trunk stood crooked and massive, covered in vines and moss. Eleon sat alone in the field, looking down at the grass, while others talked on the massive roots of the Hart Tree. Fairies fluttered around the air and mushrooms and shrubs cooed and played. This place was magnificent. He never wanted to leave here. He wished he could stay, with Chase and Kathrine and never leave for as long as they lived.

Kathrine's face appeared before him. He shook his head. She had approached him before the meeting in the Heart Tree, but he had not heard her speak. It was nearing midnight now, and they were to wake early to walk on Olympus, but nobody slept. Adam saw the flickering lights of oil candles burning within several tents. Including Kathrine's.

He was reluctant of the thought. She was awake he knew that much, and he knew that she had wanted to talk to him. But after her vision in the Heart Tree, he was unsure if that was still the case.

He cursed himself and walked over. It was still odd to him that even after all of this he had just learned, Kathrine was still important. Then he remembered what Zethus had said at the oasis. *Love.*

Raia appeared in front of him, a wide smile on her lips. She looked him up and down with her amethyst eyes. He backed up, ignoring the festering annoyance that burned in his chest.

"You're awake." She said.

Adam struggled to form words. She extended a hand and brought two fingers, like legs, up to the collar of his tunic. "I enjoyed the party, did you?"

Adam still stammered. He looked over at Kathrine's tent, the light in it still on.

"We know not of what awaits us tomorrow, perhaps we could share... one final night together." She got close to his face, and her hair smelt of heavy perfume.

She pushed her aside, "No. Stop that."

She scoffed, "you do not have to worry. I do not bite."

"I am not interested in what you offer me." Adam said, his fists clenched.

She knit an eyebrow, "Do not play fool with me, Adam. I can *make* you interested. I can make you... *very* interested."

Adam frowned, "No. You can't."

"You would still go to that girl?" She jabbed a finger at Kathrine's tent and made a sour face.

"You speak to low of her. Kathrine is my friend. You are but a poison to me. You do not seek my happiness; you search only for your own. She is not like you, and for that, I am thankful."

He walked past her and left her alone in the field. He heard a scoff as she stormed off, and took a deep breath as he arrived at Kathrine's tent.

He tossed open the curtain to Kathrine's and there she sat. Cross legged in the middle of her tent, with a flickering oil lamp lighting up her map.

She looked up with emerald eyes, and suddenly Adam could not name anything more beautiful.

He stammered to find words, "I... I couldn't sleep."

She giggled, her hazel hair falling behind her shoulders, "Neither could I." She tapped the parchment spread out before her. "Chase let me borrow his map."

"Oh. You're looking at it, the world."

"I've never imagined anything so massive. Did you know that there are more than a thousand islands in the Shattered Lands of Argana."

Adam had no idea what that meant "I did not." She smiled, and he sat next to her.

They sat there for hours, talking and looking at the map and talking more, and for the first time since leaving Alor, Adam felt as though nothing else mattered. He looked at her eyes and found himself lost in them. His mind was entranced by the swirling pools of emerald-green that were her eyes. He noticed thing she had never noticed before. Kathrine had a small scar above her top lip, and a small birthmark above her left eyebrow, and her fingers had been reddened and left bruised by her bowstring.

He pointed at the map, "Where is Alor?" He asked.

Kathrine smiled, "It's not here. Chase told me that Zethus said it was to the south of Vulna, but it is not on any maps."

Adam knit an eyebrow, "of course not. Nobody knew it existed until Norris made it there."

"We did." She laughed; the most adorable laugh had ever heard.

He laughed back, "Yes we did."

The map stared at him with invisible eyes. He thought about Alor, all the years he had lived there. All the years *they* had lived there. Compared to all of this, he missed the simplicity of it in a way. Every day he would wake and spend his day with Kathrine and Chase in the old forest. Him and Kathrine had no other friends because of Chase but Adam did not care. He always loved those days with the nymphs and satyrs. He remembered Diocles and all his lessons, and Chase's thousand stories of what nymph he had seen the night before. He missed eating stolen food Kathrine had gotten for them every day. He had always lied to her, saying that there was a better way to live than having to steal to eat, but she never listened. She got them fed and never expected anything in return. He loved that about her. She gave to him and he took and thanked, but he never gave her anything. He had pulled her from the comfort of the city to see a world they were not sure existed and had nearly gotten her killed a hundred times after. Then she found him with Raia at Silenus's lair, and everything came crumbling down so quickly, all because he went to one goddamn priestess.

He felt tears swell in his eyes and tried to blink them away but stopped when he felt them run down his cheek.

Kathrine frowned and touched his face. He took her hand, it was smooth, and wet with his tears, "I'm sorry." He held his face, taking deep breathes.

"For what?"

"Everything. I'm sorry I took you from Alor. I'm sorry I led you from your home. From *our* home. I just wanted to end these dreams. You said no! You said it a thousand times and I ignored you. We nearly died a hundred times because of me and my foolish wish. I'm sorry for Raia. I'm sorry for all of this. Alor is a pile of rubble now because of that damn army and-"

"And if we never left then we would be with that army." He met her eyes. They were caring and compassionate and she smiled faintly.

Kathrine did not know what to do now that she saw him cry. She seldom saw tears in his eyes and whenever she did, she wanted them gone. Raia had seduced him, she saw that. Up until now she always thought that Adam was to be left behind, though she had come to regret that thought. She feared forgetting him, she feared having him forget her. She wanted him in his life. She knew that now

"I know your sorry. For Alor, for Raia for all of it. But none of that matters now. We got what we wanted. We got the answers and we know what to do now. I'm not mad at you," she took his other cheek with her other hand and pulled him close, "you are the greatest thing to ever happen to me." They kissed, smooth and long. Adam felt a thousand butterflies in his stomach and lightning shot down his back. Kathrine's heart fluttered and felt Adam's arm wrap around her waist. She ran her fingernails through his hair, and they fell backwards, now lying on the ground.

Her lips were soft, and his hands were warm. They kissed for a long moment and then she pulled away. They both breathed heavily, and Adam felt both their skins fill with goosebumps. Adam felt relieved, and she smiled as she straddled him.

Her face flickered in the candlelight as her shirt came off. Adam remembered Zethus's words. He remembered Laura. He knew why he did not bed her; it was because he did not love her. Then that thought vanished. *Love* replaced it.

He felt Kathrine's hands on him, and they kissed again.

43

NORRIS WAS ANGRY. Nearly three days had passed since they had run out of wine, and not one single damn person in this entire damned garden had any more. He flung his empty skin across the skin and watched as it landed flatly on the grass. Norris sat on the roots of the Heart Tree with Akio, Zethus, Hexus and Chase. Light flickered from the small brazier in the corner and the smell of coals filled the air.

Animals and woodland spirits slept around them, bathing in the shadow of the Heart Tree. Morpheus meditated nearby, levitating, glowing in a purple aura. Norris did not like the boy. It had all been far too simple. Morpheus had explained everything in less than a moment. Norris was not sure whether to trust what he said entirely, especially after he had observed Kathrine queerly after explaining something about a prophecy.

He floated above a massive root, cross legged with his dark hands floating before him. His white eyes were shut, and his dark face was still. The only thing that moved was his billowing cape.

"The hell is he doing?" Chase asked.

"Probably spreading more dreams around." Akio chuckled.

Norris looked down and sighed. Some part of him had hoped that this had all been a dream, that he could wake from all of this whenever he liked, but he knew that was only a wish.

Norris thought about his dream he had had in the lake a few days past. He remembered the city beneath the waves and the strange creatures floating about in it. Adam saw Zeus in his dreams, the Eagle, and Theodore had seen Hermes, the young man. Norris had not seen anybody, but he remembered the voice he had heard. It was gruff and commanding, foreign to him, and yet... so familiar.

"Poseidon..." he whispered to himself. No one heard him. He would have thought it funny if he was drunk, but the thought did not make him smile. A drunken fool who hated the taste of water, connected to the god of the seas. That was the only answer he could discern. He figured that his abilities seemed to connect as well. The city was below water. Norris had heard of underwater cities in stories and myths. He had heard that they were all scattered around the earth. One was in the Shattered Lands of Argana, one was in the icy Sea of Farnörr and another in the Rainbow Fish isles to the south, if the tales were too be believed. Norris never believed in the gods, and now he had just been told that his beliefs had wrong for nearly thirty years. He wished for alcohol as soon as possible.

Norris had believed in men. He believed the world was run by man and woman and nothing else, and now, he had travelled with a goddess for a day, stayed in the company of a god another and had been receiving dreams from other gods for his entire life. His head still spun.

Norris had never heard of Morpheus before this day, but he had heard enough of the gods to know that if they *were* real, they were not to be trusted. He thought of Red Winter, the Three Kings and the weeks to come. Weeks that would turn to fortnights, fortnights that would turn to months and months that became years. He had no idea where they could end up. With luck, Volar will not be the last place he sees.

They still knew not of the third king's name, but he knew that it would come soon enough, but he knew *soon enough* would never feel like it was here.

Chase brought a waterskin to his lips, and contemplated his thoughts, "What's it like... to have those dreams?" He asked the group.

Akio pursed his lips, Zethus raised his eyebrows and breathed in, and Hexus averted eye contact. Everyone had forgotten about Chase not having the dreams until Morpheus had reminded them in the Heart Tree's cavern. Him and Kathrine both dreamed normal dreams, though with Kathrine's vision in the cavern, Norris wondered how long that tranquility would last.

"Hurts like hell in the morning." Zethus chuckled, fingering his amulet. Akio laughed. Hexus joined.

Norris thought of the question. No one had asked him that before, and now that he was forced to, the answer could not pass his mind. He could describe the pain when you woke from the sleep, and the fear that one felt when remembering the dreams. For nearly thirty years... he feared sleep, but wine did not. Wine did not fear anything and when Norris had it inside him, he did not fear anything.

"You should consider yourself lucky." Norris said. Chase looked up. "The dreams pain even the strongest of minds." He looked over at Eric's tent, the only one with the flame in the tent extinguished.

"What was he like?" Akio asked, after a long moment of silence. Norris turned back to him, "before all of this? What was Eric like?"

Chase seemed to be intrigued by that question. Zethus raised his eyebrows and crossed his beefy arms.

Norris laid back. He tried to think, but it had been so long since he had ever seen a smile grace Eric's lips. Now, Norris seldom saw his face at all.

"He was kind." Norris remembered. "He was compassionate and brave, and no matter who he fought with, no one was above or below him. He was fair to everyone, and everyone seemed to like that."

"That sounds like a different man." Chase said.

Norris sighed, feeling the heat of the brazier on his face, "It was."

The group went silent again.

"What happened?" Akio asked.

Norris sighed, "doesn't matter. That man is dead now, and this one has taken its place, for good or ill. We've all struggled, what difference does it make?" Norris crossed his arms.

More silence, Norris did not know what to make of it.

Zethus sighed, "Sometimes I think ive caused more suffering."

Chase looked at him, concern in his face, "What are you talking about."

"For as long as I can remember, I've been a soldier. I fought in the Great-West for a king I never met, doing battle with men I had no quarrel with." His voice broke.

Zethus felt tears swell in his eyes as he spoke. He had expected to never tell anyone of his past, he wanted to leave it all behind, but the words poured from him like water from a stream.

A know formed in Chase' throat. Zethus had never seemed the man to cry. Chase did not blame him. He had been surprised that more tears had not come as of late. Frowns and sadness had accompanied them into the garden, and it had only clung to them ever stronger since. Chase had never been in a moment where he could lose someone close to him, or lose his life *himself*, but now, with the army close, he knew it was close. He wanted to cry to, so Zethus's tears came with no judgment. Tears from the eyes of a man, when he is with others is a sign of courage.

"I... have done things I'm not proud of. My sword has claimed more lives than just other soldiers." He fingered his amulet. "I... I remember the dreams I grew up with... the nightmares. I remember how horrible they got. My tentmates could not sleep in the same tent I did, I moved too frantically... as if I were in battle... as if I had never fallen asleep. I remember one day.

"We were soldiers, we kept our blades nearby when we slept. I... had a mate... Merek was his name... a young lad. We had gone to sleep that night, below the roof of the same tent. I had the dream again, the mountain, the bodies... it was all... so real. I remember there was one Spartus... it jumped at me from the grass field and I jumped. When I opened my eyes, I was no longer dreaming... but gods do I wish I was..." More tears ran down his face. "When I awoke, my fingers held a knife. It was buried in Merek's chest. I had put it there... me! Not a mercenary, or a robber, or an enemy of the crown... me... his best mate.

"I remember he cried as he lay dying. He looked up at me... and he whispered... *why you?*"

The words seemed to fly away in the wind, never to be heard again. Zethus oft spoke of the horrors of war, but Chase had never pictured this. Zethus had done battle with countless men, and the one life that stayed with him... was the one of his friend... and Chase cursed himself for forgetting the name, but just like that... his name was forgotten... like so many other victims of war.

"I wonder if one day I will be punished for my crimes," Zethus said, wiping the tears from his face, "or if I will be destined to die with them lingering in my mind. I pray otherwise." He held up a finger, "I pray that before I die... I will atone for my sins... and smile at my friend once more."

He breathed heavily for a moment, then he turned to Akio.

"What about you Akio?" Zethus asked, "you were born rich. That must have been... delightful." He laughed.

Akio sighed, "you would be surprised."

Everyone looked him. "When your family is like mine, you don't get many things. Sure, you have money, and servants and all the food you could ask for, but for a child... none of that really matters. I've never had friends. I'm not quite sure I know what "fun" is." Is expression being grim, a far too common sight as of late.

"How'd you leave Halanor?" Chase asked.

"In secret." Akio said with a solemn laugh, "I'm not quite sure my parents know where I am."

"I've always felt like I've... had to prove myself to everyone." Chase said from silence, "I have always felt the need to differ myself from everyone's beliefs of me. I don't want to be a drunk, or a thief or an animal."

"You're not." Zethus put a hand on his shoulder.

Chase narrowed his vision, "I know that now." He said with a faint smile.

"You have friends now," Hexus elbowed Akio. They both smiled. The quiet peace was comfortable for a moment, before a blood curdling shriek filled their ears. Everyone flinched and turned to the woods.

Norris squinted at the leaves in the distance, which were now shaking and shivering.

Hexus stood, from the height of the roots, everyone could see everything.

"What is that?" Akio asked.

Norris stared deeper into the forest. Familiar voices came from below as everyone exited their tents. Whatever was in the woods, it was huge. Trees and canopies fell to make way for it and flocks of birds took to the night sky to escape it.

No, Norris thought, *the birds come from it.* The birds were huge, near the size of a child, with black plumage and glowing red eyes that danced in the distance like drifting embers.

Norris widened his eyes, "Nightcrows...."

"Shit..." Zethus said, already halfway down the root, "they found us."

44

THE FOREST HAD never seemed so ominous before. From deep within the thickness of the garden, cracking trees and snapping twigs echoed into the grove. Adam looked and saw the nature creatures fleeing into the cavern of the Heart Tree or beneath the roots or into the woods behind them.

Adam reached for a blade that was not there. All his equipment was in his tent, and he had barely had time to put his tunic back on. Kathrine already held a bow in her hand, her wild hair falling over her shoulders and onto her hastily put on shirt. Adam did not even have time to react to what had happened in her tent before the shrieks came.

Everyone stood before the garden, all staring into the seemingly endless darkness between the thousands of trunks. A growl came from it, then a snarl and then more growls. Howls and roars and shrieks and whales poured from the shadows, each one sending the group back a step. Everyone took their weapons in hand, and Adam still stood, his hands empty.

He turned and bolted towards his tent, running through streams and ponds, wetting his clothes in the process. He threw open his tent, rummaging through all his supplies until he felt it, the solid rod of cold, adamant. He pulled it from the piles of clothes and rushed back to meet the others, who were all in various stages of fear.

Eric stood before everyone, his nocked arrow pointing directly into the dark. Another howl rushed, but Eric did not so much as blink.

"Stay here," Ladon said, his massive, coiling body slithering into the darkness. His hundreds of other heads snapped and bit at each other no more, all growling at the shadows instead.

Everyone made way for the dragon before Hebe rushed up to him.

"Do be careful!" She pleaded, holding one massive claw.

The dragon lowered his gaze, "I will return to you, sweet." Then he turned and slithered into the darkness.

Morpheus floated down from the roots to meet them, "Return to the Heart Tree, it is safe there!" He took Hebe in his arms, floating up once again and backing away towards the Heart Tree.

A wheezing laugh came from behind them. Eleon's back faced them, from inside Quartus's howdah.

"What the hell will wood do? We need to leave!" He barked at Morpheus. "Erika!" He snapped at the group, "untie me now! We must leave here!"

His twin sister took a reluctant step forward before sighing and looking back at the group. Her eyes filled with courage.

"Asius, Theodore, ready Quartus, the rest of you, ready what you can and fall back out the other side of the garden." Everyone rushed to do what she told.

Eric never turned his sight from the garden, "Morpheus lead us out of the garden. Take us to the gate!" he ordered.

"At once!" Morpheus said, turning.

It was quicker than ever to pack everything and ready the animals. Asius lightly tugged on the reins of Pormant's muzzle to lead him along and Hexus got on Quartus with Akio and Chase, ready to leave.

A roar came from the forest once again. Everyone turned. Eric fired the arrow, and it whizzed into the shadows.

"GO!" he shouted, yelling at the others.

Ladon came from the darkness of the garden roaring and biting. His thousand jaws snapped at other creatures. Bony, skinless dragons. Adam recognized the beasts, the ones the had seen in his dreams. More skeleton dragons flooded in from within the forest, flapping their membrane-less wings and snapping at Ladon. The massive beast clawed and scratched at them, catching a few in his jaws and ripping them apart.

What flesh they once had, had corrupted away for the most part, leaving bones and few bits of rotting meat to hold it all together. The smell overtook Adam, and he gagged. The beasts were smaller than Ladon, no bigger than a horse, but for what they lacked in size they more than made up for in numbers. Dozens flew in from the woods, wild and terrifying.

"Aim for the heads!" Adam heard Zethus call. Black wolves with rotting skin and small imp-like creatures, Kobaloi, Adam remembered, crawled out from the shadows. More Spartoi came, roaring and screaming. Adam swung his blade, slicing through one Spartoi, and decapitating another.

Kathrine fired arrows at random, never missing a target and Chase howled as he flung rocks at the incoming monsters. Eric moved like a shadow, jumping silently from creature to creature, thrusting his short blades through skulls, eye-sockets and jaws. He sliced off heads and crushed them under the weight of his foot. More creatures came, and Adam heard wordless war cries. The animals roared, Tenzir mauling one Spartoi while Beta wrestled a corpse-wolf.

Adam blinked away his fear. He looked around nervously, finding something to do. Norris and Hexus fought with fire and water, and Akio sliced creature after creature with the thin Godslayer. The blade glinted in the darkness with the shine of blood. Raia's magic swirled around the field of battle and flung creatures into the air, crushing them or ripping them apart. Asius rode atop Quartus, leading the massive beast, crushing dozens of Spartoi beneath its heavy feet.

Adam turned back. Boo ripped Spartoi apart by the dozens and Minerva clenched her fists atop his shoulders, trying her best to stay on. Her eyes were shut, and vines twisted around her wrists. The vines licked out and snapped at the Spartoi, throwing them about.

Adam felt a claw on his arm. He was thrown down as a Spartus snapped at his face. He pressed his arm against the creature's collar bone, keeping it inches from his nose. The monster squirmed on top of Adam and he squirmed beneath it. The creature growled and Adam screamed. Sharp pain ran up his arm and Adam yelled. His arm spurted blood on his face as the Spartoi bit deeper into it. Its head jumped up, ripping a chunk of bloody flesh from Adam's forearm. He screamed louder. Adam thrust his sword into the creature's jaw, watching as the thin, silver blade jutted from the top of its skull, sputtering black blood around it. Thick black blood dripped down Adam's hand and arm, glistening in the dark. The body went limp and Adam felt all its weight fall on him. He pulled his sword free of the creatures' jaw.

He tossed the limp body to the side and got to his feet, already winded. He breathed heavily, sweat streaming down his neck and blood dripping off his fingers, his arm burning with pain. He felt dizzy, his head splitting. His mouth tasted of blood and his arm had lost all feeling.

"Stop!" A deep voice called, echoing through Adam's ears. He took a deep breath and found his balance again.

The creatures froze and growled as they slowly crawled back into the forest. Everyone waited, panting and sweating. The bony dragons' wings clattered together as they flapped in the air. Their rotting white claws pressed into Ladons skin, drawing golden blood. The massive dragon tried to pry himself free from the dragons' hold, but to no avail.

"No!" Hebe yelled.

Heavy breathes and groans of pain filled Adam's ears as everyone stared into the darkness of the forest.

The sound of a growling beast came from the shadows. The darkness morphed into form. The beast smelled awful, of rotting flesh and was clouded by flies. Its eyes glowed red like burning garnet. Its muzzle bared rotting yellow teeth beneath a sniffing snout. Giant bats wings sprouted from its shoulders and a snarling goats head snapped at the lion's head. A swirling snake hissed, being the tail.

"A Chimera." Norris murmured.

"You... you're... our dreams" Hexus said.

Adam felt a shiver down his spine. The rider showed himself. Cloaked in shadows, Korax emerged from the darkness, his grey, ripped cloak billowed behind him. His silver scales and armor shined, and his longsword dangled from his belt, hidden in his pitch-black scabbard. His eyes glowed red in his helm like bleeding stars.

A second creature showed itself, next to the first. About the size of a horse, with the head of a grey eagle and golden eyes. Its front legs were those of an eagle and its back were those of a horse. Massive birds' wings fluttered on its sides. Its rider was smaller than the first. It wore black scales and iron and its face covered with an iron mask, topped with a billowing white plume. Red eyes shine from inside the mask.

"A Hippogriff." Adam said, remembering it from his dream.

"Kneel!" The rider croaked in a wheeze of a voice. "You stand before Lord Ithacus Korax. The greatest conqueror who ever lived, the iron beast of Vulna, the reaper of the Great-West and king of the Great Children. Kneel before his majesty."

No one did anything. The smaller rider moved so quickly that nobody had time to react. A short silver blade was drawn from his sheath, its point glinting between Adam's eyes.

"I said... KNEEL!" The smaller rider shouted. Adam flinched. He bent his leg to kneel, but his mind told him otherwise. These creatures had destroyed so much. Adam's compliance was not about to be given to them.

"No." he said, his voice stern. He glared at the rider. His red eyes shrunk for a moment in his mask, he glared back.

"If violence is what you desire, you need only ask, boy." The smaller rider said.

"Enough." Said Korax. Everyone faced him, "You know who I am yes?"

"You were the man who started the War of the West a thousand years ago." Theodore said, his voice hoarse.

Korax lowered his head, as if he were smiling behind his helm. Theo went on, "You rebelled against the throne in the Great-West, you made your own kingdom, you called it, Araxia."

"You know your history boy." Korax hissed.

"I know you were a cruel man. You were killed in the battle of Rushing Waters."

Korax's joy seemed to fade with that, "watch your tongue, lest it be ripped out of your mouth."

"You murdered innocents by the thousands to scare the throne—"

"After I gave them a choice!" He bellowed. "I offered those who fell before me to declare me the true ruler of the Great-West, to pledge their loyalty to me, or suffer the consequences." He dismounted the Chimera.

"What is it that you want?" Theodore asked.

"You have shown your intelligence, young one." His armor rattled as his marched closer to the group, sending everyone walking back. Adam felt cold. The bite on his arm had ceased its bleeding, hardening into rivers of shining, dark red, like trails of ruby. His head spun and sweat poured down his neck and back.

Korax placed a gauntleted hand on the black hilt of his great sword, "the Great Snake brought me back to this wretched world for a reason. This world needs correction. I can give it that, we can give it that."

"Who is we?" Chase asked.

"The Three Kings." Adam realized.

Korax laughed, Adam had never heard something so terrible before, "The Three Kings will unify this world. We will correct it, by allowing only the worthy to live in it."

"Who are the worthy?" Erika asked.

"Those I deem fit. I will cleanse this world of all who seek to do it harm."

"You'll slaughter millions for a chance at power?" Adam said.

"I will slaughter millions to rectify the mistakes of the past."

Adam tightened his grip on his sword, "what mistakes?"

"For a thousand years, the Olympians have kept my people from rising. Your gods have prevented us from correcting their sins, only to ignore those same sins themselves. No longer will that law go further. You have had this world for far too long, and you toy with it as if it were a child's plaything. This world around you, famine, poverty, bigotry, unnecessary violence, that is what you have wrought. The Great Snake will rise, and when he does, those who have lived under the shield of the Olympians will die."

"You're an evil man," Zethus said, sternly.

Korax chuckled, "*Evil*, will always be a word without an owner. To an insect... a sparrow is evil.

"No!" Erika's voice cried. Zethus lumbered over, sword in hand. Korax studied him, he placed a finger beneath Zethus's bearded chin. "You are beautiful, aren't you? The first host, perhaps." Adam didn't know what he spoke of. Xuthos, the smaller rider a top the Hippogriff laughed. Korax chuckled.

Zethus spat in his face. Korax did not blink. *What the hell are you doing?* Adam wanted to cry, but his mouth did not form the words. Erika stood next to him, her breathes short, her spear broken at the shaft. Zethus stood before Korax, and as tall as may be, he was dwarfed next to the iron giant.

"As long as there is life in my breast, I will *never* bow to men like you." Zethus clutched his sword in his hand. His knuckles turned white.

Korax laughed again, "You speak as if you had a choice in the matter, there is no choice. I give everyone a choice before they meet their fate, join me or die, but I'm afraid this time, that offer cannot stand. The Great Snake had plans for none of you." Korax turned and mounted his beast again.

Adam met eyes with Korax as he mounted the Chimera.

"Nock," he said quietly. Creaks came from the darkness.

"Draw." The creaks were followed by smooth sliding. Everyone ran. Quartus trumpeted and Adam felt Kathrine's hand on his arm.

"Let's go!" Her slowed voice seemed to shout.

Adam kept his gaze fixed on Zethus, who stood motionless before then group, his body glowing a hot orange red.

"Loose!" Korax cried. From the darkness of the forest, a dozen arrows flew straight at Adam's face.

45

RED LIGHT FLASHED before everyone's eyes. Zethus held his hands out, and a dome of orange and red sparks flew from his fingers. Adam gasped in awe. The black arrows froze as they all hit the dome with loud *thunks*.

Zethus turned, rage in his eyes, "GO!" He yelled. Adam was too stunned to move. He heard the squawking of the birds and the cries of the animals. Metal clanged as it was pulled from scabbards and shouts and cries surrounded him.

Korax scoffed, "Kill them all." His red blade was pulled from its black scabbard.

From between the trunks, countless more riders emerged, followed by their beasts. Riding black, rotting horses with hoofbeats like thunder and clad in full iron and chainmail came more than twenty cloaked riders, waving silver swords in their gauntleted hands.

Waves of Spartoi followed them, collapsing on each other like toppled bricks from a fallen building. Kobaloi scurried on the grass and leaped from the trees like demonic monkeys and corpse wolves bared their teeth, foaming at the mouths.

Adam felt his feet move. He dashed across the roots of the Heart Tree, feeling his face heat up when Hexus blasted flames at the oncoming horde. Shrieks of the burned beasts echoed across the garden. Adam saw Ladon break free of the Bonedragons' hold roaring and ripping apart his skeletal captors with his thousand jaws. He heard

Raia's voice as she chanted spells, saw Minerva and vine-whips and Kathrine firing arrow after arrow alongside Erika.

The fires raged around them. Hexus blasted the forest with so much force, that trees fell over, launching embers into the air like glowing red snowflakes. Adam clutched his sword. In seconds, his surroundings became a hellish battlefield. He tried to look around him, to find a familiar face, to get some sort of understanding as to what was going on, but all he saw were the raging flames that surrounded them. He tried to look for Kathrine, for Chase, even Akio or Theodore, anybody. He heard voices yell and shout. The creatures growled and shrieked. He heard their roars and the loud scratches of their claws ripping apart the tree bark.

To his left, behind a wall of flames, Eric stood with his back to Adam, an arrow nocked in his bow. He yelled something Adam could not understand, and Adam heard a voice respond. He did not understand what it said, but it sounded scared.

Adam stared into the forest. Something moved in there. He closed his eyes less he be blinded by the flying embers. The bark on the trees snapped and creaked as it curled into burnt strands, eventually melting into thousands of dancing embers.

Adam heard a shriek from his side. He turned and an Imp-like creature threw itself at him. The Kobalos screeched as it landed in the ember covered ground next to him. The chaos roared around Adam. The trees creaked and snapped, and the embers nearly blinded him. He yelled out names; Kathrine, Chase, Eric, Hexus, Norris, and no response. He heard wild war cries and shouts of terror, but his sight was an orange blur.

The Kobalos screeched again. It was a grotesque creature, with large, triangular ears on top of its large head, big white eyes and a small, thin body, no larger than a child. It slashed its claws and Adam felt pain run up his ankle. He looked down, blood dripped down to his feet and the Kobalos stabbed another claw into his side.

He roared with pain. Adam swung his arm, knocking the Imp into the forest, it screeched as it retreated. A violent roar followed it. From the darkness of the forest, three skeletal, black skinned creatures burst from the trees, swinging swords and claws and howling a wordless war cry. Red eyes glowed in the deep voids that were their sockets and some missed bones.

A jawless Spartus swung a rusted, dented blade at Adam. He pivoted out of the way, and brought his fist down on the creature's skull, knocking it to the ground. Another attacked, this one with more skin on its bones and a much more human appearance. Its cheeks were sunken, and its arms were thin. Few hairs sprouted from its scalp and its skin was dark as coal. It bit at him with rotting teeth. Adam somersaulted to the left, landing next to a rock. The stone was the size of and apple, and he took it with his hand, flinging it at the Spartus's head. It crumpled, and Adam swung the stone at it once again, and again, and again. He did not stop until the creature's skull was no more than a black sludge. He stared at his work, not knowing whether to be satisfied with it, or horrified.

Bony fingers crept onto his shoulders. He screamed and swung his rock, hitting the third Spartus in the face. It swirled the left, clashing with the first one that Adam had knocked to the ground. They screeched collectively.

Adam heard a snap next to him. He looked up to see an oak tree, covered in flames coming down on top of him. He jumped out of the way as it crashed into the leaves below, launching burning leaves and embers into the air. The Spartoi's twitching arms danced in the flames until they slowly stopped. The fires raged on, growing hotter and hotter as the seconds past.

"Hexus!" He cried. "Stop this! You'll kill us all!"

The roaring flame continued, and the crackle of fire accompanied it. Adam kneeled in the leaves, panting and sweating. The heat was painful, and the night sky crept through the ruined canopy.

"Where are you?" Cried a voice from the flickering darkness. It was followed by a scream, a female scream.

Adam rushed past the flames towards the scream. His mind rushed, was it Kathrine? What had happened to her? He past a flaming log

and jumped over it. What was he doing? He was going to get himself
killed. He didn't care, he needed to find Kathrine before something
happened to her.

He heard footsteps louden before him, and he saw a silhouette
running towards him. He crashed into something solid, and they both
grunted. He fell backwards onto the leaves and looked forward. A tall
man wearing a tunic picked up his dropped weapon, a mace.

Eleon stared at Adam with wild amber eyes. Foam dribbled down
his beard and his face had been badly burned, embers still glowing on
his brow, beard and right cheek. Burned rope hung from his wrists,
and his owl screeched.

Adam placed his arm out to calm the clearly angry Eleon, his
eyes rarely leaving the terrifying bird, "Eleon listen to me." He said
hurriedly, "You're not thinking straight. I need you to calm down."
Eleon's ember peppered brow furrowed and he raised his mace with
a wild roar. Spit flew from his teeth as he brought the weapon down
on Adam.

Adam rolled to his side, narrowly avoiding the heavy mace. It
landed with a loud *thump* next to his face, knocking embers everywhere.
Adam took his sword in his hand and faced Eleon, who grunted as he
pried his mace from the flaming ground.

Eleon faced Adam, his burn melting the flesh off his cheek, "YOU
DID THIS TO ME!" He screamed, more spit flying from his mouth.
"YOU DID THIS TO ME YOU LITTLE SHIT! YOU BETRAYED
ME!" Dirt exploded from the ground where he finally pulled his mace
from. "

AND NOW I WILL RIP OUT YOUR GUTS AND FEED THEM
TO YOU!"

His bird attacked, its black feathers a dark blur as it blazed through
the flames. Adam felt its talons tear at his arms, he shook it off, only
to feel pain on his left cheek. Flesh tore, blood dripped into his mouth
and he spat it out. He screamed; his face smothered by feathers. Adam
brought his fist up and felt the hilt of his blade smash into something
and opened his eyes to see the bird squawk as it took to the skies.

Eleon roared, Adam looked at him, hot blood trickling down his cheek. He took his mace with both arms, and red energy crawled all around him, his amber eyes now glowing blood red. The energy swirled down to the shaft and ball of the mace and the weapon began to steam. Eleon roared as he rushed towards Adam. Adam felt his arms shake and the hairs on his neck stood up straight. He was terrified. Eleon was bigger than him, and stronger and faster. Adam thought this was where he died.

He lifted himself from the ground, holding his sword in his hand before him. He rolled out of the way of Eleon's first swing, avoiding the strike by less than an inch.

Adam swung his thin blade, cursing when it bounced off Eleon's mace with no effect. He pivoted to the left at Eleon's second strike, as it made a crater in the dirt. Eleon through it to the left and it slammed Adam in the chest.

The flames flew past his view as he flew back, his chest burning. He landed on his stomach, woodchips and twigs scratching his face. He spat blood out and coughed violently. Adam turned back, facing Eleon.

Eleon smiled maniacally as he stared at Adam, the amber returning to his eyes. He slowly walked towards him, smiling and laughing a wheezing laugh.

Adam breathed heavily, hot blood pouring down his head and mouth. His body felt lighter, and he felt his chest burn less and his arms feel stronger. The hairs on his arms stood up, and goosebumps peppered his body. He clenched his jaw then let out a scream. Blue energy crackled around him like lightning, sending sparks flying from his body. He thrusted his arms forward and hundreds of sparking tendrils shotfrom his fingers. They crackled and zapped and slammed into Eleon's chest, sending him flying back into the darkness of the forest. He screamed as he disappeared into the shadows. Adam gasped, and finally let out a sigh of relief.

The lighting retreated into Adam's arms, zapping between his fingers until they completely vanished. He took his sword and rushed into the forest. Blue lights flickered in and out of existence. Eleon's twitching body groaned and grunted. Until it stopped.

Adam stood above the body, breathing heavily and gulping repeatedly. Was Eleon dead? He refused to accept the thought. He hated Eleon, but he never meant to kill him. He never meant to blast him with the lightning, he did not even know he could do that. He pleaded with himself, with Eleon, "breath... please..." The thought of taking a life haunted him for those moments. He did not want to be a monster. This man was Erika's twin brother. He was a monster, but he was also a man. Adam kneeled next to Eleon, he put his hand out to find a heartbeat, but only felt the trembling of his arm.

Eleon took a quiet breath, and Adam was relieved. He pulled his arm away and stood up quickly. The smoking mace sizzled feet away from him, the ball cracked in half and the red energy completely gone.

Another scream came from the depths of the forest, and Adam stared at Eleon's unconscious body one last time before rushing back into the fire.

Adam ignored the scorching heat hitting his face as he rushed past the flames. Hexus was an idiot. Could he not see that all that fire could kill them all? He was scared that Hexus had already learned that. The source of the flames was long past gone, and he had not yet seen any of his friends. He cursed himself for even thinking that any of them had died. And yet the thought kept creeping into his mind.

He heard a shout again, echoing from the clearing of the Heart Tree. Adam looked up at the burning canopy of tree leaves and saw the fire eat away at the branches, revealing the Heart Tree. It was close.

He dashed between the trunks ignoring the throbbing of his limbs or his bleeding face. The clearing revealed itself. He rushed into the opening between two burning logs and looked around. Some still fought, others retreated. Quartus's howdah sat blackened from the fire. The pole that had held Eleon had snapped in half. By the massive snaking roots, Erika fired arrows while Akio sliced and slashed at oncoming Spartoi, his face bloody, and an arrow shaft jutting from his left shoulder.

"Faster!" A voice called. Adam looked around. Behind the Heart Tree, retreating into the unknown part of the garden were his friends. Hexus, Theo and Akio fended off wave after wave of Spartoi and Kobaloi, Theodore in the body of a brown bear Asius led Quartus forward with the help of Silenus and Raia and Boo and Minerva tried their best to protect them. Even Morpheus and Hebe did battle with the walking corpses, the young god spraying them with blasts of purple mist, while Hebe rode atop Ladon, who fought off the bone dragons and hellhounds. Adam called for them, but a roar overtook his voice. Charging from the opposite side of the clearing, a bear bared its yellow, rotting, teeth. It was a black, shaggy thing with arrows jutting from everywhere, making it look like an undead porcupine. Its eyes glowed black and its black fur made it near invisible. A Spartus rode atop its back, covered in rusted silver pieces of armor, holding a spear with a bent point.

Adam took a deep breath, facing the beast. The bear roared again, and Adam could feel the thundering of its heavy paws hitting the grass.

A second roar came from next to it. A brown-haired bear swung its jagged paw at the black one, knocking the Spartus off. It sheriked as it fell to the ground.

"Theo!" Adam called at the bear. The black bear landed a blow to the face, its dagger-like claws drawing blood from Theos face. Theo roared and hurled his heavy body at the black bear. They fought on their hind legs, and threw their claws at one another, each one bloodier than the last. Theo roared with pain, and the Spartus rider showed itself, its rusted spear tip pushed through Theos back.

Adam launched himself at the creature, driving his sword through its skull.

"Get the others to safety!" Theodore cried, his voice gruff and almost an incomprehensible growl.

"But you-"

"GO!' Theo cried. The black bear jumped at him, and the brown bear shielded Adam.

He ran as fast as he could across the grass, cutting down creature after creature. He swung his sword hysterically until those before him had fallen. He rushed to the roots where more people had gathered. Kathrine fired arrows while Norris bent and swung his arms in different ways, launching trails of water so thin, they resembled blades, slicing apart Spartus after Spartus. He froze the water in midair into ice, launching the icicles like a hundred arrows, then calling them back in the form of water again.

Even with arrows and missing limbs, the creatures kept coming, only stopping when their heads were destroyed or killed by Adam or Akio's sword.

Adam saw action from the corner of his eye. By the tallest root, Eric and Zethus did battle with Korax and Xuthos. Xuthos moved quickly, dodging and parrying with ease. He jumped around Eric, moving low and flashing a short dagger.

Adam called to the others, "They need us up there!"

Norris looked up and grunted, "Erika take the others to Morpheus and Hebe, get them out! We aren't far behind."

Erika opened her mouth to protest, but the shriek from a Kobalos cut her off.

Norris impaled it with an icicle, "We don't have time to argue!" Norris yelled, "Akio, Kathrine go with her!" He jabbed a thumb at Adam, "you're with me!"

He rushed past Adam and made his way up the roots. Adam locked eyes with Kathrine.

She touched his face softly, "Stay safe." She whispered.

He took her fingers and let them go, "you too."

She turned and ran after Erika and Akio and Adam took a breath. Xuthos dodged almost every attack Zethus threw at him and Korax used his sheer size against Eric. Eric's swords bounced off Korax's armor without a scratch. Korax kicked out a leg, launching Eric backwards. He collided with Zethus and Norris. They all quickly got up.

"Ahhh..." Korax chuckled, looking at Adam, "more friends. So, kind of you to join us." He held his blood-red sword in one hand.

"Eleon's gone." Adam warned the others.

"Doesn't matter now." Norris grimaced.

"The swords won't do anything." Zethus said, panting. He stared at the giant, "we don't need to kill him," he said. The others looked at him, confused. "We just need to hold him off until the others reach the end of the garden."

Grimm looks took their faces.

Norris sighed, "That's suicide." No one said anything. Nobody needed to, they all knew the truth. Adam clenched the hilt of his sword. He tightened his jaw and looked at the others, dirt and blood caking their faces. They stood, ready for battle.

Zethus' body began to glow orange, as he snapped his spear over one leg, clenching the pointed half and throwing the other aside. Eric readied his short swords and Zethus froze giant icicles to his fists like bladed gauntlets. Adam raised his sword.

"Right then," Zethus said, his eyes flashing with energy, "I got the big one."

46

THEY ALL SURROUNDED Korax and Xuthos. Four against two, to any other, their victory would have seemed obvious, but Adam was reluctant to call it so. Xuthos twirled his knife between his fingers and flourished his curved sword. Korax took his hilt with both hands, holding the red blade between his eyes.

Norris and Eric took Xuthos while Zethus lunged at Korax, Adam followed him. Korax and Zethus traded loud blows, each clang of steel louder than the last. Zethus swung his spear and Korax sliced with his sword. Zethus dodged and threw a punch with his free hand. Korax's helmet flew off with a clang. Adam gasped.

Korax looked back up, his blood-red eyes flaring with rage. Adam did not see much of his face, but the flames illuminated enough. The man had no hair and much of the skin on his face had rotted away, showing burned bone underneath. What little skin he did have was grey and decomposing, and crooked teeth twisted inside his lipless mouth. Gashes raked his head, and he no longer had ears or a nose. He slowly reached down for his helm, calmly placing it on his head again, covering his ruined face.

"Now," he said in that horrid voice, "now you know the face of the man that will kill you."

"At least I will die handsome." Zethus chuckled.

Korax readied his sword, "I assure you, what I will do to your wretched person, will make you beg for a face as beautiful as mine."

411

Zethus lunged at Korax, his spear raised above his head. Korax took it by the shaft with one hand and stabbed with his sword with the other. Zethus dodged the blow, but his hand let go of his spear. Korax tossed it aside, laughing as it clattered against the wood.

Zethus pulled his sword from his sheath and charged again.

Adam followed. His blade clanged off Korax' armor. He tried to summon his lightning, he wanted to blast Korax with the same energy that he had used against Eleon, but the lightning did not show itself.

Eric swung his short swords in twin arcs against Xuthos' curved blade. Norris launched wave after wave of water against Xuthos, jumping away as he swung his smoking blade.

"You fight with water? Quite impressive." Xuthos said.

"I could impress you even more." Norris called the water around his hands and the icicles on his arm returned. Eric flourished his blades and spat at Xuthos.

Xuthos chuckled, "there we go."

Eric jumped and slashed, landing with Xuthos behind him. He raised his second sword behind his back, hearing it clang and feeling his arm jolt with Xuthos' strike. He turned and swung his blade. Xuthos dodged, stabbing at Eric's chest. Pain surged in his breast. He looked down at his tunic, ripped and darkening with his blood. Eric took a deep breath and attacked once more, leaving openings for Norris and taking the openings Norris left for him.

They moved as a team, as they did when they were young. Norris appreciated that. He sent a volley of frozen spikes hurling towards Xuthos. The slender soldier jumped and flipped through the attack, landing before them unharmed.

Theo bounded towards the Greymen that had made it towards the roots. They crawled up the twisting cluster, trying to make their way to Eric and the others. He swung his claws, hearing the rattle of bones hitting bark as he destroyed Spartus after Spartus. He opened his jaws on the head of a Greyman, biting down on his skull and swinging him around as it were his prey. His jaws clenched, and the Greyman's head burst between his teeth. The body fell to the ground.

Theo stood on his hind legs and roared at the incoming horde. The Chimera roared back, its goat head spewing flames in the air, setting the trees and grass ablaze as it ran towards Theo.

"He's too fast." Norris told Eric, as Xuthos stood before them.

"Then we slow him down," Eric told him. Norris faced him. He was looking up, towards the branches of the Heart Tree. Norris smiled.

"Hold him off!"

Eric bounded toward Xuthos, his head low and his blades high. Norris heard the clashing of metal as he sent a sharp wave upwards. The water cleanly cut through the branch with ease, sending the massive crown of leaving swinging down towards them. The branch slowly fell like a gnarled wooden claw, creaking and crunching as it did.

"Eric!" Norris called to him. Eric stabbed at Xuthos. He had lost one sword, and his face was bloody. Eric turned when he heard his name and saw the branch. He vaulted off the wood to dodge Xuthos' first strike, and somersaulted below the second, slicing Xuthos' calf with the sword he still had.

Xuthos yelled and fell to one knee. He looked up and saw the falling branch. He took the smoking knife, the cursed blade, and lifted it to his ear, holding the blade between two fingers. The knife flew towards Norris, he dodged, with nothing but a small cut appearing on his shoulder.

Xuthos smiled, "Good luck... with *that*." The branch took him, and he disappeared behind the leaves.

Zethus and Adam swung at Korax. Adam prayed that his friends had made it out of the garden by now, he did not know how much longer he could continue fighting. His arms burned and each breath he took was heavier than the last.

Korax swung in an arc. Adam fell to the ground. He raised his sword to cut but was sent back by Korax's heavy foot. He grunted as he hit the ground. He looked up and ran back into the fight, trying his best to ignore his body's reluctance. He slid left when Korax swung right and ducked when his blade came for Adam's neck. Korax swung for his body, and Adam rolled out of the way, only standing when he heard the metal of Korax' massive sword strikes the wood.

"You avoid and evade," Korax said, his armor clinking as he turned to face Adam, "were you a real man, I could feel your steel against mine own."

"Very well then." A voice said. Korax turned, facing Eric.

They all surrounded him now. Four against one now. Adam took deeper breathes, rising to one knee, then to his feet.

Korax looked around him, realizing his disadvantage. He took his sword with one hand and reached over his shoulder with the second.

"I suppose you consider yourselves victorious now." From his back, he pulled a four-foot black rod, topped with the point of a spear, glinting in the orange light of the fire. The rod began to glow in his hand, and in an instate, it had tripled in length, nearly impaling Norris.

"The odds are against you; you couldn't possibly win." Zethus assured Korax.

Korax laughed, "if you truly believe that, you are all more pathetic than I had thought."

The spear spun in the air, and everyone lunged forward. Adam's ears rang with the sound of crashing metal and grunting and screaming.

Norris slid between the giant's massive legs and sent a jet of water towards Korax' back, freezing it. The giant jerked forward, still managing to dodge Eric's slash. He broke through the ice, sending shattered pieces everywhere. He reached between his legs and took Norris by the throat, tossing him aside. Zethus ran up behind him, slamming his fist into Korax' face. The two dealt punches than rang against each other's armor. Korax swung his sword and Zethus ducked, only to be sent flying by a kick from the iron giant.

Eric faced him with one sword, dodging each strike. Korax raised his heavy sword above his head, leaving an opening. Eric stabbed, and his sword pierced Korax' stomach. He lurched forward, grunting. Eric pulled the blade out and swung for the neck. Korax sent out an armored fist, launching Eric into the bark of the roots.

Adam felt his sword tremble in his hands.

"Why do you even try boy?" Korax asked, false sympathy in his voice. "Your comrades all tried and failed. If you attack me, you march only towards your death."

Adam stood frozen, suddenly not knowing what he could do. He couldn't possibly defeat Korax by himself. He wanted to run, to meet with his other friends on the other side of the garden. He would be safe there.

From behind Korax, Norris stood, his face pale and his eyes suddenly heavy. He dropped to his knees weakly, coughing violently.

"Ahhh..." Korax said, "it seems as though my general has defeated you."

Eric stood, his face dirty and bleeding, "Your general lies beneath a fallen tree branch."

Korax pointed at Norris with his sword, "his knife did not." Zethus pulled down on Norris' shirt. The cut that Xuthos' knife had made looked infected. The wound was pitch black, with dozens of shadowy tendrils spreading out from it like blackened veins. Norris coughed again.

"That's blackrot." Zethus said, "we need to get him out of here, he's going to lose the arm."

"Let me go..." Norris said, lazily pushing Zethus aside. He made it total of three steps before collapsing to the ground. The blackrot had made its way to his throat.

Zethus slapped his face lightly as it grew paler by the second, "Norris, listen to me." Eric rushed to his side. Adam followed. Korax allowed them to gather around their friend, as if he took pleasure in watching him die and seeing them mourn. Adam did not want to give him that satisfaction. Norris' tongue had grown a dark purple as the tendrils entered his mouth.

"You have to get him out of the garden. Take him to Erika she will know what to do." Zethus said.

Adam turned to him, "we're not leaving without you."

Zethus frowned, "if you stay here, Norris dies."

"and if we leave you will. Neither of us can take Norris alone, and you can't kill Korax on your own."

"I don't need to kill him," Zethus said, sweat dripping off his forehead, "I just need to stall until you make it out safely."

Adam could not believe what Zethus said, he told himself that his ears gave him lies.

"We are not leaving you here." Adam said.

Zethus looked down. He reached under his chest plate and untied his amulet from around his neck. He opened Adam's palm and placed the gold plate in it, covering it with his fingers.

"I'll come back for that." He told Adam. He got to his feet. "Go, I'm right behind you."

Adam was reluctant, but his mind told him to follow Eric. They were headed to safety, and Zethus had assured him. Still, Adam feared he was going to lose someone today, and he did not know if it was going to be Norris or Zethus... or both.

They made it down the roots onto the field, each with one of Norris' arms around their shoulders. He heard Zethus' voice call "Your quarrel is with me now." The metal of his sword on Korax' armor rung in his ears.

Theodore ran up to them, still in the body of a brown bear. They set Norris on his back, and Eric pushed Adam up on the bear. They dashed towards the exit of the garden; the roar of the Chimera echoed behind them.

Adam cursed himself for looking. He turned and screamed. The last thing he saw was the point of Korax' spear, piercing through Zethus armor, jutting from his back dripping with his blood.

47

ADAM' TEARS HAD almost dried by now. Theodore walked through the woods solemnly, Norris and Adam riding on his back. Eric walked along on the side. Norris groaned, the black tendrils of his cursed wound crawling up his jaw.

Norris sometimes spoke, softly and weakly, and Eric always responded. Adam heard his voice, but never said a word... his mind was stuck in the past.

He fingered the amulet in his palm, feeling as the gold grew colder by the second. His blood had crystalized, and his skin was milk white. He felt the breeze blow through his hair. His skin had gone dry, and his lips cracked when he moved them.

The sight replayed in his mind, on repeat for almost an hour.

"I told him not to do it..." he muttered, "I said he couldn't. I should have stayed with him. We both could have won."

Theodore huffed, and Norris groaned. Adam saw the tip of the spear. It was red and dripping, and part of the shaft was buried in his chest. It had even been five minutes. He had fought formidably on the tree root, but that was when all four of them faced Korax.

He was alone. He couldn't have possibly taken on Korax by himself, he knew that. He did it anyways. Zethus gave his life so that they could get out of the garden. He died so that Adam could find the gods.

The gods... Adam's rage flared. Where were the gods now? Where were the gods when they had needed them the most? Adam clenched his jaw, more tears swelling in his eyes. Zethus believed in the good of the gods, and they turned their backs on him.

"Stop." Eric told him. Adam looked at him. Even after all this time, Eric remained a mystery to Adam. He did not know where Eric came from, or how their paths had crossed to meet at this horrible moment, but somehow, seeing him, it gave Adam some shred of comfort. "The moment you begin to blame yourself is the moment his sacrifice is tarnished." His eyes were dry, as if the death of a friend were nothing new to him. Adam feared that.

"The man knew what he did, no matter how dangerous it was. It was his decision, and we must honor that decision. We'll kill the iron clad cunt soon enough."

Adam took a deep breath, and he wiped the tears from his eyes.

Norris groaned. Eric placed two fingers on his neck.

"His heart is faint. We must hurry."

After an hour had past, they had found the exit. Adam descended Theodore and he reverted to his human form. They helped Norris to his feet. Adam looked to the distance. Plumes of smoke twisted around in the dawn sky. The smoldering orange of faraway flames seemed to crackle as it they were close. The Heart Tree burned in the largest ball of fire Adam had ever seen, as if the entire tree had become one massive flame. Adam turned back, lest more tears wet his eyes.

They stood in a field, surrounded by grassy hills. Bushes and shrubs still grew here, and that made Adam smile. In the middle of the field, a few feet ahead of them, stood the gateway.

Morpheus had spoken of it, and here it was, the gateway to Olympus. It was a stone structure in the form of a massive standing ring, vines and plants breaking through the cracked rocks on all sides. The columns held up a archway of pure stone, faded, cracked words had once been read on it, but no longer could that be. It stood on a tiled platform, stone stairs leading to it. There were no torches, or guards, or light in the doorway. Adam saw the other side of the field through the space between the pillars.

"Is this the gate?" Theodore asked.

"We have to assume it is." Eric said, "line up."

Adam stood behind Theodore, to went first. They climbed the stairs and stood in front of the doorway, waiting for something to happen. Nothing did.

Theodore stepped forward, below the doorway, "Nothing." He said. "Well, shit... where the hell do we—" his body disappeared in a flash of ethereal blue light. Adam turned back to Eric who held Norris over his shoulders. He nudged his chin forward, *go*.

Adam stepped forward, his toes crossing beneath the archway of the door, and his vision went white. When his sight cleared, he was in a field of tall grass. He laid there, the sky suddenly becoming starry and black again. Adam sat up and looked around. For miles in the distance, silvery hills swept over the valley, as if the world had been covered in steel. The stars glinted overhead, and the tall grass tickled his arms.

Eric suddenly appeared beside him. Theodore and Norris were beside him.

He saw the world before him. The entire world of Alanos glowed, bright with colors of blue and green. Adam could see the white snow of the northern tundra and the deep green of the southern rainforests. He saw the swirling brown of the deserts and shining blue of the world's oceans. Below the world Adam saw a massive cloud of purple mist, like the fabled lights that shined over the north. He stared at it all, just as beautiful as it was in his dream.

"Where are we?" Adam asked.

He heard footsteps behind him. Soft arms threw themselves around his back, and he heard sobbing.

He turned and faced Kathrine, who smiled as she cupped his face. She cuts on her cheeks, and her shoulder had bled. She pulled him close and kissed him.

"I'm so glad you're alright." She said, hugging him again. The others came. Hebe and Morpheus, Minerva and Boo, Raia and Asius, Akio and Hexus and finally Erika, Chase and Silenus and the animals. Adam was happy to see them. Akio hugged and kissed Theodore and Hexus lhugged Norris.

"Where is Ladon?" Theo asked.

Hebe's expression darkened, "last I saw him, he was fighting off those skeleton dragons in the fire." Her voice cracked.

"Erika!" Eric quickly said, laying Norris on the ground. His skin was paler than ever, with black tendrils swirling around almost his entire left breast.

"Blackrot..." Erika said. She ran to Quartus and returned with healing tools. She pulled out a series of different elixirs and mixed them into one solution, which she poured into Norris' mouth.

"That should stop the effects enough to get him help."

Eric leaned over him, Norris' weasel Bugbush sniffed at his friend's forehead, "Where can we get help?"

"There." Morpheus said. He pointed to the distance.

Adam got to his feet. Everyone stared at what Morpheus pointed at. On the horizon, a castle shined in the sky. The towers jutted from cliffs topped with arrow slits. Ramparts swirled around the base of the massive mountain, topped with battlements and spotted with machicolations. Twelve shining statues lined the ivory tiled pathway that snaked through and around the mountain, ending near the peak. The main keep was a tall shining tower with a shining domed roof of gold, bronze, silver and ivory.

"Behold," Morpheus said, "Mount Olympus, home of the gods."

The words echoed in Adam's head. He saw the world, and this was the home of the gods. The tall grass was pale, almost white, and he could see endless space around him.

"We're..."

"On the moon." Morpheus finished. "The gods built their castle here thousands of generations ago to watch over the world, and here, they see all."

Adam pointed to the bright lights below Alanos, flashing like purple thunder, "what is that?"

"Atlas," Morpheus explained, "the eternal being tasked with holding up the foundations of the world for all eternity."

"Atlas," Adam said... it took him a moment to truly realize where he was. He was at the home of the gods; on the moon he had looked up to for all his life. His breath struggled to stay in his chest.

"Where is Eleon?" Chase asked.

"He broke away from his prison, when Quartus' howdah was destroyed." Akio said.

"and Zethus?" Erika said, suddenly upset. She showed no concern for her brother.

Eric, Theo and Adam stayed silent, staring at the ground.

She shook her head in disbelief, "No..." her eyes watered, "no, no it can't be... you were with him! Why didn't you help him? You could have saved him!"

Eric opened his mouth to speak, but Erika slapped his cheek. His face hardened. She sobbed. Adam knew Erika was Zethus' beloved, and to see her upset at his loss... Adam tried his best to keep his tears down.

"He gave himself up... to save us." Eric said.

Erika fell to her knees, tears flowing down her cheeks. Kathrine consoled her.

"No... please gods no... please tell me this is another dream."

"I am afraid it is not, young one." Morpheus said. "I am truly sorry for your loss, but now is no time to mourn. The longer we remain here, the more likely to lose a second friend."

Everyone looked at Norris. His breathing was heavy, but he was alive for now.

The castle was large, but not far. They carried Norris to the gatehouse. The building was constructed entirely of polished stone at the base of the mountain, with fifty-foot-tall ramparts on either side. Massive crossbows and catapults were armed and ready for battle atop the walls, with murder holes and battlements and arrow slits also decorating it.

The portcullis was down, and before it stood two guards, clad entirely in gold armor that left no skin visible. Their eyes glowed in the helms, whiter than the stars. Their helms were topped with silver crests and their white silk capes swayed in the breeze. From their waists dangled swords, and their hands held iron kite shields, polished until shining and their other hands held poleaxes. The oddest thing about them, from their backs, sprouted two massive dove wings, whiter than snow and large enough to shield a man.

Erika still sobbed, her sniffles becoming quieter and quieter. Other people began to cry as well, Hexus sniffled and Minerva pouted. Adam walked next to Chase, grateful to see his friend alive.

"We made it..." Chase said, his voice seemed to deny it, "we... actually made it."

The guards at the entrance hurried towards them, the portcullis rising. From the darkness of the gatehouse came two more people. Adam saw them approach, one was a beautiful, tall with skin a tawny gold. Long, black box braids swung from her head and her eyes shone completely white. She had dark lips with a soft nose, and she was tall. She wore a long white dress with gold ribbons spiraling from her waistline. Her chest was clad in a silver and gold chest plate and her arms were clad in rerebraces and a silver pauldron covered her shoulder. Massive, white wings lifted her from the ground, covered in glittering white feathers. In one hand she held a golden spear that glinted like her wings.

Beside her was a handsome man, most likely near 30. He had ochre colored skin, and his eyes were a soft green. His black hair was curly, and he wore nothing more than a silk chiton, tied around his waist by a golden rope. His wings were a purplish and a golden bow was slung over his shoulder, his quiver filled with arrows.

"Eros, and Nike." Hebe said, running to meet them. Her young arms were thrown around the legs of the woman, hugging tightly. The woman smiled and hugged her back.

"Eros..." Chase said, as if the word was familiar.

"The god of love." Kathrine told him.

Adam looked at the woman, "So she is Nike... goddess of what."

"Victory." She said, staring at him.

"We could have used that." Theodore said.

The young man frowned, "We heard of the battle of the garden, and we are truly devastated by the outcome. But it is good—"

"Where are they?" Adam stepped forward, eager to move along.

Eros had an expression on his face that showed he was not used to interruptions, "beg your pardon?"

Adam glared, "My friend is dead, another is dying, and your friend Ladon gave his life to get us here, so I do not have time for any of this. Where are they?"

Silenus guffawed, "I'm starting to like the boy." Everyone else was silent.

Eros leveled his vision, eyeing Alanos behind them, "follow me."

When they all past under the massive portcullis of the gate house, the portcullis was lowered again. The guards quickly came, taking charge of the animals. Eric allowed it, so long as Asius accompanied them. They left to tend to the animals, Asius left with them. On the other side of the ramparts was the city. Compared to Alor, it was small. Most of the buildings were epic golden structures with colored glass windows and bronze statues of muscular men and women that held several items in their metal hands. One woman held a shining arc colored with a thousand precious stones, rubies, sapphires, emeralds. Another held a large serpent in her arms. They even past statues of Hebe and Nike and Eros and Morpheus, and in several different positions.

"You lot always did like looking at yourselves," Silenus grumbled, his hooves clacking on the tiled walkway.

The mountain before them loomed overhead with a silent watchfulness. As they ascended the statues became bigger and more ambitious. The Olympians were sculpted with such elegancy and detail that they almost seemed real. Aphrodite, goddess of love, lifted by massive fish that sprouted from the cliffside. Ares, the god of war rode a chariot pulled by six boars, his spear lifted high and his shield glinting gold.

When they reached the main keep at the peak of the mountain, Adam felt all his courage drain from him. He wanted to curse all of the gods, he wanted to damn them all to the depths of hell, but he knew he couldn't. He was going to meet Zeus, and he did not know whether he wanted to forward into the castle, or vomit.

He turned one final time, taking in the view. Chase and Kathrine on either side of him.

The moon spread out before them, and beyond that, their home of Alanos, and beyond that, more worlds, all clad in the darkness of endless space and stars. He saw the faint shining of the sun, and he saw the cosmos that held Atlas.

"I think I might be the first satyr on the moon," Chase laughed.

"We are a long way from home." Adam said, felt his fingers lock with Kathrine's.

She sighed, "I told you not to go to the priestess."

They entered and found the Olympians. The deities argued among themselves in the throne room, as tall as Quartus. Lesser gods flew around with their wings, attending to the distressed gods. The arguing began to fade as Nike and Eros led the group into the throne room, and then it stopped.

The tallest man turned, his hair and beard white, with glowing blue eyes that locked with Adam's.

"Lord Zeus," Eros, Nike, Hebe and Morpheus all said together, kneeling.

Zeus looked down at them, his golden crown shining on his head. He sat on his massive throne and stared at Adam.

"Hello, son."

48

KORAX HAD MADE it to the gate. The ruined doorway was pitiful. Vàliëndör, they called it, the doorway to the heavens, in that disgusting tongue the Gods spoke. The gold these false gods had at their disposal, and they construct their front door of ruined stone. Korax laughed.

The forest burned behind them. The great garden, sacred to the mother goddess herself, Hera, reduced to ashes. The Olympians had not even shown themselves, what gods they were to not defend that which was sacred t them!

The altar had been set up before them, with the naked body of the host laid out on top of it. The bed of tree branches and leaves was hovered over by Pontarius, who commanded the old priestess and his assistant Kobos to gather the necessary materials for the ritual.

Korax was eager to be over with this. His king was near, he felt it in his blood.

Xuthos came beside him, "the dragon is dead, sire." He kneeled

Korax smiled beneath his helm, "Good. He will be the next to return. I want these woods searched and all the bodies of the fallen Greymen returned to me, am I understood?"

"It is already done, sire." He walked off with a limp. His battle with the children had ruined him much more than I had Korax. Xuthos had lost an eye in the battle, and the cut of the sword had damaged his leg, still, he persisted, and Korax respected that.

Korax turned, laid out before him, were his fallen troops, all ready to be awaken once more.

Xuthos walked up to him again, "with all due respect, sire, are we to wait here for these cowards to show themselves." He waved a hand at the doorway.

"They cannot stay in their castle forever." Korax said.

"The King will reward you for your work, sire." Xuthos said.

Xuthos laughed. Korax heard grunting from the forest. Two Freshs came from the darkness, another man in their grasps. He was tall, dragging his legs as they pulled him towards Korax, He placed a hand on his sword.

The man grunted and cursed, kicking weakly at the ones that held him. He had short cut auburn hair, and when they dropped him at Korax' feet, he saw the man's face. His chin was covered in an auburn beard, and one side of his face was been ruined by the fire, with the eye shut by a scar. He wore a tunic, and he reeked of piss and shit. He looked as though he had not bathed in weeks, and his good eye glowed with a golden rage. His mouth foamed and his wrists were red and bleeding.

"Who the hell are you?" He asked, panting.

"What do we do with him, sire?" Xuthos asked, looking at the man in disgust.

"What is your name, boy." Korax asked him.

"The man took a moment to answer, "Eleon." He finally said.

Korax smiled, "you are one of the children."

"Children," he said, disgusted, "are you talking about those cunts? No! No, I am not one of them! They betrayed me!"

Korax tilted his head, his hand came off his sword. The Freshs lifted Eleon. Elon ripped his arms from their grasp. He turned, and it seemed as though he had finally seen what had attacked him.

He swung a fist at one of the Freshs, and the corpses skull flew from his neck. "What the hell is that?" Eleon shouted. He reached over his shoulder for a weapon that was not there, and he lifted his fists instead. Xuthos drew his sword, but Korax stopped him.

"You're the madman who's been following us!" Eleon finally realized.

"Look around you, boy, *I* am not the madman."

"Did you kill the others?" He said, more calmly this time.

Korax' smile faded, "No. Only one." Eleon squinted his eyes.

"Which one?" Eleon asked. Korax led him to the altar, where the naked host laid.

Eleon's face went sour. He seemed confused, his breathes shaky.

"Zethus..." he said.

"You knew him?" Pontarius asked.

Eleon paused, "yes... he was the one who turned the others agsint me. He convinced them that I was their enemy, when it was you all the whole time." His eye never left the corpse of his dead former friend.

"Allow me to make you a proposition, Eleon." Korax said. He saw the anger in Eleon's eyes when he mentioned the children. Eleon hated them just as much as Korax did, and he was strong enough to knock the head off a Fresh. He was strong, and he could fight, Korax saw those as advantages.

"What?"

"You are confused, but I can fix that. I am not your enemy. Those children, the ones who betrayed you and left you here to burn with the garden... *they* are the true enemy. I can help you, and you can help me."

He nicked his eyebrows, and a faint frown tugged at his lips.

"Join me." Korax told him, "and we both of us, will destroy those who have done us wrong."

Xuthos whispered to him, "sire, I mean no disrespect, but-"

"Then remain silent, Xuthos." Korax told him. "Let the boy make his decision."

Eleon looked at the ground, slowly backing away from Korax. "They saw me as a monster... even my own sister. She never heloed me, even when I needed her." He paused, "if... if I join you... I will be exactly what they thought of me."

His mined raced. He resented the others, and he thought of nothing more than destroying them. Was he a monster? Perhaps he was. *It is not your fault,* Eleon thought, *they made you this way. They turned you into this beast.* A beast is what he will be, then. They had treated him like a monster, and now, he will show them what a monster really was. Zethus had protected them before, and now he was a corpse laying before Eleon. He wanted vengeance, and Korax will give it to him.

Korax waited for an answer, Eleon stayed silent. Finally, he looked up, "you have my loyalty," he said, laughing quietly.

Korax smiled, "welcome then, my child."

"I'm going to need a weapon." Eleon advised.

"Fear not, everything you need, will be given to you."

A Rott came near Eleon and handed him a battle axe. The shaft was short and thick, and the blade was on one side, with the other being topped with a spike. Eleon took it one hand, and red energy flared throughout his body. It flowed into the axe, and the blade glowed red hot.

Eleon turned, "I'll kill the satyr first."

Eleon took his place beside Korax, as the ritual began.

Light flashed as Pontarius chanted, and the host slowly awakened. Black smoke took the body. His skin bubbled as if something were trying to break through from within.

"Welcome, my king!" Korax shouted. They all kneeled before his excellency, and Typhon roared. His legs became long and scaly. The heads of two dragons sprouted from his feet. The beasts roared, throwing flame in the air. His back was ripped apart to make way for the massive spider legs that jutted from his shoulder blades, clicking and cracking, with tips as sharp as spears. Leathery wings, rimmed with spikes, burst from his ribs, and his spine jutted from his back with a loud crunch. His eyes became flaming pits of red light, leaving trails of fire when he moved his head, and his mouth smoked like a forest fire when he spoke. His ears became horns, and spikes sprouted from his head. His fingernails elongated into serrated claws, and his teeth became fangs in his mouth.

"Rise, my King!" Korax said. He watched as the Great Snake came forth, and his voice echoed through the night.

I...AM...HERE.

49

THE OLYMPIANS HAD looked exactly like their statues.

Zeus was a tall man, with copper skin and bright blue eyes. He looked exactly like Adam in the face. Hera had brown hair tied neatly in a bun, and her skin was pale, drawing attention to her green eyes. Poseidon was dark, and handsome with a black beard. His skin was umber, and his eyes were as bright and as blue as the ocean. Black locks fell to his waist and he held his trident with pride. Ares had dark hair, and pale skin. His eyes were red, and he wore glinting gold armor. Hephaestus was a gnarled man, with a hunched back and liver spotted hands. His beard was white, and his eyes were red, like Hexus'. Aphrodite was gorgeous, as expected by the goddess of love and beauty. Her russet brown skin glowed, and her curly black coils fell to her neck. Her eyes were a beautiful blue and her smile was flawless.

Hermes was young with pale skin and curly brown hair. Demeter had fiery hair, and she smiled at Minerva. Athena remained with a stern face. Her skin was pale, and her brow hair flowed down her back. Dionysus had curly dark hair and pale skin, and he grinned at Akio. Not everyone was here it seemed; Adam counted ten deities. Apollo and Artemis were not here.

Norris had been taken to the sickbay, where a minor goddess by the name of Hygeia took care of him. Adam had not seen him since they had carried him off, and that had been nearly twenty minutes past.

Zeus looked weary, and he looked over his kingdom. He wore silk breeches, with a cloak of blue velvet thrown over his bare shoulder. Atop his brow was a golden crown, diamonds and rubies glistening in the diadem like stars. His beard was as white as his long hair and blue tattoos swirled around his bare torso, crackling with faint electricity.

He leaned on the balcony railing next to Adam, never saying word. Adam ignored his existence. Adam tried to control the anger boiling inside him. He supposed it all made sense now. The god of the sky, fabled to wield a mighty lightning bolt, would father a boy with abilities such as Adam's. He could control the wind, and he had some control of electricity, his training with Zethus proved that.

Zethus... he pushed the thoughts away, lest his anger overcome him, and he attacks the god.

It made sense for the others as well, who had been claimed by their own godly parents.Norris was the son of Poseidon, god of the seas, explaining his power over water. Hexus was the son of Hephaestus, god of fire, explaining his fondness for flames and crafting things. Theodore was the son of the trickster god, and messenger of the gods, Hermes, as shown by his ability to change shape, a good power for a trickster to have. Erika and Eleon were the children of Athena, and the goddess of wisdom and warfare was angered to hear of her son's betrayal. Minerva was the daughter of Demeter, and Norris the son of Poseidon. Raia went to Aphrodite, and Akio to Dionysus.

There were some who remained unclaimed, however. Kathrine and Chase were born to mortal families, as were Asius and Silenus. Eric's father was Apollo, the god of archery, but Apollo was not here to claim him. Adam did not like his time with his father, but he supposed it was better than not having your father claim you. Finally, there was Ares, the god of war. It was ironic that the god that represented the worst side of humanity, fathered a caring and gentle man, in Zethus. Ares became silent, leaving the throne room when he was given the news.

Then there was Adam, the son of Zeus, god of the skies, and king of the gods. For years Adam had thought his father dead. When his mother had told him that he had died before Adam was born, he believed her... a foolish decision as he saw it now. His should have known his mother was lying, and for many years, he had wished she did, but he never met his father, and realized that it was a fool's quest to seek him out.

Now here he was, with his father, on his castle, on the moon... he wondered if he had gone mad.

"You've... grown." Zeus said, shyly.

Adam said nothing, silently brooding as he stared at the curve of Alanos.

"I'm proud of you," Zeus continued, trying to get Adam's attention.

Again, Adam remained silent, only staring at the calming colors that washed over his home in the distance. He did not want to talk to this man. To Adam, Zeus was not a god, Zeus was the man who had abandoned him. He had left him in a city filled with terrible people with a mother who never loved him. Adam could not forgive him for that. He felt betrayed, abandoned, rejected. He thought he would cry but tears never came. He was not sad, he was angry. He was furious at this man.

"I'm sorry, Adam-"

Adam cut him off before he could continue, "why?"

"Why... what?"

"Why did you leave?"

For a moment, Zeus said nothing, leaving only silence to answer Adam's question, then he sighed, "In all my centuries in Olympus, I have had many children, with many women, but none like you, boy."

"That is not an answer."

Zeus averted his gaze, "to protect you." He mumbled.

"Protect me?" Adam repeated, "I have been locked away in a city that hates me for fifteen years, tell me, how is that protection?"

Zeus looked defeated, Adam pursed his lips, "The gods are dying, Adam." The god said, "Typhon is rising and there is not much that we can do now, he senses my power, if I leave my home, I am at risk of losing my life. As would the others. We knew that our time protecting this world will soon be over, and we needed to secure our future. If my legacy would be born here, it would fall with the rest of us; But my legacy was born on Alanos, however, hidden away from the darkness that plagued my people, there was hope for the future."

Adam remembered the walls of Alor. For a century, his people had not known that the world beyond the walls and mountains existed.

"Alor was never a grand city," Zeus admitted, solemnly, "but it would do. We lifted mountains and forest around the city, and the land around it was destroyed when we sent earthquakes its way a century ago."

He grew up around stories of earthquakes shaking his city, it was odd to hear that they were never just stories.

"I decided my legacy would be born there, hidden from the world, so that one day, it could rise, and defend this world from those who sought to do it harm. We hid it away from the rest of the world." That explained why it did not appear of Kathrine's map.

"You cannot protect something you do not know." Adam said.

Zeus sighed, "there were things we could not predict. Locking a people within the confines of great stone walls for a hundred years could have some... unintentional consequences."

"Poverty," Adam grumbled, "segregation, famine. Are those, 'unintentional consequences'?" The words were poison on his tongue.

Zeus shook his head, "I don't expect you to forgive me. But I hope you realize why I did this."

Adam looked down at the castle below him. The swirling and winding steps were hypnotizing. He saw the statues dotting the pathway up the mountain, and how they glittered like the stars overhead.

"When I met you mother" Zeus said, the words caught Adam, "she was... nothing like you knew her." Adam felt the tears in his eyes, "she loved me," Zeus continued, "and when I disappeared, she was angry. She became violent, and hateful,"

"I know how she was." Adam had heard enough from his mouth. "She was cruel, and scary... for all my life, there was never a person I feared more than my own mother. I remember when she was sweet, when she was kind to me, it is hard to remember, but I can. When you 'died', she was upset. She was upset because she was stuck with a son she never wanted, and the man who had given it to her had left. She always wanted a daughter, so the sight of a boy constantly angered her, and when Kathrine left, I suppose something in her just... broke. Her life had been riddled with mistakes, and every time she saw me, she was reminded of all of them. I sometimes prayed for help, but it never came. I used to think that my prayers were simply... not heard... now I know that they were just ignored."

"I have made a thousand mistakes in this lifetime," Zeus said, "you were never one of them."

"I'm a bastard."

"You are the hidden child. As my son, you are destined to lead your people against these forces."

Adam never thought he would here this. Him and Chase had always loved the tales of the heroes, who vanquished horrible beasts and cut down evil men, and now he was one. His mind still tried to comprehend that.

"There is a war coming, and you know this. It will affect all peoples, even the Underworld. Your powers have grown more powerful over your journey, use them now."

"I do not know how."

"Focus your energy. The power resides within you as it did with all my children..." he stammered with those last words. "I first unlocked them with this." He went silent and pulled a long silver rod from his back. The rod flickered and crackled and elongated into a long javelin, crackling white and blue with lightning.

"The Lightning Bolt." Adam realized.

"Take it." He handed the bolt to Adam. He hesitated as first, but the rod crackled when his hand neared it. He curved his fingers around it and felt the energy flow through his body, filling even his toes with its immense power.

He felt no pain, nor discomfort. He felt the rod suit to his needs, fitting his hands. It was not heavy, or difficult to use.

"Whether you like it or not, you are my son, and this responsibility now lies upon your shoulders. My time here is nigh over, but your time here had just begun."

The rod crackled again, and Adam pointed it to the sky. He did what Zeus told him, and focused on the energy. The flash of lightning blasted into the sky with a *boom*. He jumped as his eyes flared blue energy. He felt more powerful than he did in the garden, but now the energy he had felt there was not wild. He could control it.

The sky *boomed* again, and he glared at it, accepting the thunderous call to battle.

Zeus stayed silent for another moment, then he said, "I suppose... I will leave you with thoughts."

The god turned, leaving Adam with his thoughts. He breathed deeply, not knowing what to do next. He held his fingers tightly, warming them up from the chilly wind. He thought of Zethus and his sacrifice. He thought of his home, he thought of the Cyclopes cave and the Lion's den. He thought of his escape from his city, and how Hexus and Norris had broken him out of prison. He heard his leather armor breath and creak and imagined his dreams with the sounds.

He remembered his dream in the prison, with the ruined remains of a destroyed Alor, and how in that dream, Zeus had given him a sword, the same sword that appeared in the coffer when he returned home. Everything he had done since leaving Alor, had led him to this point. That worried Adam.

He clenched his hand into a fist, and his breathes grew heavy.

"So, you're a leader now?" a voice said. Adam turned, Chase smiled, and Kathrine lowered her eyebrows.

"You heard all that?"

"Most of it." Kathrine said.

Chase frowned, "there isn't much to do around here."

Adam chuckled, "I'm sorry."

"There is nothing to be sorry for," Kathrine said.

They joined him on the balcony, staring out at the endless space beyond Olympus and Alanos. Kathrine linked her arm with Adam's standing tall. Chase glared at the castle below them.

"We are far from home." Chase dragged the word out. Kathrine and Adam chuckled. It was true. They had come a long way from the walls of Alor. Kathrine as no longer the thrill-chasing thief and Chase was not the hot-headed wild man. Adam had noticed even his own differences. In Alor, he never would have thought he would ever do what he did in the lion's den, or in the burning garden.

"We don't have a home anymore." Kathrine said.

Adam remembered how Korax had destroyed Alor, leaving it a pile of rubble.

"and we don't have families anymore." Chase said frowning.

Adam glared, "we have each other, and that's enough."

His fingers locked with theirs. He was glad to have them here, to have come so far with them by his side always.

Adam knew what he had to do, but he was not excited about it. He stared at the stars again, watching as they blazed in the sky.

50

THE THRONE ROOM was a colossal hall made entirely of
quartz. The domed ceiling loomed over one hundred feet above Eric's
head. The coffers alternated with colored panes that were filled with
dark colors and shadows. The columns that supported the ceiling were
tall and chipped in some places. The entirety of the room had signs
that it was once grand and mighty, but clearly, its days of power had
come and passed.

The floor was a map of Alanos. It seemed to be a separate world
below Eric's feet. Clouds blew over his toes and boats sailed in the
seas by his legs. The world moved, if one looked closely. You could the
mighty storms that covered the Pearl Sea, and the massive pods of ice
whales and that swam in the sea of Fàrnörr. The thousand islands in
the sea of isles were droplets of green against the blue water, and the
shadowy Deadlands of Kayembe oozed darkness ominously.

The room was ringed with thrones, all at the top of a short staircase.
Massive seats of gold decorated with precious stones and inscribed with
old words that represented the gods. At the front of the room was Zeus'
throne, bigger than all the rest, with the back expanding into beams
of silver like a flowerbird's tail feathers. The king of the gods sat in
his throne, not looking at anyone. His face was troubled, thinking of
things he could not share with the others. His hand covered his mouth,
and he sighed several times.

He sat on the stairs, his elbows resting on his elbows. He thought of Norris, and Zethus. He knew the battle was near, and when it arrived, he knew he wanted to place his sword between Korax' eyes.

"Was he good?" a voice said.

Eric turned. Ares was a tall man, with black hair and a shaggy black beard. His eyes were the color of fire and his arms were bare and filled with scars. He was clad in full armor, with a flowing cloak strapped around his shoulders by a golden brooch.

"The boy was brave," Silenus said. Eric realized that they were speaking of Zethus. It angered Eric that Ares knew so little of his son. It angered him that all the gods knew little of anything outside their castle.

"He gave his life, so we could live." Silenus told him.

The god of war breathed heavily, "that sounds like a son of mine." He smiled, a thin, half defeated, yet accepting smile, as he took his seat at his throne. He wanted to know Zethus, and now he never got the chance. Still, it was more than Apollo. Eric clenched his fist at the thought.

Adam, Kathrine and Chase came from one of the dozen halls that lead into the throne room. Eric eyed him. He had been reluctant to accept the boy at first, especially since he travelled with a satyr, but Eric was impressed by him. Adam had become more than Eric expected. Even the satyr was growing on him. They were still foolish children thought, thinking themselves high and mighty because of a talk.

Eric was not going to discourage the boy, though. Zethus' death had affected the boy more so than anyone else, except perhaps Erika. Still, Adam was no soldier yet.

Zeus stood up behind Eric. Adam averted his gaze, "what of Norris?"

"Hygiea is saying he is doing well. The blackrot has subsided almost entirely." Ares said.

Eric stood, "where are they keeping him?" He asked.

"Boy I am afraid you cannot see him." Ares said, extending a hand.

Eric glared, "my friend was nearly killed, because of me. I am not asking for permission. Where is he?"

Ares looked at Zeus with a face that asked *why do you allow this child to speak to me like this?* It pleased Eric to think that he had angered a god.

Ares looked defeated, "the sickbay is two levels down, Hygeia will see to it that you meet your friend."

Hexus smiled when he saw the workshop. For as long as he could see, the room was filled with fascinating objects. He saw hundreds of swords, hammers, axes and shields hung up on the walls. He saw metal machines roaring and hiss. Steam was blown by something in the distance and his face was filled with the calming feeling of heat. He heard the banging of hammers against metal, the sizzling of swords being tempered, the zooming and booming of machines he could not understand and the roaring of flames. He took a deep breath, smelling smoke and... was that incense?

"We keep it burning to cover up the smell of... other things." Hephaestus smiled, revealing yellow, crooked teeth with spaces in between. He had white hair covered his head like a cloud, and a mustache-less white beard beneath his lips. He had dark skin, and his gnarled, bony hands were peppered with liver spots. He hobbled when he walked, the clicking of his cane against the stone floor echoing through the vast workshop. He wore a woolen robe stained with ash, dirt and other stains he could not recognize.

He limped into his workshop with Hexus at his heels. He saw beautiful sets of armor hung up on the walls and flames jutted into the air in the distance. The rusted remains of forgotten machines and old automatons hung from the ceiling, and Hexus had to crouch to pass below their bronze feet.

Working on the forges and hammering at plates of red-hot metal were golden automatons. Metal humans with glowing blue eyes and limbs replaced with several working tools. One had a hammer for a hand, and another had a chisel. They passed by a metal ship with still propellers and a rusted hull. It loomed over them, covered in bronze shadow like a metal ghost.

"Forgotten designs and abandoned projects." Hephaestus said, dismissively waving his hands at the ship.

"Why abandon them?" Hexus asked.

"That's why I wanted to talk to you." The god said. They stopped by a workbench, dozens of dusty scrolls and torn design sheets rolled out.

"I am getting old, Hexus," He said, disappointed, "that is rare for a god to say, but alas, it is true. I am no longer the skilled forger I was in my youth. I am getting to weak to bring my creations to life." He rested an old hand on Hexus' shoulder, "I need my creations to be remembered. I need someone to keep my memory preserved, and I want you to be that someone."

Hexus was at a loss for words. He tried to speak but all could manage was a quiet, "yes."

Hephaestus smiled again, "this will not be here for much longer," he said, referring to the workshop. "The designs, the automatons, the creations, take them all. Complete them, create new ones, I cannot tell you what to do with them, but I know you will make the right choices."

Hexus tried to control his breathing, "I don't know what to say.'

Hephaestus laughed, "not many would." He looked down, "I loved your mother."

Hexus looked at him, "what?"

"I never wanted to leave her, but I had to. An Olympian cannot stay far from this place, I suppose it is a dept to pay for our, endless power." He said *endless power* as if it were the name of his worst enemy.

"I understand. You do not need to apologize."

Hepheastus smiled. Hexus hugged him, and he was glad. For the first time in his life, he had a father. For a moment, it was silent, even the automatons stopped their hammering, and Hephaestus and Hexus embraced each other. He was happier than ever, and he was determined to make his father proud with his creations.

"Well then, boy." The god said, "why are standing there. In a few hours, the gate will open, and our enemies will be upon us. We better get to work.

Norris had left the sickbay and entered the wine cellar. He stumbled down the endless halls, still lightheaded from his treatment. He had hoped to get more time with the woman that treated him, but his body was to sore to work with, so he sought the next best thing: alcohol.

He wandered down the quartz halls, leaning on the massive pillars. His head throbbed and his shoulder burned with pain. He licked his lips and tried to keep his eyes open.

The cellar was huge, larger than any building he had ever seen in his life. On the vast shelves, dozens of bottles laid in rows and on the ground, massive barrels sat, waiting to be emptied.

His mouth watered and he rushed over to the bottles. He emptied bottle after bottle, sweet golden honeywines, sour dry reds, vintage reds and sour blackales. He cracked open a cask of golden mead and pured it into his mouth. All the pain that once flared in his body vanished with each drop he drank.

"Norris," a voice said, commanding and stern.

He turned and saw Eric in the doorway, his arms crossed.

"What?" He slurred his words.

"You're drunk."

"Am I?" Norris laughed, hiccupping, "I hadn't noticed."

"What the hell are you doing out of the sickbay, and in the wine cellar no less."

"I thought I would..." he studied a bottle of bluewyne "clear my head... before battle."

Eric frowned, "What exactly do you expect to accomplish here? You'll drink yourself to death."

"Well... perhaps that's best!" He snapped.

Norris did not know where the anger had come from. Eric glared at him.

"You think we are going to lose?"

"Of course, I bloody think that! We don't have the men, and they nearly killed us the first time."

"It was an ambush-"

"That doesn't mean anything. That thing, that 'great snake' bastard, he is winning! We cannot do anything to stop him. That iron cunt killed Zethus, and the little one nearly killed me. You know, Poseidon showed me Atlantis when we left the Shadow City? It's a beautiful place, maybe we should flee there."

"So, you just walk away with your tail between your legs? You wish to flee. That is not what father taught us." Eric said, waiting for a reply.

"Höthör was not my father."

"But he raised you like a son. He taught us everything. That's more than Poseidon did, no?"

Norris looked at him, his mind no longer stable. "Eric..."" he mumbled, "we cannot hope to beat them."

"You don't know that."

"I knew we could not beat the Ironfangs, and I was right, wasn't I?"

Eric's furrowed his brow. Norris knew he was remembering that night, the Night of Fire. His eyes avoided Norris, and the scars on his face seemed to shimmer with new light. It seemed so long ago, but they both still felt the pain of remembering.

"We told each other we weren't fighting for anyone anymore." Norris said.

"No one except each other."

"and here we go, fighting for these kids."

"It isn't about the kids anymore." Eric said.

"Then what?"

"If we don't do anything now, then no one can do anything ever. These creatures have a goal, and they will not rest until they have that goal."

Norris sighed, "you know we're going to lose."

"We can't."

Norris stared at his wine bottle. He did not want to do this. He saw the outcome, and he dreaded it. There was no way the Olympian army could successfully defend against those creatures. What Korax had, it was not even an army, they were just... a hoard... wave after wave of horrid beasts with only one goal: death.

"You were wrong about the Ironfangs..." Eric said.

"We survived." Eric said. "That's enough."

"We aren't the Sons of the Hydra anymore."

"No..." Eric said... looking defeated. "we're just the Hydras."

"This sure looks nice," Theo said.

Minerva walked by the garden, sitting on Boo's shoulder, her mother Demeter was by her side. Beside her was Theodore and his father Hermes.

The weeping willows drooped over the walkway, and Minerva had to push the vines away with her hand to walk through. She had seen many beautiful things since leaving Lornura, but this garden had been by far the most beautiful.

The hardscape was colored stone in shades of blue, red and green and there were statues of water-spewing, and the garden keepers were winged men and women who smiled at them as they passed.

"This garden has stood for centuries, since this castle was first built." Demeter said, looking up at Olympus behind them. She wore a long emerald-green dress with golden silk sewn in the flounce and a thick brown obi belt tied around her waist. She had fiery orange hair and beautiful green eyes: she looked just like Minerva. Her face was dotted with freckles and the gold ringlet circling her head was ringed with jades and rubies.

Hermes looked less-so like his son. Where Theodore was short and plump, Hermes was tall and muscular. They both shared blue eyes and curly hairs, thought Hermes' was dark brown where Theo had golden locks. He wore a silver crown atop his head, with shimmering wings sprouting from above each ear. He wore a silk, white tunic with a leather belt tight around his waist and leather sandals, with two more pairs of silver wings flanking each heel. He held a winged staff that was ringed with two snakes in his hand.

"How long has that been?" Theo asked.

Hermes laughed, "ask her, I wasn't born yet."

"This castle is older than even your country, Theodore. You see, all life in your world started in Kayembe over a thousand eons ago. We started with life there, then let it grow, expand as it pleased."

"I suppose your regret that. The humans don't even believe in you anymore." Theodore stared longingly at Alanos. It was surreal to see the whole world like this from thousands of leagues away, but something about it made Minerva smile, it truly was beautiful.

"Humans have made many mistakes, my boy." Hermes said, "but they have done nothing that the gods did not do before them. We are eternal beings, meaning we will make mistakes for eternity."

"That doesn't sound that bad." Theo said. Minerva thought the same. She wished she could speak, she wished she could share her thoughts with everyone else.

Hermes stared at the world himself, "between us, it is more of a curse than a blessing. We have lived for centuries, watching many loved ones die. Humans somehow see eternal life as... a gift."

"It isn't?" Theodore asked.

"Something is not beautiful if it lasts, it is beautiful because you know it doesn't. You spend your whole lives leaving behind a story for others to tell when you are gone, and that... is beautiful. When you live forever, the stories run their courses rather quickly." He laughed emptily.

"Is that why you brought us here?" Theodore asked, "for our story?"

Hermes chuckled, "I'm afraid it is much more complicated than that. Everything we have done has let you to this point. We sent spirit animals to protect you all, like the owls, or the tiger, or even the mammoth. We told Eric to find Alor, where you would get Adam and his friends. I told you to find the lair of the lyre in the Lion's den, so you could give it to Silenus in exchange for his aid. Of course, the Cyclopes den was a... unwanted obstacle, but I see you made good with what you were given." The god eyed Boo, the cyclops smiled. "We needed you here, and now you are, but now so are they."

The creatures, Minerva thought.

"War is upon us children," Demeter said, her beautiful orange hair falling over her shoulder, "and we cannot survive without your help."

Minerva looked down, avoiding eye contact with either of the gods. She wanted to say it was hopeless, she wanted to prove to them that there was no way they could win. War between men is one thing but doing battle with these... these... monsters... death was inevitable.

"I lost a friend getting here," Theodore said, "and I left my family when I sailed from Analios." He looked up, "neither of those things will be in vain now. I will fight with you."

Hermes smiled, "thank you son." The two hugged.

Demeter went to her daughter, "I know I have not been in your life as much as I would have liked to, but I am here now. Your destiny is beyond this battle. I see your future, and it is bright." She cupped Minerva's face and smiled with care, "I understand if you are afraid, I am afraid, but there is only one way to get rid of the fear: face it." She kissed Boo on the cheek, the cyclops cooed. "Thank you for protecting my daughter, young one.'

Boo smiled, "I never leave forest mother."

Demeter laughed, and looked at Minerva. She nodded courageously and Demeter smiled.

The sky somehow became darker with the ever-present promise of battle on the horizon. Adam had never gone to war before, he had only ever read about it. He had always wanted to see himself on the pages of the old books, along heroes like Jessor the brave and Oden the clever, but now, as he stared at the open field before the battlements, storm clouds raging above, his stomach turned to think what he might have to pay for his name to appear in those pages.

"Adam the great," he thought trying to think of something else. "Adam the bold, the wise... the rebel... the"

"New sky." A voice said behind him. He turned, and Zeus walked towards him.

Adam frowned, "that sounds ridiculous."

"I know you do not like me, boy," Zeus said, "but admit you like something when you like it. The title suits you. I am the king of the sky, I *am* the sky, after Uranus died; and now, when I die, you will be the sky. The *new* sky. I have always liked that name."

"Adam the new sky." Adam mumbled to himself, smiling.

"I know... that nothing I say now will matter to you, Adam, but truly, I am sorry, and I am proud of you. You're a strong boy, like that satyr friend of yours. I called to him when you were in the Shadow City, and the boy listened. Strong willed, he is."

Adam stared at the open field. In a few hours the catapults and crossbows would be set up before the battlements.

"I want to give you something." Zeus said, looking at the sky.

Adam followed his gaze, something gold glided through the sky, shimmering as it flapped its large wings.

"An eagle." Adam realized.

"My symbol. Halius is his name." Zeus said, whistling.

The large bird glided down towards them. Zeus held out his arm, bent at the elbow and the bird landed on his wrist, rustling its golden feathers. It's eyes glowed blue like angry opals and its talons were like onyx daggers.

"The other children have animals that have helped them here. The weasel for Norris, the tiger and redbear for Akio and dog for Zethus. But you never received one." The eagle shared a look with Adam, and Adam could see trust in its eyes.

He took the bird on his arm and Zeus croaked, "the moments before battle are always more dreadful than the battle itself."

51

THE HOURS LEADING to the battle had everyone on edge. Hexus had been in the workshop with his father for hours working away on defensive siege weapons and gods know what else. Kathrine stood with the others in the armory. They all readied weapons and armor and had revised the plans a thousand times. Still, with all their preparations having gone according to plan, she could not shake the thought of something bad happening.

The metal clanged as they pulled weapons off the racks. The room was a large shed filled with swords, shields, spears and other weapons of war. There were barrels of hellfire and old rusted siege weapons. The bows were much larger than any she had used before and the arrows much longer. She searched and searched in the armory until she came across her weapon of choice. The bow had limbs of silver and a grip of gold. When she pulled back the bowstring, an arrow magically manifested out of thin air, the fletching between her fingers and the shaft straight through the bowstring. She released it, startled, and the arrow vanished. When she pulled it back again the phantom arrow appeared again, resting on the shelf of the bow. It glowed green, with the shaft, fletching and head all feeling as thought she had it in her hand.

"The Everbow," Athena said over her shoulder. She turned to face the goddess. She was beautiful, with almond colored skin and bright golden eyes. Her auburn hair fell over her shoulders and chest plate and

on her shoulder was perched the most majestic golden feathered owl
Kathrine had ever seen. "It once belonged to Artemis herself, but the
young goddess decided she was more well suited for traditional bows.
It is a fine weapon, a weapon meant only for those worthy enough to
wield it."

She smiled and slung the bow over her shoulder. The goddess
looked her in the eye, her golden eyes filled with care and compassion,
"I understand you are close with my daughter."

Kathrine blushed, "she taught me a lot."

Athena smiled, "I see great fortune in your future, you will be
repaid for all your sacrifice." She walked off, her silver cloak billowing
after her.

Kathrine appreciated her words, but she cursed herself for not
believing them. Her only reward in little time will be a battle, and her
sacrifices were far from over.

The armor was less glamourous than the bow. Erika strapped her
into a thin gambeson with leather padding on the shoulders, stomach
and breasts, and tightened her leather bracers and grieves and helped
her into her leather pteruges. Finally, she through over a dark green
cloak over her head and watched it flow down her back as she walked.
She could respect the Olympian's inclusion of female warriors. In Alor,
all the soldiers and guards were men. Kathrine had been teased all her
life for being around boys and not acting like a proper lady, but now,
she saw that as an advantage.

On the way out to the battlements, they passed their friends. Akio
was dressed in his halanese armor, thick, olive-green leather padding
all over the arms and torso and a thin purple silk shirt underneath.
His sword Godslayer was sheathed on his waist and his face was hidden
behind a devilish purple mask with fangs and flaring eyes. Norris had
recovered from his wound and was dressed in a blue tunic with a black
cloak thrown over top. Dangling off his waist were several water-skins
filled with his most useful weapon; water. He wore no armor, which
seemed odd to Kathrine, but he was an odd man.

Chase wore thick ring mail over a leather tunic and nothing covering his furry legs. He held both a sword and a knife on either waist.

They made it to the battlements at the front of the castle. The gatehouse was flanked by massive trebuchets and the crenels were filled by archers. Erika and Kathrine took their place on either side of Eric, who held a bow of his own, at the front of the battlements. Erika wore the same armor Kathrine did, save for the cloak and the small, adamant dagger Kathrine had sheathed to her side. Her waist was protected by two quivers and she faced the open field before them.

Eric wore leather armor all over, with a black cloak thrown over top and his hood covering his scarred face. Two short swords were sheathed at his side and a barrel of arrows was at his feet. Another barrel of hellfire sat next to Kathrine's feet.

She had been nervous to be so close to it after hearing how Hexus described it. He had spent so much time in the workshop that he had become an expert in everything there was to learn about warfare in the past hours.

"It burns so hot that not even water can put it out!" He had said with stars in his eyes. He also mentioned it blazed in several different colors, red, green, purple, blue, yellow. Kathrine had been excited to see it after that.

At the head of the center legion, in the field before them, was Adam. He stood vigilante, dressed in steel and leather and holding his thin silver sword. The golden eagle his father had gifted him stood perched on his shoulder and squawked anxiously. Next to him was his father Zeus, his tattooed arms flaring to life with blue lightning as thunder rumbled above. Some of the others were in other legions. Kathrine spotted Theo, Norris, Chase, Akio and even Silenus. The old satyr had taken up arms with the other soldiers, gripping a spear with one hand and a broken shield with the other. Some of the animals, like Quartus and Tenzir had taken their place next to their owners, ready for battle.

Quartus had been gifted a new set of armor, massive and thick enough for a mammoth of his size, and topped with a modified wooden howdah on the back, so that archers could peak from the crenels and rain arrows as the beast marched around the battlefield.

Catapults and crossbows lined the walls while trebuchets and massive wooden caltrops were set up on the front lines. The trenches were defended by the calltrops, which were covered in tar and ready to be set ablaze whenever Eric gave the answer. The gods had been generous with them all, allowing them to lead the forces as they please.

The soldiers held their spears up, silver and glimmering. They all had massive wings that shimmered as if they had been dipped through the starry night sky and their silver armor glinted.

A metal clang came from behind Kathrine. When she turned, she saw Hexus riding the most amazing contraption she had ever seen in her life.

The machine was at least fifteen feet tall, made entirely of wood and iron. It was an open wooden cage on two tall legs of wood and iron, with a tube on top that billowed black smoke. The massive feet widened out in three long, iron toes and the knees bent backwards. Two long arms extended from the bottom of the cage, one ended in a crossbow-like contraption, a spear already nocked in the string. The other was a metal cannister taller than her, sloshing with some liquid whenever the machine took a step. A small tube extended from the bottom, connected to the cannister by several metal pipes, orange with rust. The machine rumbled as it crossed under the portcullis, beneath Kathrine.

"Hexus?" Kathrine saw him fidgeting with wooden buttons and iron levers inside the cage. He wore thick rimmed goggles and full leather armor under his wide leather gorget.

The walker froze in its tracks and Hexus looked up at Kathrine, his face dark under the shadow of the cage. He smiled hysterically and waved at Kathrine.

"I call it the Flamewalker!"

After that, nothing seemed to be right again. Everyone stared at the open field, worried and waiting for something... anything to happen.

Behind the gatehouse, Hephaestus glared at the world orb; the glowing black sphere with shimmering lights in the center that formed any image he wished to see.

He glared at the gateway, with only a single, rotting Spartus, a Rott standing patiently and waiting for the gods to open the gates.

He raised his hand, and behind him, Nike's eyes began to glow. A flash of light came silently from the grey field. Then, faced with an army of the hundred thousand, the Rott rose, clicking and groaning.

52

"AIM FOR THE head!" Eric cried. The sole Rott charged at the army, and everyone readied their weapons. Kathrine heard the whistling of arrows as they flew. Kathrine counted eight, all soaring towards the Rott.

The Spartus froze as the arrows peppered its body, the final one jutting from its skull, sending it to the ground.

Everyone froze. Kathrine heard heavy breathing, and on the front lines, soldiers' iron armor clattered with their shivers.

Eric took a deep breath, "open the gate," he mumbled.

"OPEN THE GATE!" An archer beside him yelled.

A tall beam of light shot up from the field, pure and white. From the endless brightness of the beam came another Rott. Then a Dryy and a Decayer.

"Nock!" Eric cried; the archers nocked arrows in their bows. "Draw!" They lifted their arrows; Kathrine did the same. "Loose!" The archers sent a volley of arrows through the starry sky like a thousand thin black clouds. They cast a massive shadow over the Olympian army, making their silver armor glint even more.

Little by little, more and more Spartoi were taken by arrows fired from the battlements. The front lines stood still, not engaging with the action before them. Finally, when more came forward from the gate, Zeus began a wordless war cry, and little by little the rest followed.

The legions screamed as they stood their ground. Hundreds of Spartoi flooded in from the gate, sprinting at the army as soon as they laid their dead eyes on them. Hundreds became thousands, and soon, they were nothing more than a blur of black on a field of grey, charging towards the blur of silver that was the Olympian army.

She pulled back on the Everbow, but the arrows never fired. They disappeared as soon as she let go of the string. *A weapon only meant for those worthy enough to wield it*, Athena had said. Kathrine cursed and jumped from the parapets of the gatehouse onto the battlements. She armed a crossbow and launched it. The spear-sized arrow sliced through the air before finally hitting its target; impaling the Spartus through the shoulder. She armed the crossbow again, turning the crank to pull back the bowstring, and firing. Then she saw the black blur of the Spartoi and the Silver blur of the Olympian army merge into one.

Kobaloi, Spartoi and rotting bears and wolves stormed through the gateway. Chase levelled his spear, pointing towards the incoming horde. They moved like cockroaches, crawling over each other and twitching wildly. He saw their bodies in the light of the portal and heard their collective growls like one loud hiss. Chase uttered a short Senewan prayer before the wave crashed into him.

"Hold the line!" cried the legionnaire, the leader of their legion.

"Stand your ground!" yelled a soldier at the front.

"We're going to die!" cried another.

The Spartoi and Kobaloi crashed into the spears and shields, sending men flying backwards. Chase thrust the shaft of his spear forward, and landed a blow right between the eyes of an incoming Dryy. He pulled it back and thrust again, putting all his force behind his shield to keep it from pushing it back. The creatures gnashed their rotting teeth and swung their gnarled, grey claws. Chase felt the thumping and thundering of the mindless creatures banging on his shield.

He pulled and thrusted his sword until he fronts line broke. A second wave of Spartoi rammed into their shields, knocking more soldiers back, including Chase. He felt his hooves give way below him and he stumbled back, several creatures crawling over him. He had dropped his spear, and so pulled a short sword from his back and stabbed frantically at the moving masses of flesh crawling over it.

He felt the black blood pour over him like a waterfall of poison. He spat it out and continued to stab. He heard screams and clangs. Chase felt stiff claws dig into his hock and he screamed. Pain flared up his leg as he kicked wildly.

The Dryy growled again, and slobbered all over the ground as it opened its mouth to bite down on Chase' heel. Chase thrust his sword, and the blade pierced the creature's mouth, exiting from the other side of its skull. The body crumpled and Chase stood up. He saw arrows flying and heard metal clanging. The Spartoi seemed to be ripping the soldiers apart. Blood spurted and metal flashed. Chase heard screams of terror and pain and the tear of flesh, as he raced back into the battle.

Akio slashed his blade at any opportunity he could, but it seemed that for every Spartoi he cut down with Godslayer, ten more took its place. He felt the thundering bangs of the Spartoi against his armor. He did not have a shield, but his sword was thin and light. He dashed through the field of battle, slashing Godslayer at oncoming creatures that scrambled to murder him. Quartus trumpeted as he ran through the battlefield, crushing and flattening whatever creatures got caught in his path.

Akio sprinted towards the mammoth, dodging swings from rusted swords and vaulting off rocks and the bodies of Spartoi as he swung. Tenzir was with him, ripping apart more creatures by the dozens. The white fur around his mouth was stained baclk with the corrupted blood of the Spartoi.

Akio came closer to Quartus. Asius, wearing full leather and mail armor, pulled the reins, leading the mammoth into the hordes of the dead. Akio rushed towards it, vaulting off a pile of corpses with one leg and extending the other to grab a hold of Quartus tusks. He gripped the tusk with one hand and slashed at a Spartoi swinging its claws at his dangling feet, knocking its head off.

He made it to Quartus' howdah and gather the weapons located on the top. The mammoth's howdah was filled with Olympian archers, all clamoring to find arrows and launch them within a matter of seconds. Akio picked up a bow of his own, nocked and arrow, and fired at the hordes of the dead below.

Theodore was now a bear, his back swarming with a dozen Rotts, all stabbing at his furry hide with rusted swords. He shook and rolled on the ground, crushing several and throwing off several more. He swung his sharp, heavy claws at the Spartoi, shattering their dry, dead bodies.

He saw Zeus blast the dead with lightning, lighting up the battlefield. The trebuchets and catapults and crossbows launched their ammunition at the incoming waves of Spartoi. They stormed forward towards the Olympian army, shrieking.

The beam of light that was the gate flared brighter and brighter with each Spartus, Kobalos or other creature that burst through it. More and more washed from the gateway, replacing the last thousand that the Olympians had destroyed. Theo had tried to think the fight was anything but unwinnable, but his conscience told him otherwise. He saw the dead thrust their rusted swords through the Olympain forced, sending the winged soldiers to their knees, and for every creature that the Olympians killed, a thousand more would flood from the gateway.

He morphed into a massive bird, his wingspan big enough to shield a grown man from arrow fire, and took to the skies. The nightcrows that followed the army dived at the battlements, knocking archers off the ledges and through the crenels. Theodore soared their way, his talons extended. He tore one up and ripped the wing off another. Each bird he killed sent out a blood-curdling shriek now of their demise, as they plummeted to the fighting below.

He became a boy again and laid on the battlements at the feet of the archers, panting. When he looked up again, the rest of the flock of nightcrows were gliding towards him.

Hexus delighted in blasting flames at the Spartoi. They scurried and scattered as he pulled the iron levers inside the Flamewalker, launching scorching red flames at the screeching corpses. The bronze hose that jutted from the bottom of the hellfire cannister spewed the fire out, dripping glowing orange water from the tip. The Spartoi shrieked, their flaming bodies ran around the battlefield, lighting up the grass when their limp bodies feel to the ground.

He pushed and pulled the leavers, moving the heavy iron legs and crushing the Rotts and Decayers that walked below, and launched the automatically reloading crossbow on the other side of the cage. His new war hammer, Fyrestar, hung from his belt. It would seem heavy to any other person, but Hephaestus had made it only for him. The shaft was short, able to be held with only one hand. The head was large and flat on one side, for blunt damage, and the other was sharp and meant to peirce armor. It was made of what left over adamant the god had in the workshop. The metal was rare, said to fall from the sky once every five thousand years. Hephaestus had worked with the metal before, using it to forge weapons for the gods, and even Adam's sword, and now, Hexus held the last of it in his possession.

The thought gave him comfort. He tried to ignore the rising difficulty of fighting off the creatures, instead trying to focus on his future creations. *I will finish the airship!* He told himself with a grimace. The Spartoi began to crawl up the legs, gnashing their foaming teeth. *I'll build the automatons! They will be our friends! I will finish the bull, and he will build the Hellhound.*

He thought of all the designs his father had shown him. He thought of weapons, small and great, that he would make. He would become the greatest craftsmen to ever live.

The Spartoi began to claw at the walls of the cage, breaking through the wood with their claws. Hexus thrust the lever forward, and the Flamewalker sped up into a sprint. He blasted fire in all directions, praying he did not hit allies. He felt sweat trickle down his neck and back and his knees trembled. His fingers hovered the controls, not knowing what to do next. The Spartoi broke through the front bars, almost pouring from the hole they made.

Hexus screamed and jumped back, the Spartoi growling and roaring. He took Fyrestar in his hand and focused on it, his hand began to glow red hot as fiery energy crawled up the hammer. He lifted it over his shoulder and threw it at the cluster of Rotts swinging their arms through the bars.

When the hammer made contact, they disintegrated in an explosion of orange light. He rushed to the controls and called the hammer back. It zipped through the air and back into his hand, still smoking and still hot when he touched it.

Small tongues of fire licked at the ruined rim of the hole in the cage. The flames became bigger. They flared to life with colors of green, blue and white.

"The hellfire!" Hexus realized. The tank muct have been damaged when the Spartoi attacked. He heard sizzling from the fire and felt as the colorful liquid slid around the inside of the cage. The world on the other side of the bars was a blur of dark colors with sounds of clashing metal and screams. He saw flames erupt from the controls, watching as they went up in smoke. He coughed as the smoke billowed in thick plumes, blinding him. His eyes watered and he fell back.

He felt the heat around him rage on as the Flamewalker exploded, the final thoughts moving through his head before it did, *this is going to hurt.*

Adam saw the explosion in the distance. Hexus' creation burst into a bright cloud of a thousand colors. The fragments that flew from the explosion left trails of blazing colors as they flew away. White, green, blue and purple lit up the field, and there were even Kobaloi and Spartoi that were thrown into the air with the explosion, their bodies burning.

His eyes widened as he realized that Hexus was still in it. He heard an arrow fly near him, and a scream come from behind him. He saw the soaring Olympian guards fly overhead, thrusting their lances at the creatures behind Adam.

The battle raged on around him. Arrows flew, metal clashed, and he heard screams. Roars came from the gateway as more creatures flooded in. Spartoi, Kobaloi, rotting beasts, nightcrows and bonedragons. A Rott rushed towards him and he swung his blade at its head, sending it to the ground.

He turned and held out the bolt, and a blast of lightning jumped out, destroying a group of Spartoi and Kobaloi. He shot energy and slashed his sword. Zeus fought alongside him. His arms blasted thunder as his body flashed blue. He had cuts and gashes, all bleeding golden blood.

He was right, Adam thought, *the gods are near their end. They are not supposed to bleed.* Still, he did not fight like he was mortally injured, blasting his foes with strength and accuracy.

Adam glared at his own thoughts. He supposed he was harsh to this man, but he was not ready to accept him as his father yet.

He looked around and noticed the battlements. Kathrine had mounted a crossbow and fired massive arrows at the Spartoi crawling up the walls. Eric and Erika led volley after volley of arrows at the flock of nightcrows that swarmed the battlements. The Spartoi dug their claws into the bricks, pulling their rotting bodies upwards towards the crenels the hordes outnumbering their arrows.

Adam rushed over to the walls, raising the bolt to blast the creatures off.

"ADAAAAAMMMM!" A voice called, loud and violent. It echoed around the battlefield, bringing the heads of many soldiers staring at the source. Adam turned, the gateway behind him. He froze in his tracks, digging his toes in the dirt.

He turned to the source of the shout, and his eyes widened when he saw it.

Eleon stood before the gate, bloody and sweating. He breathed heavily and had the figure of a beast. His back was hunched, his eyes wild flames, his mouth dribbling and his arms and axe blade red and dripping. The flesh on one side of his face was twisted and melted where his old burned blazed.

He was dressed in his armor, with his golden lion hide wrapped around his shoulders. He raised his axe towards Adam, his jaw trembling, "I'm back... and I'm coming for you." His legs were buried in the bodies of a dozen Olympian soldiers, their chests and limbs bleeding from awe wounds.

Eleon' axe flared with red energy, like the rest of his body did. His eyes flared red as he hurled the axe at Adam. The blade spun through the air, leaving a smoking trail of red as it flew.

Adam threw himself down to the ground, dodging the blade by a hair. He turned back, and saw the axe still flying. He sucked in a breath as the axe clashed with the battlements left of the gatehouse, sending stone and dust upwards. Bodies flew and archers tumbled off the edge, their screams only ending when their bodies crunched against the ground.

Adam turned back to Eleon, his hand extended, holding an invisible weapon. He was calling his axe back to his hand. The blade curved in the air and returned to Adam's direction, destroying the battlements on the other side of the gatehouse. The crossbow Kathrine had mounted was tossed in the air, accidentally launching an arrow upwards into the sky. Her screaming face disappeared behind a cloud of dust, and Adam ducked again as the axe returned to Eleon's hand.

Norris knew this battle was lost. He walked among the bodies of the dead, breathing heavily as he saw their bleeding faces. Now Eleon had destroyed their battlements, and the catapults on the field had been destroyed by the Spartoi and Kobaloi.

He chugged another gulp of wine, struggling to keep it down. He had never had troubles with wine before, but now, seeing the faces of his fallen allies, his body was reluctant to accept the drink.

He dashed through the trail of corpses, covering his face when the flames of the hellfire burned next to him. He made it to what remained of the Flamewalker, a burning pile of ashes and colorful flames consuming wood.

He dug through the wreckage, jumping when he saw Hexus. Hexus' unconscious body laid covered in ash and scratches, under a pile of burning wood. Norris kneeled next to him, lightly slapping his cheek until the boy opened his scarlet eyes. Norris let out a sigh of relief.

"You fool!" Norris told him.

"That *did* hurt." He mumbled. Norris patted his shoulder. Lucky for Hexus, he was immune to flames.

"We need to go," Norris said, "Eleon is back."

Hexus shook his head at that, "Who? Wait, Eleon... what?"

"I know little more than you do, now come on."

Adam stood up, his breathes heavy. He was flanked by allies, he saw Chase and Akio, Theodore and Zeus. Several Olympian guards stood their ground against the ever-growing line of Greymen revived by whatever black magic they were using.

Their swords glimmered a silvery-black against their all black armor and cloaks. Eleon stood at the lead, at his side was Xuthos, the small Spartus that had infected Norris. But there was still no sign of Korax.

"Eleon," Adam called, "You don't have to do this." He pleaded. He gazed upon Eleon's face and realized his words were wasted. Eleon had made up his own mind, and the look in his eyes proved so. His axe had returned to his hand, and he gripped with one.

"I don't need to do this... I just want to." Eleon said. Xuthos unsheathed his cursed blade and flourished his sword.

More Olympian soldiers rallied around Adam, lifting their swords, ready for battle. He saw more of his friends take up arms by his side. Erika was reluctant to fight, but she stood by her mother, Athena. Raia and Aphrodite flashed magic between their fingers. Minerva sat atop Boo's shoulders as the cyclops roared. Norris froze icicles to his fists and Hexus lifted his hammer and called fire to his palm. Eric and Erika had rushed from the walls, bringing archers with them. Eric raised his bow and Erika her spear. Asius led Quartus to the front of the line and the beast trumpeted, Tenzir and Beta growling alongside him. Adam did not see Kathrine, and that worried him.

From the light of the gateway a silhouette emerged, massive and dark. Korax stepped from the beam, his gaze down and his sword sheathed. More Spartoi flooded in from the beam, nothing stopped them. Within a few moments, the Olympian army was outnumbered again, and there was nothing Adam could do to stop it.

Corpses hurled themselves towards the soldiers, and the soldiers tried their best to keep them away with spears and swords. Adam saw his army slowly being consumed by the darkness brought on by Korax' forces. The soldiers screamed as their bodies were ripped apart and their blood spurted all over.

Adam froze, petrified with fear.

"Fall back!" cried one soldier.

"Retreat!" yelled a second one. Several soldiers urged their comrades to flee for their lives. Adam felt like a coward, but he knew they were not going to win here. A Spartoi threw itself onto him and he fell to the ground. He shook the beast off, thrusting his blade through its eye, and tried to shake the body of a man next to him, laying motionlessly. Adam pulled back his hand, his palm wet and red. He jumped back when he realized he was next to a corpse.

He got to his feet and looked around him trying to catch a breath. Then he saw everyone. His friends engaged Xuthos, Korax and Eleon, trading blows with the three.

Kathrine locked eyes with him a moment later, and Adam gasped as he rushed towards her. They never took their eyes from each other, and when they met, they hugged. Adam embraced her warmth, "you're alive." He kissed her forehead. Adam looked at her eyes, the deep seas of beautiful green, and they gave him comfort.

"You need to go!" He told her.

Her smiled melted into a frown, "I'm not leaving you." She kissed his lips, "Never again."

"Then we need to fall back. We can't stop them."

"No but he can." She pointed at Korax. "All we need is him. We keep fighting the Spartoi, but we only need him. If we kill him-"

"The others will fall back. Their king will be dead."

"It is only a theory, but it is the only thing we have."

"It'll do. Let's go."

Kathrine could not decide whether she feared war, or enjoyed the rush of it. Her blood burned in her veins and her fingers tingled. She unslung the Everbow from her back and pulled the bowstring. The arrows vanished again. She focused all she could. She put her fear to the side, and she let courage replace it, what little there was. She thought of what there was to fight for. She thought of Adam, and Chase. She thought of Erika, and for her home, wherever that may be, she knew it was within Alanos. She did not yet know what this vast world had, but she intended to see it all through.

When she pulled the bowstring back again, the arrow of green light flew. The tip dug itself into the skull of a Kobalos and then shimmered into nothingness. She pulled back again and fired another arrow, then again, and again.

One by one more and more enemies fell as she rushed towards Korax alongside Adam. Then they were there. Korax swung his heavy sword, Xuthos flourished his thin curved blade and Eleon stood with his axe.

As the soldiers did battle with the dead, they did battle with the dead's leaders. Everyone Kathrine had started her journey with was with her now, all raising arms against her enemies, or in Eleon's case, against her.

Norris had frozen blades of his wrists, Hexus his hammer and flame. Theodore was in the body of a dragon, mounted by Chase and Silenus. Akio stood by Tenzir and Beta barked alongside Raia. Minerva sat atop Boo's shoulders, and the cyclops cracked his knuckles. Erika spun her spear and Eric nocked an arrow.

"I see you survived our first battle." Xuthos told Norris.

Bitterly, Norris said, "As did you."

"You may come to regret that." Xuthos said with a sly chuckle.

"As will you." Norris responded.

Xuthos' chuckle wavered, and the battle commenced.

Adam parried Xuthos first strike and ducked below his second. Norris thrust the icicles at him but the thin Greyman dodged them.

Theodore and the satyrs fought Korax, but the iron beast was far too strong.

Adam did not like the outcome of the battle. He could see where it led, but he tried to shake the thoughts. The fighting raged on, before he felt claws clasp at his neck.

"Adam!" Kathrine yelled.

"No!" cried a voice he could not identify.

Adam looked at his feet, they were now off the ground. The battlefield became smaller and smaller, getting further and further away. He heard heavy flapping above him, but the wind was against him, and he could not look up.

Finally, he stopped ascending, and turned towards what had taken him.

FINALLY, WE MEET IN PERSON, said that dreaded voice said, like a thousand screaming souls. Adam gazed upon the hellish face, and his terror had returned to him.

HELLO THERE ADAM. Zethus said, not with his own voice.

53

ELEON BROUGHT DOWN his heavy axe in an overhead arc, destroying the ground below Hexus' feet. He swung it again, and Hexus ducked below the strike and brought his hammer down on Eleon's foot. The man screamed, and tried a second strike. Hexus dodged, but when Eleon thrust the shaft as his chest, Hexus flew backwards, the air in his lungs being knocked out of him. Hexus stirred on the ground, groanin and cursing. His breathes were heavy and he saw blood drip from his mouth. He felt around for his hammer, but it was lost.

"You've been bothering me, you little prick." Eleon growled, wrapping his fingers around Hexus' neck. Hexus' eyelids slowly grew heavier as his body grew weaker. He forced himself to stay conscience, but his body screamed for him to rest. Eleon's fingers tightened, and Hexus' words became gasps and coughs and squeals. He lifted his hand and felt the invisible force of Fyrestar tug on his fingers. The shaft of the hammer slammed into his palm and he raised his arm over his head.

Eleon grunted and Hexus brought the weapon down on his head. The metal cracked on his skull, sending Eleon scrambling backwards. He dropped Hexus, and held his head with both hands, wailing as blood dripped off his fingers.

He looked up, his amber eyes like melting gold under a helm of glistening blood gushing from his scalp. "I'LL KILL YOU, YOU LITTLE SHIT!" He called back his axe and lunged at Hexus. Arms appeared from behind him, holding a spear parallel to his shoulders. The spear was pulled back, slamming Eleon in the throat. He coughed violently when he hit the ground.

Eric flourished the spear in his hand, cuts and gashes painting his cheeks red. He pointed the tip at Eleon's face, "stay down."

Eleon roared and flared with red energy. He took the blade with one hand, squeezing until his fingers and palm bled and brought his arm up, snapping the shaft in half. Eric jumped back and pulled out his sword. Hexus shook the weakness from his body and levelled his sight on Eleon. Soldiers flanked Hexus, ready to do battle with Eleon.

Eleon charged with his axe over his head. Hexus and the others howled and charged. Eleon's eyes were wild, and his teeth were red. The blood running down his face glistened in the fire.

An Olympian soldier charged back; his spear levelled. Eleon threw a punch, already drawing blood from the soldier's mouth, knocking his spear to the ground. He brought the axe down on the soldier's head, splitting his skull. Blood spurt and Hexus' face was painted red.

Another soldier ran to his left, thrusting his spear in Eleon's ribs. Eleon pulled the blade out and tugged, pulling the soldier towards him. The soldier flew forward then was knocked to the ground by another punch from Eleon. Eric stabbed at him, his blade digging into Eleon's shoulder. Eleon threw his hand back, hitting Eric in the jaw. He grunted and fell back, and Eleon howled as he stood over his, his axe in his hands.

Kathrine fired arrow after arrow, knocking Spartoi to the ground. She tried to focus on the battle, but she kept thinking of Adam. He was up there somewhere, doing battle with that... *thing*. She had not seen it well enough to make a proper shape, but she saw wings, and long tendrils jutting from everywhere. It was massive, and dark, like the shadow of a dragon.

Zeus grunted, "where is my son?" His fingers fired fractals of lightning at incoming Rotts.

"That thing took him!" Kathrine said. She saw Erika standing in the battlefield, looking directly upwards, "it's got him there!" She cried, pointing a finger to the air. Kathrine saw it, and her heart seemed to stop. The creature was massive, twice the size of any normal man. Just as the Olympian soldiers had silvery bird's wings, the creature had bony dragon's wings, snapping and cracking as they flapped. She saw spiked spider's legs and snarling dragons.

"The Great Snake." She heard a voice say. Akio was next to her, his face splattered with the black blood of the Greymen.

Kathrine shuddered. She heard the fight go on around her, but her head was in another place. She tried to keep her gaze fixed on Adam, but he disappeared behind stormy clouds. She silently pleaded in her head, and turned to join the fight.

54

HIS FACE WAS horrible, worse than anything Adam had ever seen. Horns jutted from his face like spiked warts, even covering one eyes and his teeth had become sharp daggers. Bones stuck out from his body, red and cracked at the ends. His skin had become pale and leathery and his fingernails were now claws. Bat wings had broken through his ribs and twitching, and four cracking spider legs sprouted from his back. His feet had become fire-spitting dragons, his body turning green and scaly at the waist.

IT IS TRULY A PLEASURE TO MEET YOU, Zethus said.

"You aren't him." Adam told him, still, the words sounded like lies to even him. He stared at his enemy, trying to picture another face, but try as he might, his enemy had the face of his friend. Adam's jaw trembled.

NO, I AM NOT. YOUR FRIEND IS DEAD, AND I AM ALL THAT REMAINS OF HIM. HE DIED, AND NOW YOU WILL JOIN HIM. He softly dragged two clawed fingers against Adam's face, holding Adam by the collar of his mail shirt.

WATCH, MY BOY, AS YOUR OWN WORLD BURNS IN THE FIRES OF YOUR FAILURE. YOU CANNOT STOP THIS, FOR IT IS THE FUTURE. YOU ARE BUT A CHILD. YOUR ARMY COULD NOT DEFEAT MINE OWN AND YOUR ALLIES TREMBLE WHEN IN THE SHADOW OF MY CHILDREN. YOUR CASTLE HAS FALLEM, YOUR FAMILY

466

HAS FALLEN, AND SOON... YOU WILL FALL WITH THEM. YOU THINK ME A MONSTER, BUT I AM NOT A MONSTER. I AM A SAVIOUR, I AM A GOD! DIVINE TO MORTAL EYES! I WILL SAVE THIS WORLD BY FREEING IT OF YOUR SINS, AND THE SINS OF YOUR FATHER, AND HIS FATHER. FOR EONS, THE GODS OF OLYMPUS HAVE RULED THIS WORLD, AND WHAT A TERRIBLE JOB THEY HAVE DONE. WAR AND FAMINE RUN RAMPANT IN THEIR PRECIOUS CREATIION AND WHAT DO THE GODS DO TO BETTER IT? THEY DRINK UP HERE, HIGH AND MIGHTY, DROWNING THEMSELVES IN WINE AND SEX. NOT IN MY WORLD. IN MY WORLD, THOSE WHO FOLLOW ME WILL PROSPER, AND THOSE WHO STILL CLING TO THE DARK WORLD THESE FALSE GODS HAVE BROUGH ON WILL BE PUNISHED.

"You will stop war by showing Alanos the greatest war it has ever seen?"

PEACE IS IMPOSSIBLE WITHOUT DEATH. PROSPERITY CAN ONLY BE ACHIEVED WITH SACRIFICES, AND I WILL ONLY SACRIFICE THOSE WHO REFUSE TO SEE A BETTER FUTURE FOR THEIR WORLD.

"They will not even see their world in *your* future." Adam spat at him, his fear still boiling in his belly.

THEN I WILL SHOW IT TO THEM! I WILL SHOW THEM THE SINS OF THEIR PAST AND I WILL SHOW THEM HOW TO REPENT FOR THEM. AND IF I MUST KILL EVERY LAST ONE OF THOSE FILTHY CREATIONS ON THAT WORLD THEN SO BE IT. I WILL BE A GOD TO THOSE I CREATE, THOSE I GIVE LIFE TO! AND YOU WILL BE REMEMBERED, AS THE ONE WHO TRIED TO DESTROY THEIR GOD.

His thrust was so hard, it knocked the breath out of Adam's chest. He was flung far from Typhon, far from the battlefield and far from the sounds of battle. He saw only blurs of grey and black as he flew backwards towards the castle.

He felt his back shatter the tiles of the dome roof. The debris fell to the castle below, crushing and destroying the statues of the Olympians. He gasped and spat blood from his mouth. His weak words came out as grunts and blood flowed from his lips. He had lost his sword and the bolt, and his vision was failing.

YOU AREN'T LEAVING YET ARE YOU? Typhon asked as his leathery wings flapped above him. His red eyes glowed like flaming rubies. He grasped Adams collar again, but his body disappeared in a flash of blue and white.

Adam looked up. Zeus struggled with Typhon, his glowing blue arms flashing with bolts as he thrust his weight onto the monster. His biceps were dripping golden blood and his eyes were blue with power. Strapped to his back were Adam's sword, and his silver bolt, found on the field below. He pinned Typhon against the spire atop the highest dome.

"If you touch my son again," he said, "I will rip out your entrails and feed them to you!"

ZEUUSSSSS, Typhon said, smiling. **IT HAS BEEN AN AGE, OLD FRIEND. YOU HAVEN'T AGED A DAY?** One of his spider legs jumped up and thrust itself forward. The jagged spike at the tip buried itself in Zeus' side, blood spurted, and Zeus screamed.

Adam took a deep breath and thrust himself at Typhon. He pulled his sword from Zeus' back and summoned the blade, plunging it into Typhons chest. He tried to ignore the face, lest he crumble with anguish.

Typhon roared and slapped him with a spider leg. Adam flew backwards, blood jumping from his jaw. He gripped his sword tight, making sure it did not come loose from his grip.

When he landed, he was on his stomach, blood dripping from his mouth. He looked up, and Typhon's claws were wrapped around Zeus's neck. Adam grunted and pushed himself upwards, launching himself towards Typhon.

His fingers gripped Typhon's arms and the two wrestled over the roof. He tossed Typhon off him after the beast pinned him. His body felt a rush of strength, the same strength he felt during his fight with Eleon. Adam could hear the battle below, screams and explosions.

WHY DO YOU FEAR FOR THEM? Typhon said, reading his expressions of fear, **YOU LOYALTY WILL MEAN YOU END, BOY.** He laughed maniacally, the sound of a thousand screams echoing from his throat.

Adam felt a hand touch his arm. When he turned, a blinding light took his vision. When it returned, he was in the throne room, his bleeding father beside him. Zeus fell beside Adam. He was pale and sweating, golden blood leaking down his sides. He panted; his eyes heavy.

Zeus fell on his back and looked up at Adam, his eyes filled with tears, "oh... you beautiful boy." His words were faint, almost completely silent. He gasped, and Adam tried his best to stop the bleeding with his hands. Golden god's blood poured over his hands, he saw his glossy reflection in the puddles that formed over the marble floor, and he felt his eyes swell with tears. Adam could hear Typhon's roars outside the castle, his thick leathery wings flapping as he searched for them.

"Weep not for me, my son. Weep for your friends. They have need of you now." He coughed, more shining blood painting his white beard gold, "I beg you, Adam. Do not be one of us. Be better than those who came before you, learn from their mistakes, and make recompense for ours past sins. I'm sorry... for everything. I know that is worth little to you now, but it is worth more than you can imagine to me. I am sorry this fell upon you, I am sorry I was never your father, for the dreams, for your mother, your home, all your pain. I am sorry I failed you." He wept now, tears lining his cheeks. He stretched out a shaky hand and cupped Adam's cheek.

Adam took a shaky breath, his tears splashing against the puddle blood. He had entered Olympus with anger burning inside him. He was angry with Zeus, but his anger had faded. Adam saw him as a greedy man who only cared for himself. Everyone had explained the gods to him, except for the gods themselves. He regretted his once narrowed vision. He had been told the gods were selfish and he had believed it, but now, he kneeled over his dying father, the god of the skies who had given his life to save him.

"I forgive you, father." The word was no longer bitter on his tongue.

He shared a final look with the god, and Zeus' expression went blank. His eyes stared at nothing, and his breathing had ceased. His arm went limp, and the hand that once cupped Adam's face fell to the ground.

He wiped his tears and stood up. His clothes and armor were stained now. His father was laid out before him, his eyes still open. Adam brought a hand to his face and shut his eyes. Then he turned to the exit and walked out to the balcony.

"TYPHON!" He yelled, "I am here! And I do not fear you anymore!"

He saw the silhouette of the massive beast crawl down from the tallest tower, his sharp spider legs piercing the tile and quarts and stone as if it were dirt. **MEN OFT CONFUSE FOOLISHNESS FOR BRAVERY,** Typhon said, **YOU WILL SOON LEARN THAT LESSON.** His claws elongated, and he bared his teeth.

Adam charged; Typhon lunged. When they collided, Adam felt his feet lift off the ground. Typhon flapped his massive wings, the leathery membrane slicing through the air as the ascended higher and higher. He looked down, the dome of the tallest Olympian tower shrunk smaller with every passing second.

Adam felt anger flare inside him. He brought an arm up and punched Typhon in the jaw. The beast roared and slashed a slaw at Adam's face. He guarded with his sword, slicing the spider's claw clean off. Green acid-like blood spewed from the open wound as Typhon roared with pain and anger. Another slashed at his side and dug itself into his chest.

Adam screamed. His heart echoed in his ears. Hot blood streamed down his arms. His chest burned with pain. Typhon ripped the leg out of his chest, and he screamed again, this time sounding more like a loud whimper.

YOU WILL DIE, SCREAMING. AND YOU WILL WATCH AS I DESTROY THIS WRETCHED CASTLE AND ALL WHO

CALL IT HOME. He wrapped his grotesque fingers around Adam's throat and choked him, his breathes becoming thicker with every second. Typhon looked down and laughed. They were still flying upwards, the noise of the battle below faded until it was no more than a faint sigh. Adam tried to speak, but his throat was tightening.

TAKE A BREATH, BOY. Typhon hissed, **SCREAM. WHY SAY WORDS WHEN THERE IS NO ONE TO HEAR THEM.**

His legs flailed as they searched for a solid surface. Typhon laughed. Adam stared into his eyes. The eyes he had once thought of as friendly. When he saw Typhon, only Zethus stared back, and Adam felt his eyelids grow heavy. His sword hand weakened, and the blade fell from his fingers. Typhon let go, and Adam fell to the ground below.

55

THEODORE FLAPPED HIS wings frantically to escape the swarm of nightcrows. They cawed and screeched as they chased him through the air above the field of battle. He was in the body of an eagle, and he extended his talons when a nightcrow got too close. The dream came back to him. He saw himself in the cave of the iron lion. The swarm of nightcrows ripped him apart, tearing his skin off his bones. His breath became heavy and he wished for something as sweet as a bed, a hot meal and the sweetness of ale.

The nightcrows grew closer to his tail, clawing and biting at his feathers. He dived downward and soared upward, still he could not shake the damned birds.

His eyesight had sharpened, and he gazed around the field for help. Ion, Erika's owl and Halius, Adam's eagle ripped apart and carried Kobaloi away.

He let out a loud screech. Chase locked eyes with him, and the satyr smiled smugly. He fought on the ground, swinging his sword, destroying the corpses. He let out a whoop and Ion and Halius flew towards Theo, launching themselves into the swarm of nightcrows and frantically fighting.

Theo turned to join them. Ion was much smaller than the nightcorws, but she used her talons to slash and scratch at the black birds, leaving deep, bloody gashes in their chests. Halius glided through the swarm, his golden wings flashed with blue energy, crackling like lightning. He cawed loudly and a dozen shocking blue tendrils sprouted from his body, blasting the nightcrows out of the sky.

The black birds plummeted out of the sky, their dark feathers leaving snaking trails of billowing smoke as they fell. Halius and Ion continued their fight with the nightcrows that still lived, and Theodore turned back to join them.

Hexus chucked his hammer through a Rott and the creature disintegrated. When he called it back, he let it move past him, destroying more behind him. Korax was a strong fighter, swinging his mighty blade over his head, striking down Olympian soldiers by the dozens.

Xuthos was quick and balanced. He parried Eric's attacks, and threw his own. The cursed blade had not been drawn yet, and Hexus was thankful for that. He heard the clang of metal and explosions in the distance. He looked up and saw darkness loom over them all, leaking over the tallest tower of Olympus over a thousand feet up.

They attacked Korax from all sides, striking his armor and clashing with his blade. With each touch of metal, orange sparks flew. He growled and roared as they fought. Hexus chucked his hammer at Korax' head, but the giant ducked. Eric vaulted over his back and brought a spear into his side. Korax brought an arm down, snapping it.

He heard a scream come from his left, and another from behind. He tried to keep his stance balanced, but one leg always seemed weaker than the other. He swung his hammer, but little by little, his swoops became slower.

Hexus was hot, sweat dripping down his neck. He looked around him and saw the raging battle. Soldiers fell as beasts of war roared in the distance. Fire engulfed the field, screams echoed into the endless void.

Hexus felt his breathes grow heavy. His mouth dried and his arms trembled as he saw more of it.

This isn't right, he thought, *this should not happen.* His legs stiffened and his arms became heavier. He turned to the walls of the city, swarming with Spartoi. The Rotts and Decayers and Dryys and

Freshs crawled up the walls, digging their nails into the stone. Kobaloi swarmed up, growling and gnashing their fangs. The war beasts fed on the corpses of the dead and their blood-stained mouths dripped onto the ground.

His knees buckled and his spine shivered, and he fell to the ground. His knees splattered into the ground and he felt tears wet his eyes.

Norris waved his hands over the water and the trail froze, catching the jumping Spartoi in midair. He twisted his fists and the ice followed his motions, crushing the Dryys and ripping them apart.

He turned the ice back into water and rushed it back towards him. He froze the wave into ice again, launching icicles into the charging Spartoi behind him. They crumpled and he called the water back into his waterskin.

He looked around for the others. They all fought Korax and Eleon. Eric did battle with Xuthos. He could not find Hexus so he focused on Eric. The thin Spartoi he fought was vaulting and jumping. He fought like Akio did, light on his feet and swinging his blade in elegant swaying motions. His fighting was no more than lethal dancing.

Norris ran to join the battle with Korax, throwing the Iron Giant back with continuous thrusts of freezing waves.

Korax staggered to keep his balance. He swung his heavy red blade and the ice shattered. Norris fell to the ground, bleeding and panting. He looked up and saw Korax with his great sword raised over his head. He dodged the strike and the ground cracked where his head once was. He rolled over and got to his feet. Akio came up behind, slashing at Korax' armor. Godslayer cut through his mail like wet paper. The touch of adamant on iron was like a hot knife on butter. The giant grunted and swung. Akio ducked and rolled. He got to his feet and jabbed Godslayer into Korax' side. The giant wailed and fell to his knees.

Xuthos was quick and cocky. He flourished his blade and chuckled when he parried Eric's attacks and dodged his swings and blocked his strikes. His moves were foreign to Eric, not like any fighting he had seen before. A fighting style not native to Vulna. He swung again, and Xuthos raised his blade between his eyes, blocking it.

"You are quite decent." He said, chuckling.

Eric said nothing back, instead choosing to let his blade speak for him. He shoved Xuthos back, knocking him to the ground. He brought his sword up in a broad stroke and got the Spartoi in the arm. He wailed as black blood poured from his wound, but he was on his feet quickly.

His eyes narrowed as he charged. He was fast with his strikes, his movements silent as air and his body as dark as a shadow. Eric's arm tired and nearly lost feeling. He blocked and parried and struck and swung and the battle went on.

Xuthos swiped left, and Eric jumped back. The Spartoi brought his foot up and kicked him backwards. He tumbled back, and the ground behind him dipped into the curve of a hill. He rolled down to the bottom, coughing dust when he had made it.

He looked up, Xuthos had jumped from the top of the hill, his sword ready to thrust the final blow. Eric rolled, dodging the attack. Xuthos landed and his thin, curved blade buried itself in the ground. He struggled to remove it, but the blade his itself in the rock, leaving only the hilt visible above ground.

Eric brought his fist forward. He had lost his sword in the fall. He punched Xuthos over and over, knocking his iron mask off, revealing his grotesque face.

His cheek and eyes had sunken in, leaving nothing more but dark pits. His teeth were rotting, and his lips were thin. Eric brought his fist down again, and his mouth bled. Eric pummeled him, his weakening body flat on the ground, pinned down by Eric's knee.

Eric threw another punch, then another and then another. His knuckled were white, and dripping with wet, black blood when he had stopped. Xuthos' jaw was a ruin, several teeth knocked out. His eyes had rolled to the back of his head and he lay there still. Eric rolled over to his side, catching his breath and staring at the sky. He saw the stars dotting the black abyss. He had never noticed how cold it was until now. His skin was peppered with goosebumps and the hair on his arms stood up. He laid on the ground, focusing on his breath as the battle raged on around him.

Chase dodged Eleon's strikes. He was growing tired, and his chest burned. The madman seemed to target him. His mouth foamed and his eyes flared with rage. His axe destroyed the ground around him, and he roared with every swing.

Chase brought his sword up. Eleon caught his arm and kicked him to the ground. Chase grunted as Eleon tossed his blade aside. His smile was wild, and his eyes were red. The blood colored mist clouded around him, moving up his arms and down to the blade of his axe. He lifted it over his head and roared.

Erika rushed to his side and jammed her spear in his side, drawing blood from below his ribs. Eleon dropped his axe to the ground behind him and wailed with pain. He stared at his side, blood pouring from his wound. He moved as though he had no wounds, grabbing Erika's spear and ripping it from his ribs. He snapped the weapon over his knee and threw a fist at his sister.

She grunted as she fell to the ground. He growled, foam dribbling from his mouth. She looked up at him, her cheek bleeding and her eyes watering. For a moment, Eleon froze, his gaze softening. He stared at her, the red energy fading from his body. His eyes flickered, opening and closing sporadically. His hands trembled as he unclenched his fists.

Erika stared at her brother, her lip tightening into a frown and a tear trailing down her cheek.

Eleon held out a shaking hand, "E-Erika..." he stumbled to make words.

She stood up slowly, the battle behind her still raging. Chase panted, still on the ground. He switched his eyes between Erika and Eleon, not knowing what would happen. He heard the clashing of swords and the screaming of soldiers, but none of that seemed to bother them at that moment.

Erika put a hand out, lightly touching her brothers face. Her mouth trembled and her tears glistened with a fear. She was sad, sad for what her brother had become, but she clenched her jaw with acceptance.

She pulled her arm away and nodded her head, her eyes closed. A massive green root the size of a tree trunk burst from the ground. More exploded forth from the field, cracking through the ground like earthen tentacles. They wrapped around Eleon, tightening around his arms and legs and squeezing his chest.

Eleon grunted, his expression of fear immediately melting off his face. Anger and confusion replaced it and his blood colored aura returned. He screamed and kicked, unable to move. Minerva showed herself from behind Chase, her arms lifted in the air, telling the vines what to do. Eleon was lifted higher and higher into the air, thrashing and cursing as he floated.

"I'll rip your arms off, you whore!" His words echoed in Chase's ears, and his sincerity terrified him. Minerva twisted his fingers and the vines followed suite. Eleon yelled one final time before Minerva slammed him against the ground. He fell unconscious and his body was still.

Chase laid on the ground, bloodied and panting, his arms were heavy, and his body ached. The Spartoi continued to ravage the city and the soldiers, and their screams sent his eyes to the air. He saw clouds of dust burst from the wrecked castle towers and zaps of lightening flicker from inside the massive black flock of nightcrows. Erika wept and Minerva comforted her and the battle faded into silence as he stared up at the stars.

56

ADAMS STOMACH TURNED and his chest burned. His head was almost completely empty now. He could not feel any of his limbs. *I've lost too much blood*, he thought. He was going to die when he hit the ground, or maybe even before then, but he knew it was soon. He thought his last thought, Kathrine, Chase, their journey, and everything in between. His eyes watered as his body grew colder with the wind around him.

Time seemed to slow. A thousand thoughts raced through his mind, and yet, none seemed to stay for more than a second. Still, he saw enough. He saw Alor, first the city he had grown up in, then as ruined piles of rubble. He saw Kathrine, and the love they shared. He saw his brother Chase, not born of the same parents, but still brothers, nonetheless. He saw his new friends, Zethus and Hexus and Theo and Akio. He knew he did not want to die yet. If he lost this battle, they would all die, and his father and Zethus would have died in vain. He felt nothing at all, and all he saw was black.

He took a deep breath and the air around him slowed to a stop. He felt the wind enter his lungs, exiting after a ling while. He felt energy crackle up his arms. The volts raced through his body, filling it with power as if he were a torch being lit. He felt the pain leave him and he felt power return to him. His eyes opened, and they flashed blue. He was frozen in midair, Typhon's massive body still floating so high above him. He extended his hands and called the lightning bolt and his sword to his hand, just as Hexus had done with Fyrestar.

He thrust his arms downward, and his body shot upwards like an arrow being fired. He flew, telling the air around him exactly what to do, yet not knowing how he did it. He charged up a ball of thunder between his arms and launched it at Typhon.

The demon roared as he struggled to dodge. His severed spider leg stump still bled green blood. *IT SEEMS YOUR FATHER TAUGHT YOU WELL,* he grimaced. Adam reached him. He floated, a thousand feet above the battle. He stood on the wind and balanced on air. His heart thundered in his chest, beating with the same rhythm that his lightning flashed brighter.

YOU ARE BUT A STRANGER TO THIS POWER, Typhon said, *BEFORE LONG YOU WILL DRAIN YOURSELF AND YOU WILL EXPIRE.*

Adam clenched his fists, "That will still be more than enough time for me to rip you apart." He threw himself at the demon and launched him backwards. His blood felt like fire and his body was stronger than ever. He spoke to himself silently. He vowed to kill Typhon. He vowed to end this all right now. He was going to kill Typhon and when he was done, he was going to kill Korax, then he was going to find the third king, and destroy his as well. He would create a new world, born from not the ashes of his father's world, but from the ashes of Typhon's dream.

The two wrestled atop the tallest tower. Adam held out the bolt and showered Typhon with blasts that passed through him and blew holes in parts of the mountain. Explosions rocked the castle, and Adam struggled to keep his balance.

Typhon brought up a spider leg and pierced Adam's side. One of his legs, with the heads of dragons, bit and gnashed at him. One of them bit into his leg. Adam screamed and slashed his blade. The first dragon dodged, but the second lost its head. Typhon roared.

He flapped his wings and threw a punch. Adam stumbled back, falling onto air. He stayed afloat, thrusting his body forward again.

He slammed into Typhon's chest, sending the both crashing through the inside of the mountain and out the other side. Adam redirected the course and they were headed upwards again. Typhon slashed at his face.

Adam crashed into one of the towers, sending dust everywhere with an explosion of stone. Typhon slammed an elbow into his gut, knocking the wind from his lungs. Adam brought his sword over his shoulders and thrust it through Typhon's shoulder blades. The demon roared and fell back. The second dragon head launched itself at Adam, but Adam dodged the strike and slashed at it with his blade. The lifeless head tore from the bleeding stump and down to the battle below, turning to stone as it fell.

Adam sent another strike at Typhon's chest. The beast flew back onto the peak. Adam followed, flying up to the top. Typhon laid in a pool of his own blood. It ran thick and black, like tar. Adam raised his bolt again, and pointed it at Typhon's chest.

YOU THINK YOU HAVE WON, BOY? YOU HAVE MERELY TRIUMPHED IN THIS BATTLE. A FIRST OF MANY. NO WAR HAS ENDED WITH ONE FIGHT.

"This one will," Adam told him, floating above him.

NO IT WILL NOT. I WILL SEE YOU AGAIN ADAM, AND WHEN I DO, IT WILL BE FOR YOUR FINAL MOMENTS ALIVE.

Adam ignored his words. He raised the bolt to the stars and called upon the powers of the sky. Lightning flashed as it struck his weapon, the scepter flashed uncontrollably as it was levelled towards Typhon, and finally, when Adam told it to, it released the largest strike he ever saw.

The strike exploded, obliterating the tower dome within seconds. Debris and dust flew into the air. When it all cleared, all that remained was the charred body of the deformed Typhon. He was left a statue in the rubble, his features and limbs completely blackened with stone. Upon his ugly lips, laid the faintest curves of a maniacal smile. Then he faded into ashes.

57

HER BROTHER HAD left, retreating with the rest of Korax' army. She had turned around and he was gone. Her last moments with him would never leave her.

She heard cheers and whooping around her. The battle had been won, at the cost of many fallen. The bodies still dotted the field, their armor glinting with their blood. Erika had seen the madness that had unfolded at the peak of the mountain.

The explosions had rocked the entire field of battle, like earthquakes. She cursed herself for feeling the way she did. They had come out victorious. By the morrow they would burn their dead and honor them with a feast, still, Erika could not shake the feelings. She had won this battle, but she had lost her brother. She could still hear Korax yelling to his troops as he saw the defeat of his master, the Great Snake atop the peak.

"Fall back! Fall back!" The corpses turned with expressionless dead faces and raced to the gate again. Erika still did battle with Eleon, trying to hurt him as least as possible. He threw strike after strike, each of which with the clear intent of killing her.

A tear ran down her cheek. She wiped it away. Now was not the time for this, that would come after. The soldiers rallied at the city gates and cheered for victory, she was reluctant, but she stood to join them.

Kathrine hugged Chase, the two laughing as they cheered. Swords were raised into the sky and spears were banged against shields, sending a thundering **Boom! Boom! Boom!** across the field.

They looked up in anticipation, and when Adam descended from the skies, the cheering loudened. Adam landed before them, his body a bloody mess and his face a ruin, but he was alive. He smiled at her and Chase, and they raced to embrace him.

She kissed his face and hugged him tight, "Everything is fine, now."

More soldiers rallied around him. Their chants echoed around the field as Kathrine embraced Adam. For that minute or two... nothing else mattered.

After an hour, the bodies had been collected into piles atop burial pyres. Adam seemed confused with their faces. He would have imagined fear and horror in their lifeless eyes, but instead he saw only peace. Their eyes were calm, and their faces seemed unbothered. He felt a thousand eyes on him as he held a torch of burning gold fire.

A *speech*, he thought, *they're waiting for a speech.* He felt cold hit his face. He felt a shiver run down his back as a drop of sweat trickled down his neck. He glanced over to the others. They all stood next to him, bruised and battered.

Eric gave him a stern look and stepped forward. He raised a golden torch in the air and waited as the flames crackled. Then he took a deep breath and finally spoke with a voice booming through the legions.

"We are gathered today at the feet of our fallen brothers and sisters, to honor their sacrifice. It is thanks to them that this world lives another day, and it is to them that we owe a dept that is unrepayable. For them, we live, for them we fight!"

"FOR THEM WE LIVE!" The soldiers chanted, "FOR THEM WE FIGHT!" They cheered and chanted and said their final goodbyes as they set the pyres ablaze.

The bodies shimmered into stars as they were consumed by flames. Zeus laid on the first pyre, his body still. Adam stared at his face until it was no more than a formless shingle of sparkles. Their thousand bodies glowed brighter than the apples of the Garden of Hesperides. The stars of their bodies floated up into the endless glimmer of the sky above and stopped high above the clouds. They exploded into a thousand different colors as they dissolved into the ethereal pathway between the sun and the moon, Linülién, Zeus had called it. Adam stared up at the sky, as he said goodbye to his father, and said hello to a star.

The soldiers had returned to the main castle, and there would soon be a feast in the main hall. Adam was tired and hungry, more than anything, but he knew that the soldiers would expect him to make a speech. He wouldn't know what to say. Chase helped him down the hall, dressed formally in a velvet jerkin and golden jewelry adorning his neck and wrists. Adam limped down the empty corridors, his right arm in a sling and his left arm resting on the hilt of his sword, sheathed at his side. His head throbbed and his limbs ached, and his blood boiled and screamed. He was dressed for the occasion, but he did not feel the part. He was fitted in a light blue velvet doublet, with velvet blue stockings and a leather belt with a golden buckle.

The main hall was filled with the smell of smoked chickens and fresh baked bread. Wine sloshed onto the floor as glasses clinked together. Laughter and guffaws filled the hall as the maidens brought food to their plates. Candles flickered light into the hall and music played from all corners of the room. People celebrated victory and cheered. Hexus and Theodore indulged in the feast, eating their smoked meats, roasted potatoes and sweet vegetables with tall glasses of wine and ale always being refilled. Everyone was dressed formally, a welcome difference to their usual dirty, sweaty clothes.

Kathrine sipped her beef stew as Chase fed on baked potatoes and steamed vegetables. She wore a red silk dress adorned with blue ribbons. Her hair had been done up at one point, but she had undone it recently, letting her hazel locks fall over her shoulders.

Adam looked around him and smiled. Everyone seemed happy for the first time in a long time. Silenus sang songs with the orchestra, strumming the thin strings on his new harp, which they had finally allowed him to play.

Ladies danced with gentlemen, and the felling of joy hovered over the banquet like a morning dew over a field of flowers.

Hours passed and courses came and went. Music continued playing and people kept singing and dancing. They were then called into the throne room. Adam and his friends were lined up at the head of the hall, the hundreds of soldiers and maidens and cupbearers stood before them, cheering at the sight of Adam and his friends before the thrones of Olympus. The gods sat in their thrones, flanking the group.

A dark man with white hair and blue eyes stood, his throne colored turquoise and designed with seashells and sea-life.

"Friends and allies, loyal soldiers." Poseidon said, loud and assertive. His voice commanded the attention of everyone in the massive hall. Thousands of faces stopped their cheering and stood silent. Their eyes were still on Poseidon, and Adam felt his spine shudder as Poseidon walked closer to him.

"We walk into a dangerous era. War is nigh and the gods are now mortal. The humans no longer pray to us, and so our power runs thin. The fate of our world now belongs to these young heroes," he gestured broadly to the head of the table, where Adam and his friends felt the gazes of the soldiers on them. "Our king has died, and we have much to do if we are to win this war. But today, we celebrate victory against the enemy, the first of many I assure you." The crowd erupted in cheers at that. Poseidon raised a hand to silence them, "today, we celebrate the young heroes that helped us in this battle. Their dreams led them here and they bared arms with us, and we repay their bravery with these gifts.

Gift bearers dressed in white dresses came up to them one by one handing them lovely rewards. Theodore received a beautifully designed dagger and Raia received a book of spells, a grimoire.

They rejoiced when they got the awards, but Adam was wondering what would soon end up in his palms.

"For lord Eric Mavros, the Dragonarcher, a Vàninëll of your own." A gift bearer rushed up to him holding something on a velvet cushion. Eric took the object in his bandaged hands and cradled it.

"A dragon's egg," Hexus said softly, "beautiful."

The egg was the size of a melon, with emerald and gold scales covering it. It glowed repeatedly a hot reddish color, as if each breath the whelp inside took was as hot as flame.

"May the dragon help you on your quest. A loyal and fierce companion to have in the battles to come."

They gifted Norris a golden ring. It was small, with a golden band topped with a blue stone resembling a sapphire. On the glimmering band were inscribed small words that burned a fiery red.

"For lord Norris Lazos, the ring of valor, Örrathör."

Norris eyed the band and read the inscription aloud, "he who holds the power of this ring, shall vanish from the sight of the wicked, and from the fires of malice, shall come forth a leader." He smiled and slipped the ring on his finger.

"Able to make its wearer invisible to the eye at will, the ring of valor will be a valuable tool in the future." Poseidon announced with a booming voice. Norris smiled and shut his eyes. His entire body from head to toe became air. Everyone gasped and some soldiers in the crowd cheered and clapped. Norris became visible again and in his hand was the golden ring, glowing white.

"For lady Kathrine Asker, we gift a young black bear. For your strength of will and bravery, we gift you a Vàninëll of your own."

The gift bearer came forth, a young, female bear curled in her arms. Its coat was a dark as onyx and on its forehead, was a symbol of white fur. Kathrine took it in her arms and smiled.

"An animal guardian," Chase told her.

"For lord Chase Silvergrove, we gift a young grey wolf. For your strength of mind and loyalty, we give you a Vàninëll of your own." Poseidon chanted as the young animal was gifted to him. Chase took it in his hands and the animal yawned quietly, clearly comfortable with a being of nature.

"Finally, for lord Adam New Sky, the mighty thunderbolt of the last king Zeus. Your father would be proud to see you now." He handed the staff to Adam, and he took it. His arm flickered with energy, and the staff flashed with lightening. He took a deep breath, and squeezed the staff, and his arm was calm. He looked at the crowd, who were all cheering and applauding.

Poseidon raised his hand and silence crawled over the crowd, murmurs and whispers were heard occasionally. Poseidon pinched the bridge of his nose and sighed.

The murmurs grew louder until the hall was nothing more than an echoing chamber of shouts and questions. Kathrine softly took Adam's hand and laced his fingers with hers.

"All hail king Adam New Sky." One soldier shouted. Adam felt his heart stop. His chest burned and Chase nearly choked on his food. He felt his grip tighten on Kathrine's hand as more men stood up. They lifted their arms to the air and chanted. Halius, the eagle his father had gifted him, flew to him and perched himself on Adam's shoulder.

"ALL HAIL THE NEW SKY! ALL HAIL THE NEW KING! ALL HAIL THE NEW SKY! ALL HAIL THE NEW KING!" The men shouted louder and louder. Their chanting never stopped, only growing louder and stronger every passing second. Hexus held his fist up and began to chant with them. Asius and Raia and Minerva joined along as well. Akio, Theodore and Norris chanted then Eric and Asius then Chase and Erika, and finally Kathrine her soft hands never leaving his.

They all stared at him, their eyes waiting for his response. Even the gods waited for an answer. Athena bared her arms and Hephaestus held out a gnarled hand holding a mug. Poseidon banged his trident three times on the floor, and the booming voices of the thousand chanting soldiers stopped.

"If it be the will of all you, and if it be the will of the young king, then so be it." He too paused for a response.

Adam took a deep breath. He knew where his journey had taken him, but he knew not where it would take him from her forward. He enjoyed the idea of being king. Adam told himself he was going to win this war, but he knew he could not do it alone. He squeezed Kathrine's hand tighter and stared longingly at his friends, who all smiled in reassurance. He had become a hero. Him and all his friends had become heroes, just as he had always hoped. Admirers looked on as he held the staff of his father, and he stared at them with the power of the sky coursing through his veins. He thought it funny. For all his life, he had been sure of what he was to do with it, he was not sure if it meant anything, but now, he was sure of where he was, and he was sure of where he was going to go.

He took a deep breath, and nodded surely. The crowd erupted in cheers and he looked at them with a smile, as his fathers crown was placed upon his head.

58

THE GODS HAD wasted no time in giving them orders. The Olympians were to stay on Olympus, using what power they had to keep Typhon under control for as long as possible, but Adam was to sail eastward. He was to go into the Shimmering Sea, to find the islands of Delos and Naxos and allies that will help them. The names of those allies, Adam wished he knew. Alas the gods would reveal only one name: Deadalus, the Wise. A foreign sounding name, but Adam was sure he would become familiar with it soon enough. They were to gather armies for the coming conflict, and, if fate be on their side, sail to the island of Volar to defeat Typhon.

Of course, Typhon was not their sole concern. Korax, Xuthos and Eleon were all alive, and the identity of the third king was still unknown. Adam still had questions, and he intended to solve them. His dreams still replayed in his mind, the giant, the mountain, the dragons, the battle, even Kathrine's vision in the trunk of the Heart Tree was confusing him. When Zeus had given the vision of a destroyed Alor in prison, he said they all went to the 'golden city'. He would find those who survived the massacre and help them, wherever they were. He would find answers to it all.

Adam stood on the balcony where he had once talked with his father, staring at the glowing stars that shined in the Linülién with his crown twirling between his fingers. He heard the music and cheers of the party inside, and wished he could join them, but his mind was elsewhere.

Halius stared at him with curious blue eyes, and Adam stroked the bird's neck. They had become comfortable with each other in the day they had known each other, two children of Zeus, left to carry their father's legacy.

"Why are you so gloomy, brother? There is a celebration going on for you." Adam turned to see Chase walking up to him. Kathrine was next to him, their new animal protectors at their feet.

Adam laughed, staring at the cubs, 'Their far too small to be protecting either of you." He chuckled and crouched to scratch their small ears.

"They'll grow." Kathrine smiled at him.

"Have you figured out names yet?" Adam asked.

Chase pet his wolf pup, "I like the name Killian, it always sounded like the name of a fierce warrior." He waved his finger over Killian's head, and the dark pup hopped up to grab it in his tiny jaws.

"And you?" He looked at Kathrine and her bear.

Kathrine paused a moment, staring into the soft, comforting darkness of her bear's eyes. Then she finally answered, "Vorena." Her mother's name.

Adam took her hand and smiled softly, "she would be proud to see you where you are now." He said.

Her beautiful green eyes wandered around the sky, "I hope so."

He kissed her, and they laughed. He turned to the balcony, and stared at the vast world of Alanos.

"For all my life, I had never known there was a world outside the walls of the one I knew, and now, I am to save it from... all this." He sighed. Kathrine placed a soft hand on his shoulders, and Chase lightly punched his arm.

"We aren't the same anymore, Adam." Kathrine told him, resting her head on his shoulder, "I have seen but a glimpse of what this world offers me, and I can say now, it is worth fighting for."

"I am a king now." The words did not seem right leaving his lips, "I know little about the responsibilities of a king, but I know this much: A king seldom knows who to trust, or when to trust them."

Chase and Kathrine looked at him. Adam kept his gaze fixed on the stretching world before him, but he felt their eyes on him.

"I have trusted you both for my entire life, and you have given me the best life I could ask for. I trust you both, which is why I ask of you this;" He turned to Chase and rested a hand on his shoulder. Chase smirked knowingly. Adam smiled, "Chase, you saved my life more than once on this journey, and I could never repay that dept. Will you do me the honor, of being a member of my royal guard?"

Chase smiled and placed a hand on his own chest. "It would be my honor." He said in a mocking valiant voice. He laughed and Adam laughed with him, "It would be an honor." He said it sincerely that time.

They hugged, and Adam then turned to Kathrine.

He stared at her emerald eyes, and placed a hand on her cheek. She raised an eyebrow and smiled, awaiting her gift.

Adam smiled looking at her, for a serious face would not stay. "For all my life, I have never known what love is, but I do now, and it is what I have for you. Kathrine, will you be my queen?'

She kissed him, long and tender, and his question was answered. When she pulled away, she smiled, and she took his hand as they stared at Alanos.

Adam was finally happy. He was happy to be here, staring at the most beautiful sight he could ever imagine with his two closest friends. He wanted to enjoy this moment before it would end.

He thought of his father Zeus, and Zethus, and Ladon and Diocles. All their lives had been lost to bring Adam to this place, and he would not forget that.

Chase chuckled, "there is still much we need to do."

"I know." Adam said.

"And you're ready for it all?"

Adam never lost sight of the universe around him, "Not at all."

Chase paused for a moment, "perfect."

"Perfect." Kathrine said softly.

"Perfect," Adam said, "let's go."

Acknowledgments

FIRST AND FOREMOST, I want to say a sincere 'thank you' to my parents and sisters, Charlotte and Sharon, who have stood by me and encouraged me to continue with my work through the highs and lows. Thanks to my mother, who was always interested in what I had to tell her and intrigued by the stories that came from my mind. Thanks to my father, who helped me to put my work out there and who supported me in creating an enticing, wonderous and original story.

Throughout the years that I have worked on this novel, several of my close friends have encouraged and supported me. Some have even inspired certain characters in my universe. Thank you to my lovely friends, Maurice Downey, Sergio Watanabe, Nathan Kayembe, and Taurai Lockhart, among others, who have made my novel what it is by inspiring countless characters, events and locations.

Thank you to my very first fans, Alexia Ielapi, Brayden Lavallee, Hayden Robbins, Stephanie Elasmar, Jessica Luong, Emily Champagne who, among others, have always shown wonder, curiosity and love towards my work before it was even finished. They loved what I was writing about and always asked questions about the world I had created, the world that they had loved.

I will forever be unspeakably thankful for those who have helped me along the way and continue to help me as I continue to work on my expanding universe.

- Francisco. B. Gomez, October 25th 2019.

CPSIA information can be obtained
at www.ICGtesting.com
Printed in the USA
BVHW070758030220
571272BV00001B/16

9 781796 073089